BOW STREET SOCIETY:
The Case of The Spectral Shot
by
T.G. Campbell

All characters in this novel are fictional. Any resemblance
to persons living or dead is purely coincidental.

Dedicated to A.E., K.M., and R.W.

TABLE OF CONTENTS

PROLOGUE

DEPARTMENT STORE FROM HELL EXPOSED stated
the headline from an old evening edition of the *Gaslight
Gazette*. Upon reading it, Miss Trent's mind had evoked a
buried memory of an account she'd been given at the time.
A Bow Street Society member, who'd helped bring about
the exposure, had told of a large pot atop a stove. A heavy,
pale mixture had been found inside. He, and others
present, hadn't needed to rely on mere suspicion to know
what it was.

The grandfather clock's Westminster chimes from
the hallway brought her back from her thoughts. While the
seventh hour struck, she turned over the newspaper and
slid it to her guest. They sat around her desk in the middle
of her office at the Bow Street Society's headquarters.
Signs of the former owner's taste could still be seen in the
high-grade, dark-olive wallpaper, embossed with a scroll
design, and the large, oak fireplace on the far left. While
she had the door to her back, her guest had the window to
his, its curtains closed against the night. A fire had also
been lit, and the gas wall lamps ignited, to repel the cold
darkness. To her guest's right was a filing cabinet
containing square drawers the size of index cards. An
Improved Salter 5 typewriter sat on the desk in front of
him. Had she possessed an inclination toward pettiness,
she would've insisted upon her usual seat.

"The case was solved," she stated. "Justice was
served."

"It was—as far as the court cared. I still have some
qualms about it, though."

Inspector Caleb Woolfe placed his large, clasped
hands upon the desk and leant forward, causing the wood
to groan beneath his weight. Far from being a portly
gentleman, Woolfe could nonetheless be described as

stocky—solid, even. His shoulders and chest were so broad that, as he'd moved forward, they'd entirely blocked the fire's light from Miss Trent's view. Also, despite his slouch, his shadow covered the clerk's entire form. A musty, damp odour exuded from his fur coat as it was warmed by the fire. Woolfe's brown eyes peered out from beneath a black, bushy brow as he scrutinised the stoic woman.

She was in her late-twenties and unmarried—a spinster in the eyes of wider society. Yet, Woolfe knew from experience, she couldn't be scorned and dismissed so easily. Even then, her dark-brown eyes were fixed on his. Others, he'd found, tended to wander or look to an ear while in a policeman's presence. Her tendency—no, *refusal*— to do the same was as intriguing to him as it was repugnant. It, coupled with a slight lift of her chin, made for an altogether defiant countenance—even when no emotion was expressed. On another occasion, he may have admired the curve of her waist, accentuated by her corset undergarment, and her chest above the high, square neckline of her brown bustle dress. Tonight, however, his pride forbade him.

"What we found in those rooms will haunt me until I breathe my last," he began in a solemn tone. "Calling them monstrous isn't enough to describe the absolute horror of what was done to those poor women. You'd agree?"

"I would."

"I thought so, but I'm still unhappy about what you, and your Society, did." Miss Trent parted her lips, but Woolfe immediately resumed, "The Society interfered with a police investigation, which was bad enough, but something else irks me." His eyes narrowed, and his tone hardened. "You let a vulnerable young woman investigate a room you knew *nothing* about without asking for the police's help. Those same horrors could've happened to her if the murderer had come across her there. She would be *dead,* Miss Trent. What's more, her remains would've been given the same undignified treatment as those of Mrs Roberts and her mother."

"But he didn't, Inspector," she pointed out. "Yet, even if he had, she wasn't alone. Mr Locke and Lady Owston were also present."

"Beyond earshot," Woolfe growled. "You and your Society put Miss Agnes Webster's life in danger without any thought of the risks involved—"

"*Firstly*, Inspector," Miss Trent interrupted. "The safety of the Society's members is paramount to me. *Secondly,* I have the utmost trust in Lady Owston and Mr Locke. *They* would've intervened had Miss Webster not returned when expected. Therefore, your accusations are *without* foundation. They are also symptomatic of your categorical hatred of the Bow Street Society, and of what we are trying to do."

"Which is *what*, exactly?"

"Ensuring justice is served for those who ask for it."

"And putting your members' lives at risk in the process!"

"*Enough,* Inspector!" Miss Trent stood and glared down at him.

In a heartbeat, he, too, was on his feet. Towering over her five feet seven inches with his six feet four, he bellowed, "You *will* listen to me, Miss Trent, and you *will* listen *carefully*!" Miss Trent put her hand on her hip but remained silent. "If you and your Society *insist* on facing danger *unnecessarily,* you will do so under *my* terms. You will give me a *full* list of your members so I, and the Metropolitan Police, can stop them from being *murdered*, *attacked*, and *robbed*. Try to justify what you do as much as you like, Miss Trent, but, at the end of the day, you are *all* just bloody *civilians* playing at a copper's game!"

"And yet, *we* are the ones people look to when the police *refuse* to help them," Miss Trent retorted as she stepped closer to the desk. Leaning forward, so their faces were mere inches apart, she went on, "Not every case we investigate is a crime, Inspector, and our clients *expect* discretion with the confidences they grant us. If I were to give such a list, you, and every policeman in London, would *hound* our members. You would also *watch* our every move and, maybe, attempt to infiltrate our ranks. The Society has *never* worked against the police or encouraged its clients to do the same. Yet *you* insist on treating us like criminals. Unless you treat me, and my members, with the common courtesy we deserve, *you* shall have your list when *I* breathe my last."

"It *wasn't* a request, Miss Trent. You have *one* day to give me the list, or I'll come back to tear this house apart."

Woolfe shoved his chair aside—sending it over—and took but three steps to exit the room. The clerk stood her ground until he was through the door before following. When the policeman opened the external door, she added, "Do that. But you'll find a representative of the press waiting for you."

"Are you threatening me?" he threw back with a growl.

"No, I'm trying to show you what an idiot you're being," she replied, her stoic expression returned.

Woolfe's eyes narrowed. "One day! Then I'm coming back!" The entire frame shook as he slammed the door. Hearing his heavy footfalls descending the stone steps, the clerk crossed the hallway and pulled the bolt back into place.

"What woz all that abou'?" a gruff voice—whose accent was that of London's East End—enquired from the kitchen. Turning, Miss Trent smiled as she looked to the round face of Mr Samuel Snyder in the dim gaslight. In his late forties, Mr Snyder was an older member of the Bow Street Society. His weathered features, calloused hands, heavy cloak, and broad-brimmed hat betrayed his long-standing occupation as a two-wheeler hansom cab driver. Standing in the corridor to the grand staircase's right, his extended belly, broad shoulders, and broader arms filled the space.

"Inspector Woolfe being his usual charming self," Miss Trent replied. Her smile faded as her mind replayed the conversation and she approached her friend.

The grand staircase had rounded oak balusters holding up highly polished, smooth, oak handrails on both sides. Its steps were covered by a plain, burgundy carpet, while the remainder of the hallway's floor was a black and white check like a chessboard. A second corridor ran down the stairs' left, and both led to doors into the kitchen. Four more doors occupied the space, the second on the left being where Miss Trent and Inspector Woolfe had emerged from. The walls were decorated with paper matching the carpet in colour. Its design was a repetitive, embossed floral pattern. Despite the space the room afforded, very little furniture occupied it. The grandfather clock, housed in an oak casing, stood between two doors on the right. A hat stand, complete with umbrella pan, was in the corner to one's right upon entering the house. These two pieces aside, the hallway was empty.

"I need to pay someone a visit," Miss Trent announced.

"I'll take you on my way 'ome, since no work's come in," Mr Snyder replied as he passed her.

"*No,*" she snapped. The cabman turned and, shifting his head to the side, regarded her with surprise. Sensing his confusion, Miss Trent explained, "I'll be fine, Sam, but thank you all the same. Besides, it's still early. We can't afford to have a potential client walk away because there was no one home." She smiled. "Do you mind staying here while I'm gone? I should only be an hour."

"Nah, course I don't," Mr Snyder replied and unclasped his cloak to drape it over the handrail's end.

"Thank you." Miss Trent gave his arm a gentle squeeze.

"Best make myself a cuppa, then," Mr Snyder remarked and disappeared back into the kitchen. Miss Trent meanwhile returned to her office and, taking her usual seat, plucked a black, curve-lipped cylinder from a set of prongs. These prongs were in turn attached to a long, narrow, wooden box mounted on the wall to the left of the window. In the centre of the box, at the front, was a non-adjustable, black cone. As a result, Miss Trent had to lean forward to speak into it as she pressed the cylinder to her ear.

* * *

A light drizzle started when Miss Trent crossed Trafalgar Square. Puddles from an earlier downpour reflected the occasional gas lamp or splashed hurried pedestrians' feet as they disturbed them in the pitch darkness. The familiar outline of St Martin-in-the-Fields' church tower also served as a beacon against the cloud-enshrouded sky to Miss Trent who was headed toward it.

Depicted in a painting of the same name by William Logsdail in 1888, St Martin-in-the-Fields was a well-known landmark. Distinctly Corinthian in style, one critic upon its completion described it 'as though Wren had gone to Italy.' Six pillars stood at the summit of stone steps, leading from St Martins Lane below, to form a portico. Above it was an impressive pediment depicting a carving of King George I's coat of arms, the reigning monarch at the time of the church's completion in 1726, and its churchwarden. It should also be noted St Martin-in-the-Fields' parish still includes both Buckingham and St. James Palaces, as it did back then. This royal connection did not stop at the façade either. A separate pew, adjacent to—and on the same level as—the first of two raised galleries, was reserved for the monarchy. A second, on the altar's opposite side and adjacent to the other gallery, was reserved for the Royal Navy. At the time of Miss Trent's visit, it was adorned with a plethora of naval flags.

As she passed under the pediment, through the open doorway, and into the nave proper, the sounds of her feet echoed. An effect fashioned by the acoustics which were, in turn, created by the nave's open-plan design and tunnel-vaulted ceiling. The ceiling being, arguably, the most striking feature within St Martin-in-the-Fields because of its highly decorative gilt and painted plaster by Artari and Bagutti. Pillars, identical to their external counterparts in style, framed the pews on the ground floor. These pews were separated by a wide, central aisle, and faced the altar at the far end. To the right of the altar was a magnificent pulpit. Meanwhile, the galleries—an important feature of Georgian churches—lined the edges of the church's interior, looking inward toward the pews. Containing pews of their own, these galleries were accessed by a set of stairs at their far ends, whilst their dark-wood, panelled facades were periodically separated by the pillars. Brass chandeliers, bathed in the light of their own candles, hung from the ceiling by chains. Though beautiful, their light wasn't adequate to fully illuminate the space. Thus, the church was strewn with shadows which danced in the flickering candlelight. The brilliant white of the pillars and ceiling continued to glow, however, creating the illusion of warmth where there was none.

A handful of parishioners were dotted about the pews, and a clergyman tended to the altar. No one paid heed to Miss Trent as she climbed the steps to the right-hand gallery and walked along the front row of pews. Sitting in its centre, she released a deep breath and watched the exhaled steam as it faded.

Ten—tedious—minutes passed. During which two more parishioners hurried through the portico and shook their umbrellas. The pitter-patter of rain against the stained-glass windows provided a calming, rhythmic melody in the near silence of the church.

Miss Trent pulled her coat closed as a harsh shiver shot through her. Sighing, she turned her thoughts to the warm stove that awaited her at Bow Street. Becoming lost in her thoughts, she didn't notice someone entering the gallery until she heard the pew behind creak. At once reminded of a certain inspector, she stole a glance over her shoulder. The glimpse of brown eyes and moustache was enough to expel her panic. Settling back against her pew, she smirked at her foolishness.

"You shouldn't have contacted me," the newcomer's soft voice stated, sending a steam cloud past her face.

The clergyman, having finished whatever he'd been doing at the altar, climbed the pulpit's steps and shuffled some papers there. Though minor, the rustling echoed around the church as if it were waves against rocks. Nonetheless, Miss Trent took the opportunity to muffle her whisper, "I had no choice. Inspector Woolfe came to the house tonight and demanded a full list of the Society's members." The clergyman coughed, but no sound came from behind her. "Did you hear what I said?"

"When does he want it by?" the newcomer enquired after a pause.

Miss Trent turned and stared at him.

He was in his early thirties, but the weight of exhaustion showed in the dark circles beneath his eyes. A knee-length, black coat was worn over a brown, cotton suit with matching waistcoat and tie. Upon his short, neatly combed, brown hair sat a bowler hat of the same colour. A starched, Eaton collar peeked out from beneath a hand-knitted, burgundy scarf, whilst his complexion was fair.

"Please tell me you're not *seriously* considering giving it to him," Miss Trent said.

"I didn't create the Bow Street Society to undermine the police, Rebecca," he replied as he took in her incredulous expression. "Rather to supplement it, however indirectly, when the public's confidence in Scotland Yard and its divisions wanes. Corruption and deception are already rife within the Metropolitan Police. Therefore, the Society—and its clerk—mustn't be seen to be falling into the same bad habits by intentionally obstructing those officers who have proven themselves trustworthy and dedicated to their work."

"Even when those same officers wish to destroy the only group people turn to when they can't approach the police because of the same—often open—corruption, brutality, and prejudice you speak of?"

"Is that what he told you?"

"He didn't have to, Richard. He despised the Society's part in solving the Oxford Street case, so now he wants to make sure it doesn't happen again by giving his colleagues its list of members. He told me he wanted to ensure none of our members were attacked, robbed, or murdered, but he also said he had plenty of arguments against us getting involved in a police investigation at all. He even accused *me* of putting Miss Webster's life at risk by sending her to investigate the room during the Oxford Street case."

"Her life *was* put at risk," he pointed out. "Granted, the outcome of the case was beyond anyone's wildest expectations, but the Society, including you, *must* acknowledge and respect the potential for dangerous situations during the course of investigations."

"I make *damned* sure *none* of our members are put into situations they can't handle, or which might unnecessarily put them into harm's way, Richard. You founded the Society, but chose me to run it, remember? While you are passing judgements and observations from the safety of your ivory tower, *I* am accepting commissions and managing cases under *constant* threat of exposure by Woolfe, our members, and even *you.* You *always* insist on meeting in public despite *knowing* we could be seen by a patrolling policeman or someone who knows you as a chief inspector of the Yard. I need not remind you of how *disastrous* that would be—for our future *and* the Society's. If you wish to lecture me about respecting, and acknowledging, the potential for danger, then, I suggest you look at yourself *first.*"

She rotated in her seat to, again, have her back to him, as silence fell between them. This time, it was a literal silence, too, for the parishioners were locked in prayer, the clergyman was absorbed in his papers, and the pitter-patter of rain had stopped. As the moments passed, with little sound, Miss Trent imagined the shadows across the gallery had grown. Her shoulders felt heavier the more she thought about the withdrawal of candlelight and their conspicuousness as the gallery's only occupants.

"Woolfe can't have a copy of the list," she said. Her expression hardened. "Aside from it being a means to stop our members from investigating any future cases which the police might also be looking into, the list would also confirm Woolfe's suspicions about Doctor Weeks."

"True," Chief Inspector Jones admitted. "As for your other point, Inspector Woolfe is simply doing his job. Metropolitan Police officers aren't allowed to permit *any* members of the public near a crime scene."

"Whenever our members have visited crime scenes, they've been invited by someone directly involved with the case—usually our *clients*. Our members have *never* trampled across a crime scene *or* encouraged our clients to intentionally deceive the police. On the contrary, Lady Owston advised our client in the Oxford Street case to inform the police of the Society's involvement. In short, the members of the Bow Street Society are *not* devious fools determined to ruin every police investigation they encounter. If you give Inspector Woolfe a copy of the members list, you'll be signing the Society's death warrant."

"Only if he's allowed to keep and distribute it."

Miss Trent, again, turned to face him. This time, however, her companion clasped his hands together, rested them upon her pew, and closed his eyes as if in prayer. Doing the same, but in front of her, she whispered, "Woolfe would never give the list back once he had it in his hands."

"He may, if it was a fellow police officer who gave it to him." Shifting in his seat a little as his expression became thoughtful, he continued, "The best interests of the Metropolitan Police and the Bow Street Society have to be protected. In spite of our differences, we want the same thing: justice for those who deserve it, and protection for the weak and vulnerable. Neither can openly assist the other without encountering mistrust and agitation among the Society's clients and the general populous of the Metropolitan Police Force." He frowned. "The revelation of my connection to the Society would be welcomed as warmly as a skunk in the House of Commons… What is needed, therefore, is a facilitator who has sympathies for both groups but who can also be relied upon to be discreet when required."

"Someone like Inspector Conway, you mean?" Miss Trent asked, referring to their mutual friend and grizzled head of Scotland Yard's Mob Squad, housed within the criminal investigations department. A soft hum sounded behind her. "You do realise," she began, "he would also discover the truth about Doctor Weeks if I gave him the members list to pass to Woolfe?"

"I do, but the fact Weeks is no longer active in the Society would serve to limit most of the damage. John Conway has supported the Society and its aims since its conception—despite not being one of its members. While he'll be undoubtedly shocked—even angered—by the news, he'll understand why Weeks' assistance was invaluable in these past two cases." Chief Inspector Jones straightened and made the sign of the cross. "As unpalatable as the coming storm will be, the Society's continued existence now rests upon it being fully transparent with both Woolfe *and* Conway."

"You'll be revealing your full involvement to Inspector Woolfe, then?"

"I invited such a reply," he surrendered. "Fully transparent as far as the Society's members are concerned, then."

"I'll be breaking their trust," she replied. "They expect me to keep their names and details confidential when they're not involved with any investigations. Have you considered what giving the list to Woolfe may do to the dynamics of the Society? To how the members see and treat me?"

"If you can think of an alternative solution, that doesn't involve wilful deceit and obstruction of the police, I'd be more than happy to hear it."

A heavy, exasperated sigh left Miss Trent's lips. She nonetheless analysed every possible option, and scenario, she could think of. Nothing her mind could produce fitted the chief inspector's criteria of legality and transparency, however. Dejected, she rubbed her temple and said, "I can't." Her hand fell to her lap. "I'll type up the list tonight. Woolfe said he'd return to search the house unless I gave him the list within twenty-four hours."

"And he shall if you don't," Chief Inspector Jones replied with a frown. "I'll send word to Conway to let him know I'll be paying him a visit at home first thing tomorrow morning." Taking a notebook and pencil from his pockets, he rested the first on the back of Miss Trent's pew. After writing down Conway's address, Chief Inspector Jones ripped out the page and passed it to her. He said, "This is *only* for the purposes of meeting with him tomorrow. Memorise it and destroy it."

Miss Trent folded the page and slipped it under her cloak as the chief inspector's pew creaked, this time as he stood. Miss Trent, who'd remained facing the other way, felt a gentle hand upon her shoulder. Without looking up, she said, "I've already forgiven you, Richard." She considered a moment. "And I'll burn the paper as soon as I've committed the address to memory."

"Thank you," his soft voice said from above. "Until tomorrow, Miss Trent."

"Until tomorrow."

The two bid one another good night and Miss Trent listened as he retreated along the gallery and down its stairs. Once she'd heard him pass under the portico, she looked to the address.

ONE

Bow Street was quiet when Miss Trent turned its corner. The usual music devotees had passed through on their way to the Royal Opera House, while the nearby Covent Garden Market was deserted. Life remained at the Bow Street police station, however. Attached to the magistrates court—whose windows were in darkness—the Holborn (or E) Division's headquarters were but a short walk from the Society's own base of operations.

A constable in a hefty, wax-coated cape passed Miss Trent and climbed the station's steep steps. Warm light formed a patent-leather shine upon the soaked stone as he opened one of two doors and went inside. Sickly sweet scents of manure and moss clung to the dense, cold damp of the soot-filled air—so much so it was wise to breathe through a handkerchief or, failing that, one's fingers. Yet, despite this, the silhouette of a pipe-smoking man blocked the light until it disappeared, the billowing smoke from his lungs bolstered by the steam of his breath.

"Shouldn't be out 'n' about in this weather, Miss Trent," he said when she neared. Recognising the voice as Sergeant Bird's, she knew the connotation of concern was baseless due to his tone's upward turn. Having an aversion toward *any* interaction with him under normal circumstances, she felt even less compelled to indulge in such tonight. Passing without response therefore, she next heard a loud scrape of a boot when he moved to follow. A sudden furore in the police station forced him to abandon the idea, however, and he went back inside—much to her appreciation.

Leaving the chaos of E Division behind, she quickened her pace as the sky threatened another downpour. Within seconds, she felt its first spots on her cheeks, and she lifted her skirts to hurry. Puddles splashed

when she half-jogged through them, while thunder
rumbled in the distance. Seeing the familiar gas lamp
outside the Bow Street Society's house, her determination
to avoid the rain appeared to have paid off. Until she saw
something she hadn't expected.

The gas lamp's light hit the black, varnished side
of a four-wheeler carriage. A single driver, half-cast in
shadow, sat upon an elevated box at its front. Having
halted when she'd seen the carriage, Miss Trent walked
toward it with caution. Rough hands, wrinkled by
moisture, held the reins of two white stallions between the
driver's bent knees. His heels, meanwhile, were pressed
together against the box's base while his feet jutted out at
opposing angles. So cramped, yet tall, was he, she was
convinced he was about to dive from his seat. Only when
she went closer did she see the limited space he occupied.
Nevertheless, she felt uneasy. His hooked nose and
bulging lips, barely lit by the gaslight, remained
motionless. The rest of his features were hidden by the
pitch-black shadow of his wide-brimmed hat. She went
even closer but, still, he didn't move. Another rumble of
thunder marked the shower's arrival. Droplets fell from his
hat's brim onto his bloodless hands.

"Excuse me, are you waiting for someone?" she
enquired from beneath the gas lamp.

His head turned toward her, and his hat's shadow
covered his remaining, visible features. A deluge of water
poured from his hat as the rain became torrential. Melodic
tinkles accompanied by deep, rapid thuds, of the rain
striking the metal gas lamp and wooden carriage roof
respectively, surrounded them. A strong wind also swept
between and across them, whipping up the rain and
sending her coat's skirt into a flap. All he did was tilt his
head forward until the wind dropped. At which point he
recommenced his stare.

"If you're not waiting for anyone, I suggest you
move on," she shouted over the noise. The driver's

response was to slide his head back toward his horses. Another sudden gust of wind, much stronger than the first, threatened to pull Miss Trent off balance. Bending into it, she gave the driver another moment to reply before she ran up the steps to the front door.

"You okay?" Mr Snyder enquired upon opening it.

"I will be once I'm inside." She hurried past and, while Mr Snyder closed the door, pulled the curtain of the adjacent window aside. Peering through the wall of water, she saw the driver looking at her.

She dropped the curtain and stepped back—straight into Mr Snyder. His frame was bulkier than hers, however. As a result, the impact caused her to bounce forward and stumble. She would've fallen if Mr Snyder hadn't taken a firm grip of her arm.

"Has sum'in happened?" he enquired, glancing between her and the window.

"No." She forced a smile. "I'm just letting my imagination get the better of me, that's all."

"Not like you."

"It's been an emotional night," she said and, removing her coat, hung it upon the stand. As she did so, her mind whirled with Woolfe's words, the clergyman's cough, Jones' faux prayers, and the void of a driver's face. Shivers gripped her, and she remembered she was wet.

"I'll get a blanket." Mr Snyder went past her and into the kitchen. She glanced over her shoulder at the window. Her mind, again, formed the driver's featureless face and she hurried after Mr Snyder. Though he was surprised, he didn't remark upon her joining him. Instead, he passed her the blanket and said, "We've got a guest."

"Where?" She dabbed at her cold face and wrapped the blanket around her shoulders. Its warmth enveloped her, and she took a towel from above the stove to dry her face and hands. Her coat had kept her middle and skirts dry, but her boots and stockings were beyond hope. Sitting down, she took off her coat but paused to quirk a brow in Mr Snyder's direction, and he turned his back to her.

"The parlour."

Miss Trent stood, lifted her skirts, put her foot on the chair, and rolled down the wet stocking. Repeating the process with the other, she then dropped her skirts. "You may look, now." She went to the stove and, holding her hands above it, looked over her shoulder at him. "Who is it?"

"Not him." Mr Snyder gave a soft chuckle. "Woolfe's not come back since you left."

A sudden—more intense—rumble of thunder shook the walls, followed by a flash and clap of lightning. Even at the back of the house, the two heard the startled screech and whinnying of horses coming from the street. Mr Snyder at once left the kitchen, not noticing if Miss Trent followed or not.

"Best go check on Blue-Shirt," she heard him mutter as she entered the hallway after him. When he opened the door, a tremendous gust of wind burst into the room. The gas lamps' flames bent and lurched while Mr Snyder, halfway through the doorway, took his cloak from Miss Trent. He then released the door and hurried outside, obliging her to lurch forward to catch the door to prevent it from striking the wall.

She watched as he reached his horse—the cab it pulled was parked behind the silent driver's—and took its reins to calm it. She'd forgotten about Mr Snyder's cab, so caught up she'd been in the uncanny situation she'd encountered. Looking to the unmarked carriage, she felt easier when she saw its driver lean forward to reassure his horses. The storm was too violent for her to loiter with the door open, however, so she pushed against the wind to close it.

After several attempts—as she braced her feet against the floor to put her entire body weight into each—

she succeeded. A deep exhalation left her lungs the instant she slid the bolt into place and took a rest against the door. Even then she felt the wood tremble under the wind's demands to enter. She pulled across the second bolt and, with a turn of the key, felt secure at last.

Then she felt it… the unmistakeable sense of being watched.

Bit by bit, she turned her head. What she saw made her recoil in an instant.

A silhouette stood three feet from her. No more accurate a description could ever be fathomed for what she saw. It was shrouded entirely in black, from the crown of its hat to the soles of its feet. Facial features, buttons, cloth, and flesh, all were indistinguishable against the now restored glow of the gaslight. Whether man or woman, she couldn't hope to tell.

"Are you Miss Rebecca Trent?" a voice hissed. The silhouette's head had shifted in shape as the words were uttered, but no pink gums or white teeth were seen.

"Yes," she replied, barely hearing her voice over her pounding heart.

"Bow Street Society representatives are requested at this address," the voice hissed. Uncertain which address the figure referred to, Miss Trent parted her lips to enquire when she caught sight of a white square against the sea of black. The white lifted and she realised it was in a hand. After a moment's hesitation, she tugged the paper from the fingers' grip. "They will be given further instruction upon arrival," the voice continued. "If no one arrives at midnight tonight, it shall be understood the Society refuses the commission."

"Why can't the instruction be given to me?" Miss Trent enquired, her courage returning considering the figure's vagueness. A vision of Woolfe's face also formed in her mind, followed by his voice: *And putting your members' lives at risk in the process.* Swallowing hard, she added, "I can't, in good conscience, send members into the unknown."

"You have until midnight tonight," the voice hissed as the silhouette advanced.

You let a vulnerable young woman investigate a room you knew nothing about… She would be dead

"You're not leaving until I have some answers," she demanded, spreading her legs and gripping the doorway to block it. The silhouette didn't stop, or even slow, however.

"*Midnight* tonight!" it hissed and, taking hold of Miss Trent's shoulder, tossed her aside. Landing with a grunt, she was stunned to find herself on the floor. The silhouette had meanwhile slid back the bolts and threw open the door. Violent winds and rain again erupted into the hallway, this time extinguishing the gas lamps.

"Stop!" Miss Trent yelled, scrambling to her feet as the silhouette ran. By the time she made it outside, the silhouette was almost to an awaiting carriage. The driver, who'd been so motionless earlier, leaned down and flipped open the carriage door at his passenger's approach. When the silhouette then leapt inside, the driver took his whip to his horses and the carriage jolted forward. The silhouette had to grip the carriage's doorframe to prevent him—or her—from tumbling out. In a heartbeat though—as Miss Trent reached them—the silhouette snatched the carriage's interior door handle and slammed it shut. Miss Trent attempted to grab the external one, but the carriage's speed whipped it from her fingers. Stumbling into the road—narrowly avoiding falling onto the carriage's large wheel in the process—Miss Trent caught herself in time to see the carriage slip away from the gas lamp's light and into the ferocious night.

* * *

Mr Snyder placed a London map upon the kitchen table and, smoothing out the creases, used his finger to trace a circle around an area in the map's top left corner.

"All this's Hampstead Heath." He glanced up to meet Miss Trent's gaze and tapped the map. "'Ere's *Jack Straw's Castle* inn. Next to that's the Flagstaff from the note.[1] A lot of the Heath's grass and trees."

"It doesn't make sense." Miss Trent rubbed her temples. "Why insist on meeting Society members *there* when *here* is more private?" She dropped her hands to the table. "He, she—whoever it was—didn't tell you *anything*? Not even their name?"

Mr Snyder shook his head. "They asked for you by name. When I told 'em you wasn't here, they said they'd wait."

Miss Trent sighed.

"Are you gonna send someone?"

Miss Trent knew whomever went to the Flagstaff would be as vulnerable as Miss Webster was—perhaps more so—as she had no idea about the commission. Yet, what was the Society for but to investigate crimes the police wouldn't? Clearly their potential client had their reasons for subterfuge—at least, she assumed as such. She looked at Mr Snyder's expectant face, broad frame, and knuckles. The same knuckles which had knocked out many a man during long prize fights. Mr Snyder's skill made him the perfect person to send. Nonetheless, sending him alone was out of the question. So, too, was sending any of the others to accompany him—not until she knew more about the case, at least. After further procrastination, she said, "Inspector Conway."

"What?"

"You and Inspector Conway should go. You're both more than capable of looking after yourselves, and I wasn't told not to involve the police. The only police officers we could trust with this are Inspectors Conway and Woolfe. Between the two, Conway is the lesser evil."

"I dunno. What if 'e don't wanna go?"

"We have to try." Miss Trent pulled on her boots and stood. "If you could drive me to his house, Sam, I will convince him to help us."

"Do you know where 'e lives, then?"

"Of course." Miss Trent smiled.

"How?"

"Ask me no questions, and I'll tell you no lies."

Mr Snyder chuckled and, picking up his hat, followed her outside.

TWO

The road Mr Snyder's cab turned onto was deserted. As more rain fell, sodden mud clung to the cab's wheels and Blue-Shirt's hooves like black treacle. The dry rot-infested bay windows they passed held the meagre glow of parlour fires or the dull lining of heavy curtains. Narrow front gardens, surrounded by low walls, had become waterlogged over the course of the night, while shallow porches had sheltered dark-painted doors from the storm's worst. Years' worth of ingrained soot had turned the houses' brown brickwork black under the torrent's bombardment.

Part of the East End borough of Hackney, Ballance Road was adjacent to Wick Road, near to the Hackney Union Workhouse. It housed Booth's "mixed" classification on his maps of London poverty in 1889, that of the poor and the comfortable. A stark contrast compared to the semi-vicious, criminal class that surrounded the public institution.

Past the bay-fronted houses, still on Ballance Road, were smaller abodes. Their doors—also dry-rot infested, with peeled paint—opened onto the pavement. It was outside one such residence Mr Snyder brought his cab to a halt. Its woodwork was in a greater state of decline than its neighbours. Two, square, sash windows—identical in size—looked down from its first floor, while a third was to its front door's right. Off-white net curtains hung in them all, but no fires or lamplight could be seen. Miss Trent therefore had to rely upon the cab's Davey lamp to see by, as she alighted and knocked on the door.

"Maybe 'e's not in," Mr Snyder remarked when no one answered. He sat in his seat mounted high on the cab's rear, his large hands beneath his great cloak as they held Blue-Shirt's reins.

"We can't come back." Miss Trent went to the window and, cupping her hands around her face, pressed her nose to the dirty glass. The dense net curtain, and darkness beyond, prevented her from seeing anything, however. Sighing, she banged upon the door with her fist. On the third strike, it swung open and Miss Trent stumbled forward, her hands flying out to grab the door's edge and frame to catch her.

"You hurt?"

"No." Miss Trent straightened and brushed the soot from her coat. "Thank you."

A narrow hallway, from which two closed doors led, had been revealed in the weak glow of the Davey lamp. The first was on the right. The second was at the far end beside the steep stairs which the door had hit and now rested against. Despite the bang it had caused, no sign of life materialised.

"Where you goin'?" Mr Snyder enquired as Miss Trent ventured further inside.

"I have to be sure," she replied and closed the door ajar behind her.

The hallway had sage-coloured, textured wallpaper, bare floorboards, and uncarpeted stairs. The ballasts and handrail, once varnished, were scuffed and scratched. A plain rug—flattened and threadbare—lined the floor beside the stairs. Behind the front door, a damp trilby hat and overcoat hung from wall pegs. Though not lavish, the hallway was nonetheless clean and tidy.

As Miss Trent passed the stairs, she saw a thin shaft of light beneath the far door. "Hello?" she called. When no one answered, she opened the near door and peered inside. An armchair stood against the wall to the door's right. Facing the window, its upholstery was sun-bleached, shapeless, and under-stuffed. On the parlour's back wall was an unlit, plain, iron hearth. Cream ceramic tiles, with countryside scenes painted in brown at their centres, framed the hearth on two sides. The hearth's simple, oak surround was topped by a wide mantelshelf. A pile of opened envelopes, a brass poker, and a clock stopped at twenty-five minutes past three were its sole adornments. An empty coal scuttle, dented in one side, sat on the fireplace's far side. Beneath the window was a short, oak table. Upon it was a box of matches, a month's old edition of the *Gaslight Gazette*, and a brass, police constable's whistle. Between the table and armchair—against the wall to the door's left—was a shabby sideboard. An unlit kerosene lamp, with a frosted glass shade and bulbous, brass base, was joined by a new copy of the *Police Gazette* and a pile of unopened letters on the sideboard's top. A wet latch key had been tossed onto the letters, causing the ink to run on the top one and distort its address.

The air was damp and cold against her skin, while a musty smell—laced with stale tobacco—filled her nostrils. She therefore left the parlour to venture further into the house and through the far door. Bright light from another kerosene lamp—this one in the middle of the room—caused her to shield her eyes the moment she entered.

"Don't move," a deep, rough voice warned beyond the lamp's light.

"John?"

"Rebecca?" The lamp was dimmed and the damp, middle-aged, weathered features of Inspector Conway emerged from the gloom. Despite the late hour, he was dressed in a dark-grey waistcoat with matching trousers and a white shirt. His shirt's sleeves were rolled up to his elbows to reveal his broad, red hair-covered forearms, while a starched Eaton collar framed the knot of his midnight-blue tie. His tie's tip was tucked beneath his waistcoat. The waistcoat had a brass chain running from its central button hole to a shallow watch pocket. Rain droplets sat upon his fair skin, neat, dark-red hair, and trimmed beard and moustache glistened in the lamplight. "What you doin' here?"

"I need to speak with you." Miss Trent approached the table. "I came inside when my knocking made the door swing open. Where've you been? Don't you lock your door?"

"Out the back." He set the lamp aside. "No one's daft enough to nick from a copper. What do you wanna talk to me about—and how'd you know where I lived?"

"Richard gave me your address. He intends to meet with us both, here, tomorrow morning. Didn't he tell you?"

"Yeah, he got me on the telephone just before I left the Yard, but he said nowt about you being there. What's going on?"

"I had a visit from Inspector Woolfe tonight—"

"Woolfe went to Bow Street?"

"Yes, but that's not—"

"What for?"

"If you *stop* interrupting me, John, I'll explain."

Conway straightened and, folding his arms across his chest, leaned against the butler's sink behind him. The room was a touch larger than the parlour. The chimney breast was dominated by an open range with an oven on its right, a blank, "sham" panel on its left, and a grate of cold coals in its centre. The oven was no larger than a stew pot, with a hob upon which a cast-iron teapot stood. The entire range was small in comparison to most found in domestic kitchens. Twisted rolls of newspaper kindling, and a box of matches, lined the table's edge. To the sink's right was a wooden draining board with the morning's overturned mug and plate on it. A marked—but clean—towel hung from a hook beneath the board. Opposite the range was a dresser as battered as the parlour's sideboard. Unused plates and mugs lined its shelves, while three drawers beneath held cutlery and other necessities like darning needles, thread, and candles. Two cupboards, housed below the drawers, contained basic dried goods. The remainder of Conway's meagre supplies were on a set of wall shelves to the right of the door.

"Woolfe spoke to me about something unrelated to my visit here tonight," Miss Trent continued. "That conversation will be discussed with you and Richard tomorrow morning as planned." She lifted her hand as his face contorted with anger and his lips parted to protest. "What I need to speak to you about tonight happened *after* I met with Richard." Conway closed his mouth but gave a deep, guttural groan of frustration. Miss Trent's eyes narrowed. "I had another visitor waiting for me when I returned to Bow Street," she continued in a firm voice. "He—or she—was all in black and wouldn't give either Sam or me their name."

"How come you don't know if it was a man or woman?" Conway enquired through a sigh while taking the towel from its hook to dry his damp face and beard.

"The *entire* body was covered—face, hands, even hair. The being also hissed rather than spoke." She sighed. "As well as its name, the being refused to tell me why it needed the Society's help. Instead, it gave me an address and insisted the Society's members would be given further instruction once they'd arrived there."

"Where does it want 'em to go?" Conway rehung the towel.

"The Flagstaff on Hampstead Heath."

"And they told you nowt else?" Conway gave a deep sniff as he, again, folded his arms across his chest,

"Yes. I tried to keep the being at the house, to try to garner more information from it, but it pushed me aside and ran. A carriage waited outside. Both escaped before I could reach them."

"Any markings on the carriage?"

"None."

"Dunno what you expect me to do about it, then. Do you know how many cabs, carriages, and 'buses there are in London?" Conway enquired, without expecting an answer, as he retrieved a cigarette from his trouser pocket.

"I want you to go to the Flagstaff with Sam and find out what this is all about."

"You what?" Conway stared at her. "It'll be more than my life's worth if the Yard catch me helping you lot out."

"You've helped the Society before," Miss Trent pointed out.

"Because Jones told me to. What you're talking about though, is me working for you. That's not the same as letting the Society in on one of my cases. I'm a copper, not a Bow Streeter." He put the cigarette between his lips and lit it with a match. After filling his lungs and exhaling the smoke, he added, "You don't let anyone from the Yard in."

"That was Richard's choice, not mine."

"Yeah, but it makes me look like a bent copper, giving you lot help and information when I've got no proper reason to." He imbibed some more smoke and, exhaling it, enquired, "Anyway, why send anyone? Sounds dangerous to me." Taking another draw from his cigarette, he held it in his mouth while he plucked some kindling from the table and laid it in a row within the grate. Coal was next laid on top, followed by yet more kindling. "The bloke, or woman, will come back if it's that important."

"And if they don't? Someone's *life* could be in danger."

"Now you're being daft." Conway straightened to meet her gaze.

"Am I? Whoever came to the house tonight didn't want me to know their identity, John. People don't hide who they are for no reason. If they, or someone they know, are in danger, they may have been putting themselves, and their friend, at risk by simply coming to the Society. If we don't go to the Flagstaff tonight, we may have blood on our hands come morning."

"You don't know that."

"And you don't know to the contrary." She stepped in front of him as he shook his head and tried to retrieve more coal. "Sam can defend himself if it comes to it—as you well know."

Conway, having stopped at her obstruction, rubbed his jaw at her mention of Mr Snyder's ability to defend himself.

"But I still can't send him alone," Miss Trent went on. "You have the law behind you. If something were to go wrong, you can step in. While it's true I can't accept any case without hearing its full details, I can't refuse a case for the same reason either."

"People don't like coppers." Conway crushed his cigarette against the sham panel and dropped its butt into the dust bin by the back door. "Me being there might make it worse."

"I wasn't told not to involve the police. *Please,* I'm not asking you to investigate the case for the Society, just make sure Sam comes back in one piece." She watched Conway's face closely as he glanced at the stove, ran his hand over his jaw, and sighed.

"Fine," he said finally.

"*Thank* you, John," she beamed, her smile then faltering as a thought occurred to her. "Let's not tell Richard about this."

"Not likely." Conway lifted his hand toward the kitchen door. "After you."

* * *

Described by many as the "lungs of London", Hampstead Heath's wide-open spaces—over two hundred and fifty acres worth—provided a peaceful, green idyll to the otherwise suffocating, industrialised, urban sprawl of the capital. A popular summer spot among children sailing toy boats was the pond where The Grove and Heath Street met, and where Heath Street ran into Heath End Hill. On bank holidays, thousands of Londoners would descend upon the Heath—though their fun was often too fast and furious for some.

Near the junction, and located at one of the Heath's highest points, was the four hundred and thirty-foot tall Flagstaff. Similar in shape and form to a central mast found aboard a galleon—minus main sails and crow's nest—the Flagstaff was kept in place by sturdy rigging. Nevertheless, its wood creaked and groaned against the strong winds of the storm.

Dim light emanated from street lamps on the corners of The Grove and Heath End Hill, while the distant lights of *Jack Straw's Castle* inn occasionally peeked through the dense foliage as it was lifted and dropped in waves by the wind. Famous for having been visited by many a literary man and artist in years gone by, the inn stood on Heath End Hill with another building between it and the junction. The outline of both, along with the pavements, dirt roads, pond, Flagstaff, and Heath, were undistinguishable in the pitch black beyond the lamp light's limited reach, however. Heavy cloud cover also blocked the moonlight, forcing Mr Snyder to rely upon his own instincts and those of his horse to avoid driving his cab from the thoroughfare.

The terrain upon which the Flagstaff stood, he knew, was uneven. The rain, though ended, had left its scent in the air and, in Mr Snyder's experience, its mark on the Heath as well. He therefore eased Blue-Shirt to a halt at the corner of The Grove, underneath the street lamp, and peered through the small window in the cab's roof at Inspector Conway within. He said, "We're gonna have to stop 'ere. I don't wanna risk gettin' the cab stuck in that mud."

"Yeah." Conway lifted the cab's doors from his knees and disappeared as he alighted onto the road. Mr Snyder detached the Davey lamp and lifted it down to the policeman. Both men then looked in the Flagstaff's direction. "Can you see anyone?"

"Nah." Mr Snyder glanced ahead and over his shoulder. "There's no one about. What time do you make it?"

"Ten to midnight." Conway lifted the lamp to arm's length and walked toward the Flagstaff. "Wait here."

Mr Snyder's reply was lost to the wind as a violent gust rattled the cab and rustled the trees' leaves. The Davey lamp's candle also flickered, but Conway was quick to shield it with his coat. When the threat eventually passed, he brought out the lamp and held it aloft once more.

The uneven terrain was muddier than Mr Snyder had feared. In several places, Conway had to extend both arms and adjust his footing to steady himself. Despite this, he made it to the Flagstaff in good time. Using the meagre lamp light, he guided his hand to the main pole and held it there as he looked in all directions. Surrounded by darkness, Mr Snyder's hunched figure atop his cab, illuminated by the streetlamp, appeared small. The expanse between him and Conway also seemed greater, but Conway knew it wasn't so. A prolonged creak of the wood above him encouraged Conway to relinquish his grip upon the Flagstaff and start a circuit of the immediate area.

Mr Snyder watched the dot of light from Conway's lamp float through the darkness. With a shiver, he took a flask of brandy from his great cloak and had a sip. While he was replacing the flask, however, he heard wagon wheels trundling along dirt toward him. Coming from the direction of *Jack Straw's Castle,* the sound was all Mr Snyder could distinguish of the vehicle at first. After a moment, two bright, white balls penetrated the darkness. They became larger and more intense while the trundling became louder and more distinct. Only when the vehicle entered the spotlight, emitted by the streetlamp on

36

the corner opposite Mr Snyder, was he able to see the unmarked, black, four-wheeled carriage and driver.

"Who's that?" Conway's breathless voice enquired as he ran across the Heath to the cab. Gripping both the lamp and the cab's side window, he leaned forward to catch his breath and watched the newcomer.

"Dunno, but they've just got 'ere."

"Is that the same driver who took your client from Bow Street?" Conway released the window and gripped the handle of a wooden truncheon hanging inside his overcoat. His dark-blue hues kept their gaze fixed on the carriage. Its driver remained still, however, and no passengers alighted.

"I couldn't tell you, Inspector." Mr Snyder shrugged his shoulders. "I was too busy gettin' Blue Shirt to the livery to take the time to look at him."

"Someone's getting out."

True enough the carriage door opened, and a figure alighted. Even in the weak lamplight, Mr Snyder and Conway saw the figure was covered by black cloth. Though the distance wasn't great between them, it seemed the figure was walking at a slow pace. Whether it was due to caution or arrogance, neither man could tell. Mr Snyder therefore kept a tight grip on the reins while Conway kept a tight grip on the truncheon, both poised to act should this uncanny stranger make it necessary.

The figure stopped a few feet from Blue-Shirt and hissed, "You are from the Bow Street Society?"

"'E is." Conway gave a sideways nod to Mr Snyder. "I'm Inspector John Conway of Scotland Yard."

"*What?!*" the figure snarled as its shoulders jerked upward like hackles. "You have no *business* being here!"

"Nah, I don't," Conway agreed. "That's why I'm only here to make sure 'e"—another sideways nod to Mr Snyder—"gets back to Bow Street safely."

"What's the instructions?" Mr Snyder enquired.

"I can't give them to *him,*" the figure hissed.

"Now look 'ere," Mr Snyder began. "We've done nowt but cooperate with you. You've told us nowt, but we're 'ere and we wanna help. That's all."

"You will be secret with me, then?" the figure enquired, addressing the policeman.

Conway glanced at Mr Snyder but, after a brief hesitation, nodded. "Yeah."

"Very well." The figure's shoulders eased. "That which concerns you isn't here, however. You must put your trust in me, and I will take you to it."

"Nah, you tell us what you've got to say here, or we're going," Conway said.

"Have your bloke lead on and I'll follow," Mr Snyder said.

Conway stared at him in disbelief. "We're not gonna—"

"Take your horse and cab to *Jack Straw's Castle*," the figure interrupted, ignoring Conway's glare. "When you return my driver will take us to where we need to be." The figure's cloth-enshrouded head turned toward Conway as it hissed, "Come, Inspector. You may wait in my carriage."

"I'm not going anywhere until I get a name," Conway growled.

"All in good time," the figure replied. It stepped aside as Mr Snyder geed Blue-Shirt and the cab lurched into motion. Seeing he had no choice but to comply, since it was obvious Mr Snyder intended to do so, Conway sighed and gestured for their 'host' to lead on. Removing his hand from his overcoat, he followed the figure to the carriage and climbed inside ahead of him.

By the time Mr Snyder joined them, Conway sat in the corner of the carriage's interior with a wide, black length of cloth covering his eyes. Needless to say, Mr Snyder had been startled by the sight. The figure gestured to him to join Conway, however, and—given the apparent risk to the policeman—Mr Snyder felt obliged to obey. No sooner had he settled himself upon the plush, burgundy bench, however, was he, too, blindfolded. A firm knock upon the carriage's ceiling reached the two men's ears a heartbeat later, and the carriage began its journey to destinations unknown.

THREE

Without further explanation from their 'host', Conway and Mr Snyder were forced to sit in silence for the journey's duration. Each had paid close attention to how the carriage had leaned and turned, however—with varying degrees of success. While Mr Snyder had formed a fair idea of the route they'd taken in his mind, Conway was lost after the initial half hour. Instead, he'd chosen to concoct various possible plans of escape from the carriage, none of which concluded with an injury-free outcome.

The termination of the uneventful, two-hour carriage ride increased their chances of escaping unscathed but, so far, there had been no indication of immediate danger. This changed when Conway attempted to remove his blindfold, however.

"Keep it on," the figure hissed.

"Why?"

The door beside Conway opened, and a strong hand gripped his wrist. It yanked hard upon his arm and dragged him from the carriage. A second hand at once took hold of his upper arm and Conway's entire appendage was twisted and pressed against the small of his back. Grunting, he pulled the truncheon from his overcoat and attempted to swing it. A firm shove by his captor sent the weapon hurtling from Conway's grip. The policeman heard it land in gravel nearby, but his captor continued onward. With their full weight against his back, Conway was propelled along with them.

"'Ere, what's all this?!" Mr Snyder's voice demanded from the carriage's other side. More gravel was disturbed as he attempted his own resistance, but was soon overwhelmed and led away, too.

"No harm will come to you," the figure hissed between Mr Snyder and Conway when the four ascended some steep steps. A warm blast of air next enveloped them as Conway and Mr Snyder felt the ground soften beneath their feet. Conway had been held back a moment, too, while Mr Snyder had been pressed onward at a greater pace. Familiar sounds, made foreign by their lack of sight, reached the men's ears, yet disappeared as quickly as they'd come. The chiming of a grandfather clock, the tapping of their feet against hard tiles while they crossed, the clicking of locks followed by the creaking of hinges, and even a piano being played in the distance.

Then the sounds died away completely, leaving only silence in their wake. Conway and Mr Snyder had also stopped. The hands, which had kept a vice-like grip upon them for so long, slipped away, too.

"You may remove your blindfolds," the figure hissed and a door behind them opened and closed with a shuffling of feet in between. By the time Conway and Mr Snyder had reclaimed their vision, both the figure and driver were gone. Instead, they were faced with a pale-complexioned man. He was gazing into a great fire housed within an even greater marble fireplace. So immense was its size, it occupied three-quarters of the vast room's wall.

The room itself was long yet wide. Opposite the fireplace were floor-to-ceiling French windows covered by cumbersome, plum-coloured curtains. The plush carpet matched the curtains in colour, as did the flock-embossed, fabric paper adorning the walls. There were two crystal chandeliers hanging from the high ceiling, but the only light in the room was emitted by the fire. As a result, the curves, peaks, and troths of the raised, plaster fresco that adorned the ceiling cast shadows which stretched and danced in the flickering firelight. The furniture was a plethora of antiques and modern pieces imported from around the world. Yet, neither Conway nor Mr Snyder could confess to possessing knowledge of such things. All they could've remarked upon were the dust sheets covering several large, flat, square objects on the wall. An exchanged glance between them was enough reassurance they'd both noticed this strange arrangement. A further glance across the room, by Conway, confirmed no other dust sheets were present.

The—yet unidentified—man turned toward them and smiled. His severe, angular cheekbones, extended, square chin, and narrow, pointed nose made the gesture more sinister than pleasant, however.

"Good evening, gentlemen," he said, his voice rich in tone. A heavily waxed moustache—split down the middle with tips curled into points—bobbed when the man spoke again. "I must apologise for the way you were manhandled. I can assure you stern words shall be had." He extended a slender hand toward a straight-backed, shallow-cushioned sofa. "Please, sit."

"Not until we get a name," Conway growled.

"Of course," the man replied with a dip of his head and a show of black, wavy hair. When he straightened, neither man saw wrinkles, sagging skin, or weathering upon their host's face—unlike their own features. "My name is Mr Terrence Partridge."

"Woz you the bloke who came to Bow Street?" Mr Snyder enquired.

"Dismiss all thoughts of him," Mr Partridge replied. Shifting his gaze to Conway, he added, "I understand you're an officer from Scotland Yard, Inspector Conway. While it's regretful the police have become involved, I'm nonetheless aware of my own failings in the matter." Mr Partridge gave a weak smile. "I should've given clearer instructions." Walking to a chair, he gestured toward the sofa, again. "Please, now shall you sit?"

"Okay," Mr Snyder agreed. Approaching the indicated sofa, he first removed his cloak and hat before settling on its edge. He was careful to keep his wet things on his lap. Conway, on the other hand, sat without such precautions. Mr Partridge's lip twitched as he looked upon the damp patch that appeared beneath the policeman.

"I know it's late, so I shan't hesitate in getting straight to the point," Mr Partridge began. "The matter I'd like the Society to look into relates to a doll of considerable age and a collectible of the highest value—"

"You *what*?" Conway growled and leaned forward. "You send us to the Heath in the middle of the night, blindfold us, and bring us all the way here for a *doll*?"

"Not for the doll, Inspector," Mr Partridge retorted, firmly. "But for the danger it poses."

"What do you mean?" Mr Snyder enquired.

"The last two gentlemen to own the doll have both died. Though each was unknown to the other, the circumstances surrounding their deaths are uncanny in their similarities: both were killed by a single gunshot wound, and both were alone in locked rooms. In each death the doll was close by, grinning from behind its glass case."

"And how do you know all this?" Conway enquired.

"Not from the auctioneer," Mr Partridge stated. "When the doll was purchased no mention was made of its history—either by the auctioneer himself or in the catalogue description. It wasn't until a short while later— after the doll had been brought to the house—a dinner guest remarked upon it being the 'Cosgrove curse' one. When he was pressed to elaborate, he told of Professor Benjamin Cosgrove's death—he being the doll's first known owner to have died—and Mister Edgar Elmore's. According to our storyteller, Mister Elmore purchased the doll from an auction house around six months ago. The doll hadn't been in the Elmore household but twenty-four hours before he, too, was killed."

"A load of clap-trap if you ask me," Conway remarked.

"It's true," Mr Partridge replied. "Whether you choose to believe it is neither here nor there. This isn't a matter for the police's interest but the Bow Street Society's." Mr Partridge shifted his gaze to Mr Snyder. "At first, the story was regarded with condescension. That is, until a window near to the doll was smashed, without rhyme or reason, when the house was locked up for the winter."

"Someone broke in," Conway dismissed.

"Nothing was stolen and the glass from the window was on the *outside*, Inspector. Whatever had broken it could've only come from *within* the room."

"Maybe a servant broke it by accident and didn't want to say?" Mr Snyder offered.

"No, there was only the groundsman here at the time and he had no way of entering the house. He was simply charged with patrolling the grounds and checking all was secured from the outside."

"So, someone tells a ghost story, and your window gets broke, and that makes you think the doll's dangerous?" Conway challenged. "If you've got nowt else for us but that, I'm going 'ome." He stood but neither in his company moved.

"Thank you for that perfect example of why I didn't want the police involved," Mr Partridge stated through a sigh. Addressing Mr Snyder, he enquired, "The Bow Street Society undertake cases the police refuse to investigate, correct?"

"Yeah, that's right," Mr Snyder replied.

"Good." Mr Partridge rose to his feet, followed at once by Mr Snyder. "If you would like to follow me, then, Mr Snyder, I will take you to the doll. I will have you escorted back to the carriage to wait, Inspector."

"Nah," Conway growled as he stepped in between them. "Wherever 'e goes, *I* go."

"I see now why the newspapers call you 'Bulldog'," Mr Partridge remarked, drily. "Very well. This way, gentlemen. After the incident with the window, it was decided it would be safer for the doll to be put out of harm's way."

Mr Partridge led them to the back of the room to another door. With a glance at Conway, he unlocked it and went inside. Beyond was a much smaller room with considerable, wooden-framed windows on five of its angular walls. These walls followed the contours of a traditional hexagon's top left quarter and right half. Where the hexagon's bottom left quarter should've been was a ninety-degree-angled corner. The door, through which they'd entered, was located on the hexagon's bottom side. There was sturdy brickwork on the bottom third of the room's walls as windows occupied the remaining two thirds. Thus, the whole room appeared to sway under the strength of the ferocious wind outside. Creaking—reminiscent of the Flagstaff—filled the limited space. Even the coned roof above their heads—with its many exposed beams and great, iron nails—groaned and complained like a man's deep voice. A draft had hit the three the moment they'd entered, too. Since the door had been left open, both Conway and Mr Snyder stepped back toward the fire's warmth. Mr Partridge, meanwhile, stood his ground.

Against the wall in the far-left corner was a tall, glass case. Within stood a brown-haired, brown-eyed doll approximately three feet tall and wearing the distinctive red tunic of a British Army officer's uniform. Over its chest was the criss-cross of white cotton straps, while its feet wore black, leather riding boots. The doll stood against a painted backdrop of the English countryside. Once brightly coloured, the scenery was now pale and faded. Only the portion of backdrop against which the doll stood had retained its vibrancy. The doll stood on a wooden base painted and carved to resemble grass. A taxidermy, infant bunny lay curled at the doll's feet, while wax flowers were stuck to the faux ground. Around the doll's waist was a broad, white belt and hip holster. In the doll's right hand was a revolver pointed downwards. It rested on the doll's outer thigh as the doll's arm was flush against its side. The doll's left hand was flat and fixed to its opposite leg. Varnished leaves, affixed to carved sticks of wood, formed a bush to the doll's right. Beneath the glass case was a block of wood no deeper than two inches and, below that, the table upon which the entire thing stood. Conway and Mr Snyder could see beneath this table, through to the brick work behind. The table was around four feet tall.

"Here is the window which was broken," Mr Partridge announced, indicating the window opposite the doll. "As you can see, gentlemen, there are no doors leading from this room to the outside. These others"—he looked behind him—"are solid and can only be opened from the inside."

"Do you always keep the doll in 'ere?" Mr Snyder enquired as he moved toward it. Leaning forward, he peered at its harsh cheeks, sharp nose, and pale, thin lips through the glass. Its eyes, though large, failed to reflect Mr Snyder's face. Instead, their brown depths stared at him—emotionless, flat… soulless.

"Yes," Mr Partridge replied and joined Mr Snyder at the case. "I'm actually rather fond of it." He met Mr Snyder's questioning gaze. "The intention isn't to sell it, Mr Snyder. It's to be shipped to America for a thorough valuation."

Conway grunted from the door but, despite both men glancing at him, neither Mr Snyder nor Mr Partridge responded. Instead, Mr Partridge continued, "I know it sounds simpler than it is, but all that is required is for the Society to determine if the doll does indeed pose a physical threat to anyone."

"If the doll's shooting people, why's the glass not broke?" Conway questioned.

"I have no idea, Inspector," Mr Partridge replied. "The case is sealed, as far as one can fathom." He looked between them as he pressed his chin against his Adam's apple a moment. "Therefore, the prospect of possible supernatural forces influencing the doll should also be explored by the Society."

"You think the doll's haunted?" Mr Snyder enquired, his bushy-brows raised.

"The household would feel safer if *all* possibilities were explored," Mr Partridge replied.

Another grunt sounded from Conway.

"Okay, Mr Partridge," Mr Snyder said. "Other Society members will have to see the doll, too, then."

"I understand, but they can't come here," Mr Partridge replied.

"Why not?" Conway interjected. "And what's with all the secrecy? Blindfolding us and all that."

"As I said earlier," Mr Partridge said. "The doll is highly valuable. If it was to become known it may be cursed, its value may diminish considerably. Hence, the Bow Street Society's involvement, and the cautionary measures employed." He addressed Mr Snyder, "I'll have the doll brought to your Miss Trent in the morning." His smile faltered. "The Society will be liable for any damage caused to the doll while in its care, of course."

"It'll be well taken care of, sir," Mr Snyder replied. "You have my word."

"Jolly good." Mr Partridge's smile grew. "If you need to contact me again, stand under the Flagstaff, and you'll be collected within the hour." Mr Partridge stepped around Mr Snyder and returned to Conway at the door. "I hope you're satisfied enough about Mr Snyder's safety to stay away during his next visit, Inspector."

"We'll see, sir," Conway stated.

Mr Partridge's lips pursed together as he glared at Conway a moment. "*Well*," he began in a terse voice.

"Unless you have any further questions, Mr Snyder, I'll have you taken back to *Jack Straw's Castle.*"

"Nah, I've got nowt else to ask," Mr Snyder replied. "Inspector?"

"Just one. If you was gonna send the doll to Bow Street all along, why bring us 'ere?" Conway enquired.

"To see where it was kept, of course," Mr Partridge replied. "One cannot appreciate the uncanniness of the window's breakage without seeing the room for oneself. Don't you think so?"

"Nah," Conway replied, tersely. "But I'll take it for now."

Mr Partridge's lips pursed together once more as his glare returned. "*Please…* make yourselves comfortable, gentlemen." Mr Partridge followed them into the larger room, closed the door, and locked it as a fierce gust seized the wooden walls and rattled the windows. "And please put your blindfolds back on. I shan't be a mo—"

A tremendous bang ripped through Mr Partridge's words. Throwing his arms above his head, he ducked behind the sofa and crouched upon the floor. Inspector Conway and Mr Snyder—who'd both jolted at the noise— soon joined him.

"What was that?!" Mr Partridge cried, his voice strangled by his body's tension. He gripped the sofa's back and his knuckles whitened from the strain. With wide eyes, he looked from his guests, to the door of the hexagonal room, and back again.

"A gun shot," Conway growled. Slowly moving upward, he peered over the sofa's top at the closed door. "*Don't* move," he ordered. Keeping his knees bent and his head low, he moved around the sofa and toward the curtains. Mr Snyder, who'd followed Conway to the sofa's edge, crouched behind the arm to watch his approach of the room. The deep whistle of the wind reverberated around them, with an occasional interruption of a snap or crackle from the fire. When Conway neared the locked door, still bent down low, the wind strengthened. It howled with ferociousness akin to contempt as Conway peered through the keyhole and felt a shiver sweep through his body, like the lightning bolt that illuminated the room beyond.

"What did you see?" Mr Snyder enquired when Conway leapt to his feet and held out his open hand to Mr Partridge. Though the colour had drained from his features, Conway didn't speak as the key was pressed into his palm. Instead, he strode back to the door. Both Mr Snyder and Mr Partridge followed, the latter huddled behind the former. Another lightning bolt illuminated the interior of the hexagonal room when Conway threw open its door. While the ensuring thunder rumbled through the house, the three men could only stare in disbelief at what they saw.

FOUR

The rain had cleared by the next morning and blue skies
prevailed over London. With them came milder air and a
low sun that bathed the capital with brilliant, white light.
On Bow Street, a gentleman disembarked from his
carriage and went to the Society's door. Rather than
knock, however, he took a moment to inspect his reflection
in the nearby window. His duck-egg-blue frockcoat—with
its silk, black lapels, cinched waist, and wide skirt—
matched the colour of his cravat and waistcoat's
embroidered roses. The background colour of the
waistcoat was midnight blue. His trousers—tailored to a
standard as high as his other clothes—were black cotton.
As he leaned forward, he pulled down his high
cheekbone's flesh with a black leather clad fingertip to
peer at the puffy, dark area beneath his eye. A brief
inspection of the other eye confirmed it to be the same.
The gentleman therefore removed his gloves and smoothed
the lead-based powder—applied to the remainder of his
complexion—over the offensive sight. Once complete, he
checked his reflection again, furrowed his brow at the
trembling of his scratched hands, and replaced his gloves.
Only then did he lift his cane's silver handle to knock
thrice upon the door.

"I was starting to suspect you wouldn't arrive, Mr
Locke," Miss Trent remarked upon seeing him. "We're in
the meeting room." She indicated the second door on the
right of the hallway.

Removing his hat, Mr Percy Locke hung it upon
the stand and slid his cane beside the one present in the
umbrella pan. The other was ebony—like his—with a
skull-shaped handle made of silver. It warranted closer
inspection but, before he could sate his curiosity, Mr
Locke was drawn to a sound behind him. Akin to the

shuffling of feet, it had originated from the room beside Miss Trent's office. With a renewed sense of intrigue, Mr Locke silently approached and peered through the gap between the frame and door—the latter having been left ajar.

The room beyond was, as far as Mr Locke could tell, unfurnished. With his back to him was a man who, though short, had broad shoulders and tremendous biceps. His brown hair—flecked with grey—was cut close to his head, while his posture was perfect. The cut and material of his charcoal-coloured tail coat, beige, cotton trousers, and black, leather riding boots were of a high quality.

"The *other* room, Mr Locke," Miss Trent said at his side. Her voice prompted both men to look around.

The—yet unidentified—man was revealed to be in his late thirties. Burn scarring covered the right side of his jaw and cheek, while his right hand was a wrought-iron contraption. Though it had the correct skeletal parts, the false limb rested, motionless, against his side. His dark-brown eyes grazed Mr Locke's face before settling upon Miss Trent's. In a soft, Dublin accent, he said, "I'll be right wit you, Miss Trent."

"Whenever you're finished is fine, Mr Skinner," Miss Trent replied. Stepping back, she watched Mr Locke with expectant eyes.

"Good morning, Mr Skinner," Mr Locke said, acknowledging the Irishman. With a subtle tug upon his glove's cuff, he added, "Lead the way, Miss Trent."

Miss Trent glanced at the gloves but didn't request they be removed. Instead, she strode past him with a rustle of skirts and entered the meeting room. Once the unfurnished space adjacent to the parlour, the room now had a table down its centre. Chairs—of various styles, sizes, and repair—lined its edge. Teapots, cream jugs, and sugar bowls were arranged upon it, while teacups and saucers were set before each place setting. A blackboard, scratched and stained with chalk dust, was on the wall to the door's left. At the opposite end of the room was a cast-iron hearth housed within a large, intricately carved oak fireplace. While the walls were papered with a brown and cream stripe, they boasted no adornments other than an embossed, diamond patterned wallpaper on their lower halves. A plain, oak dado rail separated the two. Floorboards, whose dark varnish was thinned and marked, were left exposed. To the blackboard's left, a four-paned, sash window overlooked the well-tended garden at the building's rear.

"Mr Locke," Miss Trent began. "This is Mr Virgil Verity, a retired schoolmaster and spiritualist. Mr Verity, this is Mr Percival Locke, an illusionist who also owns the Paddington Palladium."

"'Ow do's," Mr Verity replied in a broad, Tyneside accent while his skeletal-like hand shook Mr Locke's slender one. Despite the leanness of his appendage, the rest of Mr Verity was well-built. He was clothed in a tweed suit and black waistcoat, the latter's colour complementing the earthen shades of the former. A chocolate-brown tie was tucked under the waistcoat, while Mr Verity's broad neck was hidden by the wide, starched collar of his white shirt. A wholesome, off-white beard and moustache then, in turn, hid much of his tie and collar. His grey complexion, meanwhile, was wrinkled and riddled with age spots—"probably enough for each of my sixty years!" he'd often jest. Yet, despite his advanced age, he'd kept a full head of thick, silver hair which he'd back-combed and tucked behind his ears.

"Well, thank you," Mr Locke replied.

"You've already met our freelance artist, Miss Georgina Dexter, our resident cabman, Mr Samuel Snyder, and solicitor, Mr Gregory Elliott," Miss Trent said, glancing to them.

"Indeed," Mr Locke replied, extending a hand to Mr Elliott. He'd not spoken to him since the Dorsey case. Yet, despite the passage of time, Mr Elliott's complexion had remained translucent-like in its appearance. Though Mr Elliott and Mr Locke were both in their late twenties, the stoicism of the Mr Elliott's green-brown eyes and slender face gifted him a gravitas usually found in men of more advanced years.

"A pleasure to make your acquaintance again," Mr Elliott remarked as he shook the offered hand.

"The feeling is mutual," Mr Locke replied, reclaiming his hand to shake that of the cabman. "Mr Snyder."

"Good mornin', sir," Mr Snyder said, his large hand dwarfing Mr Locke's.

"Good morning, Mr Locke," Miss Dexter said. Rather than a handshake though, she gifted him with a warm smile.

"Miss Dexter, a pleasure as always," Mr Locke replied, sending the eighteen-year-old into a blush.

At only five feet tall, Miss Dexter was markedly shorter than Mr Locke. Despite this, her physical proportions and poise were perfect. Sat on the far end of the table, between Mr Snyder and Mr Elliott, she kept her small, clasped hands in her lap. The firelight to her right heightened the fairness of her complexion, in addition to giving her curled—yet pinned—red hair a halo-like glow. Her attire consisted of a plum-coloured dress with straight skirts, high collar, and long sleeves. Simple lace, that matched the dress in hue, formed a 'v' over her bosom. It also edged her cuffs and collar.

"Please, take a seat, Mr Locke," Miss Trent invited as she indicated a vacant chair beside Mr Verity. The elder man had taken a spot on Mr Elliott's other side but had pushed his chair back to angle it toward the hearth.

"Thank you," Mr Locke replied and took the offered seat.

"Tea, Mr Locke?" Miss Dexter enquired.

"No." He smiled. "Thank you, anyway." Addressing Miss Trent then, he enquired, "And Mr Skinner is…?"

"The bodyguard of Lady Mirrell, and former officer with Her Majesty's British Royal Navy," Miss Trent replied and checked her pocket watch. "Once our final guest arrives, I'll explain everything—" The sound of knocking interrupted her. "That should be him now." She stood and, on her way out of the room, added, "Make yourselves comfortable, everyone, as we'll begin as soon as I'm back."

"Mr Verity," Mr Locke said as he scratched the back of his hand over his glove. "Since you are a spiritualist, do you also support the practises of mediums?"

"I both support and condemn them," Mr Verity replied. "There's folks who'll just as easily cheat you about death as cheat you in life. I don't care for them. A maid who has her candle blown out when there's no wind, or a widow who talks to her dead husband in her dreams— *they* are the ones I care about."

"Incidences which may be attributed to a draft, and the loneliness of an old woman suddenly widowed after many years of happy marriage," Mr Elliott remarked in a monotone.

"Yeah and no. There's plenty of evil under the sun, Mr Elliott, as you know. Not'll of it can be thrown in Newgate, or explained by science, or"—Mr Verity looked to Mr Locke—"exposed as fraud by magicians."

"Sorry I'm late," Mr Maxwell said as he entered the meeting room. He stilled, however, as Miss Dexter's angelic appearance seized his vision and hushed his hearing. An ephemeral recollection of her lips pressed against his swept through him, leaving in its wake an intense longing. He approached an empty chair and, holding its back, watched Miss Dexter.

"*Mr* Maxwell," Miss Trent's voice urged.

"Yes…?" he responded, his dark-green eyes widening when he saw Miss Trent's scowl. Looking to the others, he realised they were also watching him. Small beads of sweat formed on his forehead as he swallowed. "I was just—"

"Not listening?" Miss Trent interrupted and placed her hand on her hip.

"Yes," Mr Maxwell replied. "I mean, no. I mean—"

"Sit down," Miss Trent said.

Mr Maxwell swallowed harder and, pulling back the chair, dropped down onto it.

Like Miss Dexter, he sported a head of red hair. His was wavy and parted at the side, however. The two shared a fair complexion, but his was sickly in appearance. His defined cheekbones were also covered in freckles. In comparison with the gentlemen of the room, his attire would be considered cheap. A coarse, black frock coat covered his black trousers and waistcoat. A dark-green cravat sat pride of place in the centre of a starched collar too large for his slender neck. His thin fingers were spotted with ink blotches, and his shoes were scuffed and worn.

"As I was saying," Miss Trent resumed. "This is Mr Virgil Verity, Mr Maxwell. He's a retired schoolmaster and spiritualist. Mr Verity, this is Mr Joseph Maxwell, a journalist with the *Gaslight Gazette.*"

"Sir," Mr Verity said and extended his hand across the table.

Having blinked at the unexpected sound of the man's accent—and the nature of his work—Mr Maxwell wiped his hand upon his frockcoat and gave Mr Verity's a limp shake. "Good morning." When their handshake ended, Mr Maxwell stole a glance at Miss Dexter. At such close quarters, he could see every facet of her delicate features as she looked toward Miss Trent who'd returned to the table's head.

"You've all been invited here today because the Bow Street Society has accepted a new commission," Miss Trent announced.

Miss Dexter's shoulders rose as she filled her lungs. Her exhalation was soft, accompanied by a gentle relaxation of her jaw muscles.

Mr Maxwell felt his heart lift at the sight. A glance to Mr Snyder nearby expelled his exuberance, however.

Mr Snyder—who'd watched Mr Maxwell for as long as he'd watched Miss Dexter—scowled when their eyes met. The sight—so rare upon the features of the otherwise jovial Bow Streeter—was enough to avert Mr Maxwell's gaze and turn his stomach.

Miss Trent, having caught the hostile look out the corner of her eye, waited a moment before she continued. When neither Mr Snyder nor Mr Maxwell spoke, she made a mental note of the incident and said, "Last night, a man dressed in black visited the Society."

"Not I," Mr Locke interjected with a smirk.

"I didn't say it was," Miss Trent retorted. "In fact, it's unclear at the moment exactly *who* he was, since his face, hands, and hair were also concealed by the fabric."

Mr Locke's smile faded as he reclined within his chair.

"Though he refused to give me his name, he made a request for members of the Bow Street Society to meet with him at the Hampstead Heath Flagstaff at midnight. Once there, he said, the members would be given the full details of the case he wanted the Society to investigate." Miss Trent paused as Mr Skinner entered the room and sat. "Once my visitor had left, I spoke to Mr Snyder and he agreed to honour the arrangement."

"You went alone?" Mr Elliott enquired from Mr Snyder who looked to Miss Trent.

"No," she replied for him. "Inspector John Conway went as well."

"Is Scotland Yard also investigating the case, then?" Mr Elliott enquired.

"No." Miss Trent paused to inhale and release her breath as a soft sigh. "Inspector Conway went because I asked him to, to ensure Mr Snyder's safety."

"You thought the masked man might hurt him?" Mr Maxwell queried.

"Yes," Miss Trent replied. "At the time, I didn't have enough information to know either way, or even to help me decide whether or not to accept the commission. Mr Snyder was willing to meet with the man and Inspector Conway agreed to make sure Mr Snyder returned safely."

"Despite the fact it was Inspector Conway who struck Mr Dorsey while he was in police custody," Mr Elliott remarked.

"Mr Dorsey refused to pursue the matter, Mr Elliott," Miss Trent reminded him. "Besides, Mr Snyder came back in one piece, so your disapproval of the inspector's assistance last night is irrelevant."

With an uncharacteristic scowl, Mr Elliott pursed his lips.

"I don't put much stock in a copper's word either," Mr Skinner remarked to him. Sitting bolt upright in his chair, Mr Skinner's actual hand toyed with a toothpick while his iron one rested on the table top.

"When we got to the heath," Mr Snyder commenced. "We woz the only ones there at the Flagstaff. The inspecta wandered over to it, with my cab's lamp, and then come back as another carriage came up to mine. The bloke in black got out and talked to us. 'E wasn't pleased to find I'd brought the inspecta but he agreed to take both of us along. I put my cab in the livery at *Jack Straw's Castle* but, when I got to the bloke's carriage, I saw the inspecta blindfolded. I was blindfolded, too, and the carriage took us away to a house—I think it was a house, anyway. We woz still blindfolded when we got there and kept like that until we got to a room where Mr Partridge woz."

"Could you retrace the carriage's journey?" Mr Locke enquired.

"I thought I kept it right in my head. There woz a lot of goin' around in circles, but... I lost it at the end," Mr Snyder admitted with a frown.

"This Mr Partridge," Mr Locke said. "What did he have to say?"

"'E wants the Society to find out if a doll 'e's got is dangerous to people who go near it," Mr Snyder replied.

Miss Dexter stifled a gasp, while Mr Maxwell almost choked on his tea.

"P-Pardon?!" Mr Maxwell exclaimed, red faced as he put down his cup with a clatter. Coughing to clear his airway, he was surprised to see Miss Dexter's concerned expression directed toward him.

"Two gentlemen—Professor Benjamin Cosgrove and Mr Edgar Elmore—who owned the doll at different times, were killed by a gunshot wound while alone with it in locked rooms," Miss Trent explained, drawing Miss Dexter and Mr Maxwell's attentions back to her. "That was the story Mr Partridge had told Mr Snyder and Inspector Conway, anyway."

"I see," Mr Locke said, the corner of his mouth having twitched at the name 'Cosgrove'. "And where did Mr Partridge purchase it from?"

"An auction house," Miss Trent replied.

"Can't we ask the auctioneer about the deaths?" Mr Maxwell enquired.

"Nah," Mr Snyder replied. "Nowt woz said about the doll's history when it was bought. It woz a dinner guest to the house who told 'em about the curse."

"Mr Partridge revealed he intends to have the doll sent to America for valuation," Miss Trent continued. "But he wants to ensure it's safe before he does so." She clasped her hands together upon the table and leaned over them. "Hence the reason for Mr Skinner's presence. Like the rest of you, he's a member of the Bow Street Society. His knowledge of firearms, and other weaponry, is second to none. He's therefore studied the gun in the doll's hand—but only through the glass of its case."

"I thought they mostly used cannons in the Royal Navy," Mr Snyder remarked, intrigued.

"They do," Mr Skinner replied. "But I had a revolver as an officer, too. The groundsmen at Captain Mirrell's estate taught me the rest."

"And what were your conclusions?" Mr Elliott enquired.

"The gun in the doll's hand's a Webley Mark I revolver. I could've told ye that in my sleep," Mr Skinner replied. At Mr Elliott's inquisitive look, he went on, "It's the same revolver I was given in the Navy as my service firearm. It takes six black powder .455 British service cartridges that fire lead bullets. The bullets aren't fired that fast, but still do enough damage when needed. If I could get close to the t'ing, I could tell ye if it's fully loaded or not. It breaks open and sends out any cartridge cases, so I could tell ye how many times it's been fired since it was loaded, too."

"Weren't there any in the case?" Mr Elliott enquired.

"None," Mr Skinner replied and put the pick between his teeth.

Mr Elliott made a note of the information given and pressed his pencil's tip against his lips. "Are we looking for a murderer with a Royal Naval connection, then, Mr Skinner?"

"Maybe," he replied. "But a man could've come back from sea and sold it on to fill his belly."

"Did you?" Mr Elliott enquired.

"I had no need to," Mr Skinner replied. "I keep mine right here." He turned in his chair and pulled aside his coat to reveal the service revolver sitting in a hip holster. Dropping the coat back into place, he leaned forward. "And I had no reason to murder two men."

"Where is the doll now?" Mr Locke enquired as he smirked at the Irishman's wit.

"In the room beside my office," Miss Trent replied. "Miss Dexter has already taken photographs of it, which she'll develop and bring to our meeting this evening."

Miss Dexter gave a polite smile as everyone looked at her.

"Why may we not simply see it for ourselves now?" Mr Locke enquired drily.

"I don't want to be shot," Mr Maxwell confessed.

"Very well," Mr Locke said through a sigh. "Why may *I* not see it for myself now?"

Miss Trent looked from Locke to Mr Skinner and back again as she considered the request. After a few moments, she stood. "Very well. This way, Mr Locke."

"Surely, you're not going to allow this, Miss Trent?" Mr Elliott challenged as he, too, stood. "You said yourself, two men have died while in the doll's vicinity."

"I am no stranger to danger," Mr Locke pointed out. "Besides, if I should die, I shall take full responsibility."

"Mr Skinner has spent the last twenty, or more, minutes alone with the doll, Mr Elliott, without suffering any injury," Miss Trent explained and cast a black look at Mr Locke.

Without acknowledging her disapproval, or awaiting Mr Elliott's response, Mr Locke strode past Miss Trent and out the meeting room. Crossing the hallway, he, again, tugged upon his gloves' cuffs and opened the door in question. Standing with his hand upon its knob, he gazed into the room beyond. Only a moment passed, however, before he went inside and disappeared.

Mr Elliot at once moved around the table, while the others simultaneously hurried to follow. Before Mr

Elliott had even reached the grand staircase though, Mr Locke had re-emerged.

"Did you change your mind?" Mr Locke enquired as he met Mr Elliott in the middle of the hallway.

"This is not one of your performances, Mr Locke," Mr Elliott replied. "I'd ask you not to treat it as such."

"I was doing nothing of the kind," Mr Locke replied. "The light within the room was insufficient for me to see anything from the hallway so I went inside. And, as you can see, I am unharmed." Stepping around his fellow Bow Streeter, he returned to his seat in the meeting room.

The others, who had gathered by that room's door, parted to allow him to pass before following his lead. Miss Trent was the last to take her seat once she'd closed the meeting room door after Mr Elliott.

"It is as Mr Skinner stated: the doll is in a glass case," Mr Locke observed. "The glass of which shows no damage—from a bullet or otherwise. I must therefore conclude that, unless the glass was replaced after each death, the doll is not dangerous at all." He smirked. "Even *I* cannot pass a bullet through solid glass and leave it in one piece."

"How do you explain the gunshot it done last night, then?" Mr Snyder enquired.

"Pardon?" Mr Locke responded with a lofted brow.

"Me, the inspecta and Mr Partridge went in this room where the doll was kept. We looked at it, then left, and Mr Partridge locked the door. We talked for a bit and then heard a gunshot come from in the room. The inspecta got the key from Mr Partridge, went in, but found no one. 'Cept the doll and a broken window." Mr Snyder leaned over his broad arm. "Which is the same as what happened when the house was locked up. A groundsman found a broken window with the glass on the outside, too. The doll was in that room, too."

"Perhaps the entire case was replaced?" Mr Maxwell suggested.

Mr Snyder's scowl returned. "Nah, that's the same case as woz on the doll last night." When he shifted his gaze to the others, his countenance softened. "I looked at it myself when it got 'ere this morning. But, even if it woz, it couldn't of been replaced in the time when we woz stood outside the room. There woz *no one* in there. I'd swear that on my life."

"There's no gun I know that can shoot a bullet through glass and not shatter it," Mr Skinner interjected.

"It sounds like we must look to unearthly causes, then," Mr Verity said. "Spirits of the dead usin' the doll as a vessel—demons, too. *Cursing* the doll and *all* who own it."

"B-But how do we make sure that's the case and, more importantly, get it out of the doll?" Mr Maxwell enquired.

"By doing a séance and an exorcism," Mr Verity replied, ignoring the roll of Mr Elliott's eyes. "We can do both tonight."

"T-Tonight…?" Mr Maxwell enquired with wide eyes as he looked between Mr Verity and Miss Trent. "Would we *all* have to do that?"

"In the best of worlds, yeah," Mr Verity said. "We need everyone's help to call forth the spirit and banish it."

"I would like to excuse myself from such an endeavour, if I may," Mr Elliott said. "My interest is in scientific fact and physical evidence, and *not* in abstract imaginings of spirits, possessions, and curses."

"As a member of this Society, you're obliged to investigate all leads in a case, Mr Elliott," Miss Trent pointed out. "Regardless of how ludicrous a lead may appear to be."

"Is it safe…?" Miss Dexter enquired in a subdued voice.

"Miss Dexter's right," Mr Maxwell interjected and gripped his Adam's apple between his thumb and forefinger.

"Don't worry, Mr Maxwell," Mr Verity said. "My Da was a priest. He taught me everythin' he knew—hopin' I'd follow him into the church. I became a schoolmaster instead, but I know how to exorcize a spirit if need be."

"Oh… good…" Mr Maxwell said and allowed his concern to carry off his voice. With a trembling hand, he picked up his cup and drank down the tea in one mouthful.

"Mr Maxwell—" Miss Trent began.

"Yes?" he interrupted with yet another clatter of china.

"Would you be able to search the *Gaslight Gazette's* archives for information about the deaths of Professor Cosgrove and Mr Elmore?" Miss Trent enquired.

"W-Well, I don't know if Mr Morse would be happy about that," Mr Maxwell replied. "But I can try, yes."

"Good," Miss Trent said.

"Since the Act for the Registering of Births, Deaths, and Marriages in England was passed in 1836," Mr Elliott began, his stoicism regained. "There has been a requirement for each occurrence of these life events to be recorded by the local registrar overseeing their registration district. In March, June, September, and December of each year, the records kept by these registrars are collated into indexes and sent to the Registrar General at Somerset House in Central London. In 1875, enforcement of compulsory registration was introduced. I'm therefore confident both Mr Elmore and Professor Cosgrove's deaths would be recorded in the national indexes kept at Somerset House. Unfortunately, as I'm not a relative of either man, and I have no professional connection to the original cases, I very much doubt I'd be granted access to the deaths' index entries and corresponding certificates.

Once Mr Maxwell uncovers the newspaper articles about their deaths, I may be able to identify the coroner's districts in which they died. Consequently, I could isolate the coroner who oversaw their inquests and send written requests to see their inquisition and deposition records. Unlike the registrars, coroners retain the documentation from the inquests they've overseen."

"I thought the inquisition was Spanish?" Mr Maxwell enquired, confused.

Mr Elliott replaced his cup upon its saucer. "The inquisitions I'm referring to are usually one-page documents containing the coroner's verdict, the name of the deceased, date of death, time of death, cause of death, and the signatures of the jurors present."

"Oh," Mr Maxwell replied and felt his cheeks burn.

"By comparison, depositions are the statements given by witnesses during the course of the proceedings. I shall first attempt to access Mr Elmore and Professor Cosgrove's death certificates but, for our purposes, the inquisitions' and depositions' documents are likelier to bear fruit."

"Take as long as you need, Mr Elliott," Miss Trent replied. "It certainly sounds like a lengthy process."

"The doll also requires a closer examination," Mr Locke remarked as he watched Mr Elliott write his notes.

"Regardless of the cause—which I don't believe for one moment is spiritual in nature—we must take the possibility of the doll being dangerous to heart," Mr Elliott said. "At least until we have concluded our investigations—"

"*All* our investigations," Mr Verity interrupted.

"*All* of our investigations," Mr Elliott echoed. "And discovered a definite answer either way."

"If the doll is not possessed, however, we must nonetheless identify the means by which it is murdering people, the identity of whomever implemented them, and

64

why," Mr Locke retorted. "To eliminate the possibility they intend to bring harm to our client."

"We shall investigate that further once we have conducted the séance and gathered more information," Miss Trent said.

"Mr Snyder," Mr Elliot said, shifting his disconcerted gaze from Miss Trent to Mr Snyder as he attempted to expel his irritation with a change in topic. "Did Mr Partridge explain his reasoning behind the measures he employed in soliciting the Society's help?"

"'E said 'e didn't want folk findin' out abou' the curse, 'cause it would cheapen the doll's worth," Mr Snyder replied.

"I see." Mr Elliot considered a moment. "Extreme measures to protect an investment though, nonetheless—a disguised man, blindfolds, and sending the doll here."

"And the covered-up paintin's," Mr Snyder remarked.

"What covered-up paintings?" Mr Locke enquired, intrigued.

"In the room where me and the inspecta woz took to see Mr Partridge. There woz sheets hangin' from some square things on the wall. I wasn't sure what woz under them until I thought about it later."

"How very curious," Mr Locke commented.

"Indeed," Mr Elliot said. "It would appear there are two mysteries to be unravelled here."

"There are?" Mr Maxwell enquired as he felt confused for a second time.

"Mr Partridge was hiding the paintings for a reason," Mr Elliot replied. "It may be possible they would have identified his true name or, at the very least, the location where Mr Snyder and Mr Conway were taken."

"Currently, Mr Partridge is paying for the Society's services, however," Miss Trent pointed out. "While we must keep in mind his suspicious behaviour, and discreetly seek out an explanation for it, our initial priority is uncovering the truth about the doll."

"If we were able to identify, and locate, the masked man who visited you," Mr Elliott began, "He may tell us more about Mr Partridge's intentions."

"'E works for Mr Partridge," Mr Snyder replied. "Doubt 'e'd tell us out."

"And it could prompt Mr Partridge to become uncooperative or, at the least, suspicious of our investigations," Mr Locke pointed out. "I suspect we shall uncover who the masked man was when we confirm Mr Partridge's identity."

"I agree," Mr Verity said.

"Very well." Miss Trent checked the time once again. "Unless anyone has something further to add, I'd like to end the meeting here. As there's a great deal to be done—by Mr Elliott especially—I've decided to postpone our next meeting until tomorrow evening. That gives the remainder of today and most of tomorrow."

"Thank you, Miss Trent," Miss Dexter said as she slipped her small box camera into her satchel.

"I have to escort Lady Mirrell to the opera tomorrow night," Mr Skinner said as he stood and pocketed his toothpick. "You know where to find me when you decide to take a better look at the doll."

"Of course, thank you, Mr Skinner," Miss Trent replied and allowed the bodyguard to depart.

"I shall endeavour to be here this evening," Mr Locke said as he stepped to give Mr Verity enough space to wander past.

"Be sure that you do," Miss Trent replied with a glance to his gloved hands. The look didn't go unnoticed by Mr Locke, who pursed his lips and slipped from the room to retrieve his hat and cane. Though her eyes followed him, Miss Trent didn't attempt to prevent his departure. Waiting until he stepped into view again, she added, "Take care, Mr Locke." Her tone was sympathetic which gave Mr Locke cause to pause in his movement and look her way. Reading her expression, he gave a small nod and brief lift of his cane before following Mr Verity outside.

"Good day to you, Miss Trent," Mr Elliott uttered with a nod. Putting his satchel upon his shoulder, he departed the meeting room to wait for Mr Maxwell in the hallway.

Mr Maxwell, having stood, was once again looking to Miss Dexter, however. With a wipe of his hand upon his frockcoat, he cleared his throat and said, "Miss Dexter…?"

Miss Dexter stilled. Her gaze then looked everywhere but Mr Maxwell as she replied, "Yes, Mr Maxwell?"

"Erm…" He cleared his throat for a second time and felt his cheeks burn. "…Are you well?"

Miss Dexter's eyes shot up to meet his. Staring at him, her lips parted, she then blinked several times as she turned her head away.

"*Please*," Mr Maxwell said and moved toward the hearth as she did the same.

"Haven't you done enough?" Mr Snyder growled from behind, causing Mr Maxwell to jump and stare at him with wide eyes.

"It's quite all right, Sam," Miss Dexter said. When she looked to Mr Maxwell, her shoulders were squared, and her chin lifted. "Thank you for your thoughtfulness, Mr Maxwell. I'm well, and I appreciate your asking me." She swallowed and, as she spoke again, her voice trembled. "Sam, I'd like to go home now."

"I'll take you in the cab," Mr Snyder replied.

Miss Dexter gave a small nod and, turning upon her heel, left the room.

As Mr Snyder went to follow her, Mr Maxwell's hand stayed him.

"She told you what passed between us?" Mr Maxwell enquired, stunned.

"She's told me nowt," Mr Snyder growled. "But seein' her cry her poor heart out when she come outta yours woz enough for me. Anyways, you've stopped the wrong person."

Mr Maxwell's eyes widened.

Mr Snyder meanwhile shrugged his hand off and strode from the room, muttering a good day to Miss Trent as he went.

FIVE

Miss Trent regarded the parlour for the third time. The transformation since the previous night was remarkable. A fire burned in the hearth, the old *Gaslight Gazette* was gone from the table, and the damp pile of unopened envelopes was cleared away. The sounds of Ballance Road in the daytime also drifted through the—now pristine—window. Children played, carts trundled by, and housewives conversed while they swept their front steps.

"The doll is now at Bow Street?" Chief Inspector Jones enquired. At Miss Trent's nod, he remarked, "Mr Snyder shouldn't have gone to Hampstead Heath alone. Anything could've happened."

"What's that?" Inspector Conway's gravelly voice enquired as he entered with a tray of mismatched cups, a swollen teapot, and cracked cream jug.

"I was just telling Richard about the Society's new case," Miss Trent replied. To Chief Inspector Jones, she said, "Mr Snyder knows how to defend himself. Doesn't he, John?"

"Yeah," Conway replied, plonking the tray down upon the table to prepare the drinks. The first was passed to Chief Inspector Jones—who sat in the under-stuffed armchair—and the second to Miss Trent sitting on a borrowed kitchen chair opposite. While he poured his tea, Conway enquired, "Is that what's brought you both here, then?"

"No," Chief Inspector Jones replied and placed his cup on the sideboard. He waited until Conway sat and explained, "Inspector Woolfe went to Bow Street last night."

"Did 'e now," Conway commented and took a mouthful of tea while stealing a glimpse of Miss Trent over his cup's rim. "What's that got to do with me?"

"He wants a full list of Bow Street Society members," Miss Trent replied.

Conway lowered his cup. "So give it 'im."

"Don't you wish to know why he wants it?" Chief Inspector Jones queried.

"Woolfe'll have his reasons," Conway replied and put his cup on the tray. "'E's a good copper."

"He is. A very obstinate one, too," Chief Inspector Jones said. "Which is why giving him the list *isn't* a good idea. During the Society's investigation of the Oxford Street case, Woolfe made his dislike of their involvement abundantly clear."

"Nowt off about that," Conway remarked.

Miss Trent's eyes narrowed but she remained silent.

"On the face of it, I would agree with you," Chief Inspector Jones replied. "When coupled with Inspector Woolfe's reasoning behind his request for the list, however, one has to contemplate the depth of his dislike."

"What do you mean?" Conway enquired.

"He wants the list, so he may keep Bow Street Society members safe during an investigation. Now…" Chief Inspector Jones pointed at Conway. "You know from experience *none* of the Bow Street Society members make a habit of concealing their identity, or connection to the Society, from a policeman investigating a crime they, too, have been commissioned to look into."

"Except Doctor Weeks," Conway hazarded.

Chief Inspector Jones' lips parted, yet no sound came out. Instead, he looked to Miss Trent, who returned his stare and gave a slight shake of her head. At once, the chief inspector's mouth closed, and his Adam's apple bobbed as he swallowed and shifted his attention back to Conway.

Though Miss Trent's movement had been subtle— and their exchange had passed within seconds—Inspector Conway had seen it all. His hand clenched into a fist upon

70

his knee. "*Don't*," he growled when Chief Inspector Jones, again, opened his mouth to speak.

"Don't what?"

"Don't bloody lie to me."

"Hold your tongue," Chief Inspector Jones warned, his eyes narrowed. "Aside from the fact there's a lady present, you should remember who you're speaking to."

"I know who I'm talking to," Conway replied with a glower as the ligaments in his wrist bulged. "A lying bastard—"

"*Enough*," Chief Inspector Jones ordered. "I'm your superior officer. As such, you will speak to me with due respect. Do I make myself clear?"

"You *knew* Weeks was working with the Bow Street Society—"

"It is a simple yes or no answer, Inspector."

"*Yeah*," Conway barked. At the hard look from Chief Inspector Jones though, he broke his gaze and dug his fingernails into his palm. "Yes… *sir*," he added.

"Good," Chief Inspector Jones replied and glanced at Miss Trent, who had begun to drink her tea. "Now, returning to the matter at hand, John. Yes, I'll admit I knew Doctor Weeks was working with the Bow Street Society, *but* I never communicated with him *or* gave him authorisation to pass information onto the Society—unlike I have with you. Furthermore, I was not involved in the doctor's recruitment into the Society and he, like all the others, has no knowledge of my connection to Miss Trent or of me being the group's founder."

"Chief Inspector Jones knew nothing of Doctor Weeks' joining the Bow Street Society until I informed him of it after the fact," Miss Trent said. "By that point, I'd already approved his membership, so it was impossible to expel him without raising awkward questions. His choice to share his medical findings with the Society was entirely his own, Inspector."

"You still should've told me," Conway said as his clenched fingers separated.

"And said what?" Chief Inspector Jones enquired. "The Yard's preferred surgeon is assisting a group perceived to be one of the Metropolitan Police's many enemies? You would've been as delighted about it then as you are now. Besides, there was nothing to be done about it."

"But what about now?" Conway enquired. "Woolfe's got the idea in his head that Weeks' been helping the Society—and 'e has. Sumin' like that can ruin a bloke. As much as the lushington rubs people the wrong way, 'e's too much of a good surgeon to be put out like that."

"Nonetheless, the truth must come out," Chief Inspector Jones replied, his voice and expression grave. "I want *you* to show Inspector Woolfe the member list, but for it to stay in your possession. Doctor Weeks' name will be recorded as a retired member, so Miss Trent may at least argue there's no further risk of him sharing information he shouldn't."

"There'll be no need for that," Miss Trent interjected. As both men looked at her, she said, "I haven't brought the list."

"I *beg* your pardon?" Chief Inspector Jones replied, stunned. "Whyever *not*?"

"You said you wanted transparency between the Bow Street Society and the Metropolitan Police," she reminded him. "There's another way we can achieve this *without* exposing Weeks *and* our other members to Woolfe's wrath."

"How?" Conway enquired.

"Assign John as the investigating officer for the Bow Street Society," Miss Trent said.

"Me?"

"He *is* the Head of the Mob Squad and therefore the logical choice for keeping an eye on the Society's activities," Miss Trent pointed out.

"I'm not gonna lie for you," Conway said.

"And I don't expect you to," Miss Trent replied as she finally looked at him. "Whenever the Society accepts a new commission, I'll inform you of who is investigating the case, so you may pass their names onto the investigating officer. It will then be down to his judgement whether he inhibits the Society's efforts on the grounds of their safety—Woolfe's alleged concern—or Scotland Yard's regulations."

"But, if you're gonna do that, why does it matter if you give the list to Woolfe?" Conway enquired.

"Inspector Woolfe wants to have the list so he may hound our members and drive the Society out of business," Miss Trent explained.

"And that would be bad because…?" Conway probed.

"You know why, John," Chief Inspector Jones replied.

"The Society makes us honest coppers look as bad as the bent ones in the eyes of the man in the street. When all's said and done, *that's* what me and the other lads have to face when we go out there, doing our work."

"I know," Chief Inspector Jones replied as his expression and tone turned sympathetic. "That is why we need your help. You are uniquely placed to act as facilitator since you are a part of—and empathise with—each side. Besides, we are all trying to achieve the same goal—justice for all. Of course, I want there to come a time when a group, like the Bow Street Society, is no longer needed. A time when the public has enough confidence in the police to seek *us* out when trouble comes their way—rather than the *police* being the ones causing their strife." Chief Inspector Jones frowned. "Unfortunately, now isn't that time. Violence, drunkenness, debauchery, and corruption are rife among our ranks, John. I am doing all I can in my capacity as chief inspector but I'm only one man. Yet, the demand for justice is never-ending. Now, those able to meet that demand are only a handful of honest coppers and the Bow Street Society."

"But aren't what we're doing corrupt?" Conway enquired in a soft voice.

"You're far from being a saint as it is," Miss Trent pointed out. When he shot her a questioning look, she added, "Dorsey?"

"The bugger fell," Conway muttered.

"Onto your fist?" Miss Trent retorted with a lifted brow.

"*Enough,*" Chief Inspector Jones ordered as he cast a glare at them. "*No one* in this room is sinless." To Conway alone, he continued, "But I have *never* passed any confidential files to the Society, nor used my influence at the Yard to assist them."

"You're using your influence now though, aren't you? By asking me to do this," Conway said.

"All I'm asking you to do is your duty as a policeman," Chief Inspector Jones retorted. "I agree with Miss Trent about Inspector Woolfe; his intentions aren't as clean cut as he would have us believe. Irrespective of that fact, however, is the one already raised: as a group operating outside the confines of the Metropolitan Police, the Bow Street Society should be treated the same as the other criminal gangs your detectives investigate. As a result, you have a duty—as their head—to lead those efforts. Or would you deny such a duty exists?"

"Nah," Conway replied after a long pause. "But I'm not gonna make things easier for 'em at the Yard. Like I said before, I'm a copper, not a Bow Streeter."

"As you shouldn't," Chief Inspector Jones said.

"I wanna know sum'in." Conway paused to toss back the remainder of his cold tea. "What happens if Miss

Trent is done in? She's the only one who knows who all the Society's members are."

"Each member has an index card assigned to them within the locked filing cabinet in my office at Bow Street," Miss Trent explained.

"Inspector Woolfe intends to search the Society's house today," Chief Inspector Jones said. "I want you to tell him of Miss Trent approaching you with her proposition. You were the investigating officer in the Dorsey case—the first major case the Society accepted— so it would be only natural for her to seek you out. Once you've outlined her terms to Woolfe, I suspect he'll abandon the idea of searching the property."

"And if 'e don't?" Conway enquired.

"Then we may *all* be exposed," Chief Inspector Jones replied.

SIX

"Inspector Conway from A Division to see you, sir," the constable announced as he entered and stepped aside. Woolfe pushed back his swivel chair from the window and stood to take Conway's hand when he arrived a moment later.

"That'll be all, Constable," Woolfe said.

"Yes, sir," the constable replied and closed the door as he left.

The second-floor office was among a handful which overlooked Bow Street. The police station's stone steps, and the law court's corner entrance, were visible from the small sash window that was opened a few inches. A glass ashtray, filled with spent cigarette ends, sat on the stone ledge beneath. Woolfe's fur coat hung from a stand against the back wall, while a squat chair faced the desk that monopolised the room. The earlier sunshine had been suffocated by dense cloud, prompting Woolfe to repel the gloom by increasing the supply of gas to the lamps.

"Which blighter has brought you to E Division, then?" Woolfe enquired once the two sat with their pleasantries made. "I've not heard about any degenerates on the Mob Squad's list wandering into Holborn." His chair creaked as he settled back into it, its sides snug against his hips.

"I've not come about them, but the Bow Street Society." Conway put his hat beside a file stack. "And the search you're gonna do of their place today."

"Are you offering to help?"

"Nah, I've been sent to tell you to leave 'em be."

"By who?"

"Chief Inspector Jones," Conway said and watched Woolfe's brow furrow.

Yet, the Holborn inspector's contorted features soon unknotted as he digested the revelation. He opened his desk's top drawer and took out a packet of cheap cigarettes that he then tossed onto the desk. Taking his time as he closed the drawer, picked up the packet, and took out a cigarette, he then put it between his lips and lit it with a match before imbibing the smoke. "If this is an official intervention," he began through a cloud. "Why isn't he here, instead of you?"

"Because it's *not* official," Conway replied and ignited one of his own cigarettes. "The clerk of the Society—Miss Rebecca Trent—come to me and said what you wanted from her—"

"Why'd she come to you?"

"I worked on the Dorsey case, remember?" Conway tossed his spent match into the ashtray. "There was times when I had to talk to her." Conway dropped his gaze to Woolfe's lips. "She don't want to give you the member list."

Woolfe sneered.

"But she said she'll tell me which one of 'em's working on a case so I can give their names to the investigating officer," Conway said, lifting his eyes as he imbibed more smoke.

"Are they working on anything now?"

"Nah. They've been thrown a hatchet about a doll putting people's lights out—nowt worth you doing anything about."

"All the same, those meddlers are on *my* patch. *I* should be the one to root them out."

"The list's not gonna be there. You can tear the place apart, but you'll find nowt." Conway lowered his voice as he leaned forward. "Think about it, mate. You go in there with a bunch of peelers and the 'papers will drag you through the mud. We've got a hard-enough time as it is without putting us coppers in an even worse light. You'll just send more people the Society's way."

"Does Chief Inspector Jones think the same?"

"Yeah." Conway sat back. "Because I've already got the clerk's trust, 'e wants me to keep an eye on what the Society gets up to and let 'im know."

Woolfe grunted.

"We've just gotta bide our time," Conway said.

"And if one of them dies because they've poked their noses where they shouldn't? Like Miss Webster sneaking around, or their cabbie taking fares from suspects. They've got no place in an investigation."

"They've helped catch two murderers," Conway pointed out.

"They're *not* coppers!" Woolfe snarled. "And you're forgetting where your bloody loyalties lie."

"You *what*?"

"You heard me."

With a harsh scowl, Conway lessened the gap between them. "I don't like what they're doing any more than you do," he growled. "But these are the chief inspector's orders—go against me, you go against '*im*."

Woolfe remained silent.

"And this is from me." Conway stood and put the flats of his hands upon the desk. "Say that about me again…" He leaned over his hands to place their faces inches apart. "…and I'll break your jaw." Maintaining his glare, he waited for a response. When none came, he snatched up his hat and headed for the door.

"Never thought I'd live to see the day a woman had Scotland Yard by the pisser," Woolfe remarked.

Conway kept on walking.

"I won't do the search," Woolfe relented as Conway started out the door. Conway stopped and half-turned as he waited for his friend. "Orders are orders, after all," Woolfe added when he'd reached him.

"Yeah," Conway muttered.

"But tell me this, John," Woolfe began and closed the door ajar. "Did helpful Miss Trent mention Doctor Weeks?"

Conway hesitated. "Nah… Why?"

"He's been passing privileged information to the Society."

"You know that?"

"No, but I'm as sure as I can be without catching him in the act. I found a packet of cigarettes—the same he smokes—at the Society's house."

"That don't say much."

"Not on its own, but he looked like a scared rat when I told him what I'd found and where."

"I'll keep an eye on 'im."

"And the rest?"

"And the rest."

Though he kept his eyes on his fellow inspector, Woolfe lifted his hand and waited. Conway straightened but, after a moment's consideration, accepted the peace offering and gave his friend's hand a firm squeeze.

* * *

Glass eyes stared up at Miss Dexter as they emerged from the solution. Dragging the paper back and forth, she was careful to keep her fingers clear of the poisonous chemicals and on the tweezers. Within moments, the remainder of the photograph had appeared from the depths. Lifting it from the tray, she pegged it to a piece of string suspended between the two walls in the corner of her bedroom.

"I'm only thinking of you," her mother's voice said from the other side of the door.

"She needs a ring first," her father interjected from downstairs. "And there's still the matter of making sure she's financially secure—two things which are more important than setting a date."

"But we *can't* make any arrangements, Henry," Mrs Dexter retorted. "And *everyone* has been asking what they can do to help." Several knocks sounded upon the wood. "What are you *doing* in there, Georgina? Come out, so we can talk properly."

"Keep on talking, love, and the hinges'll soon come off," Mr Dexter remarked, his voice travelling from the parlour.

"Maybe if you put down that newspaper, Henry Dexter, your daughter might—*there* you are, Georgie!" Mrs Dexter exclaimed as the door opened and Georgina Dexter emerged. Mrs Dexter was a short woman in her late forties with wide hips. Her brown eyes crowned sagging cheeks, while her chin hid her throat. Pinned into a bun at the base of her neck, her dark-grey hair was coarse and streaked with white. Black, A-line skirts hung to her broad ankles and a cream, high-necked blouse covered her ample bosom. A white apron—clean on that morning—was tied around her waist.

"I truly haven't given it much thought, Ma-Ma," Georgina Dexter confessed. "And I must take these other photographs to Miss Trent at Bow Street before I give my class tonight." Georgina Dexter held the dried photographs to her breast as she crossed the landing.

"Time is marching on, Georgie," Mrs Dexter replied, pursuing—and passing—her on the stairs. Taking hold of the handrail to block her daughter's descent, she enquired, "Maybe a summer wedding—early July?"

"She'll choose a date when *he* has given her a ring," Mr Dexter remarked from behind his newspaper. Though only a little taller than his wife, he was considerably slimmer. A man in his mid-fifties, he had lost most of his hair. The hair which was left sitting around the base of his skull in a closely cut line of light grey. His impressive grey whiskers peeked out from the newspaper's sides, but his—still hidden—moustache and beard were equally remarkable. A senior accountant at a firm in the city, he wore a black suit of acceptable quality with a matching waistcoat. His pressed, white shirt had an attached, starched, Eton collar, and was finished off with a black tie.

"August, perhaps?" Mrs Dexter said.

"Please, Ma-Ma, I must be leaving. Mr Snyder will be knocking for me at any moment."

Two loud thuds then sounded from the front door, causing Mrs Dexter to turn and thus create enough space for Georgina to pass. Gasping upon seeing her daughter suddenly in front of her, Mrs Dexter resumed her pursuit. "Promise me you'll give some thought to the date, Georgie!"

"I promise, Ma-Ma," Georgina replied and opened the door to greet Mr Snyder.

"By the way," Mr Dexter boomed from the parlour. Rustling newspaper next reached Georgina's ears, followed by her father's footsteps as he came into the hallway. After a brief hello to Mr Snyder, he addressed his daughter, "I've invited your Mr Maxwell to dine with us on Monday. So he and I might discuss the financial matters still outstanding."

Georgina felt a shiver as her entire body turned cold.

"Pardon us, please," Mrs Dexter said to Mr Snyder with an exaggerated smile. When he stepped back onto the porch with a polite smile, she closed the door and approached her husband. "*Really,* Henry," she scolded. "I *wish* you'd tell me your plans."

Georgina held her breath and looked between her parents.

"I'll have to wash the best china, press the table linen, *and* use that nice bit of mutton I was saving for Sunday," Mrs Dexter finished.

"Then do so," Mr Dexter replied.

"But I…" Georgina interrupted. When her parents looked to her though—her mother with pride, her father with concern—she felt her courage desert her. She thought of her mother's tears and her father's disappointment— neither of which she could stomach, for all they were mere imaginings.

"…Mr Snyder is waiting…" She slipped her lithe form between her confused parents and joined Mr Snyder outside.

"But what of your supper?" Mrs Dexter called as she hurried to the door. Georgina and Mr Snyder were already halfway down the garden path, however. Hearing hushed voices nearby, Mrs Dexter glanced at Mrs Halifax and Mrs Kelp conversing at Mrs Kelp's gate. Bidding them a good afternoon with, yet another, exaggerated smile, she retreated inside and slammed the door.

SEVEN

The cold wind pulled at the fire in the hearth, elongating the flames and shaking them like a terrier with a rat. Mr Verity, having succeeded in exorcising the chill from his bones, withdrew from the fireplace and into a vacant chair at the table. It had been almost forty-eight hours since he'd last occupied a place amongst the Bow Street Society members, but his enthusiasm for their commission, and what this evening promised to bring, hadn't waned.

"Sixth of April, 1896," Mr Maxwell began from the other side of the meeting room. Clearing his throat, he adjusted his grip upon the oversized volume and continued, "Evening edition of the *Gaslight Gazette*." He peered over the book's top edge to search for something to lean it against. Finding nothing suitable, he lay the book down and shook his wrists beneath the table. "Mystery Surrounds Sudden Death," he said. Looking down the table at his fellow Bow Streeters, he added, "That's the headline." When no one responded, he felt a twinge of intimidation—since they were *all* looking at him—and a heat around his cravat. "I'll just read the article… An—as yet, unidentified—gentleman died in mysterious circumstances last eve at his home on Gloucester Place. According to a local police source who, for reasons of anonymity wishes to be known only as *P*— here, the gentleman was alone in his library when a single gunshot was heard. The gentleman's wife and son, who were in the house at the time, were startled by the unexpected sound and hurried to his aid. They discovered the door to the library was locked, however—much to their horror. The family's groomsman—a stout fellow with the strength of an ox—broke into the room at the family's behest. The scene which met the three upon entering was, in the groomsman's own words, one "no man would wish to see in the darkest hours of night." The tragic gentleman lay upon his back in an increasing pool of blood on the floor. His son immediately rushed to his side and, dragging him into his arms, pleaded for him to speak. With an insipid countenance and trembling hand, the gentleman slowly lifted his arm and pointed over his distraught son's shoulder. The hand then dropped as the poor man breathed his last. All present were at once rendered speechless and unmoving, as the terrible realisation set in. For, beyond the son, lay nought but a locked window and an antique figurine, newly acquired into the home. Housed within its solid, glass case, the crafted British soldier gazed down upon the scene with empty eyes and a maniacal smile."

"The gentleman was Mr Elmore…?" Doctor Locke ventured. Despite sitting side by side, the inch height difference between her and her husband was notable. Their ages were equally as close, with she being the elder by two years. Also blond haired, Lynette's was darker in colour, and pinned into an elaborate sculpture of curls atop her head. A chocolate-brown, cotton jacket covered the olive-green blouse she'd tucked into her belt, which was positioned over the high band of her matching brown skirts, emphasised her waist's inward curve.

"Mr *Edgar* Elmore, yes," Mr Maxwell replied. Turning the pages, he muttered, "There should be another article here somewhere… no, that's not it. I was certain it was… yes, here are." From his saucer, he took a biscuit that he then dipped into his tea and had a bite of while he scanned the page. "The evening edition of the *Gaslight Gazette* from the twelfth April, 1896." He swallowed the biscuit morsel. "Inquest Held into Elmore Death." He paused to wash the biscuit down with a sip of tea. "The inquest into the mysterious death of Mr Edgar Elmore was held yesterday in the back room of the Gilded Rose public house in the parish of St. Marylebone, London. Prominent and local business owner, Mr Xavier Dennis, oversaw the hearing in his usual capacity as coroner for that area. The entire inquest lasted but a few hours—during which time Mr Elmore's wife, Mrs Edgar Elmore, Mr Edgar Elmore, Jr., his son, and groomsman, Mr Dent, gave their depositions. A verdict of suicide was returned by the jury, despite there being no weapon found in the vicinity of Mr Elmore, Sr.'s body. A great furore erupted from the public seating as the verdict was read, prompting Mr Dennis to threaten clearing the room. Once the perpetrators were calmed, Mr Dennis accepted the verdict given, closed the hearing, and dismissed the jurors. Mr Edgar Elmore shall therefore be buried in un-consecrated ground in a private ceremony sometime in the coming days." Mr Maxwell put the remaining biscuit into his mouth.

"As predicted, I was prohibited from seeing the death index entries for both Mr Elmore and Professor Cosgrove," Mr Elliott said. "From the information uncovered by Mr Maxwell, I determined Mr Dennis' district and located him in the Post Office Directory. Upon receipt of my written request, he sent a reply by way of messenger, inviting me to his place of business yesterday evening after closing. Impressed by my occupation and reputation, he granted me a loan of the inquisition and deposition documents from Mr Elmore's inquest with the understanding I would return them tomorrow morning." Mr Elliott passed a file across the table to Doctor Locke. "There is only a brief mention of the doll within Mr Elmore, Jr's deposition. When I enquired after it during my short conversation with Mr Dennis, he dismissed its involvement as ridiculous. I suspect he had the same reaction during the inquest."

A brief hush fell upon the room while the Lockes read the documents and the others waited to do the same.

"I would like to scrutinise the Elmore's library," Mr Locke remarked as he gave Mr Verity the page once he'd finished it. When he brought a cigarette to his lips, Mr Locke noticed a slight tremble to his hand. He therefore rested its heel upon the table and watched his wife's smaller hand cover it a moment later. The two then exchanged a knowing glance but neither remarked upon it.

"Me, too," Mr Verity said as he came to the end of the page.

"The doll's location in the library may also be crucial," Doctor Locke said. "A deposition from Doctor Wren—the attending doctor on the night of Mr Elmore's demise—describes Mr Elmore's wound and cause of death." She paused and, to Miss Trent at the table's head, said, "It's rather gruesome."

"I'm certain we may stomach it," Miss Trent replied. "Please, read it aloud."

Miss Dexter—sitting diagonally from the doctor—looked to her tea cup and focused on the sound of the rain hitting the window behind her.

"Superficial examination of the corpse, while still at the location of passing, revealed a single bullet wound," Doctor Locke began. "The use of a bullet probe upon the corpse further revealed the bullet had entered the torso at an angle of approximately two hundred and forty degrees. The trajectory then grazed the left ventricle, thereby piercing the heart, and ended when the bullet became lodged in the deceased's rib. If the wound was inflicted by another person, they would have had to have been at least seven feet tall to achieve the bullet's angle of entry. This is a supposition based upon the angle itself and the fact the measured height of the deceased is five feet.

"A full post-mortem examination failed to uncover any symptoms of disease which may have led to death. As the stomach was empty, it's my opinion poison wasn't a factor either. I therefore have no alternative but to categorise Mr Edgar Elmore's cause of death as a self-inflicted gunshot wound to the chest." Doctor Locke frowned. "I see Doctor Wren's thought process and reasoning. Yet, I can't agree with it." She set the deposition aside for her husband to read. "If a person's intention is suicide, he, or she, wouldn't point the gun at such an impractical angle. The most damaging places to aim a gun at are the head, specifically here." She pressed the tip of her index finger against her temple. "And here." She moved the same finger to the underside of her chin. "In both instances, the bullet is highly likely to hit the brain. Death is—almost—guaranteed."

"Could Mr Elmore have not intended to kill himself?" Mr Elliott queried. "In your medical opinion, that is. Practically, his choice of venue was ill suited if he wished to be saved before it was too late."

"I'm a doctor, not a telepath," Doctor Locke replied. "If I can see, precisely, where the doll was standing when the deadly shot was fired, I may be able to match the angle of the bullet wound to any angle created if the doll was the one that fired the gun. Miss Dexter, could you sketch the library's layout and bring a ball of string?"

"I could," Miss Dexter replied in a quiet, yet clear, voice.

"Good. Then you and I, my husband, and Mr Verity shall all go together."

"The Elmores' address is in their depositions," Mr Elliott pointed out. "There is also a brief deposition from the police constable who was called to the house on the night of Mr Elmore's death. He discounted Mr Elmore's death as being anything other than suicide, however. Contrastingly, Mrs Elmore and her son strove to convince Mr Dennis of their kin's stable state of mind and strong Catholicism."

"We shall keep that in mind, then," Mr Locke replied and imbibed some smoke before exhaling it away from the table.

"Wot abou' Professor Cosgrove?" Mr Snyder enquired as he folded his broad arms across his chest and rested them upon his stomach. Sitting beside Miss Dexter, he'd pushed his chair back to have a full view of the table.

"I have something about him here," Mr Maxwell said as he stood and consigned the first volume to the table's centre with one hand while his other pulled a second toward him. "Mystery of Cosgrove Murder is the headline from the morning edition of the *Gaslight Gazette* from the twenty-third of October, 1890. The world of academia has been left in a state of shock this morning following the sudden, violent death of respected Professor of Antiquities (retired) Benjamin Cosgrove at his residence on Oakley Street in Chelsea. A full police investigation is already underway, with early reports suggesting Scotland Yard has sent an inspector from T Division to look into the matter.

"According to an eyewitness who was at the Cosgrove residence last eve—and who wishes to remain anonymous here—Professor Cosgrove was found, deceased, in his locked study following a single gunshot. A window was open in Professor Cosgrove's study, but an inspection of the ground outside revealed no footprints. Your correspondent will, of course, keep you informed of any further developments pertaining to this case."

"The inquest into Professor Cosgrove's death lasted for several days," Mr Elliott stated as he passed its documentation to Miss Dexter on his right. "And it ended in a verdict of wilful murder by a person, or persons, unknown. Unlike Mr Dennis, the coroner who oversaw the professor's hearing—Mr Jebediah Crumple—would only relinquish the inquisition and deposition documentation to me once I'd proven my membership of the Law Society and presented him with twenty pounds." Mr Elliott looked to his notebook and read aloud as he held his pencil's tip above the paper.

"The inquest was held at the Plough public house in Chelsea. Professor Cosgrove's wife, Coral Cosgrove, his nephews Ned and Norman, and his secretary, Miss Henrietta Watkins, all gave depositions. The records of these are frustratingly brief, however. According to Mr Crumple, they were considered above suspicion due to their intimate connection to the deceased. In my—

arguably—humble opinion, such a connection places more suspicion upon an individual rather than less." Mr Elliott's pencil moved down a line, "the professor's servants, Mr Ian Lane, his butler, and Miss Daisy Price, his parlour maid, also gave brief depositions." He tapped his pencil against the paper. "A moneylender, with whom the professor had a disagreement, was also questioned under oath. Specifically, about a heated argument he was overheard having with the professor mere hours before the professor's death. His name is Mr Paul Bund. The catalyst of this confrontation isn't fully disclosed in his deposition. Mr Bund's account is evasive at best and intentionally misleading at worst." He looked around at his associates. "The disagreement may have no bearing upon Professor Cosgrove's death, but Mr Bund's reluctance to speak of it marks him as a person of great interest. I'd therefore like to question him on the matter."

"Very well," Miss Trent agreed. "Mr Maxwell will go with you."

"Are their addresses in 'ere, too?" Mr Snyder enquired as he passed the documents from Miss Dexter to the Lockes.

"Yes, they're recorded as being at Professor Cosgrove's residence," Mr Elliot replied.

"That woz six years ago," Mr Snyder pointed out.

"Coral Clarence—a headline act at the Paddington Palladium for a season—married a Professor Cosgrove," Mr Locke said as he tapped the excess ash from his cigarette into an ashtray and imbibed some more smoke.

"I don't recall ever meeting her," Miss Trent stated and ignored the subsequent, intrigued expressions on the others' faces.

"It was in 1886." Mr Locke smiled. "When my parents owned the Palladium. I have heard her name uttered from time to time within the theatrical circles since then. She relocated to Brighton, I believe."

"You didn't think to mention this before?" Mr Elliott probed.

"I was not certain it was the same lady," Mr Locke replied. "I am still not. Which is why I think it would be wise if *I* were to visit upon her." He placed his hand upon Doctor Locke's. "With my wife, of course."

"Of course," Doctor Locke repeated with a hint of sarcasm.

"Miss Dexter will also accompany you," Miss Trent said and, addressing her directly, continued, "Mrs Cosgrove might have seen someone in the grounds on the night of her husband's murder. If that's the case, she can describe them for you to sketch."

"Yes, Miss Trent," Miss Dexter replied. "I should be able to create a sketch of the study, too… if Mrs Cosgrove, or anyone else in the family, can recall it."

"Perfect," Miss Trent said with a smile.

"Mrs Cosgrove might know where the others are," Mr Snyder suggested.

"Ned Cosgrove frequents the gambling houses around Piccadilly," Mr Locke stated.

Mr Elliot gave an audible tsk. "Is there anything further you'd like to share with us?"

"Not to my knowledge," Mr Locke replied with a slight shake of his head.

"You've met 'im, then?" Mr Verity queried.

"Once or twice," Mr Locke replied. "Good fortune is a stranger to him at the roulette table, however."

"And when was the last time you met him?" Doctor Locke enquired, her tone hard despite her best efforts to stifle her discontent.

"Around eight months ago," Mr Locke replied with a sidelong glance to his wife. "When I last visited a gambling house."

Doctor Locke scowled and reached for the teapot to refill her cup.

"Do you remember which one it was, Mr Locke?" Mr Maxwell enquired with eagerness.

"I do…" Mr Locke replied and glanced, again, at his wife as he crushed out his cigarette in the ashtray. "I recommend having someone who possesses a considerable disposable income to accompany you—if your intention is to pay the establishment a visit, that is."

"There'll be no gambling on the Society's time," Miss Trent warned.

"I-I really wasn't intending to—" Mr Maxwell began.

"If Mr Cosgrove is playing roulette, he shan't be interested in disturbing his game to speak with us," Mr Locke pointed out. "I propose that I and Mr Elliott accompany Mr Maxwell."

Miss Trent considered the three gentlemen with a degree of concern. Concluding Mr Elliott wouldn't permit Mr Maxwell to gamble with what he could not afford, however, she reluctantly agreed. "Fine, but ensure you show Miss Dexter's photograph of the doll to anyone you speak to, as well as asking after the other witnesses' addresses, and the professor's study."

"We will," Mr Elliott acknowledged.

Doctor Locke watched her husband with irritation. A glance to his trembling hand deepened her disapproval of the proposed visit to the gambling house. Nonetheless, she held her tongue and sipped her tea. She had her pride, after all.

"Woz there a trial for the Cosgrove murder?" Mr Snyder enquired.

"There's no record of one in the newspaper, so I would assume not," Mr Elliot replied.

Mr Verity poured some more tea and stirred the mahogany-coloured liquid. Tapping his spoon against his cup's rim, he placed it on the saucer and accepted the second transcript from Mr Locke. Applying his pince-nez, he began to read it.

"Like the Elmore inquest, there's a deposition from the attending doctor regarding the cause of death," Doctor Locke explained as she retrieved the relevant page from Mr Verity. "Doctor Walters concluded a single gunshot wound to the back of the head was responsible." She located the relevant passage and read aloud, "The deceased was found slumped over his desk with his right arm dangling and his left raised above his head. Neither hand held a gun, nor was a gun found in the direct vicinity of the corpse." She made a circle with her hand. "Doctor Walters' preliminary examination of the corpse—while it still sat at the desk—using a bullet probe revealed the bullet had entered the skull at an approximate ninety-degree angle. There was significant skull, tissue, muscle, and brain damage caused by the impact, however, so Doctor Walters was unable to be fully certain about the angle of entry. An internal examination revealed some damage to the tissue of the lungs, but this damage wasn't sufficient to cause the deceased's death. No further symptoms of life-threatening diseases were found, either."

"What time did both men die?" Mr Maxwell enquired.

"Doctor Wren gave an approximate time of between three thirty and five thirty in the afternoon for Mr Elmore's death—" Doctor Locke began.

"But the inquisition placed the time of death at four o'clock, as this was when the gunshot was heard," Mr Elliott interrupted.

"And Doctor Walters gave an approximate time of between eight o'clock and ten o'clock in the evening for Professor Cosgrove's death," Doctor Locke said.

"And that inquisition placed the time of death at eight thirty as, again, the gunshot was heard at that time," Mr Elliott stated. "This, superficially, grants us the luxury of accurate times of deaths. We must proceed with caution, however, as a gunshot may be fired at any time and muffled—either through a pillow or some other thick material. A second gunshot may then be fired to confuse matters."

"Is there any such suggestion in the inquisition or depositions?" Mr Locke enquired. "…Or in any further *Gaslight Gazette* articles?"

"No," Mr Elliot replied.

"After the article covering Mr Elmore's inquest, there wasn't another until a month after his death." Mr Maxwell frowned. "It describes the horror of the bloodstain in the library and how Mr Elmore was discovered, but little else."

"I agree with Mr Elliot; we mustn't ignore any possibility," Miss Dexter said.

"*Exactly*," Mr Maxwell added and pointed at her with a broad smile as he looked to Mr Locke.

Neither Miss Dexter nor Mr Locke echoed his good humour, however. While she pursed her lips into a frown, he replied, "Anything is possible, Mr Maxwell. I was merely enquiring if there had been any physical evidence found at either location to support Mr Elliot's supposition." He gave a polite smile to Mr Elliott. "Alas, I suspect we shan't be able to answer that question until we have spoken with those involved."

Mr Elliot gave a curt nod and returned to his notetaking.

"Wouldn't the police be in a position to tell us such information?" Doctor Locke enquired from Miss Trent.

"In an ideal world, yes," Miss Trent replied. "Unfortunately, their willingness to cooperate with the Society is patchy at best."

"Perhaps Inspector Conway could assist us?" Mr Locke suggested. "In my personal experience, he is considerably more approachable than Inspector Woolfe. Furthermore, he has already participated in this case by accompanying Mr Snyder."

"Approachable, yes—unless you give him reason to use his fists," Mr Elliot remarked.

"The Metropolitan Police doesn't exist for the Society's convenience, gentlemen," Miss Trent said. "We must investigate ourselves—for *that* is what we've been hired to do. Currently, this is purely conjecture on your parts. I will speak with Inspector Conway when I have a need to do so."

Mr Locke raised his hand a little. "As you wish, but you have reminded me of a question I wished to ask. Was our Mr Partridge mentioned in any of the articles, inquisitions, or depositions you found?"

"No, not at all," Mr Elliott responded for the both of them.

"Only one line about the doll," Mr Verity remarked as he peered through his pince-nez at Miss Price's deposition. "The same as the Elmore inquest…" He removed his pince-nez and tapped them against his vast beard. "Did Mr Elmore or Professor Cosgrove have any very young children?"

"Not that any of the records mention, no," Mr Elliott replied.

"What about deceased children?"

"The doll isn't haunted," Mr Elliot rebuked.

"We've not discovered that, yet," Mr Verity stated and lowered his head to peer across the table at him. Mr Elliott looked away with a soft tut. Unperturbed, Mr Verity swapped his pince-nez for his teacup and settled into his chair. "Since the year of our Lord, 1882, a children's toy maker in the Midlands called Joseph Maskelyne & Sons has been making dolls for use in séances. Bereaved parents use them to try to encourage their deceased children to come forward. Unlike china dolls you find in toyshops, or porcelain, Frozen Charlotte dolls you get given in little coffins, these dolls are solid clay. They're also blessed by the spiritualist church, and—to stop evil spirits from using the doll—have salt mixed in with their clay for purification

94

purposes. Not many have been made, and most go over to America—in fact, Mr Partridge saying he was going to send our doll there is what made me think of these séance dolls."

"You suspect our doll was made for a dead child?" Doctor Locke enquired with great concern.

"No," Mr Verity replied. "From what I can see in Miss Dexter's photograph, the doll's not made the same as Maskelyne's. *But*"—he took a mouthful of tea and set the cup down—"Someone could've tried to use our doll in such a séance and, because it wasn't blessed or purified with salt, an evil entity took control instead of the intended child. It was then *this* entity that killed the two men."

"Are you quite certain you're not confusing yourself with memories of the theatre, Mr Verity?" Mr Elliot said with condescension.

"*John Nevil* Maskelyne is the performing partner of fellow magician George A. Cooke, not *Joseph*," Mr Locke interjected. "Admittedly, I find it amusing two men with remarkably similar names have connections with dolls and spiritualism. Maskelyne & Cooke famously exposed the spiritualist Davenport Brothers as frauds in 1865, however. Now that we are on the subject, I would like to, again, put forth my proposal for the doll to be more closely examined—preferably by a clockmaker."

"A clockmaker?" Mr Maxwell queried.

"Yes, to determine if there are any mechanisms which may enable the doll to be controlled from afar," Mr Locke explained.

"Is that possible?" Mr Snyder enquired.

"Indeed, it is," Mr Locke replied. "One of Maskelyne & Cooke's many, impressive, feats includes the doll, *Psycho*. It was showcased as possessing the ability to not only play cards, but think about its next move. Audiences were kept astounded—and confounded—for months. Until, that is, a patent was filed and the key to Psycho's success was revealed."

"What was the key?" Miss Dexter enquired.

"The air within the tube, upon which the doll sat, was manipulated off-stage using a set of bellows. The control of the air resulted in the control of the doll's movements. It was rather ingenious, since the tube was in plain sight of the audience at all times and yet no one had ever made the connection."

"You think whoever's murdered these men, done it by shootin' a gun from outside the room, usin' the doll?" Mr Snyder enquired as he looked sideways at Mr Locke.

"It's only a theory, until I am satisfied the doll holds no further secrets," Mr Locke replied.

"Even Mr Partridge?" Mr Snyder enquired, confused.

"Perhaps," Mr Locke replied.

"Why?" Mr Elliott stated.

"Pardon?"

"Why would Mr Partridge go to such lengths? What has he to gain from such theatrics?" Mr Elliott pressed.

"Every gentleman must have a hobby," Mr Locke replied as the corner of his mouth lifted.

"I'll arrange for a clockmaker to visit, Mr Locke," Miss Trent said as she closed her notebook. "But that shall come *after* we have *all* participated in Mr Verity's séance. If you'd all like to follow me, then, we'll begin."

EIGHT

"I had expected to see more paraphernalia," Mr Locke remarked as he sat at the large, round table in the hallway. The others had done the same while Mr Verity—who'd taken the chair opposite Mr Locke—laid the cards out. Those marked with a capitalised letter of the alphabet were put along the table's edge with gaps in between. Four further cards— *YES*, *NO*, *HELLO* and *GOODBYE*—were positioned in a square of four in the table's centre. In the middle of this square was a wooden planchette on wheels. "The spirit cabinet is a particular favourite of mine. I have always wanted to inspect the ropes binding the medium once they have been placed inside."

"I'm not a medium, sir," Mr Verity replied as he took a bible from the bag beneath his chair. "There'll be no need to tie me up."

"Perhaps, we should bind his feet to the chair, if we begin to hear knocking," Mr Elliot remarked with a cynical tone. "That's what alleged mediums do, isn't it, Mr Verity? Use their big toes to tap upon the floorboards."

"Now, Mr Elliot," Mr Verity replied. "What good would it do me to do that? *None*. You don't believe any of this, and that's your right. But I, for one, believe in a life after death. All this, and all I do, is only me trying to find proof of it. *Real* proof, not charlatans. If we hear knocking"—he nodded—"*IF* we do, it won't be me." Setting down his bible, he licked his finger and thumbed through its thin pages.

Beyond Mr Verity was the door, stood ajar, to the doll's room. The sound of the rain seemed louder both in there and the hallway. The wind from the chimney also made the gaslight flicker until it seemed like a fire was in the hearth, casting shadows and bursts of light against the walls. The doll's face, too, was illuminated one moment and plunged into shadow the next. Throughout, its eyes appeared to sparkle behind the glass case. Despite almost twelve feet between the doll and them, the Bow Streeters had a clear view of the uncanny light show.

The sight sent a chill down Mr Maxwell's spine, followed by a shudder of his heart. As he rubbed his chest with a slender hand, and swallowed the lump in his throat, he urged himself to look away. Yet, the more he stared at the ill-omened figure, the more he was drawn to it.

Doctor Locke was just as fascinated by the antique, this being the first time she'd laid eyes upon it. When she'd read the word 'doll' in Miss Trent's invitation to investigate the case, Doctor Locke had presumed she'd find a delicate, porcelain lady with rosy cheeks and fine clothes. The reality had therefore been altogether unexpected. Unlike Mr Maxwell though, she felt no trepidation while sitting so close to something so— arguably—dangerous.

Miss Dexter filled her lungs as the hallway became gloomier and cavernous when Miss Trent and Mr Snyder dimmed the gas lamps. Miss Dexter had the staircase to her back, but her nervousness made it feel like a gigantic precipice into the unknown. When Mr Snyder put his hand upon her shoulder therefore, she felt her throat constrict and her chest tighten. Upon seeing his worried expression, she forced a smile. "I'm fine… Thank you, Sam."

"First, a blessing on our gathering and a request for Him to protect and keep us," Mr Verity announced to bring everyone's attention onto him.

"P-Pardon…?" Mr Maxwell said as his sickly complexion paled further and his grip upon the table tightened.

"We'll be asking for anyone, Mr Maxwell," Mr Verity said. "So, we *could* call forth *anyone*—good or evil."

"Oh…" Mr Maxwell replied.

"Now, let me see…" Mr Verity tilted his head back to peer through his pince-nez at the Holy Book's minute text. After a moment of reading, he took a small, glass bottle from his bag and held it out to Mr Locke. "Could you uncork this for me, please? Fingers're not what they used to be."

Mr Locke took the bottle and, slipping the cork free between gloved fingers, set it aside.

As he sniffed the liquid, Mr Verity snatched the bottle out from under his nose and warned, "*Don't* contaminate it. It was only blessed this afternoon."

"Holy Water?" Mr Elliot enquired. When Mr Verity gave a nod, he rolled his eyes and leaned back in his chair. "I suppose you have salt in your bag, too?"

"Yeah," Mr Verity replied. "Which reminds me, would you mind, Mr Locke?"

"Not at all," Mr Locke replied. He set back his chair and, plucking the bag from the floor, placed it upon his lap. Taking out the vessel of salt to give to Mr Verity with one hand, he kept his other within the bag. "Do you require anything else?"

"No, thank you," Mr Verity replied. Mr Locke cast a sideways glance at Miss Trent but slipped the bag from his lap and deposited it beneath the table. For all the preparations which had gone into it, the blessing was brief. The call for protection was also executed within moments. "Please, put your index fingers upon the planchette but *don't* push or pull on it. Just lightly *place* your finger," Mr Verity instructed as he stretched his hands and leaned forward to put his own finger on the pointed piece of wood. While the others did the same, he closed his eyes and said, "Absolute silence, now, everyone." He lifted his head and, in an authoritative voice, enquired, "Is there anyone here with us, who is not of the living?"

The rhythmic tick of the grandfather clock, intermixed with the strum of rain against glass, filled the hallway. Everyone's gaze remained fixed on the stationary planchette as they waited. Mr Locke switched his trembling hand with his other as the contrast between his and the others' hands became stark.

"Please, if you are here with us now, come forward," Mr Verity continued. "We mean you no harm."

The planchette was still.

"If you are a child, or an adult, spirit who is bound to the doll, please come forward," Mr Verity went on. "We can help you pass over, to your friends, to your family."

"Listen…" Miss Trent said in a hushed voice.

The pitter-patter of the rain continued on the glass, and the wind resumed its howling in the chimney breast. No other sounds reached the Bow Streeters' ears, however—despite Mr Maxwell straining to catch any.

"I just hear the wind and rain," Mr Snyder answered.

"Precisely," Miss Trent replied. "The grandfather clock has stopped."

Everyone turned toward the noble timepiece. Its pendulum had stilled mid-swing, and the distinct tick was absent.

"It must have wound down," Miss Trent suggested.

No one moved.

"If that was you, we thank you," Mr Verity said as his voice reached the rafters. "Can you, please, move the planchette?"

Mr Elliott stared at the piece of wood as he willed it to stay still but feared it may not. Soon, his mind wandered onto imagined scenes of panic and carnage caused by demons and spirits. He closed his eyes and forced the images from his mind. When he opened them again, he was relieved to find the planchette still in the table's middle. "I think my point has been proven—"

A crash from Miss Trent's office tore through his words.

"What was that?" Mr Maxwell enquired as he leapt to his feet and spun around to stare into the dark passageway. "Is... isn't that where Palmer was-was...?" He held onto the table for dear life.

"Wait 'ere," Mr Snyder said and left the group as Mr Locke joined him. Doctor Locke and Miss Dexter had stood, while Miss Trent set about turning up the lamps with Mr Elliott's assistance. Mr Verity had remained seated, though. With a broad smile, he shouted, "Thank you!"

The wind shrieked through the windows' frames.

"A rat knocked off a cup," Mr Snyder said as he and Mr Locke stood in the office's doorway. He pointed to the shadow beneath the filing cabinet. "Saw it run under there." The two made their way back to the others as he added, "I'll put some poisoned bread down before I go 'ome tonight."

"As I was saying," Mr Elliott said from the bottom of the staircase. "My point has been proven. The doll is *not* haunted, which makes this whole charade an utter waste of our time."

"I disagree," Mr Locke replied as he crossed the hallway to retrieve his coat, hat, and cane from the stand. "The séance has given us sufficient grounds to eliminate a spectral influence from our investigation. That, in itself, is worthy of our time." He retrieved his wife's coat from the stand and took it to her. "Which is becoming increasingly limited."

Doctor Locke offered a comforting smile to Miss Dexter and moved to join her husband. She allowed him to hold her coat as she slipped her arms into its sleeves. When he'd lifted it onto her shoulders, she fastened it and said, "Thank you for making me a part of this, Miss Trent. I've found the entire evening fascinating. Percy and I shall do as instructed and tell you what we find at the earliest opportunity." She smiled at the others. "Good night, everyone."

"Good night," Mr Locke interjected with a slight bow of his head before he put on his top hat, unbolted the door, and held it open for his wife to leave first. Stepping out after her, he closed the door and checked his pocket watch. Their private carriage was due to return at any moment.

"That's my part in all this done, then," Mr Verity remarked as he heaved himself out of his chair and bent down for his bag.

"Not at all," Miss Trent replied and picked up the bag for him to put on the table. "You still have the visit to the Elmore residence to do, and I'd like you to assist the clockmaker in—safely—examining the doll."

"*Well,* now," Mr Verity beamed. "I'd be honoured, Miss Trent."

"Excellent," she replied as she handed him the bible, Holy Water, and salt. "I'm glad we didn't have any reply. I have to sleep here tonight."

Mr Verity chuckled.

"I'll take you all 'ome," Mr Snyder announced as he went for his cloak and hat.

"Thank you," Mr Elliott replied with a curt nod. While Mr Verity and Miss Trent finished putting away Mr Verity's things, he returned to the meeting room for the inquests' documentation and notebook.

"Oh," Mr Maxwell said, surprised. "Th-Thank you, Mr Snyder."

Mr Snyder tossed Mr Maxwell a scowl. "Can't have you goin' out in that weather to find a hansom."

"I'll just fetch the newspaper volumes, then," Mr Maxwell said and stepped past Miss Dexter to follow Mr Elliot. The sight of her jogged his memory, however, and he retraced his steps to face her. "Miss Dexter…" He glanced at Mr Snyder who was keeping a close eye on him. "Your father has invited me to—"

"Yes, I know," Miss Dexter interrupted. She glanced downward and toyed with her skirts. "I shall inform him you're unable to attend."

"No, no," Mr Maxwell replied and closed the distance between them.

Miss Dexter met his gaze, hopeful.

"I shall write him to give my apologies."

Miss Dexter felt a weight sink to the depths of her soul. "…Y-yes…" She gave a nod while simultaneously averting her gaze. "…Of course."

"You haven't told him of…?"

"No, I…" Her voice caught in her throat. "…I, perhaps, hoped it would change."

"I'm sorry it came to this, Georgina," Mr Maxwell said, repentantly. "If it was down to me—"

"Down to you?" she repeated as she looked at him with wide eyes. Though she searched his sombre features and dejected gaze for reassurance, she could find none. Her mind instead presented the memory of the intimate moment she and Mr Maxwell had shared in another hallway. Mr Maxwell had retreated from her mere moments after. Miss Dexter felt her throat restrict, compelling her to cast her gaze downward. She mumbled, "How could I have been so foolish…?"

"Pardon?"

"I understand now, Joseph," she said, forcing herself to look at him.

"You do?"

"Yes… You must do what you think is best."

"I didn't think you knew."

"How could I not?" she said, her voice shaking.

"I'm *truly* sorry, Georgina," Mr Maxwell urged. "If things were any different—"

"*Please*," she whispered. "Please, Mr Maxwell… it is *done*, and it can't be *undone*." She turned from him. "I wish you happiness, Joseph…" She pressed her knuckles to the underside of her nose and hurried into the kitchen.

"Georgina—" Mr Maxwell called, but was prevented from going after her by a firm hand upon his shoulder.

"That's enough," Mr Snyder said.

Mr Maxwell shrugged off the hand and glared at him. "Someone should go to her."

"I will," Miss Trent said as she looked at the two with a sombre expression. Crossing the hallway, she paused with her hand on the kitchen door. "I'll send her to the cab when she's ready." Miss Trent then went into the kitchen to embrace her friend, while Maxwell and Mr Snyder exchanged irritated glances and completed their preparations to leave.

* * *

Doctor Locke passed her coat to their butler and answered his questioning look with a small nod. While he hung her coat, and went to light a lamp in her office, she turned toward her husband who'd begun to climb the stairs. "You haven't any more, remember?"

Mr Locke's foot stilled, and he placed it on the higher stair.

Doctor Locke watched him bring the other foot up to join the first and stand to his full height. She strolled over to the foot of the staircase and looked up at his back. "Yet, your body is craving it." Her arms folded across her chest. "I'm surprised no one noticed your trembling tonight."

Mr Locke's gloved hand withdrew from the rail. "If they had, they are too polite to remark upon it," he replied as he turned upon the stair to face her with a smile—despite the clenched hand held against his breast. "And you are *far* too observant, darling." He descended the stairs to stop upon the last, his hand uncurling as it extended toward her.

104

"Why didn't you mention you knew Mrs Coral Cosgrove before?" Doctor Locke enquired and turned her back to obstruct his path. "And the gambling houses?" She lifted her chin. "Am I to be destitute, as well as apprehensive?"

"You are being melodramatic—"

"Do *not* think to patronise me, Percy Locke." Doctor Locke strode into her office. "I am tolerant of many things, but I *shan't* tolerate you mocking me."

The click of a lock opening reached Mr Locke's ears. Stepping from the stairs at a brisk pace, therefore, he entered the office. When he saw the half-filled needle in his wife's hand, he slowed and stopped a few feet from her. Doctor Locke laid the needle upon her desk as she watched his eyes follow it. To their butler—who had stood by the window—she said, "You may leave us, now, Lyons."

The servant bowed his head and left, pulling the door closed as he went.

"I ask you again, darling," Doctor Locke said with her hand across the needle's glass chamber. "What was your reasoning for not disclosing you knew Mrs Cosgrove earlier, and how many times have you frequented the gambling houses?"

"I have already given my explanations and assurances once tonight." Mr Locke's voice and demeanour were tense as he watched her hand.

"Very well," Doctor Locke said and picked up the needle. When she moved toward her medicine cabinet with it, her husband followed.

"But I shall—naturally—give them again." Mr Locke gave an unnatural smile while his eyes fixed upon the needle. "I have not, in all actuality, visited upon a gambling house in the last few months. Poker and roulette have little to attract me; their risk is too contrived for my liking. As for Mrs Cosgrove…" He lifted a hand but kept it close. "I spoke to a veteran employee of the Palladium this afternoon to confirm such a lady had sung there when I was seventeen. I was uncertain prior to the conversation; my recollection of that time is marred by what happened."

"Amongst *other* things," Doctor Locke remarked. "Was she the one?"

"I cannot be absolutely certain until I speak with her face to face."

"Of course." Doctor Locke held up the needle. "But was she the one who introduced you to your… 'medicine'?" Mr Locke's hand sprung for the needle, but his wife pulled it out of reach. She watched him retract his hand and rub it with his other. "I shan't have you speaking with her again if it equates to you indulging in your shared vice."

"No," Mr Locke replied as he continued to stare at the needle. "She was not the one."

"If you have lied to me…"

"May the curse of the doll strike me down." Mr Locke's hand, again, reached for the needle. "Now, permit me to have it, darling." Once more, his wife kept it from him and moved away from the cabinet with it. Like a shadow, he followed her around the room. When she paused by the window, his whole demeanour became entrenched in panic. "I *swear* it, darling. She is *not* the one."

Despite her trepidation and suspicion, Doctor Locke's love for her husband weakened her resolve at the sound of his pleas. "Do you honestly believe I would have tossed it from the window?" she enquired, saddened by the insinuated low opinion of her from his reaction to her standing by the window. When he could only provide her with an abashed silence, she sighed and gave him the needle. "This is your only dose tonight."

"I understand." He gripped the needle with both hands and, moving closer to her, planted a brief—but passionate—kiss upon her lips. "Thank you, darling."

"It is only because I love you," she replied softly. She rested her hand on his cheek and caressed it a moment before forcing herself to pull away. "I shall see you at breakfast." Stood by the window, she watched her husband's reflection as, with the needle still clutched in his hands, he left her office and went upstairs to his study.

NINE

A short walk from Regent's Park was Gloucester Place.
Though not as splendid as the Hanover and York Terraces
which adjoined that beautified piece of London, it
nonetheless earnt the accolade of genteel from authors
Henry Mayhew and John Binny in 1862. Built between
1800 and 1808 (approximately), it comprised of
impressive, multi-storey private homes with wrought-iron
railings and narrow balconies which overlooked the
cobbled road. Each had sturdy, wood-panelled, double
doors footed by single, stone steps and crowned by half-
moon windows. Wide paths, adorned with large mosaics,
bridged the gaps formed by the basements' steps located
between the street and the houses' front elevations. These
external staircases descended in the direction of the main
doors, with their access being through gates in the railings
on the opposite corners. Originally, gardens would have
brought colour and greenery to the otherwise urbanised
facades. By 1896, these had been removed to widen the
road.

Miss Dexter and Mr Verity were therefore able to
take in the well-to-do frontage of the Elmore residence
with ease, as Mr Snyder's cab slowed to a halt outside.
Similarly, the Lockes were able to identify their intended
destination from their private carriage. Having followed
the Society's vehicle all the way from Bow Street, the
carriage drove around it to park parallel to the Elmore's
front door. The servant's childish behaviour only served to
amuse Mr Snyder, however.

"Not what I'm used to up north," Mr Verity
remarked.

"Whereabouts in the north?" Miss Dexter enquired
as she unfastened the doors and pushed them open with his
assistance. Since she was closest to the pavement, she

alighted first. Doctor Locke and Mr Locke soon joined her, but Mr Verity was unsteady on his feet. Grasping the edge of the cab, he pressed his cane against its floor and attempted to step down. Missing the kerb with his foot, however, he trod air until Mr Locke offered his arm.

"Thank you, sir," Mr Verity said as he accepted the support and vacated the vehicle. Taking a moment to straighten his coat and reposition his cane on the pavement, he answered, "County Durham."

"Is that place not full of coal mines?" Mr Locke questioned. Swinging out his own cane, he walked across the ornately tiled path toward the door.

"Is London not full of cathouses?" Mr Verity countered.

"Forgive me, I meant no offence," Mr Locke replied.

"I'm sure, but don't think to know a place by its industry. County Durham has a canny cathedral, and hardworking people. They're a lot friendlier, too," Mr Verity explained.

"*That* I shall grant you," Mr Locke replied. He lifted his cane and used its silver handle to tap thrice upon the door. Doctor Locke and Miss Dexter—who were side by side behind the gentlemen—exchanged amused glances at the others' minor altercation.

"Did Miss Trent not inform the Elmore's we would be here this morning?" Doctor Locke enquired when no one answered. Her husband looked to her over his shoulder.

"I very much doubt she had the time," he replied and knocked again. After another few moments without a response, he said, "I could get us inside without any trouble. The lock seems simple enough."

"We are not so keen yet, darling," Doctor Locke replied. Moving back to the street, she peered over the railings at the basement door. "Perhaps the family are abroad? It is winter, after all." As she looked up at the house, she saw an ashen-faced woman glaring at her from a second-floor window.

"*Begone*!" the spectre cried, raising her fist to thump the glass. Hands grasped her shoulders, however, and pulled her away from view. A heavy curtain then fell over the window.

"Who was that?" Miss Dexter enquired, alarmed, at her side.

"I haven't the foggiest—" Doctor Locke began, her words cut short by the sudden sound of the door being unlocked. Lifting her skirts, she hurried to re-join her husband and Mr Verity on the path. Miss Dexter, who'd followed her lead, came to a halt behind her just as the door was opened and a man in his late thirties emerged. The quality of his white shirt, and contrasting black trousers, waistcoat, frockcoat, and cravat indicated he was—at the very least—a visitor rather than a servant. His brown eyes took in the crowd upon the doorstep with tense agitation.

"Yes?" he enquired. "Can I help you?"

"Mr Percy Locke, Doctor Lynette Locke, Mr Virgil Verity, and Miss Georgina Dexter from the Bow Street Society," Mr Locke introduced as he offered his calling card. The man didn't take it, however.

"What is this?" he enquired.

"Is this the Elmore residence?" Mr Locke enquired.

The man's face contorted into a scowl. "Have none of you got any decency?"

"I think you misunderstand—" Mr Locke began.

"No, it's *you* who has misunderstood—*all* of you." The man glared at the others. "This isn't a side show, and my mother and I aren't some *bloody* penny dreadful. Leave us alone!"

The man retreated and Mr Locke at once put his cane inside.

"*Sir*," he said. "My associates and I are *not* here to gawk at you, or your home. We are neither tourists of the macabre, or journalists. We are *detectives*, and we are investigating the doll Mr Edgar Elmore was in the vicinity of when he was tragically killed."

The man, furious at finding he couldn't close the door, had advanced upon the illusionist. Mr Locke's words struck him at his core, however, and he stared at him, stunned. The tension melted away from his face and eyes as, with a quiet voice, he stammered, "W-Who did you say you were again?"

"The Bow Street Society," Mr Locke replied.

"And we are here to listen," Doctor Locke added.

The man looked at her with utter bewilderment. Unable to drag his voice from his throat, he instead studied each of their faces in turn. Slowly, the shock left him as sorrow made its home. Moving aside, he indicated the open doorway. "Please…"

"Thank you," Doctor Locke replied with a weak smile.

The hallway beyond was around four feet wide but fifteen feet long. At its end, a wooden staircase on the left snaked downwards, while a second staircase snaked upwards on the right. Each step was steep, and a high window on the right permitted natural light to flood most of the hall. Plaster cornices—moulded into flowers and leaves—lined the tops of the walls. Further into the hallway, on the right, was a closed, panelled door. On the ceiling, before one came to the door, was a plaster arch with further mouldings—of feathers and simple, square cornices—at its tips. A narrow, forest-green rug ran the length of the hallway to cover dark, polished floorboards. Paper, identical in colour and embossed with a leaf vine design, covered the walls' lower halves. The tops, meanwhile, had cream and forest-green vertical striped wallpaper.

Doctor Locke was the first to enter, followed by her husband, Mr Verity, and, finally, Miss Dexter. The man, who'd answered the door, stepped inside and took their coats. Indicating the closed door, he said, "We may speak privately in there."

* * *

"I've neva heard owt as daft as that," Mr Paul Bund remarked with a wiggle of his finger in his ear. Drawing out a lump of brown wax, he wiped it upon his desk's edge. "Cosgrove was breathing when I left him."

The dingy office had a low ceiling, grubby window, and scarce enough room to hold the desk and chairs which occupied it. Mr Bund sat upon one chair, his back to the window, while Mr Maxwell was on the other, pinned between the desk front and the wall. Mr Elliot stood at Mr Maxwell's left, by the door. Foul odours drifted from the street, despite the window being closed.

"You don't deny being at his home, then?" Mr Elliot enquired, maintaining his stoicism and monotonic voice.

"Why should I?" Bund replied.

"You were heard to have an argument…" Mr Elliott said.

"I have lots of spats with them who owe me money," Bund replied. "I likes to talk to them myself first when the debt comes overdue. Cosgrove had the monies but didn't wanna pay the interest. Two hundred interest against a debt of one was fair, I told him. He said it was robbery. I showed him the bill of sale—that *he* signed in these *very* offices, sat where you are now. He said he didn't know about the interest."

"What did you say?" Mr Maxwell enquired.

"When he still said he wouldn't pay, I told him I'd be back the next day to take what was mine."

"Pardon?" Mr Maxwell enquired, confused.

"Professor Cosgrove's possessions," Mr Elliot clarified. "To be sold at auction to cover the debt. No doubt at a reduced price, to fellow money-lenders, with whom you split the profits after the sale."

"What I do's with the items, and who I sell's them to, is for my mind alone, Mr Elliot," Bund replied. "All you need's to know is I didn't kill Cosgrove."

"Where were you when he died?" Mr Elliot enquired.

"At church," Bund replied with mirth. "Next."

"Was the debt paid?" Mr Maxwell enquired.

"Like I said, Cosgrove wouldn't pay," Bund said.

"By someone else, then?" Mr Maxwell pressed.

"That'll be between me and them, won't it?" Bund countered.

"Does the name 'Terrence Partridge' hold any significance for you?" Mr Elliott enquired. He'd been doubtful of the chances Bund also knew Partridge, and his doubts were confirmed by the shaking of Bund's head.

"Don't know him from Adam," Bund said.

"We're not going to find out anything more here," Mr Elliot stated, drawing Mr Maxwell to his feet.

"I don't like questions asked in my office," Bund said to pull the Bow Streeters' attention back to him. "Come here again, you won't be walking out."

* * *

"My name is Mr Edgar Elmore, named after my father," the man said.

They were gathered in a parlour on the ground floor. Gloucester Place could be seen through the immense window, while muffled voices and the sound of walking was heard overhead. The parlour itself was drab and unhomely, despite the fire in the hearth and the soft furnishings. Above the fireplace was a square of vivid red where the wallpaper had been protected from the sun.

There were no well-thumbed books, or unfinished sewing one may expect to find in a heavily used parlour. Miss Dexter concluded the ornaments, coal scuttle, and cushions had all been displayed rather than arranged. The ornaments were grouped with the finest at the forefront, the scuttle was pristine with no dust anywhere to be seen, and the cushions were wrinkle free and plump. Put simply, the room was not lived in.

"Ever since his death, we've had people coming to our door wanting to know the details and asking to see his library," Mr Elmore, Jr. continued. "We were so troubled by the frequency of such visits, we invited a journalist into the house to write our story and publish it in his newspaper. Unfortunately, he focused entirely on the horror of that night and not on the burden of grief we've had to endure ever since. As a result, the visits have only increased…" Mr Elmore, Jr. wrung his hands. "…My mother isn't herself. The shock of losing my father…" He looked across at the others on the sofa. "…We refuse to accept he took his own life, but the weight of not knowing *who* killed him or *why*… it is slowly crushing us both."

"May you tell us if this is the same doll your father bought?" Miss Dexter enquired, holding out a photograph in her dainty hand.

Mr Elmore Jr. glanced over it and gave several, curt nods.

"It is," he said and took in a deep, shuddering breath. "May it be damned."

"We have reason to suspect the doll may, in fact, have been responsible for the fatal gunshot wound inflicted upon your father," Doctor Locke said. "I've read the medical evidence given by Doctor Wren at the inquest, but I still have some questions. Would it be possible to see the library, then, and where the doll was kept?"

"The room has been sealed since the journalist's visit," Mr Elmore, Jr. explained. "And I'm confused as to how the doll could've shot him. Its glass case was still intact."

"Yes, it is a puzzle that has been confounding us, too," Mr Locke remarked.

"Where did your Da get the doll?" Mr Verity enquired.

Mr Elmore Jr. was visibly taken aback by the Tyneside accent, and had to take a moment to fathom what was said. At last, he replied, "Milton's Auctioneers. I don't recall their address."

"How long was it between your Da getting the doll and him dying?" Mr Verity enquired.

"A few hours," Mr Elmore Jr. replied. "He went to the auction in the morning, returned at midday with news of his purchase, and received delivery of it from the auctioneers at around one o'clock. The men who brought it carried it upstairs to my father's library, put it in its place, and left. My father spent the next half an hour with my mother and me in the dining room while we had lunch. At two o'clock, my mother took her visitors in the parlour, I wrote some correspondence, and my father worked in his library."

"And the gunshot was heard… when?" Mr Locke enquired.

"Four o'clock," Mr Elmore Jr. replied, resolutely.

"You seem very certain," Doctor Locke observed.

"The moment shall be forever etched into my mind," Mr Elmore Jr. replied.

"What happened then?" Miss Dexter enquired from her corner of the sofa.

"We went to him, of course," Mr Elmore, Jr. replied.

"We…?" Mr Verity probed.

"Yes, my mother and me. When we found the door was locked, we had Mr Dent, our groomsman at the time, break it down. My father was on the floor, bleeding, by the time we got inside. I rushed to him, took him into my arms, and then…" He averted his gaze to look upon their feet. "…He pointed to the doll behind me and passed on."

"Could we speak to Mr Dent?" Miss Dexter enquired.

"Quite impossible, I'm afraid," Mr Elmore, Jr. replied through a deep sigh. "He died of a weak heart two months ago."

"And the library…?" Mr Verity began. "May we see that?"

Mr Elmore, Jr. rose to his feet, prompting the others to do the same. "I'll have to find the key, but it's upstairs, if you'd care to follow me."

"Ladies first," Mr Locke said with a smile to his wife. Doctor Locke gave a wry smile of her own but, nonetheless, strode forward to tail Mr Elmore, Jr. out the room. Miss Dexter hurried after, with Mr Verity having a steadier pace that compelled Mr Locke to shuffle along behind.

As they began to ascend the stairs, however, a handsome gentleman in his mid-forties emerged onto the narrow landing above them. He was attired in a black, knee-length coat over black trousers, a white shirt with starched, Eaton collar, and a plain, burgundy waistcoat with matching cravat. His wholesome, pitch-black hair was impeccable, while his well-formed sideburns stopped halfway down his jawline. Hazel eyes, crowned with naturally neat eyebrows, regarded the gathering.

"Good afternoon," he said. To their host, he enquired, "May I have a moment?"

"Of course," Mr Elmore, Jr. replied. Climbing the remaining stairs, he went to the far corner of the landing and spoke to the handsome man in hushed tones.

Nonetheless, Doctor Locke picked up the words "sedative" and "a few hours". Noticing the Gladstone bag in the gentleman's hand, she enquired, loud enough for him to hear. "You wouldn't be Doctor Wren, by any chance?"

Mr Elmore, Jr. and the man half-turned toward her.

"I am," the latter confirmed.

"These are members of the Bow Street Society, doctor," Mr Elmore, Jr. explained. "Mr Verity, Miss Dexter, Mr Locke, and his wife—"

"Doctor Lynette Locke." Doctor Wren smiled. "I've heard much about your work in Edgware. It's most commendable—and courageous."

"Because I'm a woman?" Doctor Locke enquired, her tone hard.

"No, anyone with coin would be reluctant to enter the streets you do," Doctor Wren replied. Traversing the short distance to her, he extended his hand. "If rumours about you are to be believed, you are a formidable foe against those who try to cross you."

"I only defend myself," Doctor Locke replied as she accepted the hand and gave it a firm squeeze.

"The Society is here to look at Father's library," Mr Elmore, Jr. said.

"Is that so?" Doctor Wren glanced between them all, his brow lofted.

"We don't believe Mr Elmore committed suicide," Doctor Locke added and watched the way Wren shot his attention back to her.

"I'll fetch the key," Mr Elmore, Jr. stated as he slipped past them all to ascend the next flight of stairs and disappear through a door at the top.

Doctor Wren, who'd kept his gaze upon Doctor Locke, said, "I'll show you where the library is in the meantime." Allowing Doctor Locke to walk ahead of him, he glanced at Mr Locke as he attempted to push past him. The two gentlemen exchanged brief—yet, polite—smiles before Mr Locke was granted access to the staircase by Wren. Waiting a moment to allow a gap to form between them, Wren then began his climb. Miss Dexter and Mr Verity followed in that order.

"I wasn't entirely satisfied with my original diagnosis," Doctor Wren stated once they were on the first floor. Leading them to a door at the back of the landing, he turned toward them. "But I couldn't give definite proof it was murder, either. Mr Elmore was alone, in a locked room, when he died. If there had been someone else with him, it would've been impossible for them to enter or leave."

"Was the key still in the lock when the door was broken down?" Mr Locke enquired as he squatted before the door to peer through its keyhole. He could see three floor-to-ceiling bookcases beyond, and a large, dark-brown stain on the burgundy rug that covered most of the floor. Slipping a magnifying glass from his pocket, he inspected the external, brass casing of the lock for scratches. There were none.

"I believe so," Doctor Wren replied.

"Here we are—" Mr Elmore, Jr. began as he approached with a key. He stopped, however, upon seeing where Mr Locke was. Waiting for him to straighten and step away, Mr Elmore, Jr. finished, "…The key." Approaching the door, he unlocked and opened it. "I hope you'll forgive me for not going inside."

Doctor Wren gave the back of Mr Elmore, Jr's shoulder a reassuring pat as he passed him to enter the room. There was a heavy mustiness to the stale air of the library. The bookcases occupied the entire back wall, while an impressive desk stood in the corner to one's right as one entered. The only window in the room was largely blocked by the bookcases, causing only a small amount of natural light to penetrate the gloom.

Miss Dexter toyed with the brooch pinned to her dress's high neck as she stepped around the offensive stain. Mr Locke, meanwhile, went to the left and waited for everyone to be inside before he half-closed the door

118

and inspected the interior casing of the lock. Like its external counterpart, it was free of any scratches. Straightening once more, he began to gently tap upon each of the door's six panels to test their rigidity.

"Before your Da's death, had anyone died violently in the house?" Mr Verity enquired, leaning upon his cane and looking to Mr Elmore, Jr. through the gap in the door.

"That's a trifle insensitive, don't you think?" Doctor Wren interjected, stunned.

"Not at all," Mr Verity replied, looking over his shoulder at him. "Violent deaths can bring violent spirits. According to a Plymouth newspaper, there's a house near Chard, where a farm labourer was murdered by his wife in 1879. Blood appears on the floor where the deed was done. The murderess is seen often, and his face looks in the windows at those inside."

"Have people been murdered by the spirits?" Mr Elmore, Jr. enquired.

"Not there," Mr Verity admitted. "As far as *I* know, anyway. 50, Berkeley Square in Mayfair's a different matter. *Mayfair* magazine reported, in 1879, about a gentleman who was found, dead, in the middle of that home's famously haunted room."

"Such was never proven," Doctor Wren pointed out.

"You've heard the story, then?" Mr Verity enquired.

"Heard it and dismissed it," Doctor Wren said.

Mr Verity gave a small nod but, looking sideways at the medical man, said, "*He* was a disbeliever, too."

"I don't know of any murders here before my father's," Mr Elmore, Jr. interjected. "And there have been no hauntings here, either before or since."

"Where was the doll?" Doctor Locke enquired as she moved to the far side of the stain. Glancing around, she couldn't see any tables near the stain.

"On a table, where you're standing now," Mr Elmore, Jr, said, pointing at the spot.

"Could you show me how high it was, please?" Doctor Locke enquired. With a warm smile, Wren assented and held his hands, flat, before him.

"Around four feet tall, I'd say," Wren said. "The doll… three feet…?"

"Where is the table now?" Miss Dexter enquired.

"Sold with the doll at Stafford's Auction House a month ago."

"Your father died approximately six months ago, correct?" Mr Locke enquired, though his eyes were on the doorframe, where he was running his gloved hand over the wood and the indentation for the lock.

"Yes," Mr Elmore, Jr. replied.

"Why did you wait five months to sell the doll?" Mr Locke turned toward the younger Elmore with a questioning look to his eyes. "If it were I, I would have wanted to be rid of the dastardly artefact at the earliest opportunity."

"My mother was reluctant to—at first. She said it was the last item my father purchased, and one he had been very proud to own," Mr Elmore, Jr. explained. "She felt she would be betraying him if she sold it."

"And now…?" Mr Locke probed.

"Now, Mrs Elmore is far from in her right mind," Doctor Wren interjected. "She is under a great deal of strain from the interest her husband's death has created. Whatever light the Society may shed on the matter could only serve her well, in my opinion."

"Do you still stand by your original opinion, now you are here again, Doctor?" Doctor Locke enquired.

"As far as the entry angle of the bullet and the cause of death are concerned, yes," Wren replied.

"If the doll was here," Doctor Locke began, taking the place of the doll and lifting her hand to point her index finger at the empty space. "It could have created the

120

correct entry angle for the bullet that killed Mr Elmore. Darling." She looked to her husband. "Could you fetch over the steps from the bookshelves?"

"Certainly, darling," Mr Locke replied, plucking up the steps and setting them down before his wife.

"Miss Dexter, you are around the right height. Could you stand upon this lowest step and extend your arm, please?" Doctor Locke enquired. "Also, did you bring your ball of string as I asked?"

"Yes," Miss Dexter replied, slipping the item from her satchel and passing it to Doctor Locke. While Miss Dexter climbed the steps and turned inch by inch to face the others, Doctor Locke sized up the gentlemen.

"Mr Verity," she announced. "You are close to Mr Elmore's height. Would you be so kind as to stand in front of Miss Dexter, please?"

"Absolutely," Mr Verity replied, crossing the room and standing where indicated. Straightening his back as much as it would allow, he looked up at Miss Dexter who raised her hand and allowed Doctor Locke to form her fingers into the shape of a gun. Once she was in position, Doctor Locke unravelled the string and wrapped it around Miss Dexter's finger. Its loose end was then gripped by the artist's tucked digits. As Doctor Locke pulled the string taught and pressed its other end against Mr Verity's chest, she and Doctor Wren followed the line with their eyes.

"That looks about right," Wren remarked. "But what of the glass case? It wasn't broken."

"We are working on that," Mr Locke interjected, the desire to expose the antique's secret becoming stronger in his breast—if only to silence the singular question that kept arising.

Mr Verity gave Miss Dexter his hand as she descended the steps.

Mr Locke, having walked behind the steps, began to examine the books on the shelves. Each appeared normal, and even the shelves behind sounded solid beneath his tapping. A soft hum left his lips. Squatting once more, he ran a hand across the stain and pressed down, firmly, in its centre. At last, he declared, "This room is utterly impenetrable."

"May I make some sketches, sir?" Miss Dexter enquired from Mr Elmore, Jr., who'd ventured a few steps into the library. A brief nod and wave of his hand was given to indicate his consent and the artist at once retrieved her sketchbook from her satchel. Looking about the room, she made a simple sketch of its layout and labelled each item of furniture accordingly. Next, she set down her sketchbook upon the desk to retrieve her handheld, box camera. A brief look to Mr Elmore, Jr. garnered the necessary permission she needed to take photographs.

"Did your Da have any enemies?" Mr Verity enquired.

"No, none," Mr Elmore, Jr. replied.

"Not even a man named Terrence Partridge?" Mr Locke hazarded.

"Who?" Mr Elmore, Jr. looked confused.

"Was he in debt, into the drink, or the opium?" Mr Verity pressed.

"Certainly not," Mr Elmore, Jr. snapped. "On all three counts."

"Mr Elmore was in perfect health, too," Wren interjected.

"Thank you," Miss Dexter said upon capturing the last photograph. Returning both her camera and her sketchbook to her satchel, she slipped the satchel back over her head to rest upon her hip.

"Did your father say why he purchased the doll?" Mr Locke enquired.

"He simply liked the look of it," Mr Elmore, Jr. replied.

"I've seen all I need to," Doctor Locke announced. Turning to her fellow medical practitioner, she said, "It was a pleasure to meet you, Doctor Wren. Where may we reach you if we have any further questions?"

"At my home," he replied. Taking a card from his pocket, he turned it over and leaned upon the desk to write down his address. Giving it to Doctor Locke with a smile, he noticed her husband watching from behind. Expelling the smile from his features, therefore, he gave a small bow to Mr Locke and bid the group goodbye, citing appointments he had to attend. A second hushed conversation was had with Mr Elmore, Jr. as Wren departed.

TEN

"The doll's facing the wall," Miss Trent said as she rested her hand upon her hip and eyed the offensive antique. The backside of its case was, by all appearances, solid wood. Mr Maxwell always lingered at her side with his back to the wall and the case in full view. He tapped a pencil against his notebook's top while he watched Miss Dexter walk Mr Verity to a chair and ready her box camera. Mr Locke strolled in behind and went past the doll to stand by the window where Mr Skinner sat. As he heard a familiar voice outside, he pushed aside the net curtain and peered out at Mr Snyder and Sergeant Bird. The latter spoke to the former with the odd gesticulation toward the opera house. Mr Snyder uttered one-word responses here and there but otherwise rolled his shoulders and stretched his arms.

"Miss Bernice and Brenda Kershaw have a shop in Cheapside," Miss Trent said.

Mr Locke pulled back from the window to be struck by the sight of two identical ladies setting down a large box on the floor. They were—at least—thirty years old with oval faces, fair complexions, golden-brown hair, and bespectacled, hazel eyes. Their thick heeled shoes supplied an additional inch to their six feet height. Mr Locke listened to Brenda Kershaw introduce herself to Mr Verity and then the others as she traversed the room exchanging pleasantries. The sister who kept her arms folded and muttered a blunt "hello" whenever Brenda referred to her had to be Bernice, Mr Locke assumed. He watched her polish her spectacles with her skirt and dip her head to replace them upon her nose. The entrance of Mr Elliott caught both ladies off guard, however. While Brenda stumbled over her words, Bernice crossed the room to thrust her hand toward him.

"Hello, Mr…?" she enquired.

"Elliott," the solicitor replied. He glanced between them with his usual stoicism. "You're the clockmaker?"

"My sister and me, yes," Brenda replied.

"Misses Brenda and Bernice Kershaw," Miss Trent introduced. "I was telling everyone about their shop in Cheapside. It's highly recommended by London's watch and clock connoisseurs."

"The name is familiar to me," Mr Elliott said. "But belonging to two brothers."

"A necessary deception," Brenda said.

"One that has served us well," Bernice added.

"Deception, of any kind, is abhorrent," Mr Elliott said. "And rarely do the ends justify the means."

Bernice's lips pursed as her spectacles slipped. She pushed them up and replied, "And rarely do the ends meet when one is an unmarried woman, striving to carve her path through London's rock."

"Minor deceptions oft weaken the conscience, until a person has no morality to keep them from overstepping the line of the law," Mr Elliott replied without emotion. "I've encountered the aftermath of such degradation enough times in my work as a solicitor to recognise its symptoms." His mask of stoicism faltered as, with a tilted head, he gave a slow nod. "But… I'll nonetheless concede necessity is the mother of invention. As is most commonly the case, wider society is responsible for creating, and enforcing, the distasteful situations which compel people to utilise deception as a necessary means of survival."

"Indeed," Bernice said.

"Miss Bernice, what are your first impressions of the doll?" Miss Trent interjected.

The twins looked to one another and turned toward the antique.

"It has the characteristics of the clockwork figurines we've seen in the past," Bernice said. "Brenda, could it be one of Fernand Martin's, perhaps?"

"It's too large."

"Oh, yes, of course."

"Who's Fernand Martin?" Mr Verity enquired.

"A highly talented maker of clockwork toys in Paris, France," Brenda replied.

"His works are something to behold," Bernice added.

"You subscribe to the theory the doll has a clockwork mechanism, then?" Mr Locke enquired as he came forward and scratched at his gloved hand.

"We subscribe to no one's theory," Brenda stated.

"But form our conclusions on what we observe," Bernice said. The sisters stood on opposite sides of the case and traced its edges with their fingertips. When they reached the summit, they ran their hands over the topmost pane and touched in the middle.

"Solid, Bernice."

"Impossibly so, Brenda."

"There are no visible hinges," Mr Locke remarked. "I have already conducted a search for them." His irritated hand rested against his side while he indicated the doll with his other. "No hidden pressure pads, loose connections, or gaps between the frames, either. The table, upon which the case stands, is as mundane as the next."

"Any mechanism is likely to be concealed within the doll, the base, or wooden frames," Bernice remarked.

Mr Maxwell paused his notetaking. "How can you be so sure?"

"There is insufficient space elsewhere," Brenda replied. "Mark this, Bernice." She sidestepped to her right and pointed at the interior of the case's front, left corner. "Is that a hinged panel?"

"It is," Bernice replied. "And a sturdy, iron pin stood, perpendicular, beside it."

"Where?" Mr Locke enquired as he peered through the glass. "I see no pin."

"It is hidden by the taxidermy rabbit," Bernice said. "Do you have the magnifying glass, Brenda?"

"Third compartment, left side, Bernice."

Bernice knelt beside the sewing box and turned an elongated handle on its top. She paused to look over her shoulder and, seeing Mr Locke was close by, waited for him to move. At first, he was resolute in his silent refusal to budge. A subtle touch of his elbow by Miss Trent persuaded him to relent, however. Bernice watched him walk away but still shifted to one side to block the box's contents.

Mr Verity strained his neck to peer over Bernice's shoulder, but the angle prevented him from seeing anything at all. Miss Dexter, uninterested in the box, instead took a photograph of the pin through the glass. Mr Maxwell swallowed as she neared and lifted his pencil-wielding hand to garner her attention. When she didn't see him, he parted his lips to coax her away from the antique. He didn't speak though for, as if sensing his fear, Miss Dexter returned to Mr Verity before he could.

"Thank you, sister," Bernice mumbled as Brenda moved aside from the case. Bernice tilted her head and body to the left to peer through the magnifying glass at the pin. "There is a hollow, thin, circular line cut from the carved grass in the base, beneath the rabbit. The pin disappears into this hollow." She passed the magnifying glass to Brenda. "Agreed?"

Brenda conducted her own inspection and returned the glass. "Agreed."

"Such a pin is likely to serve one purpose, Brenda."

"Absolutely, Bernice."

"Our course of action is clear, then?"

"I see no practical alternative."

In unison, the twins turned to face the others.

"We are going to activate the mechanism," Bernice announced.

"To demonstrate how a bullet may pass through solid glass," Brenda said.

"You may stay to watch, if you wish," Bernice added.

"No, absolutely not," Miss Trent said as she stood before the twins. "As I explained in my note, two of the doll's past owners have *died*. I'm not going to allow you to mimic their mistake by leaving you alone with it. Nor do I want you tinkering with what is, in all likelihood, the cause of their deaths. Your assurance of the hidden mechanism's existence is enough. Mr Callahan Skinner is a former officer with Her Majesty's Royal Navy, and now a bodyguard." Miss Trent looked past the twins to the man in question. "He therefore has a great deal of knowledge regarding guns and other weapons."

"Good day to you," Mr Skinner said as he stood.

"Sir," Bernice replied but looked to his scars rather than his eyes. Bernadette, meanwhile, was distracted his iron hand.

"Mr Skinner, please could you tell Miss Brenda and Miss Bernice your conclusions?"

"The gun in the doll's hand's real," he replied and rested his iron hand upon his stomach as he peered through the case. "A Webley Mark I, used in the Navy. Like I told ye before, I could say if the guns been fired, and how many times, if I could get close to it."

"Then we *must* activate it," Brenda interjected.

"The doll poses a very real threat," Miss Trent replied. "One we must respect." Woolfe's words echoed around her mind and her stomach clenched. Her fear was both unexpected and unwelcome. "But I trust the knowledge, expertise, and judgement of everyone in this room." Irritated by her own reaction and trepidation, she dismissed Woolfe's voice and held her head high. "Misses

Kershaw, Mr Skinner, you have my permission to do what needs to be done."

"If we're gonna fire the gun, ev'ryone should leave," Mr Skinner said.

"But, if we are right in our assumptions—" Brenda began.

"*If* we are right," Bernice interjected.

"Yes, *if* we are right," Brenda continued, "then we should have plenty of time to halt the doll's mechanism before it has an opportunity to harm anyone."

"How're you going to do that?" Mr Verity enquired.

"With this." Brenda held up her magnifying glass.

Mr Skinner gave a loud tut and shook his head. "You're mad."

Brenda scowled and dropped the magnifying glass to rest against her skirts. "We're not going to stop a flying bullet with it, sir."

"This *isn't* one of Mr Locke's shows, after all," Bernice interjected.

"We shall lodge it in the mechanism to obstruct its movement," Brenda said.

"Forgive my impertinence, ladies, but we are still without a keyhole," Mr Locke said. "I would therefore like to see your intended means of activating the purported mechanism."

Bernice gave a wry smile and slipped her fingernails beneath the right edge of the case's back panel. As she pushed against it, a soft click sounded, and she slid back the panel to reveal a small keyhole surrounded by a brass disc. "On occasion, the keyholes are hidden to make the case more pleasing to the eye."

"But we've still not got a key," Mr Verity said.

"I believe I may be of assistance," Mr Locke replied. From his frockcoat he took a black, velvet roll that he carried to the window sill and unravelled. Amongst the wires was a short, thick rod with bumps and grooves on one end that Mr Locke took out and compared against the keyhole. He smiled as he found it to be the correct size.

Mr Maxwell pointed at the doll with his pencil. "Pardon me, but… wouldn't it be safer to simply… break the glass?"

"We might damage the mechanism," Bernice replied.

"And inadvertently set it off," Brenda added.

"Guns can be unpredictable," Mr Skinner interjected. "Best not to mess with 'em."

"Ah," Mr Maxwell said and dropped his gaze to the iron hand as he wondered how Mr Skinner had lost his other. The thought of it being a gunshot wound turned his stomach. He therefore diverted his gaze to Miss Dexter to distract himself. She took a photograph of Mr Locke's odd key, and then several photographs of the doll. Her proximity to the antique served to worsen Mr Maxwell's agitation rather than relieve it.

"Don't worry, Mr Maxwell," Mr Verity said with a smirk. "We're not in any danger here. Besides," he pointed up, "we've got Him looking over us."

"Yes, of course…" Mr Maxwell replied with a weak smile as he put his pencil and notebook away. With a wipe of his sweaty palms upon his frockcoat, he forced down the lump in his throat, and willed Miss Dexter away from the doll.

"Miss Dexter, please join Mr Elliott and me over here," Miss Trent instructed.

To Mr Maxwell's great relief, Miss Dexter stood in front of Miss Trent and Mr Elliott. She then held her box camera against her skirts and peered through its top to check she could see the entire doll.

"Whenever you're ready, Mr Locke," Miss Trent said.

"I'll assist him," Bernice said. "If only to ensure he doesn't break the mechanism's delicate balance with his…" She eyed the rod. "…Whatever that is."

130

"A master key of my own design," Mr Locke explained. "And I would be glad of your assistance, Miss Kershaw."

"I'll stay 'ere, too," Mr Skinner said. "Just in case."

Bernice went closer to the case and lifted the magnifying glass. "Let us begin, then, Mr Locke."

Mr Locke's brow lofted as the obvious question presented itself. Deciding to trust the clockmaker, however, he stepped behind the case. With a tug of his gloves' cuffs, he leaned down to peer into the keyhole. He had neglected to request a candle—an unwelcome failure on his part. Yet, the tense atmosphere of the room was too intoxicating for him to break by requesting one. He therefore resolved to continue without it.

Positioning the rod's end against the keyhole, he straightened, and placed himself parallel to the doll. The resistance the rod encountered—as it was inserted—told him at least one tumbler was present. He gripped the table's edge, stilled the remainder of his body, and slowed his breathing. His gaze fixed upon the wall opposite but, soon, shifted to his mind's eye. To better feel the slight variations in pressure as he manipulated the rod's transit, he also muted his hearing.

Several moments passed as he worked, during which the room fell silent.

Mr Locke tilted his wrist and pushed, and the rod drove home with a loud click. Withdrawing from his near meditative state, he looked across at Bernice. *Her stoicism could rival Mr Elliott's*, he mused. *So could his*, he added as he saw Mr Skinner's stony-faced expression. With his hand on the rod, he waited a moment to savour the anticipation before turning the rod with a sharp flick of his wrist and a dramatic sideways slide of his feet.

Metallic whirling filled the room, followed by ticks and rhythmic clicks. Interspersed with these were the rapid clicks of Miss Dexter's camera as she pressed its button to capture the moment. Bernice's grip on the magnifying glass tightened at the steadily increasing volume—and number—of sounds.

Mr Locke, who'd moved to the doll's left, watched the interior pin jerk forward and follow the path of the hollow circle—just as the Kershaws had predicted. He smiled. *One cannot be correct all the time.* As the pin approached the case's front panel, it pushed against the brass plate affixed to its frame. This, in turn, caused another loud click to fill the air, and the panel began to open. To begin with, only a few millimetres' gap appeared between the front and side panels' frames. Another click, identical to the last, then sounded. Mr Locke peered through the ever-widening space and saw a blackened, metal hinge emerge between the front and far frames. This hinge, he fathomed, was opened by another—still hidden—mechanism.

Intrigued, he studied the case's interior. A thick mustiness, with a hint of gunpowder, filled his nostrils. The scent also affected Mr Skinner as he, too, peered inside.

The clicks and ticks became louder. A prolonged whirl then bounced off the glass. Mr Locke searched the doll and base but found no trace of what had caused the sound. That was, until he caught the movement of the doll's arm out the corner of his eyes. Previously, it had rested against the doll's side. Mr Locke watched as it was lifted into a horizontal position. In its hand was the revolver that, with each passing moment, was being aimed at the wall.

"Miss Kershaw," Mr Locke said as he kept his eyes on the gun. When Bernice didn't respond, he looked across the case and found she, too, was entranced by the doll's motion.

"Miss Kershaw?" Mr Skinner enquired.

"Miss *Bernice*!" Miss Trent urged.

132

The doll's arm bounced and locked into place with a clunk. Mr Locke—having heard the shift in sound—had looked in time to see a slither of light slide down an otherwise invisible length of fine wire. The revolver's trigger was being compressed as the wire tautened. Without hesitation, Mr Locke reached into the case to take the gun, while his other hand went for the rod.

"*No*!" Mr Skinner cried as he attempted to pull Mr Locke from harm's way.

A tremendous bang exploded from the revolver.

Silence reigned in the immediate seconds which followed. A cacophony of shrieks and strangled gasps then erupted from the room, while screams, shouts, and hollers for the police filled the street.

"What happened?!" Mr Maxwell shrieked as, knelt upon the floor, he trembled. Mr Skinner—who'd ducked behind the doll—stumbled to the window. A loud ringing in his ears made him deaf to Mr Maxwell's question, however. Instead, he struck each ear with the heel of his hand and shook his head.

Bernice, meanwhile, used the table to pull herself up onto her knees. Her sister went to her at once to help her to stand. On the way to the door though, they were drawn back by the sight of Miss Trent running toward the doll.

"Mr Locke!" she cried.

"Oh my God," Mr Elliott said as he also bounded to his feet.

Mr Locke lay upon the table's edge with one arm raised above his head. His other arm was motionless at the case's rear. No response came to Miss Trent's cry and everyone held their breath. When she and Mr Elliott reached him, however, a deep—yet distinct—groan sounded from Mr Locke.

Miss Trent could've fainted from the sudden rush of relief. She grasped Mr Elliott's arm to steady herself and said, "Help him stand." She put her other hand upon Mr Locke's back. "I thought you were dead."

"Open up, this is the police!" a male voice shouted from the hallway, followed by several loud thuds.

"I am sorry to disappoint," Mr Locke remarked with a weak smile. With Mr Elliott and Mr Skinner's assistance, he lifted himself from the table. A weight was against his wrists, however, and, as he gave it a gentle tug, he felt the entire case rock. "Ah." He put his right foot behind him and twisted his arm. As he pulled upon his wrist though, a sharp pain shot up his arm. "As much as I am loathed to admit it," he said. "I appear to be trapped."

"I said, *open up!*" the voice shouted again, prompting Mr Elliott to leave the room to answer the door.

Miss Trent turned on the twins with a fierce scowl. "What the *bloody* Hell *happened*? You were supposed to stop it."

"She didn't *intend* for Mr Locke to trap his hand in the case," Brenda replied as she stood between Miss Trent and her sister.

"I was attempting to take the gun," Mr Locke stated, "in the hope it would prevent it from firing."

"Take it from me, Mr Locke, that don't work," Mr Skinner said as he lifted his iron hand.

"I don't care what you say, I'm comin' in," Sergeant Bird insisted from the hallway.

"I wanted to see what the doll would do," Bernice admitted in a subdued voice. "The best way to fathom a clockwork mechanism is to see its motion in full. I'm sorry, Mr Locke."

"What's going on in 'ere?" Bird demanded as he walked into the room, followed by Mr Snyder—who'd asked another to watch his cab—and Mr Elliott.

"I heard a gunshot," Mr Snyder said.

"Thank you for your concern, Sergeant," Mr Elliott stated as he helped Mr Maxwell off the floor. "The gun was fired accidentally." He next assisted Miss Dexter

134

and Mr Verity, who were huddled behind the latter's chair. "But we're all unharmed."

Sergeant Bird pointed at Mr Locke. "What 'bout 'im?"

"I am perfectly fine, thank you," Mr Locke reassured.

"Nothing to see 'ere," Mr Skinner interjected.

"We're sorry to have wasted your time," Miss Trent said as she moved in between Mr Skinner and Bird, since it was clear Mr Skinner's accent had roused Bird's suspicion.

"Whatever you say, Miss Trent," Sergeant Bird replied with a large dose of sarcasm. "I don't mind bein' put out. Not. At. All." He looked around the group. "Any more 'shots though, and it'll be down the station for the lot of you."

Mr Snyder followed Sergeant Bird outside.

"We are all in a great state of shock, and therefore unable to think clearly," Mr Elliott stated once he heard the front door close. "I therefore propose we focus our efforts on freeing Mr Locke. Are you injured?"

"No," Mr Locke replied. "The bullet must have missed by a mere hair, however."

"It's in the wall," Mr Skinner said. Sure enough, there was a round, black singe in the wallpaper. The wall also had a dip in it where a flattened, metallic disk sat.

"If someone would be so kind as to turn the rod, I should be able to—" Mr Locke began.

"*Wait*," Miss Trent ordered to halt Mr Skinner as he reached for the tool. "We are *not* setting this thing off again. We'll just have to find another way of freeing him."

Mr Locke leaned toward the window and tried to push the door open with his free hand. It moved half an inch and rebounded. Mr Locke sighed. "I really do think turning the rod is the best course of action in this instance." When he reached for it though, Miss Trent plucked it from the keyhole and slipped it into her pocket.

"I said, *wait*," she scolded.

"You are being unreasonable," Mr Locke said. "It is but a simple matter of—"

"Risking your life?" Miss Trent questioned with a lofted brow.

"As I have already done so—on *several* occasions—for this Society, you mean?" Mr Locke smiled. "No, I was going to say: it is a simple matter of turning the rod, setting the mechanism in motion, and preventing it from reaching its pinnacle, by lodging Mr Verity's chair beneath the door."

"W-Was it the doll that fired the gun?" Mr Maxwell enquired. His trembling thumb and forefinger were either side of his Adam's apple.

"Yeah, just as our hero 'ere was reachin' fer it," Mr Skinner replied. "Bloody daft t'ing to do, and all."

"Do you think the revolver was given to the doll when it was made?" Mr Verity enquired from the Kershaws.

"Don't be absurd," Brenda rebuked.

"Earlier…" Miss Dexter began. As the others turned toward her, she continued. "I noticed the doll's hand is shaped as if it was intended to hold something."

"Which means… there *could* have been a faux firearm previously, but someone has added a real gun, and tampered with the mechanism to ensure it is fired, correct?" Mr Elliott mused aloud.

"Looks that way," Mr Skinner agreed as he eyed the weapon.

"Perhaps," Brenda said.

"We can't *know* until we open the doll," Bernice added.

"There is a fine wire tied around the gun," Mr Locke said. "It pulled the trigger back. I suspect the wire's other end is attached to the interior mechanism. Correct me if I am wrong, Misses Kershaw, but I would suppose such sabotage would not be too difficult to execute, even for an ignoramus in the field of clock making."

"Your supposition is correct," Bernice replied and shifted her gaze to Miss Trent. "Yet, depending upon the complexity of the mechanism, one couldn't apply the wire in mere moments. It would be time consuming. Anyone wanting to add the wire, then, and the revolver, would have to know they wouldn't be disturbed for at least ten minutes."

"And know how to handle a gun without settin' it off," Mr Skinner interjected. "That wire's got to be strong, too, to pull a trigger like that."

"These are all questions which may be answered by a simple examination of the doll," Bernice said.

Miss Trent felt all eyes upon her. Putting her hands upon her hips, she sighed. "Very well," she said and gave Mr Locke the rod. "I'd like to ask you all to wait in the meeting room, please. Miss Brenda, Miss Bernice, once Mr Locke is freed, and the mechanism locked, you may properly inspect the doll."

"Thank you, Miss Trent," Bernice replied with a weak smile. She slipped her arm around her sister's and walked with her from the room. Miss Dexter—after retrieving her camera from the floor—followed suit, while Mr Maxwell accompanied Mr Elliott. Mr Verity approached Mr Locke, however, and extended a hand to him.

"May God be with you," he said.

"Thank you," Mr Locke replied as he gave his fellow Bow Streeter's hand a firm shake. "I shan't be in need of Him, however."

"Still, best to be prepared!" Mr Verity announced. Giving a nod to Miss Trent, he too left to occupy his usual spot by the meeting room's fire.

"I'll stay," Mr Skinner informed Miss Trent.

"Only you could do this," Miss Trent remarked, softly, to Mr Locke once the others had left and Mr Skinner had the chair ready.

"I shall accept that as a compliment," Mr Locke replied as he slipped the rod into the keyhole and manipulated the lock until it was released. For a second time, the doll's mechanism clicked, whirled, and ticked. Like before, the door eased open. Mr Locke waited until the gap was wide enough before he slipped his hand free. "Now."

Mr Skinner lifted the chair with his actual hand and slipped it beneath the case's door to place it in front. The clunk of the doll's arm sounded a moment later, followed by a loud, metallic click. The door then swung closed, struck the chair and locked in place against it. The three looked at one another in silence.

"It didn't fire," Miss Trent remarked.

"It did. I heard the click of the hammer," Mr Skinner said. "Chamber must be empty."

"Thank God." Miss Trent looked at the weapon, and then at Mr Locke as he rubbed his wrist. "I'll fetch Bernice and Brenda."

ELEVEN

The doll's inner workings were a jumble of brass cogs set within a hollow, tin body and wooden base. To describe it as 'complex' would've been an understatement. Gathered around its table, and reinvigorated with tea, the Bow Streeters observed the Kershaws at work. Brenda guided Miss Dexter's sketch through explanation of each component's placement and purpose. Miss Dexter had taken photographs but suggested a detailed, labelled sketch would provide an excellent reference point. Bernice, meanwhile, worked to untangle the fine wire from the cogs and rods. As she watched, Miss Trent considered Mr Snyder's account. "How is it possible the doll's mechanism was set off in an empty, locked room?"

"If there was still some tension in the springs, minute movement, or change in temperature, could, theoretically, initiate the mechanism," Bernice replied.

Miss Trent hummed. "The gun has been fired twice when the doll's been unattended: once when the house was locked up and, more recently, when Mr Snyder accepted the case on the Society's behalf. Could there be enough tension in the springs to allow these two incidences, despite the length of time between them?"

"Perhaps," Brenda replied.

"But there's no way we can be certain," Bernice added.

Miss Trent gave a slight frown. "I see… thank you."

"If, as was remarked earlier, the wire took more than a moment to apply," Mr Locke said. "And—judging by how long it is taking to remove it—a longer period is likelier than a shorter, I propose a member of the Cosgrove household was responsible. Their presence in the doll's vicinity, for an extended amount of time, would not be

139

questioned. Furthermore, I would like to draw your attention to the professor's study door. It was locked at the time of his murder. Presuming he took such a precaution to eliminate the risk of his domestic staff helping themselves to his valuables, we may narrow the circle of suspects to those with legitimate reasons for having a key. Naturally, we should make certain of *who* the key holders were, but, for now, the natural choices are: Mrs Coral Cosgrove, the professor's wife, and his secretary, Miss Henrietta Watkins. By association, we may also include the nephews, Mr Ned and Mr Norman Cosgrove." Mr Locke rubbed his wrist. "Then, we have the question of the whereabouts of the original key for the doll's mechanism. Our client did not give it with the doll. Mr Elmore, Jr. may have it still, perhaps?"

"Or our murderer," Mr Elliott remarked.

"Talking about the wire, the professor might've bought the doll with it inside, like Mr Elmore did," Mr Verity suggested and wiped tea from his lips with his handkerchief. "We don't know if it was made like it."

"It's *hardly* likely," Brenda countered.

"And the automata makers' relentless efforts to surpass one another has never included wilful murder," Bernice said.

"I could look again b-but, when I searched, there were no articles about other owners of the doll dying," Mr Maxwell said as he looked between the Kershaws and Mr Verity while he kept a firm grip of the saucer nestled in his lap.

"The trail *must* begin at the Cosgrove residence, then," Mr Elliott said.

"A chilling thought," Mr Verity remarked. "A demon would've been *less* uncanny. Someone *took* the time to make the doll into a *weapon*…" He shook his head. "…It's the devil's work, y'nah."

"Wrought by the hand of man," Miss Dexter murmured. Her mind drifted to a crowded Oxford Street and the mutilated corpse of a fallen woman.

"And smelted by us," Mr Maxwell replied, softly.

Miss Dexter looked to him and saw a quiet determination in his eyes. It sent her wretched memories into the ether, as if they were steam from a teapot's spout. As she felt a calm descend upon her, she permitted a smile to flutter across her lips. "Indeed, Mr Maxwell."

"It's even more important we find, and speak with, *everyone* connected to the Cosgrove residence at the time of the murder—including any domestic servants," Mr Elliott urged. "Whoever put the wire into the doll is not only responsible for the professor's death, but also Mr Elmore's. Whereas the first was, undoubtedly, their intended victim, the second was not. Yet—"

"Yet, they didn't stop the doll from being sold at auction," Mr Maxwell interrupted. He stood and crossed the room to set his cup and saucer down upon the table. With his back to the others, he bowed his head and spoke in a quiet voice, "Or had even written to Mr Elmore to warn him of the danger."

"A most reprehensible act of cruelty," Mr Locke remarked.

"The revolver had four cartridge cases in it," Mr Skinner said and wedged his teacup between the fingers and thumb of his iron hand. "That what killed the professor, that what killed Mr Elmore, the thurd that Mr Snyder heard, and this one. The man who gave the doll a gun was gonna get the professor—sooner or later."

A heavy silence—brought on by unanimous, quiet reflection—fell upon them. Bernice, Brenda, and Miss Dexter slowed in their work and the light sought to mirror to their mood. Dense clouds were pushed across the sun by strong winds and the room was plunged into gloom.

"Mr Maxwell…" Miss Trent ventured and waited for him to meet her gaze. "Would you and Mr Elliott like to tell us what you discovered during your visit to Mr Paul Bund?"

Mr Maxwell peered over his shoulder at Mr Elliott. With a swallow, he wiped his palms upon his frockcoat and faced the others. "Y-yes… of course. He told us he hadn't murdered Professor Cosgrove, b-but that the professor owed him monies. Mr Bund made his visit, to the professor's house, when the debt became overdue."

"Namely, a loan of one hundred pounds with one hundred percent interest added," Mr Elliott said. "Professor Cosgrove refused to pay the interest, and the two argued. From Mr Bund's account, and what was said in the other witnesses' testimonies at the inquest, it is safe to assume the money lender was never left alone with the doll."

"Shall we eliminate him as a suspect, then?" Miss Trent enquired as she looked between them. Mr Maxwell returned to his chair and straightened the knot of his cravat several times while he directed anxious eyes toward Mr Elliott.

Mr Elliott, though conscious of the less-than-subtle hint posed by Mr Maxwell's behaviour, maintained a vigorous stoicism. "I think it would be wise, yes."

Miss Trent wrote down the decision in her notebook but, no sooner had she done so, did Miss Dexter's voice reach her.

"And Mr Partridge…?" Miss Dexter enquired. "We know very little about him, and we still have no idea why his paintings were covered, or the name of the man in black who came here."

"Mr Bund hadn't heard of Mr Partridge," Mr Elliott stated.

"Nor had Mr Elmore," Mr Locke added.

"The Cosgrove family might've," Mr Verity said. "He might've been the one to put the wire in the doll, and that's why he wanted the Society to take it. Once it's gone from his house, he can say he knew nothing about it."

"And hope the blame for the professor's murder was put on the Cosgrove family…" Miss Dexter said. "…That's *terrible*."

"*If* true," Miss Trent pointed out. "Continue asking after Mr Partridge. Dependent on what is said, I shall arrange for us to pay him another visit. He gave Mr Snyder instructions on how to reach him, but we must be careful. As Miss Dexter said, we know very little about him. If we act in haste, he may do something desperate or, at the very least, cut all communication with us. Both outcomes will do little to help us solve this case."

Miss Dexter felt warmth wash over her. She was pleased their odd client wouldn't be forgotten, but her happiness was eroded by thoughts of meeting him herself. When Brenda said their sketch was complete, Miss Dexter felt her anxiety disappear. "I'll have the new photographs sent over this evening, Miss Trent."

"And *we* shall seek an appointment to see the professor's study when we speak with his nephew," Mr Locke interjected with a smile. "If it achieves nothing else, it shall draw him away from the roulette table."

* * *

"Devious blighters," Inspector Conway remarked. Granted, the sketched workings were beyond his understanding, but he'd recognised the gun and wire. "What about what happened at Partridge's place?" He looked to Miss Trent. They stood in the shelter of a burnt-out warehouse on the East end of St. Katheryne's Docks. Dark-coloured water poured from the top of the open doorway as yet more rain soaked the capital. The innumerable ships on the Thames—and workers who loaded and removed their cargo—weren't slowed by the inclement weather, however. The cacophony of yells, horns, engines, paddles, and splashes swallowed the sound of rain. Even in their secluded corner, Conway could just about hear himself think.

"The Kershaw twins believe latent tension in the springs could've been responsible," Miss Trent replied. She watched as Conway passed the sketch to Chief Inspector Jones. "But they can't be certain." She wrapped her coat around herself as she shivered. The heavy cloud had made the air milder, but the relentless damp had chilled her core. While Chief Inspector Jones studied the sketch, Miss Trent retrieved a hip flask of brandy from her pocket and took a sip. At Conway's glance toward it, she held it out. The grizzled policeman stole a sideways glance at Chief Inspector Jones but, seeing he was engrossed in the sketch, took the flask and had a swig. The brandy's warmth, as it slid down his throat, made Conway cough a little. Nonetheless, he had some more before he returned it to Miss Trent.

"Give me that," Chief Inspector Jones stated as he looked up from the sketch and held out his hand. Miss Trent, who'd attempted to slip the flask back into her coat before he saw it, gave a sigh but did as instructed. While Chief Inspector Jones took the flask, she had the sketch, and watched him unscrew the cap to have a sniff.

"Sam swears by it to keep back the cold," Miss Trent said.

"We have plenty of that," Chief Inspector Jones replied and took a half mouthful. With a shake of his head to shrug off the burn, he replaced the cap and returned the flask to Miss Trent. "Just don't make it a habit."

"Of course not," Miss Trent replied as she caught Conway's relieved eyes.

"The doll being rigged to cause harm does make Mr Elmore's death a murder, rather than suicide," Chief Inspector Jones remarked. "Since the Society can trace the origins of the doll's deadly additions to the Cosgrove residence though, then the entire case falls back under the remit of the Metropolitan Police. Especially as the

144

Cosgrove murder remains unsolved and is therefore an open case in the police records."

"You want me to tell the investigating officer, then?" Conway enquired and lit his cigarette.

"Is that *really* necessary?" Miss Trent interjected. "The case is six years old."

"Transparency, remember?" Chief Inspector Jones replied.

Miss Trent sighed. "Yes, I remember…" She rubbed her red nose with her handkerchief. "Just *please* don't tell me Woolfe used to work in that division."

"Nah, 'e's always been at Holborn," Conway said as he exhaled the smoke into the wind. "Chelsea… that's T division."

Chief Inspector Jones hummed. "Inspector Gideon Lee. He was likely the investigating officer on the Cosgrove case, too."

"What's he like?" Miss Trent enquired.

"Thinks 'imself a gent," Conway replied. "From what I've seen."

"Can you arrange a meeting?" Miss Trent enquired, still addressing the Head of the Mob Squad.

"'E won't have your lot in his station house," Conway replied. "But, yeah, I can do that. Who you thinking of sending?"

"I have someone in mind. I'll arrange for them to meet you at the A.B.C Tearoom, John," Miss Trent said with a smirk. "So you may introduce them to Lee."

Conway stared at her. When he looked to Chief Inspector Jones, he didn't reject the suggestion. "Okay. Let me know when, but don't think you'll get much." He finished his cigarette and tossed it onto the ground to crush under his shoe. "Or that I'll push 'im to give it."

"The meeting will be on an official basis, John," Chief Inspector Jones replied. "I'd expect you to act within your official capacity, as you did with Inspector Woolfe. Speaking of which, did he search the house, Miss Trent?"

"No, I didn't hear a word from him, or his constables," Miss Trent replied. "Which was great. I had expected to receive at least a telephone call from Doctor Weeks about Woolfe's newfound knowledge, however."

"Likewise," Chief Inspector Jones said.

"Why you both looking at me?" Conway enquired.

"You *did* inform Woolfe of Weeks' involvement with the Society, didn't you?" Chief Inspector Jones enquired as he watched Conway pace in an apparent effort to stay warm. The fact he wasn't shivering did give him pause for thought. Yet, Conway's firm nod gave Chief Inspector Jones further cause for hesitation. "What was his reaction?"

"'E was angry," Conway said. "But I got him to leave off doing something about it."

"How?" Miss Trent enquired, surprised. "Woolfe's not the type to listen to reason."

"We're *mates*," Conway growled as he shot her a black look. When she lifted her hand in surrender, he looked back to Chief Inspector Jones. "And because what I said was done unofficially, sir. I also said I'd keep an eye on Weeks, along with the rest of the Society."

Chief Inspector Jones' mouth formed a hard line. "That's *not* what we agreed, John. Weeks' involvement with the Society will need to be openly dealt with—"

"*Past* involvement," Conway interrupted. "Sir." When Chief Inspector Jones' eyes remained hard, Conway softened his expression. "Weeks' retired from the Society, you said so yourself. Woolfe's happy with what I told 'im, and what's being done about it, so where's the harm?"

"John's right," Miss Trent interjected. "We shouldn't kick the hornet's nest if it's not absolutely necessary."

Chief Inspector Jones turned over the arguments in his mind. The rain also weakened, allowing them to hear the dockworkers' shouts more keenly. "Very well. But I want to be told if Weeks returns to the Society."

"Of course," Miss Trent replied while Conway gave a soft grunt of agreement.

"Is that all?" Conway enquired. "I dunno about you two, but I'm about ready for a cuppa." He held down his trilby, pulled up his coat's collar, and strode from the warehouse. Miss Trent smirked but, at Chief Inspector Jones' indication for her to go ahead of him, walked out also.

* * *

"I request an *immediate* moment of your time, sir," Mr Dexter announced the moment Mr Maxwell alighted from Mr Snyder's cab. Mr Maxwell raised his hands to his chest and stepped back when Mr Dexter then thrust an envelope into his face. "About *this*."

"Wh-what is it?" Mr Maxwell enquired with wide eyes. Mr Snyder, who had recognised the man stood outside the *Gaslight Gazette* office, shifted forward in his seat to listen. At Mr Maxwell's question, Mr Snyder leaned sideways to see what Mr Dexter held.

"*Your* letter, sir," Mr Dexter replied. His expression was hard but, thus far, he'd kept his composure. "What is the meaning of your breach of promise to my daughter?"

"P-Pardon?" Mr Maxwell said, his hands elevated, still.

"Your breach of promise!" Mr Dexter repeated.

Mr Maxwell remained confused, however.

"*Marriage*, sir. *Marriage*! You sat at *my* table, dined on *my* good hospitality, and asked for *my* daughter's hand in marriage. Now, you *refuse* my hospitality and *breach* your proposal to Georgina, with *no* explanation."

"Georg—I mean, Miss Dexter, sh-she told me she understood," Mr Maxwell said as he lowered his hands and glanced at the Gazette's first floor windows. His fellow journalist, Mr Baldwin, watched him from there and, with their other colleagues, sniggered. Mr Maxwell frowned at this but then gasped when Mr Dexter gave his chest a firm prod.

"Never mind what she said!" Mr Dexter cried. "She's thinking with her heart, not her head. *You*, sir, have a *lot* to answer for, and you *will* answer for it. I'll have you in court before the week is out."

Mr Maxwell blinked as a cold flush swept over him. Staring after Mr Dexter as he strode away, Mr Maxwell then hurried to catch him up. "Sir, wait!" He caught his foot on the pavement and stumbled. Thankfully, he grabbed a nearby lamppost and stopped himself from falling into Mr Dexter's arms. Out of breath, he maintained his grip on the cold, wet metal. "I love your daughter, but circumstances have changed. I would put it right if I could, but—"

"Good intentions won't clothe my daughter, Mr Maxwell," Mr Dexter interrupted. "Prepare your defence, for I'll be *eager* to hear it. *Good day*!" Mr Dexter stepped around Mr Maxwell to put his foot on the edge of Mr Snyder's cab. "Home, please, Mr Snyder!" Mr Dexter climbed inside and slammed the doors.

"Yes, sir," Mr Snyder replied. He geed the horse with a flick of the whip and, with one last cold look cast at Mr Maxwell, drove the cab into the flow of traffic.

Mr Maxwell stepped away from the lamppost and watched them go. His stomach tightened as he thought upon Mr Dexter's words. It then flipped, however, as he imagined his own father's reaction. To his colleagues' great amusement, Mr Maxwell bent over the curb, and emptied his stomach into the gutter.

TWELVE

Widely regarded as the heart of London's west end, Piccadilly Circus was then—as now—a stone's throw from the clubs and theatres frequented by the wealthy elite. Being the point at which many major thoroughfares converged, and omnibus lines crossed, the Circus had earnt a deserved reputation for being chaotic. Even past sunset, when the bitter-cold wind coiled around Coventry Street and Shaftsbury Avenue. Hansom cabs and private carriages lined the road outside the London Pavilion, and Criterion Theatre and Restaurant, with pedestrians headed to both. Amidst the fur-wearing ladies and top hatted gentlemen were the emaciated pocket-dippers and rouged ladybirds who openly plied their trades.

Mr Maxwell was fascinated by the spectacle. His green eyes took it all in as he followed Mr Locke and Mr Elliott along Coventry Street. So distracted was he, he'd failed to notice his associates had stopped outside a book shop. He therefore walked into Mr Locke and grunted as he was propelled backward. Mr Locke was also forced into a forward step by the sudden collision.

Mr Locke turned on his heel and peered down at the red-faced Mr Maxwell. "Please be more observant."

"Begging your pardon, Mr Locke."

"It is granted. Especially as I am not obliged to check my pockets for the presence of my watch and handkerchief." Mr Locke smirked and indicated the shopfront with his cane. "This way, gentlemen."

Mr Maxwell felt an immediate disconcertion when he stepped inside. The small establishment was dominated by a mahogany panelled counter, behind which stood a scrawny, apron-wearing man. Shelves full of old books covered the opposing wall. Three gas lamps—suspended from the ceiling down the shop's centre—illuminated their immediate vicinity. The remainder was left to the mercy of the dark and cold alike. While Mr Maxwell stopped and stared, Mr Locke swept up his cane to greet the proprietor, and led the way to the shop's rear. Mr Elliott followed at a brisk pace, obliging Mr Maxwell to do the same.

"I thought we were visiting a gambling house?" Mr Maxwell whispered to Mr Locke.

"We are," Mr Locke replied and pulled upon a bright-knobbed bell. It reacted with a muffled clang that went unnoticed by the proprietor, followed by silence. Mr Maxwell worked at loosening his cravat's knot with one finger while he watched the door. By contrast, Mr Locke offered a cigarette to Mr Elliott—who declined—and returned the silver case to his pocket. After a moment, the scrape of metal was heard as a gigantic bolt was slid back.

A middle-aged man in a forest-green suit, cream shirt, and brown tie eased the door open. Without making eye contact, he touched the brim of his black, bowler hat and nodded to Mr Locke. "Good evenin', sir."

"Good evening, Roland," Mr Locke replied as he walked past him. "These are my guests, Mr Gregory Elliott and Mr Joseph Maxwell. Their pockets are heavy with coin, and they are eager to lighten them."

"Very good, sir," Roland replied and gestured for Mr Elliott and Mr Maxwell to go through the door. As they complied, he bid a good evening, and slammed the door shut behind them.

The compact room beyond was windowless with a single, wall-mounted gas lamp. Opposite was a second door covered in green baize and boasting a greater bulk. In its centre was a small, glazed aperture that slid back to reveal beady, brown eyes peering out at them. The rest of the viewer's face was in shadow. The sight caused Mr Maxwell's gut to tighten and his palms to moisten. Wiping his hands over his frockcoat's skirt, he glanced between his fellow Bow Streeters in front. A grunt from beyond the aperture brought his attention back, however, and he watched as the door was opened.

A set of deep-red, carpeted stairs was revealed beyond. Their bannisters were wrought iron leaves and vines crowned with a polished, oak handrail. Gold and cream-striped paper adorned the upper halves of the walls, while oak panelling covered their lower. As he followed Mr Locke and Mr Elliott, Mr Maxwell scanned the area for their mysterious observer. Finding no sign, he reached to close the door.

"Leave the door, sir," a gruff voice said from behind.

Mr Maxwell reeled backward as if burnt. "P-Pardon me."

"Best move on, sir," the voice replied.

As he heard Mr Locke and Mr Elliott climb the stairs, Mr Maxwell hurried to join them.

At the top, they passed through an open doorway into a long room with identical décor. The differences being the high, plaster ceiling covered in ornate roses, the tall windows, and duo of tables stood, side by side, in the room's centre. The first table held a roulette wheel, while the second played host to a game Mr Maxwell recognised as hazard. Both tables were covered by white cloths.

Well-turned-out gentlemen sat around each, while two younger men occupied the space between. Attired in long-sleeved, white shirts with plain, burgundy waistcoats, they occasionally called "no more bets" and swept their hooked walking sticks across the tables' surfaces. Beyond the croupiers was a second open doorway and, through this, Mr Maxwell saw gentlemen dining on a supper of cold chicken, joints of ham, and salads, *et cetera*.

"Mr Elliott?" a venerable voice enquired from the Bow Streeters' left.

"Judge Lowood," Mr Elliott replied and shook the hand of a gentleman at the roulette table.

The judge was in his seventies, with thinning, white hair, and tremendous whiskers. His grey eyes took in Mr Elliott's face as he gave his hand a firm squeeze and placed his other on top. "I hadn't marked you as a gambling man."

"I'm not," Mr Elliott replied. "I'm here as the guest of Mr Percy Locke. This is our mutual friend, Mr Joseph Maxwell."

"Pleased to meet you, sir," Lowood said. "And it's been some time since we saw you last, Mr Locke. What is it… five… six months…?"

"Eight," Mr Locke clarified with a smile and glanced at the table's remaining occupants. "May we join you?"

"Yes, of course," Judge Lowood said.

Mr Maxwell hesitated before he took his seat, however. With a hard swallow, he whispered into Mr Elliott's ear.

"A very good question," Mr Elliott replied as he looked to Mr Locke. It was the judge who answered, however.

"What is?" he enquired, loudly.

"Mr Maxwell was just asking after your reputation, judge," Mr Elliott lied with greater ease than Mr Maxwell would've expected. Nonetheless, the judge beamed and embarked on a speech about his pin-sharp memory for those convicts whose trials he'd resided over. While he spoke, and Mr Maxwell listened, Mr Elliott whispered behind Mr Maxwell's back. "Is our mutual friend here, Mr Locke?"

"He is," Mr Locke replied but kept his eyes on the croupier. "On the far end, left-hand side."

Mr Elliott looked down the table at the gentleman in question. He was in his forties, as attested by his skin's coarseness and his belly's extension. His moustache and hair, meanwhile, were identical in their blond wildness. The former had its tips twirled, while the latter had a strict, central parting. At first, Mr Elliott couldn't distinguish Mr Ned Cosgrove's facial features due to a cloud of smoke that engulfed him. When the cloud eventually dissipated though, he identified its cause as a long cigar gripped between Mr Cosgrove's thumb and forefinger. Studying the man's face, Mr Elliot noted the minute, brown eyes, and swollen jaw disappearing into the thick neck. The fatty rolls of which bounced and jiggled as Mr Cosgrove's deep boom of a laugh drowned out his fellow gamblers. Mr Elliott watched as Mr Cosgrove counted out three five pound notes to place onto the black marker.

"No more bets, please," the croupier announced.

The wheel was spun, and the ball sent on its way. A hush fell upon the table—including Judge Lowood—as the ball flew around the wheel thrice and glided downward to bounce across several numbers. When it was finally caught by red twelve, a cacophony of groans, mumbles, and gleeful chuckles erupted from the table. The croupier at once swept the monies from the markers and distributed the winnings.

"Excuse us," Mr Elliott said as he stood. Placing a hand on Mr Locke's shoulder, he then walked with him to take the newly vacated seats beside Ned Cosgrove.

Mr Maxwell's attempt to join them was foiled by Judge Lowood gripping his arm, however. "Of course, I'll never forget the Winslow Baby Carriage case."

Mr Cosgrove, meanwhile, had placed a half crown on red.

"Lady Luck has deserted you, Mr Cosgrove," Mr Locke remarked as he put a guinea on the black.

Ned narrowed his eyes and puffed upon his cigar. "The night's still young."

"I was not referring to roulette," Mr Locke replied.

Mr Cosgrove's face was again concealed by smoke. "What was you speaking of, then?"

Where Mr Locke's gloved hand had been empty a moment prior, it suddenly held Miss Dexter's photograph of the doll. He placed it upon Ned's coin pile. "This doll that you sold through *Milton's Auctioneers* six months ago is responsible for a man's death."

"That's *demmed* nonsense!" Ned barked. "Dolls don't kill people."

"This one did," Mr Locke replied. "Mr Edgar Elmore, to be precise. Slain in his locked library while alone with this doll." Mr Locke tapped the photograph. "*Your* doll, Mr Cosgrove."

"*Demmed* auctioneers!" Ned barked. Sticking his cigar between his teeth, he gathered up his monies and stuffed them into his pockets as he stood. "I had nothing whatever to do with anyone's death, Mr Locke." Ned looked down at him. "And *Milton's* had no right to give my name."

"They did not," Mr Locke replied and stood as Ned stared at him. "Perhaps it would be more appropriate to continue our discussion in the supper room…?"

The three left the gambling tables to head in that direction. When Mr Maxwell joined them a moment later, and all pleasantries were taken care of, they took a table by the window.

"You've a devious mind, Mr Locke," Ned stated after a few puffs of his cigar. "But, I suppose that's why you're the most famous magician in London, eh?" He smiled as he chewed his cigar's end. "But you must take my word when I say I wasn't responsible for Mr Elmore's death. The doll was perfectly mundane when I sold it."

"Why did you sell it?" Mr Elliott enquired.

"I hated it: ugly thing. It was worth a few bob though," Ned replied.

"Did you not think to test its mechanism prior to placing it into a sale?" Mr Locke enquired as he took a cigarette from his silver case and tapped off the excess tobacco.

"What mechanism?" Ned enquired through another smoke cloud.

Mr Locke placed Miss Dexter's sketch before Ned. "As you can see, the doll contains a complex mechanism of cogs, springs, and rods." Mr Locke's gloved finger slid down the sketch's centre. "This is a fine wire—much like a fishing rod's line—that has been added to the mechanism to fire a loaded revolver held in the doll's hand."

"The front of the doll's case opens when the mechanism is activated," Mr Elliott interjected. "Thus enabling the bullet to hit its target without damaging the glass."

"We—that is, the Bow Street Society of which we are all part—strongly suspect your late uncle, Professor Benjamin Cosgrove, was killed by this method," Mr Locke said as he watched Ned's reaction. "The same method that killed Mr Edgar Elmore."

Mr Cosgrove brought the sketch closer to pick it up and study in silence. Chewing his cigar from one corner of his mouth to the other, he then removed it to rest in an ashtray. "The police were sure my uncle was murdered by a housebreaker," put the sketch down.

"According to a newspaper article written at the time, the door of his study was locked," Mr Elliott said. "A window was open, but no footprints were found on the ground outside." He put his finger upon the sketch. "But a housebreaker didn't do this. Given the time required to string the wire around the doll's mechanism, it's most likely your uncle was murdered by someone *inside* his household."

"Not *me*," Ned replied. "I wasn't there when he died." He tossed the sketch at Mr Locke. "Talk to the police, talk to the inspector who investigated." Ned glanced away for a moment. "Inspector Lee, that's his name. Talk to him. He'll tell you I wasn't there, and that I *insisted* on talking to him, too. Now, I ask you, does *that* sound like the actions of a guilty man?"

"You'd be surprised," Mr Maxwell remarked.

"Why did you insist upon it?" Mr Elliott enquired as he ignored Mr Maxwell's tactlessness.

"I didn't blend well with my uncle, nor did my brother," Ned replied. "Him more so than me though, mind you. I knew people would suggest *I* had something to do with my uncle's death because I inherited the lion's share of the estate. I wanted to get ahead of the game by clearing my name first."

"Where's your brother now?" Mr Elliott enquired.

"Three across and six down," Ned replied. At Mr Elliott's perplexed expression, he added, "Dead, sir. From consumption, last year."

"Did your brother inherit nothing from your uncle's estate, then?" Mr Maxwell enquired as he looked up from his notetaking.

"That's none of your business," Ned retorted.

"Did you reside at your uncle's house at the time of his death?" Mr Locke enquired as he kept a close watch of Ned's face. When Ned shook his head, he enquired, "Where were you?"

"Here," Ned replied. "I won quite a few wheels that night. Inspector Lee asked after it at the time, and Roland confirmed I was here."

"Of course, on consideration of *how* the doll was manipulated, the murderer could rely on Professor Cosgrove activating the deadly mechanism," Mr Locke pointed out. "Therefore, as you may have already guessed, Mr Cosgrove, you being away from the house at the time is—put quite simply—irrelevant."

"Same can be said about Norman, then, and everyone else that went into the place!" Ned barked. "My uncle was always having learned men calling upon him."

Mr Elliott studied Ned's reaction to the accusation. It appeared genuine, but he had been deceived before. Also, given the man's track record at the table tonight—and the observations about Ned's luck which Mr Locke had aired at the Society's meeting—Mr Elliott wondered if the inspector had checked Ned's bank account. He was clearly a prolific gambler, and such creatures often attracted mountains of money or mountains of debt. "Have you ever had any business transactions with a Mr Paul Bund?"

"No," Ned replied. "But, now that you mention him, he's the likeliest murderer in my opinion."

"Why's that?" Mr Maxwell enquired.

"Coral," Ned replied. "The day after uncle Benjamin died, she told me a moneylender had come to the house the day before and argued with my uncle. She thought he might've been behind the murder. Inspector Lee disagreed, though." Ned plucked his cigar from the ashtray and, finding it had gone out, put it back between his teeth to reignite with a match. Taking a few puffs from it, he exhaled the tremendous cloud of smoke into the table's centre. Both Mr Elliott and Mr Maxwell coughed, the latter waving his notebook to try to disperse the toxic fumes. Mr Cosgrove, ignorant of their discomfort, puffed upon his cigar a few more times and added yet more smoke to the air. "I didn't murder my uncle. But I would shake the hand of the fellow who did; using the doll like that's *demmed* ingenious."

"The revolver was issued to those serving in Her Majesty's Royal Navy," Mr Elliott said in his usual monotone. His displeasure at Ned's compliment translated into his tone becoming even less animated. "Have *you* ever been an officer, Mr Cosgrove? Perhaps, another in your uncle's employ, or your brother?"

Ned's fatty rolls jiggled and wobbled as his booming laugh filled the supper room. "*Me*?! In the *Navy*?! Ha-ha! *No*, sir! Good *heavens*, no!" He laughed and, with a shake of his head, puffed some more on his cigar. "And my brother was as unseaworthy as I." He smirked, chuckled, and cleared his throat. "But… now that you do mention it… Mr Lane, uncle's butler, was in the

Navy, oh, years back. Not firing guns, mind you. I think he was the Captain's valet, or some such."

"Did he have a gun, though?" Mr Maxwell enquired as he leaned forward.

"Couldn't tell you," Ned replied. At once though, he held up his hand. "*Wait*. Yes, yes, he did. Kept only in case of housebreakers, of course. He showed it me once."

"Was it kept locked away?" Mr Locke enquired. "In Mr Lane's room, perhaps?"

"Not at all," Ned replied. "Kept in a cupboard in the kitchen, I think. In the flour. Can't tell you where it is now."

"According to the inquest transcripts," Mr Elliott said as he checked his notes. "Your uncle had a secretary. Miss Henrietta—"

"Henrietta Watkins, yes," Ned replied with a nod. "Don't know what happened to her after uncle's death. I had no use for her, and Coral went down to Brighton."

"Coral being your uncle's second wife?" Mr Locke ventured.

"Yes, that's right," Ned replied. "She and Miss Watkins were in the house when uncle died. Not sure where Norman was…"

"Norman being…?" Mr Elliott enquired.

"My brother," Ned stated.

"Was he angry when you inherited?" Mr Maxwell enquired.

Ned narrowed his eyes and, glaring at Mr Maxwell, replied, "He wasn't best pleased, no. But *I* inherited what was due. Coral got her share, and Miss Watkins was given a small legacy. Norman should've been nicer to Uncle Benjamin when the old man was alive."

"Did anyone possess clock making knowledge, at all?" Mr Locke enquired. "Including you and your brother."

"No," Ned replied and eased himself to his feet. "Now, if that's all, I'd like to get back to my game."

158

"Just one more thing," Mr Locke replied. "*Two*, actually. The first: have you any recollection of a Mr Terrence Partridge in connection to your uncle? The second: as it is quite late, may we call upon you tomorrow morning to see your uncle's study?—presuming you reside in the same house, of course."

"The man's a stranger to me," Ned replied. "And I'm still there. The study's a library now. *Not* that I do much reading, but people respect you more if you're learned. I'll be up and about around eleven, so call then."

* * *

Miss Trent regretted opening the door as soon as she saw her visitor. She put her weight onto her right foot and, holding her left hip, looked up at him. "I've a good mind to slam this door in your face."

"You won't," Inspector Woolfe replied. "Your curiosity won't let you." Driving his own weight forward as he stepped inside—thereby forcing her to move—he took the door from her and closed it. "I've been told by Sergeant Bird that gunfire was heard here today."

"That's right," Miss Trent replied as she folded her arms across her chest. "But no one was hurt so we sent Bird away—which you would've *also* been told. Which begs the question, Inspector, of 'why are you here'?"

"We've already discussed this, Miss Trent," he replied and went past her to peer through the open doorways leading off the hall. "Are you here alone?" He turned to face her. "Where's your cabbie?"

"At home, not that it's any of your business," she said. She then moved closer to him with defiant eyes. "You feigned concern for the Society's members' welfare to create a method by which you could undermine us. I presume *that* is the discussion you are referring to? As far as I'm concerned, that matter was resolved."

"Yeah," Woolfe's eyes narrowed. "You did well in pulling the wool over Conway's eyes." He advanced toward her like a lion stalking an antelope. "I only agreed to stay away because he's my friend and working under orders from the Yard to watch you lot." He moved closer, still, until Miss Trent could smell his whiskey-drenched breath. "Know this though: you won this battle, but there's a long way to go before the war's over." He leaned down to look in her eyes, their faces mere inches apart. "I can't look over your shoulder every minute of the day, but that doesn't mean I'm not watching you. Conway has his orders, but this is *my* patch. You so much as soil those pretty skirts of yours and I'll know about it. One way, or another, I'm going to uncover the truth behind the Bow Street Society."

Miss Trent remained silent as her hard eyes bore into him.

"Something to think about," he said with a wolfish grin. Strolling past her as he lit a cigarette, he then slammed the door shut when he left.

THIRTEEN

Joining the Albert Bridge across the Thames to the east, and neighbouring the Chelsea Work House to the west, Oakley Street echoed Gloucester Place's affluence. The style of architecture adopted by its terraced houses also mirrored Mr Elmore's street. Mr Locke stood at the arched, first floor window of one such house. The temperature had dropped during the night to below freezing. Snowflakes therefore danced upon the brisk wind and settled on every available surface. Mr Locke's focus was on what was beneath the window, however. Stone steps led from the street, via a set of wrought iron railings, to a narrow walkway. At its end was a thickset door leading—Mr Locke presumed—to the basement kitchen.

He next studied the window's construction and swing arm lock. The swing arm lock being a typical choice for a sash window such as this. The lock's function was to prevent a housebreaker opening the window from outside. Comprised of two halves, screwed into the frame and sliding sash respectively, it had a rounded hook on a pivot. The hook would slide downward into the deep recess of the lock's other half attached to the frame. The point of the hook would then 'catch' the recess' edge. To test his theory, Mr Locke attempted to lift the window's lower half with the lock was applied. Even with all his strength, he couldn't budge the window. He therefore lifted the arm, to release the hook, and pushed the window open.

A cold blast of air struck him as he poked his head outside and scrutinised the wall beneath. It was sheer, without lead pipes or damage to the stone work to provide foot holds. The distances between the window, railings, and walkway below were beyond the reach of an average housebreaker.

A second—shorter—flight of stone steps led from the pavement to the raised front door. Mr Locke gripped the window frame and reached out to touch the steps. When he found a gap of at least four feet between them and his fingers, he withdrew his arm and crouched upon the window ledge. He stretched his leg toward the steps and, though his toes scraped against their side, he found no nooks or crannies to hold onto. He considered a leap from the railings to the window and vice versa. Aside from the obvious risk of impalement, the space afforded by the opened window was insufficient for a housebreaker to slip through in one leap. When the window was closed, its external still provided a three-inch-wide ledge. If a housebreaker was unscathed from the railings, succeeded in the execution of his leap, and had sufficient upper body strength for his arms to hold his full body weight against the external sill, he would still have the problem of a locked window to contend with. The glass could be broken, but such an act would create noise, and require the use of a much-needed hand. Not to mention the housebreaker would be dangling from a window in plain view of the street.

Mr Locke withdrew into the Ned Cosgrove's library and closed the window. "Has this window been replaced since your uncle's death?"

Ned Cosgrove sat with Miss Dexter on a sofa opposite. While she'd sketched, he'd described the contents and layout of the room when it was Professor Cosgrove's study. "No, there wasn't any need to," he replied. "Is that important?"

"Very," Mr Locke replied. "The space afforded by this window, once opened is not sufficient to accommodate a grown adult's form, irrespective of his— or her—slight build. Considering this fact with the numerous risks involved in entering—or escaping—via this route, I am inclined to suspect the window was opened, in the moments following the professor's death, to detract suspicion away from the doll."

"We're finished," Miss Dexter announced. She took her sketch to the desk and waited for Mr Locke, Doctor Locke, Mr Verity, Mr Maxwell, and Mr Elliott to join her. Ned had also stood but retrieved a box of matches from the mantelshelf to light his cigar.

While Ned's tremendous smoke clouds consumed his head and threw Mr Elliott and Mr Verity into a spate of coughs, Mr Maxwell tapped Miss Dexter on the shoulder and enquired, "Has your father mentioned me, at all, since receiving my letter?"

Miss Dexter looked across her shoulder at him. His words had brought sorrow to her eyes. "He's disappointed." She averted her gaze back to her sketch. "We all are. But…" She took a deep breath. "…You're a forbidden topic of conversation."

"I-I—" Mr Maxwell replied, stunned.

"Here is the professor's study as described by Mr Cosgrove," Miss Dexter interrupted as she addressed the rest of her fellow Bow Streeters. "The room's shape is the same—a wide rectangle. The door"—she glanced at the one stood in the back, right corner—"is also the same. Then, like now, it led into the hallway."

Floor-to-ceiling, mahogany bookcases dominated the dark-green wallpapered walls of the library. A curved, step ladder—pushed along a horizontal bar that ran across the bookcases—stood in the corner. Its once shining brass was rendered dull by a generous layer of dust. A Turkish rug—dark-green, black and cream in colour—protected the polished floorboards with a pristine pile. The large desk, with a chair behind, stood before the window to face the room. The green, leather blotter on its top was unmarked, while the shade of its kerosene lamp contained as much dust as the ladder. Between the window and door was a simple, stone surround fireplace.

"Here are the window and fireplace." Miss Dexter pointed them out on the sketch. "And the professor's desk." She pointed to the desk on the sketch and then laid the same hand upon the item of furniture. "*This* desk." Miss Dexter walked around to the desk's other side but left the sketch in place for the others to examine. "The doll was kept over there," she indicated the space to the right of the window. "And Miss Watkins' desk was here." Miss Dexter walked to the bookshelves opposite the fireplace and indicated the spot with her open hands. "She sat with her back to the fireplace and, beside her desk, here." Miss Dexter sidestepped to the right. "The locked cupboard where she kept the typed pages of Professor Cosgrove's memoirs. Two bookcases were beside the cupboard."

"The doll was within touching distance of the professor's chair, but not Miss Watkins," Mr Elliott mused.

"On principle, it supports my theory," Doctor Locke said. "But to certain, I'd like to test the angle of entry for the bullet. Miss Dexter, did you bring your string? I utterly forgot to make the request."

"I have it," Miss Dexter replied. Moving to stand in the doll's place, she took the loose end of string from the ball and gave the rest to Doctor Locke. "Should I be stood on something?"

"Here," Mr Locke said and placed the chair where Miss Dexter had stood. With her hand in his, she stepped up onto it and held the string taut while Doctor Locke adjusted the angle to match that from her notes. Once she was satisfied it was as close to the original arrangement as possible, Doctor Locke peered down the line of string and hummed.

"Yes… it matches. Thank you, Miss Dexter," Doctor Locke said as she took her hand to keep her steady while stepping off the chair. "By my calculations, the doll fired the fatal gunshot to the professor's head."

"*Demmed* thing," Ned mumbled.

Mr Snyder looked across to Mr Elliott. "I'm happy to come by and talk to the butler, if you want."

"I think it would serve us well," Mr Elliott replied.

"And Miss Dexter can talk to Miss Price, too," Mr Snyder said with a nod to her. "If Mr Cosgrove don't mind."

"I don't know what they can tell you, but go ahead," Ned replied and returned to the sofa to finish his cigar.

"How long have they been in your service, Mr Cosgrove?" Mr Verity enquired.

"I inherited both Mr Lane and Miss Price as part of my uncle's estate. They offered to stay on, so I let them."

"And they're…?" Mr Snyder enquired.

"Out, it's their morning off," Ned replied. "I'm not normally at home during the daylight hours. There's a few good card games to be had at the gentleman's club."

Miss Dexter looked out the window as Mr Locke and Mr Maxwell studied her sketch. Though the snow was majestic, her thoughts were on the doll. A shiver coursed through her at the recollection of a motionless Mr Locke, accompanied by the relentless tick and click of the mechanism. *A rather loud mechanism*, she thought as she looked to where she'd stood on the chair. "Doctor Locke, if Professor Cosgrove heard the doll's mechanism, why was he shot in the back of his head and not the front?"

"My uncle's hearing wasn't the greatest," Ned replied as he took an even larger puff of his cigar.

"And he wouldn't have needed to turn around if he'd set the doll off," Mr Maxwell pointed out.

"But why set it off at all, if he wasn't going to watch it?" Miss Dexter enquired. "Isn't the point of owning a curiosity to sate one's own?"

"Unless someone—or something—caught his eye at the window and he opened it to look out," Mr Verity said. He eased himself from the chair by the fire to join

Miss Dexter at the window and peer through its frozen glass. Rooftops, cobblestones, lamps, and railings were all covered by a thin layer of snow.

"The bullet wouldn't have struck the back of the professor's head if he stood at the window," Doctor Locke replied. "As the angle is wrong."

"It does not stretch the imagination too far to suppose our murderer turned the doll's key prior to leaving the study," Mr Locke said. "Was your uncle in the habit of locking himself in here?"

"Yes, of course, aren't most gentlemen?" Ned replied.

Doctor Locke looked to her husband as she recalled his last study visit. "Indeed, they are, Mr Cosgrove."

Mr Locke met his wife's gaze as he felt hers upon him. "Quite," he said in a subdued tone. He allowed his eyes to linger until his own sense of guilt became too much. At which point he cleared his throat and walked toward Ned while rubbing the back of his gloved hand. "And who were the key holders for this room?"

"My uncle…" Ned frowned. "…I don't know who else. I was never given one."

"Can you at least recall who the last person to see your uncle was?" Mr Elliott pressed.

"I can't—it was blooming six years ago," Ned replied. "Have you spoken to the inspector? He can tell you."

"A meeting has been arranged for later today," Mr Elliott interjected. "Who were the likeliest visitors to your uncle's study, in your opinion?"

Ned frowned. "Miss Watkins was here most; she was helping him write his memoirs. Coral, maybe. Norman and me, not so much." He sighed. "I wasn't here, *dem* it."

Mr Elliott's expression remained emotionless at the answer. Walking behind the desk, he then took a seat and reached for the topmost drawer.

Having watched him, Ned stood and crossed the room to slam his hand against the drawer. "What do you think you are doing?!"

"I was merely checking if a copy of your uncle's Last Will & Testament was inside," Mr Elliott replied in his usual monotone.

"I've already *told* you about that. Stop poking your nose in where it's liable to get bruised." Mr Elliott withdrew his hand and settled back in the chair. Ned puffed out his chest in triumph and, with a smirk, added, "Besides, it's with my solicitor." Ned wagged his finger at Mr Elliott. "And *you're* not getting a copy!"

FOURTEEN

"You've gotta be havin' a lark."

"I'm as surprised by this arrangement as you are, Inspector," Mr Elliott replied. He'd slowed the moment he'd seen the grizzled policeman upon his approach from Euston Square railway station. Their meeting point—arranged by Miss Trent—was the A.B.C. tearoom on Euston Road. Housed above a branch of the Aerated Bread Company (hence the name), the tearoom was favoured by most for its smart interior and respectable reputation.

"She could've sent someone else," Conway muttered. He moved away from the shop's door and cupped a hand around his cigarette's end to shield it from the wind while he lit it. "He's not here."

"They're occupied elsewhere," Mr Elliott replied with a waft of his hand to dispel Conway's encroaching smoke. "You may wish to freeze out here, but I certainly don't." He opened the door and went inside.

"Bloody Trent…" Conway growled as he tossed the half-spent cigarette into the snow and strode after Mr Elliott. "…Of all the people…"

* * *

Mr Maxwell adjusted his cravat for the sixth time and wiped his hands upon his trousers. He listened to a maid as she swept out the fireplace beyond a close door to his left. The sounds of horses' hooves, wagons' wheels, and muddled chatter reached him through the front door to his right. He heard nothing from his father's study door opposite, however.

Forty-five minutes earlier, his mother had informed his father of his arrival. Oliver Maxwell had barked a reply at her, and she'd emerged paler than when she'd entered. She'd then told Mr Maxwell his father was busy, but he could wait if he wished, and disappeared into her drawing room with a muttered, "I must rest my poor nerves".

During the ensuing three-quarters of an hour, Mr Maxwell had tried to recall a time when his mother didn't have a nervous disposition. He'd also applied the same aim to recollections of his own life. His heart had sunk when he'd realised he couldn't think of any examples. He knew he'd inherited his mother's nerves, of course, even putting them to good use during a case he'd investigated with Mr Elliott. Yet, he was at a loss when it came to a reason for his and his mother's perpetual states of hysteria.

The rapid thud of heavy feet then granted him his answer. His heartrate accelerated, his brow moistened, and his stomach clenched. When he heard the doorknob turn, he leapt to his feet and fumbled to straighten his frockcoat, cravat, and waistcoat. His father's cold eyes, and harsh countenance, were enough to render him speechless—at least for a moment.

"I'm being taken to court for breach of promise. I proposed to Miss Georgina Dexter before it was arranged for me to marry Miss Poppy Lillithwaite, and I told Miss Dexter I couldn't marry her, and she understood, but her Father is angry at me and doesn't allow her to talk about me. I need your help. I don't know what to do, and courtrooms frighten me, and I never meant to hurt anyone, but things just happened and now I have no idea how to make things better." Mr Maxwell wrung the hem of his frockcoat's skirt. "Father."

Oliver's face twisted into a horrific scowl as his hand shot out to grip his son's cravat and pull him clean off his feet. Keeping a firm hold upon him—even as his son stumbled—Oliver dragged him into the study and threw him into an armchair.

"I warned you about your whore, boy," Oliver growled as he towered over his son's trembling form and unbuckled his belt. He wrapped its end around his fist and watched Mr Maxwell slide down in the chair and hold up his arms.

"P-Please, Father. I-I didn't mean—Argh!" Mr Maxwell cried as the belt struck his forearms. He pressed his body against the armchair's corner, but his father unleashed another strike nonetheless.

"I should have strangled you at birth." Oliver sneered as he watched his cowering son with cold eyes. Tossing the belt onto his desk with a clatter, he then sat behind it. "Get out of my sight."

"B-But the breach of p-promise, Father!" Maxwell exclaimed while he fought to hold back his tears. "Th-the marriage to-to Miss Lillithwaite!"

"I will deal with it," Oliver said. "Now, get out… before I rectify my mistake."

"Y-Yes, F-Father," Mr Maxwell half-fell, half-stumbled from the armchair and fled from the room with his arm held tight against his chest.

* * *

Due to the severe weather, Mr Elliott and the inspector were obliged to wait ten minutes for a table. When they were finally seated, it was by a window that overlooked Euston Road. Conway fidgeted on the dark-green cushion of the high-backed chair, while Mr Elliott perused the menu.

"I'll have a pot of Earl Grey, please," Mr Elliott told the young woman assigned to their service after several more moments of perusal.

"Me too," Conway added.

"Have you ever had Earl Grey tea before?" Mr Elliott enquired once they were alone.

"Nah, but as long as it's wet, it'll do," Conway replied and fidgeted some more. "My back's gonna be in a knot by the time Lee gets 'ere."

170

"I don't quite understand why you are here," Mr Elliott remarked. "Unless you and your colleague are going to see to it I have an 'accident', of course."

"Leave off," Conway grunted. "I'm 'ere 'cause you lot are lookin' into an open, police case, and I've been told by the chief inspector to keep an eye on you."

"Just as long it is only your eyes," Mr Elliott replied. Noticing a gentleman as he approached, Mr Elliott then stood and shook the offered hand. "Inspector Gideon Lee, I presume?"

"Indeed," the newcomer confirmed. Striking, dark-blue eyes regarded Mr Elliott with warmth. Inspector Lee's broad shoulders were also relaxed, while his words had been spoken in a rich, yet smooth, voice. His teeth, fingernails, eyebrows, and fair complexion were all flawless—despite Mr Elliott placing his age in the late fifties. Even the cut of his midnight blue suit, with a waistcoat and tie to match, was of a higher quality than most policemen could afford. Being the same height as each other—six feet, to be exact—the two gentlemen were on perfect eye level. Conway was dwarfed by an inch, and it was his hand Lee shook next. "It's a pleasure to meet you, Mr Elliott. Good to see you again, Inspector. I see A Division is still taking its toll upon you."

"I see you're still playin' at being a gent," Conway retorted.

"Touché," Lee replied with a partial grimace. "Shall we sit?"

Another chair was brought over, and the three men sat. As the young woman returned and served up the two pots of Earl Grey, she took Lee's order. Choosing the same as his fellows, he passed the menu back and allowed her to hurry away. The mild disgust upon Conway's face, as he sniffed the perfumed beverage, brought a smile to Lee's own.

"I was pleased to read of the Society's interest in my most enduring case," Lee began as he addressed Mr

171

Elliott. "Inspector Conway's correspondence lacked detail, however."

Mr Elliott passed Miss Dexter's sketch of the doll's mechanism to the Kensington Division inspector.

The warmth in Lee's eyes, and the smile upon his lips, remained strong even once he'd scrutinised the sketch and returned it. "The possibility of the doll playing a part in the murder was considered at the time but dismissed."

"Why?" Mr Elliott enquired.

Inspector Conway, having taken a sip of his foul-tasting tea, pushed his cup and saucer aside.

"The glass of its case was undamaged," Lee replied. He gestured toward the sketch as it lay upon Mr Elliott's notebook. "Your discovery has certainly given me food for thought, however. Thank you."

"We have made other discoveries," Mr Elliott said. "The subsequent owner of the doll, Mr Edgar Elmore, was also fatally shot by it. My fellow Bow Streeters and I have concluded his death, although unplanned, should be placed at the door of Professor Cosgrove's murderer."

"Naturally," Inspector Lee replied in a sincere tone.

Taking a moment to digest the lack of defensiveness coming from the policeman, Mr Elliott glanced at Conway with the passing thought he could learn a thing or two from Lee. If he had not known to the contrary, he would have never placed the two men in the same profession. Returning his gaze to Lee, who was being served his tea by the young woman, Mr Elliott waited until she'd departed their table before continuing. "We've also identified the murder weapon as a Webley Mark I revolver, the kind issued to those serving in Her Majesty's Royal Navy."

"And her Army," Lee pointed out.

"That I did not know," Mr Elliott replied, and Lee's smile grew. "The Society has also inspected the

172

rooms where each man died and spoken to Mr Ned Cosgrove, Professor Cos—"

"Professor Cosgrove's nephew. Yes, I remember," Lee interrupted with the same degree of sincerity in his voice. He added cream and sugar to his tea before he stirred it. "Has he managed to gamble away the family estate, yet?"

The corner of Mr Elliott's mouth lifted. "No, not yet. He refuses to disclose the contents of Professor Cosgrove's will to us, however. He is also confused about some of the details of the night of the professor's murder. We were hoping you could assist us in this matter, as you were the investigating officer at the time."

"Don't mean 'e's gotta tell you out," Conway remarked.

"Inspector, *please*," Lee said, disgusted. "Show some respect." He waved away Conway's remarks. "Pay him no heed, sir. Manners were not part of his street education."

Conway's eyes narrowed. "Watch it, Lee—"

"Pardon me, sir, but this has just arrived for you," the young woman interrupted. In her hand was a folded piece of paper. When Conway didn't acknowledge her or it, however, she held it closer. "*Sir?*"

"What?" Conway barked, looking from her, to the note, and back again.

"It's for you, sir," she replied.

The anger dissipated from Conway's expression. "Oh… thanks." Taking the note, he read it and muttered a curse. "I've gotta go." He announced as he stood and put on his trilby. Without another word to his fellows, he gave the young woman enough coin to pay for his tea and left.

When Mr Elliott looked back to Inspector Lee, he found a smirk upon his face. "Does something amuse you?"

"It does," Lee replied and took a sip of tea. "Inspector Conway shall be disappointed to find his trip to

H Division is a wasted one. I simply cannot tolerate his uncouthness for longer than ten minutes." He replaced the cup upon its saucer. "It is far better he is elsewhere; we may converse more freely that way." His warm smile increased in size for a moment. "As I was saying…" He set his tea aside. "I must be aware of my own obligations to not only the Metropolitan Police, but to those involved in the Cosgrove case. Despite the passage of time, emotions still run high where that matter is concerned." He picked up the sketch to glance over its contents. "Nonetheless, I would like to meet with you again." He lowered the sketch. "Not here, and *certainly* not at T Division's police station. The walls there have grown ears. If it is convenient, Mr Elliott, I'd like to invite you to dine with me this evening. I shall endeavour to have my personal files on the case ready for you to examine, if you bring whatever else the Society has discovered. Does that seem fair?"

"It does," Mr Elliott replied. He opened his notebook at a clean page and slid it across to Lee with a pencil.

The inspector smiled as he took a pen from his pocket and wrote down his address. "Naturally, your wife may accompany you if you wish."

"That shan't be necessary. I'm a bachelor."

"I see." Lee smiled, and the warmth of his dark-blue eyes intensified. "As am I." He slid the notebook back to Mr Elliott. "The fare shall be simple, therefore, but tasty."

"I'm certain it will be satisfactory, sir."

"Excellent." Lee pulled his tea back in front of him. "I look forward to it."

FIFTEEN

Miss Henrietta Watkins fuelled her parlour's fire with another lump of coal and pushed it down with a poker. She drew her black, woollen shawl tighter around her shoulders and returned to her armchair. In her fifties, with a narrow, drawn-out nose and pointed chin, she looked like strictness personified. The pallid flesh of her forehead was pulled taut by her scraped back, grey hair. This, in turn, was plaited and coiled into a rigid bun. The unpleasant smell of rose and carbolic also lingered about her. She wore a modest black dress beneath her shawl, and an oversized, ivory brooch with a man's silhouette pinned to her breast.

The parlour's walls were covered in a jumble of framed, countryside landscape prints. The mustard wallpaper opposite the window was sun bleached, while that above the fireplace was stained with soot. The vast, iron hearth was without a surround and dominated the wall to the left of Miss Watkins' armchair. A well-swept rug of greens, mustards, and browns covered the floor at her feet. The remainder of the room had chipped and scratched, exposed floorboards. To the right of Miss Watkins' chair was a narrow, under stuffed sofa. Miss Dexter, Mr Snyder, and Mr Verity were packed onto it in that order. Beyond them were a china cabinet, bookcase, plant stand, and sideboard squeezed into the remaining space.

"Now," Miss Watkins began as she took a cup of sweet tea from the table. "Who did you say you were again?"

"The Bow Street Society," Miss Dexter replied. "If we may, we'd like to speak to you about your late employer, Professor Benjamin Cosgrove?"

"Employer and friend," Miss Watkins corrected as her fingers brushed against the brooch's silhouette. "He was a good man—a generous man."

"We were told he'd left you a legacy," Mr Verity said with a soft smile.

Miss Watkins stared at him. "I would not trust their recollection." She crossed the shawl's corners over her chest. "His will did contain a gift for me—heartfelt words which held a greater value than his money ever could."

"You were his secretary for many years?" Mr Verity enquired as he stirred his tea.

"I'd served him for fifteen years at the time of his death," Miss Watkins said.

"And you got nothing for it?" Mr Verity pressed.

"The professor's money didn't interest me," Miss Watkins replied. "The same couldn't be said about the second Mrs Professor Cosgrove; she made a cuckold of him. He knew, of course, though he never spoke of it. He was too much of a gentleman to discuss such intimate matters, and *I* was but his secretary. More's the pity."

"You woz fond of him, then?" Mr Snyder enquired.

Miss Watkins looked down her nose at him. "I *respected* him. Honoured him as his wife should have done."

"Who woz she makin' him a cuckold with?" Mr Snyder enquired.

Miss Watkins took a sip of tea. "It's really not my place to say." She put the cup onto the table to warm her hands by the fire. "You'll have to ask his widow." She wrapped her shawl around her hands and settled back in her armchair. "May I ask why it's you who've called upon me and not the police?"

Miss Dexter passed her teacup to Mr Snyder and retrieved a photograph from her satchel. When she held it up for Miss Watkins to see, the elder woman's grip

176

tightened upon her shawl and she enquired, in a hushed voice, "What is the meaning of this?" Her gaze shifted to Miss Dexter's face. "I *demand* to know."

"You know it?" Mr Verity enquired as he peered around the photograph at Miss Watkins.

"I would know it anywhere," Miss Watkins hissed and snatched the photograph to toss it into the fire. Miss Dexter leapt to her feet, but it was already too late. The paper crumpled as the flames took hold. "Your presence here is no longer welcome." Miss Watkins stood and, blocking the fireplace, cast a scowl upon her guests. "I don't know what your purpose is here, but I shan't listen any longer."

"Miss Watkins," Mr Verity began as he, too, heaved his weight from the sofa with the aid of his walking cane. "Someone gave that doll a loaded revolver and put some wire in the mechanism to pull the trigger. The professor was murdered by it, but you know that, don't you?"

"He had great admiration for it," Miss Watkins replied as her lower lip trembled. "When Mrs Cosgrove and I found the professor, he was sitting by the doll. There was the gun in the doll's hand… but then Mrs Cosgrove pointed out the open window…She assumed someone had come in…" Miss Watkins retreated to her armchair. "…I apologise for tossing your photograph into the fire… I realised, long ago, no one would entertain the idea of a doll murdering a man…"

"Two men," Mr Snyder said as he set down both teacups beside Miss Watkins'. "Mr Edgar Elmore bought the professor's doll from an auction. Hours later, 'e was shot, too, and found dyin' in his library by his family."

"But… that cannot be…" Miss Watkins said and grasped the oversized brooch.

Mr Snyder glanced at the others. "Why's that, then?"

"The doll's key…" Miss Watkins' fingertips pressed against the brooch's porcelain face. "It went missing after Benjamin's death."

The three Bow Streeters exchanged glances, yet it was Mr Verity who enquired, "Are you sure, Miss Watkins? You couldn't be mistaken…?"

"*Certainly* not," Miss Watkins scolded. "I remember it distinctly. Its second tooth was chipped, and there was a rose on its handle."

"I don't recall reading about it your deposition from the inquest," Miss Dexter remarked as her eyes showed concerned at their host's flushed complexion.

Miss Watkins' hand dropped from the brooch and her mouth formed a hard line. "As I've already explained, it was assumed a housebreaker was responsible. I didn't think it proper to mention the doll at the inquest." Miss Watkins retrieved her cup and peered into the depths of her remaining tea. For a moment, her face crumpled. "I *should* have mentioned it. Mr Elmore… the *poor* man…" She poured the tea into her mouth and held it there as her eyes closed. When she opened them again, she swallowed and set her cup down on the table for the final time. "What his family must be going through…"

"You mentioned it was Mrs Cosgrove who pointed out the window…" Miss Dexter gently reminded.

"Yes… Yes, that's correct." She straightened as she cleared her throat. "She suggested a housebreaker could've been sent by that *horrible* Mr Bund, the moneylender. He had tried to wring money from the professor, but he had remained resolute."

While Miss Watkins spoke, Miss Dexter took her sketch from her satchel. With trepidation she turned it around and kept it tight against her chest. "This is what the Society found when we examined the doll. Did you know it could move?"

Miss Watkins' complexion paled this time, but she remained silent.

178

"Yes," she eventually replied in a subdued voice. "My reaction was most amusing to him when she showed me how it worked…" She tore her gaze from the sketch to lift the teapot to check its weight. "…But it fired a cork, then."

"The revolver given to the doll was a Webley Mark I," Mr Verity said as Miss Dexter put the sketch away and he returned to his seat. "Did anyone in the house own one?"

"I think Mr Lane, the professor's butler, had some sort of weapon but I wouldn't want to commit myself to one in particular," Miss Watkins replied. "It was stolen some time before the professor died." She gathered up the teacups and stood. "Excuse me."

As the door closed behind Miss Watkins, a gust of wind howled within the chimney breast. The gas lamps also flickered in their sconces, compelling Miss Dexter to place her hand upon Mr Snyder's broad arm. Mr Verity, on the other hand, gave a satisfied smile.

"There's something here," he said. "Feel how cold it is, in spite of the fire." Once again, he used his cane to pull himself to his feet and hobbled around Miss Watkins' armchair. Behind it was a high—yet narrow—table with a wooden board and wheeled planchette. Mr Verity prodded the planchette. "A well-used talking board—"

"A gift from Benjamin," Miss Watkins said from the door.

"My apologies, Miss Watkins. I meant no harm," Mr Verity replied.

Miss Watkins looked from Mr Verity's face, to his hands, and back again. Finding he'd not picked up the planchette, she permitted her initial annoyance at his inconsideration to ease. "Apology accepted." She approached the board as, while she inspected it for damage, Mr Verity moved to stand behind the sofa. Satisfied all was as it should be, she turned to her guests. "Professor Cosgrove was a man of science. He believed death resulted in the flesh turning to dust." She placed her hand atop her armchair as she walked around it. "Yet, he respected my beliefs about life after death. He was also grateful for my discretion when practising my Spiritualism." When she sat, she took a moment to straighten her shawl. "One morning, I found the box on my desk. Its card was unsigned, but *I* knew the truth…" She cracked a smile. "…It was his gift to me."

"Talking to our departed loved ones is comforting, isn't it?" Mr Verity enquired as his smile mirrored Miss Watkins'.

"It can be," she replied. Her stony expression returned. "But Professor Cosgrove hasn't come through."

"You've tried torkin' to him?" Mr Snyder enquired.

"Of course." Miss Watkins turned hard eyes upon him. "When you've lost someone to death's embrace, Mr Snyder, you may judge me. Until then, refrain from mocking what you don't understand."

Mr Snyder's expression dropped as, with apologetic eyes and a gentle tone, he replied, "Pardon me, Miss Watkins. I've not come by people who tork to the dead, is all."

"Spiritualism is revered and reviled in equal parts," Mr Verity remarked in a sombre voice.

Miss Watkins gave a brief nod as she touched the brooch's silhouette. "It's only the professor I want to speak with, however. To ensure his spirit is at peace after…" Her hand closed about the brooch. "…I can't stand the thought of him trapped in limbo, crying out for justice and going unheard."

"Could the professor give the name of who murdered him…?" Miss Dexter warily ventured.

"Out of the question," Miss Watkins snapped and dropped her hand to her lap as she glared at Miss Dexter. "He was shot by the doll. How could he *possibly* know who was really responsible?" She shifted her weight

180

toward the edge of her chair. "Spiritualism is about communication, not divination."

Miss Dexter's cheeks flushed. "I only wondered because… well, it's difficult to dismiss accusations made by a murdered person, isn't it?"

Taken aback, Miss Watkins' scowl vanished. "Yes…" She was quieter than before. "…But their forgiveness is the light to lead them to eternal life… Vengeance is God's domain."

"Amen," Mr Verity murmured.

Miss Watkins smiled. "Amen."

Mr Snyder cast an uncomfortable look Miss Dexter's way, only to find she'd done the same. They averted their eyes to their teacups, but it was Miss Dexter who cleared her throat and enquired, "Miss Watkins… you mentioned you were the professor's secretary…?"

Miss Watkins nodded. "He'd write his memoirs and give me the pages to type."

"Woz there out in 'em that could've made someone want to hurt him?" Mr Snyder enquired.

"No," Miss Watkins replied with a furrowed brow. "His memoirs were about the archaeological expeditions he participated in while abroad. He'd study and catalogue the artefacts as they were unearthed. Nothing he wrote about was either scandalous or controversial, and he was a gentleman besides. He didn't have a cross word for anyone."

"Except his nephews," Mr Verity interjected.

"Ungrateful leeches, the pair of them," Miss Watkins said. "Pardon my speaking out of turn, but the professor would agree with me. Ned was the worst for it, gambling away money as if it were matchsticks."

"And Norman Cosgrove…?" Mr Snyder ventured.

Miss Watkins hesitated. "He had more than his fair share of sins. Practically all of them self-inflicted. Yet, he maintained a righteous arrogance nevertheless." Her hand returned to her brooch. "Even in the presence of his uncle. Norman was a source of great shame to the professor, and Norman knew it. He wasn't aggrieved by his uncle's disowning of him, though." Miss Watkin's mouth formed a hard line. "Knowing Norman as I do, I'd say he relished the moral shaming of his uncle in the eyes of his fellow professors." Miss Watkins' grip tightened on her brooch. "Yet, it had all come out of Norman's sin, not Benjamin's."

"What had?" Miss Dexter enquired.

Miss Watkins looked at her sharply. "Nothing you need concern yourselves with." She folded her arms across her chest and gripped the corners of her shawl. "It was over long before Benjamin's death."

"Have you torked to Mrs Cosgrove, or the nephews, since the professor died?" Mr Snyder enquired.

"*Certainly* not," Miss Watkins snapped. "Nor do I *wish* to."

"You wouldn't have heard that Norman died last year, then?" Mr Verity enquired.

Miss Watkins' mouth twitched but her hard expression remained as, in a cold tone, she replied, "No. I'll say a prayer for him."

"You don't want to talk to *his* spirit, too?" Mr Verity ventured, delicately.

"We have nothing to say to one another," Miss Watkins stated.

"You said you discovered the professor's body," Miss Dexter began, her voice gentle. "May you recall what passed in the hours before?"

Miss Watkins stilled a moment. Unfolding her arms, she rested one hand upon her knee while the other touched the brooch's silhouette. "It was six years ago, but I still remember it like it were yesterday… I was the last to see him alive…" She stroked the silhouette as she looked past Miss Dexter. "I was finishing the day's pages when Mrs Cosgrove came into the study. She was set on speaking with Benjamin in private. I, naturally, left them

182

alone." Her stroking stopped, but her fingertips remained upon the brooch. "There was shouting—hers, mostly. When she came out, I slipped in behind her to return to my desk and finish my typing." Her face fell while her fingertips pressed against the silhouette. "Benjamin's mood had soured considerably…" She grasped the entire brooch. "He shouted at me to leave—something he'd only ever done once before—so I complied." She released the brooch to rest clasped hands in her lap. "When I left the study, I heard him lock the door behind me." Her gaze shifted to Miss Dexter's satchel. "I must have walked as far as the front door when I heard the shot…"

"Can you remember who unlocked the door?" Mr Snyder enquired.

"No… I'm afraid not," Miss Watkins replied with a brief shake of her head and her gaze upon his feet.

"What woz Mrs Cosgrove like when you got into the study?" Mr Snyder enquired.

Miss Watkins took a deep breath and, releasing it as a sigh, looked to Mr Snyder. "She was distraught—lingering around the doll with tears streaming down her face. It was more passion than I would have ever expected from her. At least, as far as the professor was concerned."

"Did you have a key for the study?" Miss Dexter enquired

"No, the professor would usually be in his study when I'd arrive in the morning," Miss Watkins replied as her stony face returned. "Mr Lane had a spare key, I believe."

"Where woz that kept?" Mr Snyder enquired.

"I don't know," Miss Watkins replied. "I was only the professor's secretary. I wasn't privy to the household's routines."

"What time did you find the professor?" Mr Verity enquired as he hobbled around the sofa and sat with a soft sigh of relief. His walking cane was leaned against the sofa, but he kept a firm grip of its silver handle.

"A little after eight thirty in the evening," Miss Watkins replied once Mr Verity was settled.

"Would you often work late?" Miss Dexter enquired.

"I would work for as long as was required of me," Miss Watkins replied. She warmed her hands by the fire. "Will that be all? It'll be dusk soon and I plan on holding another séance."

"I can help you speak to the professor," Mr Verity said. "I have some experience in these matters—"

"No," Miss Watkins snapped. "Thank you."

Miss Dexter pulled her satchel onto her lap and took from it the study's floorplan sketch. "May you look at this, please, Miss Watkins, and tell us if it is as you remember?" She held it out to her.

"There was a globe here," Miss Watkins said and pointed to an empty space on the sketch after she'd studied it. "Otherwise it's as I remember."

"Thank you," Miss Dexter replied with a soft smile and added a simple drawing of the globe to the sketch. While Mr Verity and Mr Snyder stood, she put the sketch away and joined them.

"Do you know Mr Terrence Partridge?" Mr Snyder enquired.

"No. I don't," Miss Watkins replied as she stood also. "Who is he?"

"No one," Mr Verity replied with a smile and accepted the arm of support from Miss Dexter. "We'll be making a move, then. Good night, Miss Watkins."

* * *

Conway tilted his head and looked upon an antique sculpture cast of two male wrestlers. Both were naked, with the top wrestler holding the other's arm behind his back. The sculpture hall, in which Conway stood, was in the south corridor of the South Kensington Museum.

184

Sculptures of various figures—either stood or sat on dark, box plinths—lined the corridor's central aisle. Arched windows on the right mirrored the deep alcoves opposite in shape. These alcoves contained the taller, and more elaborate, sculptures of classical figures. Despite it being a day allocated to free public entry to the museum, the harsh snowfall had kept most away. There were only two others aside from Conway in the corridor therefore. While he remained by the wrestlers, they strolled amongst the sculptures at the far end. Their footsteps upon the tiled floor echoed around the vast space as they did so. It was the footsteps which approached from behind which caught Conway's attention, however. He glanced over his shoulder at the newcomer and resumed his 'admiration' of the sculpture. "Good evening, sir."

"Where's Miss Trent?" Chief Inspector Jones enquired once they stood shoulder to shoulder.

"Woolfe went to see her again yesterday. She thought 'e might follow if she came."

Conway stole a sideways glance at the other visitors before he pulled a document from his overcoat. Wrapped in brown paper and tied with string, the document was only a few pages thick. He turned toward Chief Inspector Jones and used his body to block the view of the packet as he passed it across.

Chief Inspector Jones slipped the document into his own coat. "Why was Woolfe there?"

"A gunshot was heard coming from the Society's house."

Chief Inspector Jones' brow lofted.

"She's put it in that report," Conway said. "But it was the Cosgrove doll that fired the shot. Sergeant Bird was there first and, later, 'e told Woolfe about it. Woolfe went to the house to make sure everything was okay."

As he heard the other visitors walk into the next room, Conway approached the sculpture sat opposite the wrestlers. "'Cause I'm keeping an eye on 'em now, I read the report before I gave it you. I'll go see Inspector Lee tomorrow, too; let 'im know what the Society's found out."

"I understand." Chief Inspector Jones followed Conway and stood closer to him than before. In a hushed voice, he said, "Thank you for delivering it. The fact this whole situation has put you into an awkward position hasn't escaped me, John. I wanted to make clear how important your continued support is to me."

"I know." Conway walked around the sculpture to look out the window. The sky had darkened as the sun slipped further behind the dense clouds to make way for night. He watched Chief Inspector Jones' reflection as he joined him. "It's why you've still got it." When he walked in front of him to head for the door, he added, "Just don't make me pick sides."

"I'll do my best, John," Chief Inspector Jones replied and watched Conway's reflection as he stopped, looked back, and walked around the corner to leave.

*　*　*

"Delicious," Mr Elliott said as he set down his knife and fork. He then reached for his glass as he dabbed at the corners of his mouth with a napkin. Inspector Lee poured some more wine into both their glasses and, as Mr Elliott took a sip, he felt his cheeks flush from the alcohol. "Forgive me." Mr Elliott gave a weak smile as he concentrated on keeping his hand steady while he put down his glass. "It would appear I have reached my limit."

"You surprise me," Lee replied. "Does not the Law Society consume copious amounts of alcohol every evening?"

"Undoubtedly," Mr Elliott said. He dabbed at his lips, again, and returned the napkin to his lap. "But my time there is spent in the library, rather than the lounge."

They sat in the inspector's parlour. Half the size of the adjacent dining room, it was filled with antiques from around the world. Their table was in the centre of the room, beside two armchairs which were turned inward toward the large fireplace. The bay window at Mr Elliott's back was concealed by dark-brown, damask curtains, drawn to keep the draft out. The entire floor—except a foot around the edge—was covered by a soft carpet to match the curtains. The walls, meanwhile, were covered by tan paper with an embossed dark-brown flock design.

Though there were modern, electrical lamps, Lee favoured candlelight while dining. As a result, Mr Elliott's complexion appeared even more translucent. The dance of shadows across his face, from the flickering firelight, also gave his cheekbones a more severe definition. Inspector Lee regarded these anomalies with appreciative eyes. Their presence granted his guest with the look of a ballet dancer in the limelight. "Your thirst for knowledge is admirable. It shows a dedication seriously lacking in my profession—as well as demonstrating fearlessness by the acknowledgement of your flaws."

"No one man can know everything," Mr Elliott replied. "But it's the duty of all educated men to at least try."

"How so?" Inspector Lee enquired, curious.

"We are the privileged ones. Our wealth and status afford us the luxury of time. At least, it does for most. My time is greatly limited by my work as a solicitor, and my involvement with the Bow Street Society. Nonetheless, I have more time than others. It's also unnecessary for me to break my back, undertaking physical labour, simply to make ends meet. Thus, I must repay the privilege afforded to me by expanding my mind, so I may assist the less fortunate in whatever way I can." Mr Elliott picked up his glass to peer at the wine but set it aside untouched. "Which brings me to the purpose of my visit."

"Indeed, it does," Lee replied and took his glass, and the bottle of wine, as he stood to wander around to Mr Elliott's side of the table. When he took the empty chair beside his, he set the bottle down and turned to enable their knees to touch. His dark-blue eyes fixed upon Mr Elliott's while he rested his glass upon his guest's knee. "Unfortunately, I have nothing to show you."

Mr Elliott's eyes darted from Lee, to the wine glass, and back again. "I don't understand."

"You're an outsider, Mr Elliott. And, as such, you are a threat to the genteel echelons who reside in Chelsea. As their protector—and, yes, their friend—I can't allow you and the Society to disrupt their idyllic existence with awkward questions and unfounded accusations." Lee put his hand on Mr Elliott's other knee. "Inspector Conway believes I merely play at being a gentleman but, being gentlemanly yourself, you undoubtedly see that isn't the case."

Mr Elliott felt the hand but maintained his stoicism. "I do. Yet, as much as I respect your loyalty to those you serve, it doesn't alter the fact one—or more—of them are guilty of two murders. Awkward questions have already been asked and will continue to be asked until we fulfil our commission by uncovering the truth."

"Ah yes, of course," Lee said and took a sip of wine. His hand remained upon Mr Elliott's knee, however. "Who is your client?"

"The Society's clients' identities are confidential information. But, even if they weren't, I have nothing to gain by sharing the name."

"Mr Elliott, *please*," Lee said, disgusted. "I'm an officer of the law. Besides that, I have *very* wealthy and influential friends who would ensure you *never* worked in the Inns of Court again. I know you don't want that." He put his hand to his chest. "*I* don't want that." He dropped his hand back onto Mr Elliott's knee and smiled. "Tell me who your client is."

"Mr Ned Cosgrove claims he wasn't in the house at the time of his uncle's murder, is that true?" Mr Elliott enquired after a long pause.

Lee sighed. "You're a very stubborn man." He put down his glass. "Who clearly thinks I'm bluffing." He leaned forward to put both hands on Mr Elliott's knees. With his dark-blue eyes fixed on his, he gave them a firm squeeze. "I can assure you I'm not."

"I hadn't doubted it for a moment."

"Then why do you persist in poking the lion?"

"It's my duty."

Inspector Lee at once straightened in surprise and stared at Mr Elliott. "I see." He removed his hands and reached for his wine glass. Rather than pick it up though, he rotated it upon the table. "I don't know if your unwavering integrity is courageous or foolish…" He regarded Mr Elliott and smiled upon seeing the strength in his eyes. "No." He lifted his glass and put his other hand back onto Mr Elliott's knee. "I mustn't mock you." He took a few sips of wine and returned the glass to the table. "Instead, I should admire you. True integrity is becoming an increasingly rare trait these days." He smiled with genuine warmth as his fingers squeezed the knee. When Mr Elliott permitted it for a second time, he went to rubbing the knee while he spoke, "Mr Ned Cosgrove was gambling with money he didn't have in the rooms above the book shop on Coventry Street. When we found him, he was almost £500 down with ten 'I Owe You' notes in his gambling partners' possession."

"And his reaction to his uncle's death?"

"Denial, at first." Lee removed his hand and refilled their wine glasses. "And a strong desire to finish his poker game. When I showed him my warrant card though, he was genuinely shocked." Lee passed Mr Elliott his drink. "Now…" He took a sip of his own. "The name of your client, please."

"Mr Terrence Partridge," Mr Elliott replied and watched the inspector's reaction. Lee's expression showed no hint of recognition, however.

"And who is he?"

"We're not certain," Mr Elliott said. "He's as much of an enigma as the murderer. You didn't encounter him during your original investigation, then?"

"No."

"And the revolver…? Ned Cosgrove mentioned the professor's butler, Mr Lane, owned such a weapon."

Lee swilled his wine around its glass as he gazed over Mr Elliott's shoulder. After a few moments, he said, "I recall some mention being made of it, yes. Mr Lane claimed it had been stolen some weeks before the murder, so I dismissed it."

"With all due respect, Inspector, it appears as if you dismiss a great many things which may, potentially, be of great importance."

"I've seen enough of life to know when I'm chasing shadows, Mr Elliott," Lee replied with a smile. As he leaned forward, his hand rubbed Mr Elliott's knee once more. "You'll stay for dessert, of course?"

"Of course," Mr Elliott replied with a ghost of a smile. "After you've answered one more question." Lee gave a soft chuckle but reclined in his chair and gestured for his guest to proceed. "Miss Henrietta Watkins, the professor's secretary, has informed us the key to the doll's mechanism went missing after the murder. Was this the case?"

"The doll was never mentioned beyond the initial consideration of its involvement when I first arrived at the residence," Lee replied. A smile formed upon his face as, with a twinkle in his eyes, he reached forward to put his hand a little higher up Mr Elliott's leg. "That is enough talk of business for one evening. If I may be so bold, Mr Elliott, you have the look of a man who requires a decent dessert in his belly."

Mr Elliott chortled at the remark, "It has been some time since I last indulged, it's true."

"Allow us to remedy that, then," Lee replied and slid his hand down the inside of Mr Elliott's thigh to come to rest on his knee once again.

"Yes," Mr Elliott replied as he looked into the inspector's intense eyes. "Let's."

SIXTEEN

Located on the south coast of England, Brighton was a popular travel destination due to its easy accessibility by railway from the capital. Its piers, luxury hotels, seafront entertainments, and fresh air also attracted people from further afield. Having taken the ten o'clock train from London that morning, Miss Dexter and the Lockes were welcomed by brilliant blue skies over calm seas, a cool breeze, and pleasant sunshine. Sat sideways upon a bench at the far end of Brighton's west pier, Miss Dexter looked out to shore.

Middle-aged ladies—adorned in traditional full body bathing suits and mop caps— paddled in the shallows. Among them were ladies, in everyday wear, who held up their rolled skirts. Children also played in the water and sand, while bowler hat-wearing men and straw-hatted young boys, with trousers rolled to their knees, sailed toy boats.

Groups of bathing huts were scattered across the beach, some at the water's edge and others against the promenade's sea wall. Made of wood, each hut had brightly painted stripes on its sides, and a door at its rear. A primitive set of steps—ladder-like in their appearance— allowed one to climb inside. Windowless, the huts provided a private space for bathers to change clothes. Due to their mobility, the huts were pushed to the water's edge to allow bathers to enter the sea without the painful inconvenience of crossing the shingle-covered sand barefooted. A platform at the hut's front provided enough space for a bather to sit and ease themselves into the— often cold—waters. Miss Dexter couldn't help but smile when she saw the startled expression of one lady bather who dangled from a platform to dip her foot into the murky depths.

The promenade was located below the main thoroughfare of King's Road that ran along the seafront. Red-bricked archways, set into the promenade's back wall, contained the frontages of shops and amusements, e.g. a Jungle Shooting Gallery. Above each wooden doorway were arched windows—which could be opened at leisure—and numerable flagpoles and signs. Ladies with parasols strolled arm in arm with gentlemen in straw hats along the promenade. While well-dressed children stood at the promenade's edge, entranced by the beach entertainers and puppet show.

Visitors, happy to watch the world go by, stood at the criss-cross, iron railings which overlooked the promenade. Beyond them was the line of single horse drawn carriages which awaited passengers, the opposing streams of traffic, and magnificent Hôtel Metropole and Grand Hotel. The Metropole stood out against its neighbours due to its redbrick façade, striped canopies, and white balconies. Miss Dexter recalled, from Mrs Cosgrove's correspondence that Mr Locke had read aloud during their train journey, that she resided in a suite at the Metropole. Yet, Mrs Cosgrove had stated she'd prefer to meet at the end of the west pier. Thus far, she'd failed to honour the arrangement.

"She is twenty minutes late," Mr Locke remarked as he snapped shut his pocket watch and slipped it back into his waistcoat pocket. "Excuse me." He went across the hexagonal area to study the faces of those who approached along the pier's main promenade deck.

Miss Dexter watched Mr Locke for a moment before she looked back to shore and filled her lungs with the crisp, sea air. "Isn't it simply wonderful?" she enquired as she glanced at Doctor Locke at her side. "Not at all like London." Miss Dexter closed her eyes to feel the sun against her face and, with a broad smile, sighed. "There's such life and happiness here." She opened her eyes and leaned forward to grip the railing and peer at the swirling foam beneath. "I wish I had the time to sketch everything."

"Surely you have seen it all before?" Doctor Locke enquired with a bemused expression.

Miss Dexter's cheeks burned as she brought her hands together on the railing. "This is my first visit to the seaside," she admitted. "Pa-Pa says the beach is far too rowdy a place for respectable people like us."

"Well," Doctor Locke said with a smile as she slipped her arm around Miss Dexter's and stood with her. "You may tell your father the health benefits of sea air are widely accepted by medical practitioners. Furthermore, on the advice of one such practitioner, you intend to take the air at least once a month."

"Thank you," Miss Dexter replied with a broad smile.

The approach of Mr Locke distracted both ladies, however, for his stride was swift and his expression serious. Upon reaching them, he tucked his cane beneath his arm and announced, "I have just caught a glimpse of Mrs Cosgrove in the crowd. She should be here any moment."

"You recognised her after all this time?" Doctor Locke enquired with a lofted brow.

"I know. Uncanny, is it not?" Mr Locke replied with a twinkle in his eyes.

Before the two ladies could respond though, a third emerged from the crowd and extended her hand to Mr Locke. In her mid-thirties, she had a small, round, delicate face with curls of strawberry-blond hair which peeked out from beneath a cream bonnet. A broad, burgundy ribbon ran around the bonnet behind its brim, while a cluster of red roses and silk leaves were pinned to the bonnet's side. Her cheeks were tinged with rouge, while her lips were painted a cherry red. The severe inward turn of her waist betrayed the presence of a tight corset beneath her mutton-sleeved, cherry-red dress.

194

Though its neckline was low, her ample, tightly packed bosom was covered by transparent, cream netting. A white, fox fur stole was draped around her arms, while a cream parasol, with lace trim, served as a makeshift walking cane.

"Percy, *darling*!" the woman cried as she allowed him to take her hand and kiss her knuckles. "You haven't changed at all. How many years has it been? Three? Five?"

"Ten," Mr Locke replied.

"*Heavens*! Has it *really*?" the woman replied. She pulled one side of her stole up onto her shoulder and tilted her head back. "Why yes, of course it would be." She placed a slender hand upon Mr Locke's arm. "I was *most* distressed to hear of your mother's death—and then your *father's*, too!" She released a deep breath. "*Such* a tragic accident."

"Quite," Mr Locke replied with a frown and a swift clearing of his throat before he turned toward the others. "Mrs Cosgrove—"

"Coral, *please*!" Mrs Cosgrove interrupted. "You and I are on far more intimate terms than that." She gave him a sideways wink.

"This is my wife," Mr Locke hastened to say. "Doctor Lynette Locke."

"Mrs Cosgrove," Doctor Locke replied as she tried to conceal her distaste. "Percy's told me a lot about you."

"Don't believe it!" Mrs Cosgrove cried before she gave a soft chortle.

"Far from it," Doctor Locke said. In a dry tone, she added, "You are precisely what I expected."

"And this is—" Mr Locke began as he indicted Miss Dexter.

"Your *daughter*?" Mrs Cosgrove interrupted and clasped her hands together with a broad smile. "*How* charming."

"Miss Georgina Dexter of the Bow Street Society," Mr Locke corrected. "Now, Coral, you *really* must permit me to finish."

"Don't I always, darling?" Mrs Cosgrove replied with another sideways wink.

"*Mrs* Cosgrove," Doctor Locke began as she stepped in between her husband and the other woman. "As Mr Locke has already stated in his prior correspondence, we wish to speak with you about your late husband, Professor Benjamin Cosgrove."

Mrs Cosgrove tensed, and her smile melted away. Pulling the other side of her stole onto her shoulders, she strode over to the benches and gazed out to sea. A handful of yachts and fishing boats dotted the horizon and intervening space. Mr Locke moved to join her, while his wife followed with her arm wrapped around his. Miss Dexter, on the other hand, kept a respectable distance on Mrs Cosgrove's other side. The crowd had begun to disperse on the pier since many were returning to their accommodations for luncheon. Seeing they were practically alone therefore, Mrs Cosgrove turned her back to the sea and said, "I'd hoped you had forgotten about that."

"Unfortunately, as pleasant as this reunion is, we nonetheless have a duty to perform for our client," Mr Locke replied. "A Mr Terrence Partridge…?"

"Who?" Mrs Cosgrove enquired, confused.

"No matter," Mr Locke said, satisfied with her response. "Tell us of your husband, Coral. Of your marriage, and the night he was so cruelly taken from you."

Mrs Cosgrove opened her parasol and rested it against her shoulder as she sat on the bench behind her. The Lockes and Miss Dexter moved to occupy the benches which framed hers. "Taken, yes… Cruelly, perhaps," Mrs Cosgrove replied. "Ours was a loveless marriage, Percy." She smiled. "Before we were married… He was very romantic. He would send me roses each day and tell me I

196

was an angel sent from heaven." She looked sideways at Percy with a wry smile. "He made love like an animal." Her eyes drifted over his form. "And… in so doing… made me feel alive."

"What changed?" Doctor Locke enquired in a hard tone.

Mrs Cosgrove diverted her gaze from Mr Locke to his wife—albeit with reluctance—and replied, "He put a ring on my finger." She stood, walked a few steps, and turned to face them. "The passion drained from him like rain down a pipe." She strolled across to some empty benches. "Is it little wonder I fell into the arms of another?" She turned sharply upon her heel to look upon Percy. "Oh, I knew it was *wrong* of me, but Norman was there with a shoulder to cry on. He also offered the warmth I'd lost from Benjamin. How was I to know Norman would murder my husband?"

"Pardon?" Miss Dexter enquired, stunned.

"Norman was the professor's nephew, correct?" Doctor Locke enquired.

"Yes," Mrs Cosgrove replied. As she returned to them and reclaimed her seat, the sun became hidden by the clouds. She therefore closed her parasol and rested it against her knee. "He denied it, of course, but how *could* I continue with the affair? I told him it was over and came down here to Brighton. I've not heard from him or his son since."

"Did you say Norman had a son?" Mr Locke enquired, intrigued. "This is the first we have heard of him."

Mrs Cosgrove shrugged a shoulder. "It does not surprise me. Norman told me the mother died in childbirth, but he'd only found out she was expecting when her sister arrived on his doorstep with the child. She told him she'd been able to keep the secret of her sister's shame from their father and was *very* keen to keep it that way. It was to the baby farm, or Norman, for the innocent child." She gave Percy a soft smile. "Norman, being the good man he was, took the child in and raised him."

"An unusual decision on his part," Doctor Locke remarked. "It would've proven far less scandalous for him if he'd denied the child's parentage. I've seen it countless times before, unmarried women bearing the bastard babies of their wealthy employers, only to be cast out with no way of proving what they know to be true in their hearts."

"Norman wasn't like other men," Mrs Cosgrove snapped. "Besides…" She smiled at Percy once more. "I only discovered Adam's existence by chance. He was home from boarding school when I called upon Norman one day."

"When was this?" Mr Locke enquired.

"Oh, hmm," Mrs Cosgrove considered a moment. "I remember it was a sunny day as we sat in the garden drinking some lemonade. Adam would have been… seven… eight, perhaps? Around 1888." Mrs Cosgrove frowned. "Naturally, I was shocked when I discovered Adam's relation to Norman. I asked Norman who the mother was, but he became angry and told me not to interfere. He then made me swear not to tell Benjamin. I agreed because I was actually rather fond of Norman." She looked back out to sea. "Which is what made his betrayal of Benjamin and me all the more unbearable."

"You had already betrayed the professor by having an affair with his nephew," Doctor Locke blurted out, much to her husband's obvious displeasure.

Mrs Cosgrove pursed her lips together. "If you had been married to such a selfish man, Mrs Locke, then you would have done the same." Her expression softened as she ran her fingertips over Mr Locke's gloved hand. "I'm glad to say you didn't have that misfortune." Mrs Cosgrove's hand slipped down to rest upon Mr Locke's knee. "Percy was always so very kind to me. Weren't you, darling?"

198

"You argued with your husband on the night of his murder," Doctor Locke said as she clenched her hand beneath her coat. "What did you argue about?"

"I can't recall now," Mrs Cosgrove replied with a dismissive wave of her hand. "Possibly about Norman. Benjamin was always so frightfully angry at his nephews. I understood his displeasure at Ned—he was the gambling type—but Norman had true affection for his uncle." Mrs Cosgrove lifted her hand from Percy's knee. "You know, you've made me remember the will. Benjamin was rarely civil to Ned and, yet, *Ned* inherited *everything*. There was *quite* the to-do. Benjamin's spinster secretary—what was her name?" Mrs Cosgrove inclined her head as she thought a moment. "Miss Watson… no… Miss Botkins… ah, Miss Watkins! Yes, that's right." Mrs Cosgrove gave a self-satisfied smile. "She was *particularly* annoyed by the news. Probably because she was as fond of Benjamin as I was of Norman at the time. No doubt she expected to inherit a legacy, or some such thing."

"Did Miss Watkins tell you of her feelings?" Miss Dexter enquired.

"*Heavens*, no. She was too much of a prude to admit such a thing. All one had to do was see the way she looked at him though, to know the truth of it," Mrs Cosgrove replied.

"You hardly seem upset about it," Doctor Locke observed as she fought the urge to roll her eyes.

"It's been six years, Mrs Locke," Mrs Cosgrove reminded her. "And I'm not the sort to allow jealousy to fester in my bosom." She turned admiring eyes toward Mr Locke. "There are plenty of handsome gentlemen waiting to put their heads there."

"Weren't you unhappy about not inheriting anything?" Miss Dexter enquired as she tried to divert the conversation away from the scandalous topic.

"I was…" Mrs Cosgrove replied. "…At the time. When I came here and met lord Gelding… well, he soon pushed all thoughts of Benjamin from my mind." She smiled as the playful twinkle returned to her eyes. "I had little reason to contact anyone from back then, so I didn't. Has Norman confessed to the murder? Is that why you're here?"

"No," Percy began. He looked from Coral, to his wife, and back again. "I'm sorry to have to be the one to tell you this, Coral, but Norman Cosgrove died last year from consumption."

Mrs Cosgrove's eyes widened, and she rose a few inches from the bench. Her arm swept up, and her parasol clattered to the floor, as she cried, "good *gracious*!" and fell into Mr Locke's arms in a near faint. Mr Locke caught her with ease and, as he cradled her, Mrs Cosgrove gave a weak smile. "Thank you, Percy…" She rested her hand on his cheek. "…You always were such the gentleman…" The foul stench of smelling salt then filled her nostrils and caused Mrs Cosgrove to retch and cough with a flurry of fur and arms. "*What* was *that*?!" she demanded as she sat on the bench beside Mr Locke.

"Smelling salts," Mrs Locke said and recorked the bottle. "You fainted, Mrs Cosgrove."

With her fur stole pressed against her nose and mouth, Mrs Cosgrove stared at the insolent Mrs Locke a moment. "Yes… yes, I did. You did not have to *suffocate* me with such a *vile* smell, however." She turned her back on her and dropped the stole to take several deep breaths. "*Poor* Norman!" She gave a singular sob. "Such a *horrific* way to go. Even if he *did* murder my husband."

"Mrs Cosgrove… When did you tell Mr Norman Cosgrove you wished to end the affair?" Miss Dexter enquired.

"The night before Benjamin's funeral," Mrs Cosgrove replied. "I saw him and Miss Watkins leaving Benjamin's study. After she had left us, I told him, in no uncertain terms, I would not share a murderer's bed."

"Do you know why the two were in your late husband's study?" Mr Locke enquired as he lit a cigarette with a slight tremble to his hand.

"I never thought to ask," Mrs Cosgrove admitted. "Is it important?"

"Perhaps," Mr Locke replied. "Miss Dexter, will you show Mrs Cosgrove your two sketches and the photograph, please?" While Miss Dexter did as was asked, Mr Locke continued, "We believe the antique doll, that your husband had recently purchased, was given a loaded revolver and set in motion to shoot him." He fell silent as Mrs Cosgrove glanced at the photograph and studied the sketch of the doll's inner workings with obvious disquiet upon her features.

"I… I don't quite understand…" Mrs Cosgrove muttered.

"It is really rather simple," Mr Locke replied. "Someone added wire to the doll's inner mechanism and switched its wooden revolver for the real thing. Were you aware of the doll's ability to move?"

"He may have mentioned it, once… I can't be certain," Mrs Cosgrove replied. "I don't even recall seeing the doll when I spoke to Benjamin."

"The doll had a key," Miss Dexter said. "Do you remember it at all?"

"A small thing, with a rose on the handle…?" Mrs Cosgrove enquired, unsure.

"We believe so," Miss Dexter replied. "It went missing after the murder…?"

"I don't know about *that*," Mrs Cosgrove replied with a weak smile. "Benjamin kept a key with a rose on it upon the window sill. I never knew what it was for."

"The revolver was a Webley Mark I," Mr Locke explained. "Did your husband own such a gun?"

"He may have. I didn't take any interest in his sport," Mrs Cosgrove replied, flustered. "This is… it is too much to grasp all at once. *Who* could have done such a thing?"

"Someone within the Cosgrove household," Mr Locke replied. "That is the theory we are following at the moment, at least. Please, may you look at Miss Dexter's next sketch? I would not make the request if it was not important, Coral."

"It's a plan of the study as described by Mr Ned Cosgrove," Miss Dexter explained as she passed over the sketch. "Is there anything you think should be changed?"

"I… uh…" Mrs Cosgrove said, her voice shaking, as she looked over the drawing. "I… I do not believe so." She met Mr Locke's gaze. "But there was a housebreaker. *He* killed my husband. The window was open… the police…"

"Miss Watkins said you'd noticed the window when you both found the professor's body," Miss Dexter said. "May you recall who unlocked the professor's study door?"

"Was it locked?" Mrs Cosgrove enquired.

"Miss Watkins told us Professor Cosgrove had locked it after he had instructed her to leave," Mr Locke interjected after he exhaled his cigarette smoke into the breeze. "She also denied having a spare key."

"I must have unlocked it, then," Mrs Cosgrove remarked.

"Did not Mr Lane have the spare?" Miss Dexter enquired, recalling another of Miss Watkins' explanations. Mrs Cosgrove further studied the sketch of the study's floorplan. Yet, her eyes darted back and forth across it as if it were a looking glass.

"He wasn't there," Mrs Cosgrove announced, finally. She lowered the sketch to her lap and placed her hand upon it. "He *did* arrive soon after Miss Watkins and I entered the study, but it was only the two of us when the door was unlocked. I'm sorry, Percy, I *wish* I could remember more for you."

202

"Do you recall a Mr Bund, at all?" Doctor Locke interjected in a hard tone.

"The name rings a faint bell…" Mrs Cosgrove passed the sketches and photograph to Miss Dexter. "Something about money, wasn't it? I can't remember."

"Where were Ned and Norman Cosgrove when the professor died?" Mr Locke enquired as he smoked some more of his cigarette and kept a close watch of Coral's body language and facial expression.

"They may have been there, they may have visited earlier in the day, or they may have been hiding in the wardrobe," Mrs Cosgrove replied and forced a smile. "While I enjoy being questioned by you, Percy darling, I must throw myself upon your mercy." She took his cigarette, had a deep pull from it, and exhaled the smoke over his shoulder. "Time, and a *frightfully* virile lord, has cast my recollection of that God-awful period clear from my mind." She leaned closer to Mr Locke and slipped the cigarette between his lips. "You can surely sympathise with that, can't you…?"

"Thank you, Mrs Cosgrove," Doctor Locke interjected and stepped closer to her husband. "We'll be in touch should we require anything further." She looked to Mr Locke. "Shan't we miss our train to London if we don't depart for the station soon, darling?"

"Ah, yes…" Mr Locke replied and stood to slip his arm around his wife's. "Please write if you recall anything further concerning your late husband's death, Mrs Cosgrove."

"Wait a moment!" Mrs Cosgrove cried and leapt to her feet. The Lockes both stepped back and exchanged wary glances. Yet, Mrs Cosgrove's expression wasn't malignant. It was the opposite, in fact. "*Norman*… yes, that is right." She smiled. "*He* must have had a key to Benjamin's study. You see, after I spoke to him outside the door—on the night of the funeral—I had to fetch something, but the door was locked. I remember now…

yes, I heard the door being locked as he and Miss Watkins left."

"How can you be certain it was Norman who locked it?" Doctor Locke enquired.

"I'm not, but you said Miss Watkins hadn't a spare, so it must've been Norman, correct?" Mrs Cosgrove replied.

"It is possible…" Mr Locke said as he looked sideways at his wife with a lofted brow.

SEVENTEEN

"In a case filled with doubts, there is one fact we may all be reasonably certain of. Professor Benjamin Cosgrove held a key to his study," Mr Locke said. He'd chosen to sit with his back to the fire so didn't hesitate to dab his forehead with his handkerchief whenever a wave of heat erupted from his core. The draft from the chimney—provided by London's latest tempest—offered further subterfuge for his trembling hands. He clenched his damp handkerchief in one and held it against his thigh beneath the table. "It may sound ludicrously obvious when said aloud. But his possession of a study key is not only the most logical but the most probable. The remaining key holders are mere potentials until we can determine the mundane routines of the Cosgrove household." He tubed his lips as he felt the first peaks of warmth, which often preceded the imminent arrival of a penetrating, fever-like state, and wiped his forehead. "Mr Lane, the professor's butler, Mrs Coral Cosgrove, his wife, and Mr Norman Cosgrove, his nephew, are those potentials."

"Are you well?" Miss Dexter enquired, from Mr Locke's left, as she placed her hand beside his elbow to lean forward and see his complexion against the fire's glare. When she saw the sheen of sweat, she recoiled. "Mr *Locke*, you've a *fever*."

"It is merely the heat of the fire," Mr Locke reassured with a weak smile.

"But you're *shivering*," Miss Dexter retorted as she looked to his trembling hands.

Miss Trent, sat at the opposite end of the table, pursed her lips and exhaled through her nose when she witnessed the exchange. "Doctor Locke," she said in a steady tone. "I think you ought to go home with your husband."

"I agree," Doctor Locke replied. Her firm tone echoed Miss Trent's.

Mr Locke's brow lofted as his wife stood and all eyes turned toward him. He looked from his fellow Bow Streeters to Doctor Locke when she placed a hand upon his shoulder. Though he parted his lips to protest, the arrival of his fever stayed his words. He therefore stood and accepted his wife's arm. "My apologies, everyone… Miss Trent."

Miss Dexter stood and watched Mr Locke's back with concerned eyes as he left the room with his wife. When Mr Snyder followed to see the Lockes out, she sat and observed. "He seemed quite well in Brighton."

"He's in safe hands," Miss Trent stated as she returned to her notes to read a few lines. "Now, Mr Locke did raise an important point regarding the study keys. Since Mr Ned Cosgrove is already aware of our intention to speak with his butler and maid, I think it would still be appropriate for you to speak with them, Mr Snyder and Miss Dexter. The butler should be able to shed some light on the keys' ownership and storage."

"We'll do that tomorrow," Mr Snyder replied from Miss Trent's right.

"I would like to read the professor's Last Will & Testament," Mr Elliott said with his pencil poised over his own notes. "Mr Ned Cosgrove was rather fierce in his resolve that we should not see it. Miss Dexter, you were present when Miss Watkins and then Mrs Coral Cosgrove were spoken to. Did either of them mention the professor's will at all?"

Miss Dexter's petite hands toyed with the excess material of her skirt. "Yes. Miss Watkins said she was given heartfelt words by the professor. Mrs Cosgrove told us Mr Cosgrove—that is, Mr Ned Cosgrove—inherited it all."

"A clear contradiction of what he told us," Mr Elliott remarked and made a brief note of the revelation.

"Miss Watkins and Mrs Cosgrove could be lying… Were either evasive in their answers, or did they look away while speaking?"

"Not that I saw or heard," Miss Dexter replied. "And I was watching them as carefully as I could."

Mr Elliott hummed. "We would know for certain which—if any—is lying once we read the contents of the will. I doubt Mr Ned Cosgrove's insistence it is with the solicitor. If it was, he wouldn't have been so quick to prevent me from opening the desk." Mr Elliott's stoic expression cracked into a frown. "If Mr Locke wasn't unwell, he could've accessed the library's desk with ease."

"I shall telephone him in the morning," Miss Trent interjected with a cool tone.

"I doubt he'll be recovered by then," Miss Bernice Kershaw remarked from between Mr Elliott and her sister.

"Especially if he caught it from the waters at Brighton," Miss Brenda Kershaw added.

"He didn't take the waters though," Miss Dexter replied.

"I shall telephone him in the morning," Miss Trent repeated, her tone firm.

The Kershaws exchanged troubled glances, while Mr Elliott cleared his throat and made further notes. Mr Verity, who had listened in silence thus far, shifted forward in his chair and said, "Miss Watkins said about the doll's key going missing after the professor's death. *She* thought the Elmore's must've had a copy made, just like Mr Locke suggested before. We should go back and ask Mr Elmore's lad about it."

"Inspector Lee admitted the doll wasn't mentioned beyond his initial consideration—and dismissal—of its involvement," Mr Elliott said. "The alleged disappearance of its key is certainly a line of enquiry that has yet to be explored by the original parties. If the Elmore's made a copy, and the original went astray as Miss Watkins claims, the possibility of our murderer still having it in their possession becomes more probable."

"Glad we can agree on something," Mr Verity remarked with a warm smile.

Mr Elliott straightened, but retained his stoicism. "Perhaps you would like to return to the Elmore residence with Mr Maxwell, Mr Verity?"

Mr Maxwell swallowed his tea and replaced his cup upon its saucer while he looked from Mr Elliott, to Mr Verity, to Miss Trent, and back to Mr Elliott. "I-I can do that," he replied when neither Miss Trent nor Mr Verity showed any resistance to the idea. "After I've put the Adam Cosgrove advertisement into the *Gaslight Gazette*."

Miss Trent's jaw tightened. "How did you know about him? I've yet to bring up that aspect of Mrs Cosgrove's interview."

"D-Doctor Locke m-mentioned putting in the advertisement b-before the meeting started," Mr Maxwell explained as his complexion paled under Miss Trent's glare. "She said I sh-should invite Adam Cosgrove to contact the Society as soon as p-possible. W-Was she not s-supposed to tell me yet…?"

Miss Trent shifted her weight upon her chair but shook her head with a sigh. "No, but I like everyone to know the context behind the things we do. Miss Dexter, could you tell everyone what Mrs Cosgrove said, please?"

Miss Dexter gathered her thoughts a moment and, with her hands clasped in her lap, said, "According to Mrs Cosgrove, Norman had a son… Adam, as Mr Maxwell said. Norman Cosgrove was unaware the mother was expecting until after she'd died bringing Adam into the world and her sister brought the baby to him. Norman took the baby in and raised him, but he refused to tell Mrs Cosgrove who the mother was. Mrs Cosgrove said she met Adam, by chance, in around 1888 when Adam was seven or eight years old. Norman persuaded Mrs Cosgrove not to tell her husband about Adam."

208

"If the child's mother was dead, why strive to keep her identity a secret?" Mr Elliott enquired.

"She'd kept the pregnancy a secret from her father—with her sister's help—and her sister wanted to keep the confidence, despite the mother dying," Miss Dexter replied. She then furrowed her brow. "I was as confused as you, Mr Elliott. If Norman cared about Mrs Cosgrove enough to have a forbidden romance with her, why wouldn't he want to bring her into his confidence? He could've still persuaded her not to tell the professor."

"Maybe he did tell her," Mr Maxwell suggested. "And she's keeping the secret by not telling us."

"Or Mrs Cosgrove is Adam's mother," Miss Bernice Kershaw interjected. When everyone turned their attention to her, she continued, "We've only heard the story from Mrs Cosgrove's lips, after all."

"And she could've fabricated it, so we wouldn't suspect her," Miss Brenda Kershaw added.

"Devious," Bernice said.

"Very," Brenda added.

"I may be able to identify Adam's mother by tracing his birth certificate," Mr Elliott said. "I suspect I would have as much success requesting it from the Registrar General's records at Somerset House as I did with the death index records. I shall nonetheless make the attempt, in addition to checking the baptism records in Chelsea. It's likely Norman could have seduced a local woman."

"Wot about Norman Cosgrove's death?" Mr Snyder enquired as he rested his broad arm upon the table. "Miss Watkins didn't know he'd passed. Did Mrs Cosgrove?" Miss Dexter shook her head. "We've just got Ned's word that he's dead, then?"

"Looks like it," Mr Maxwell replied.

"Unless you want to try another séance," Mr Verity suggested.

"I woz thinkin' more of seein' Mr Partridge again," Mr Snyder said. "There woz pictures covered when we woz there last. Wot if Partridge's workin' for Norman Cosgrove?" Mr Snyder tapped the table with his stubby finger. "Wot if Norman and Ned done in the professor between 'em, with the idea of gettin' all his monies, but Ned conned Norman outta his share? Norman could be wantin' to get back at his bruvva by usin' the Society to make sure 'e swings for the murder."

"Are we not allowing ourselves to be carried away by supposition?" Mr Elliott enquired with a heap of cynicism to his tone. "We must gather the facts and form a theory to fit them, not the other way around."

Mr Snyder leaned forward as, in a hard tone, he said, "We'd get the fact it's Norman Cosgrove who Partridge's workin' for, or not, when we go see 'im." He turned toward Miss Trent. "I'd wanna take Mr Skinner with me though. Now I know what I'm goin' into, the inspecta's not needed."

"I'm fine wit dat," Mr Skinner remarked.

"May I go with you?" Miss Dexter enquired. "I think it would help us if I could sketch where the doll was kept when you first saw it, Sam."

Mr Snyder frowned. "I dunno if Partridge'll like that, and I dunno if I like you comin' with us."

"Me either," Mr Maxwell interjected and his features creased with worry.

Miss Dexter ignored his obvious concern, however, and instead addressed Mr Snyder's. "A sketch of the room may help us explain why the doll's mechanism was set off. Mr Partridge said he wants to ensure the doll is safe enough to send to America. Surely he can't deny our request on that basis?"

"Seeing what the doll was stood against would be useful," Bernice Kershaw said.

"And anything else nearby," Brenda Kershaw added.

210

"I'll be safe as long as I'm with you, Sam," Miss Dexter resumed.

Mr Snyder continued to frown, but knew he'd never let any harm come to his fellow Bow Streeter. If nothing else, she reminded him of his own daughter. "Okay," he said, finally. "But you've gotta be careful when you're there."

"I will," Miss Dexter said as she beamed.

"Now it's settled," Miss Trent began as she made a brief note. "I'd like you three to visit Mr Partridge tomorrow night. I'm assuming, Mr Elliott, you'd expect to have no success gaining access to Norman Cosgrove's death records, either?"

"Correct," Mr Elliott replied. "While I search the parish records for Adam's baptism, I will also search for Norman Cosgrove's interment, however."

"Perfect," Miss Trent said. "Mr Maxwell, I'd like you to search the obituaries for Norman Cosgrove. I'd like us to be confident all roads have been explored before accusing Mr Partridge of deception."

"I'll put an apprentice on it when I visit the offices in the morning," Mr Maxwell said. "I can do that now, you know." He smiled at Miss Trent, but it faded when her expression remained stoic. "That w-way I can go with Mr Verity… and Miss Dexter in the evening."

"*Pardon*?" Miss Dexter said, wide eyed.

"I've not stopped caring for you," Mr Maxwell replied.

"You're not needed," Mr Snyder growled as he glared at Mr Maxwell.

"Stop it," Miss Dexter demanded. "Joseph—Mr Maxwell, *please*. It has already been decided."

Mr Maxwell felt his throat tighten as he saw the sadness in her eyes. The sadness *he* had created but could not put right. He rubbed his arm as the memory of his father's belt made it throb. When he tore his eyes from Miss Dexter, he replied, "Very well… Miss Dexter… Mr

Snyder…" His gaze dropped to his cold tea. "My apologies."

"If Mr Partridge just wants the doll to be safe," Mr Skinner began. "Ain't we done dat already?" He looked to the twins. "By takin' out the wire and gun?"

"He's right," Bernice said.

"Mr Partridge might want an end to our investigation," Brenda added.

"And the doll returned," Bernice said.

"He may," Miss Trent replied. "I doubt Inspector Lee would allow it once I've informed him of our further discoveries, however."

The Kershaws exchanged glances but were, nonetheless, reassured by Miss Trent's reply.

"But let's try to ensure it doesn't come to that," Miss Trent added.

* * *

"Are you going to tell me, or does Lyons have to do another search?" Doctor Locke enquired while she peeled the sweat-soaked frockcoat from her husband.

Mr Locke slouched in the corner of their carriage, once he was freed from the garment, and loosened his cravat. The window was open, so he turned his face toward the cool breeze coming through it. "I have not indulged since last night." He gripped the interior leather strap above his head. "This is merely a malady brought on by exhaustion."

"You forget to whom you are speaking," Doctor Locke said while she checked his frockcoat's pockets. From them she took his cigarette case and matches, which she put on the seat beside her. "Your body is craving the drug." She looked down at him with hard eyes. "Where's the rest?"

"Cease your pestering, Lynette."

"I shall, when you cease your lying," she replied. "Your cravings were not as severe when you were denied the drug the other day, and the dose I gave you should have been sufficient to waylay them until tonight. I shall therefore ask you again, *darling. Where* are your other doses hidden?"

Mr Locke remained silent as he stared out the window. His wife felt a heat of her own rising within her bosom as she watched him. Tightening her jaw as she shoved his possessions back into his frockcoat, she then tossed it at him. "You have tried my patience for the last time, Percy Locke." She took out a compact mirror and checked her hair. "If you wish to disappear into oblivion, so be it. Just do not expect any more of my help or support." She snapped the compact shut and slipped it into her bag before she settled against the cushioned seat.

"There is no more," Mr Locke said after a long pause.

Doctor Locke considered his response. "I don't believe you."

"Fine, Have it your way. Tear our home apart if it eases your mind."

Doctor Locke pressed her fingers against her temples. "You are *infuriating."* She dropped her hands into her lap and looked down at him. In a voice strained with desperation, she said, "Can't you see I'm worried *sick* about you?" She cast her eyes upwards. "The only thing that would ease my mind is the removal of your dependency. Yet, as that is unlikely to happen, I can only manage your cravings." She looked back to him. "I can't do that if you are self-medicating."

Mr Locke regarded his wife as a violent shiver tore through his body, followed by another wave of intense heat. "I know," he replied though his voice lacked its earlier edge. He put his gloved hand upon her shoulder and sat up to pull her into an embrace. Doctor Locke held him in return and, as she pressed her chin against his damp shoulder, her cold expression disintegrated. "And I know how hard it has been for you. I am truly sorry, my darling."

Doctor Locke leaned back to wipe the sweat from his face; her gaze was one of sadness and admiration. "I know you are," she whispered. "But, please." She held his cheek and looked into his eyes. "Tell me the truth. Are there any more doses?"

"There was," he admitted with some hesitation. "I injected the last this morning."

Doctor Locke's face crumpled. "Oh, *Percy…*" she whispered, devastated, as she bowed her head to hide her tears. "…*Why* would you…"

"I was weak," he replied and lifted her chin with his trembling, leather-clad thumb. "But I *promise* you, my darling, it shan't happen again."

Doctor Locke pulled away with a sob. "I've heard it all before, Percy." She turned pleading eyes upon him. "And you haven't kept your word yet."

"I shall this time. I cannot continue to indulge as I have, my darling. I was almost exposed to the Bow Street Society tonight but, more importantly, I cannot lose you." His voice faltered as his own desperation manifested. "You are *everything* to me, Lynette. Without you, I may as well surrender to oblivion."

Doctor Locke put her hand on her husband's quaking shoulder as she searched his feverish gaze for any hint of deception. When none were found, she forced back her sadness and said, "Very well, I'll carry on helping you." She took a moment to gather her strength. "We'll continue with the same number of doses, but I'll lessen the amount each time. The weakened potency may ease your dependency. In my opinion though, you'll have to stop injecting altogether to give your body time to recover."

Mr Locke's smile wavered. "…Yes… of course…"

Doctor Locke's hard eyes locked onto her husband's. "This is your last chance, Percy." Mr Locke's smile evaporated as he gave an incoherent nod. Overcome with shivers then, he sat back and dragged his frockcoat over him. Doctor Locke's rigid tone and expression remained stanch, however. "Do *not* disappointment me."

"I shan't…" Mr Locke replied. Overcome with trembling as well, he felt his muscles constrict and ache with growing ferocity.

Recognising this deterioration, Doctor Locke put her arm around his shoulders and eased him into the foetal position. Ensuring the small of his back was flush against the bench, she cradled his head in her lap. When her free hand then stroked his sweat-covered cheek, she wiped away the remaining powder to expose the dark circles under his eyes and pallid complexion.

Mr Locke gripped the frockcoat with clenched fists and stared into the abyss. "I swear…"

* * *

Mr Maxwell tucked his slender fingers into his armpits as rain poured from the hansom cab's roof and down the doors over his legs. Having hailed the cab minutes before, he was reminded of the mounting fare by the creaking of the driver's seat, and the impatient bobbing of the horse's head. Nonetheless, he kept the vehicle on the other side of Bow Street. Seeing a shaft of golden light as the Society's door was opened, followed by Mr Snyder hurrying to fetch his own cab, Mr Maxwell leaned forward. Stray droplets of rain caught his unkempt, auburn hair and dampened his freckle-covered cheeks.

Yet, his heart leapt when the door opened again, and Miss Dexter emerged with Miss Trent. Holding the top edge of the cab's doors, he leaned further forward and watched. Even with a veil of water between them, he could see Miss Dexter's auburn halo as the porch lamp's light illuminated her hair. When she then faced his direction, Mr Maxwell threw himself upon the seat and held his breath.

"You awight?" his cab's driver's voice enquired from above.

Mr Maxwell lifted his head to peer through the square opening in the roof. "Yes… th-thank you."

A gloved hand then gripped his shoulder and dragged him upright before Oliver Maxwell growled into his ear, "I thought I might find you here."

"F-Father, wh-what are you—?"

"*Stop* stammering and move," Oliver commanded with a firm shove against Mr Maxwell's shoulder. "Open the doors!"

"Y-Yes, Father." Mr Maxwell slid the bolt back and pushed the doors outward. He shuffled across the seat while Oliver clambered inside. When Mr Maxwell heard the approach of Mr Snyder's cab, his eyes widened as he realised his voyeurism could be exposed. Without waiting for his father to settle, therefore, Mr Maxwell slammed the doors and struck the roof. "Let's go!"

The driver's whip cracked against the horse's flank and the vehicle lurched forward with such force, Oliver's top hat tumbled from his head. As it rolled down the cab's front, Mr Maxwell fumbled to catch it. His fingers slipped, however, and the top hat flipped off the doors and into the path of an oncoming wagon.

"You clumsy *wretch*!" Oliver bellowed and backhanded Mr Maxwell across the back of the head. His nose was slammed against the doors as a result. "I will have your *hide* for this!"

"N-No, F-Father, please!" Mr Maxwell begged as the blood poured between his fingers as he held his nose. "I-I'll pay for a new one!"

"With *what* funds, may I ask?" Oliver growled and threw the door's bolts into place. "The rag you call a newspaper barely pays enough to put clothes on your back.

216

It's *my* money you live on, Joseph! *My* money you press into the palms of whores whom you promise to marry!"

"She's not a whore, Father!" Mr Maxwell cried, which earned him another backhand from Oliver. This time his head was driven into the cab's wall, and he grunted as the rain drowned out the thud. Huddled in the corner, Mr Maxwell draped his arm over his head and clutched his bloodied nose as Oliver gripped the doors and leaned over his son.

"Whores are paid for what's between their legs," he said, disgusted. "And your whore's been paid handsomely for your enjoyment of what's between hers." Oliver's other hand grasped Mr Maxwell's shoulder and squeezed. "We'll be hearing no more threats of court from her *or* her father." Oliver listened to his son's snivelling a moment and yanked him from the corner to hold him close by his side. "You had better hope she didn't make you barren. Otherwise, Poppy Lillithwaite's father will cut off more than your money."

Mr Maxwell's stomach tightened, and a wave of vomit filled his gullet. He pursed his lips and swallowed it, however. "Y-Yes… F-F-Father…"

Oliver's grip eased upon his son's shoulder and he removed his hand completely a moment later. "And I would allow it." After he straightened his tie, he knocked on the cab's roof and instructed the driver to take them to his address first.

"Yes, sir," the driver replied from above. If he'd witnessed the confrontation, he was doing a good job at hiding his reaction.

Mr Maxwell eased himself away from his father and back along the seat. He retrieved his handkerchief as he went and pressed it against his nose. Fortunately, the bleeding had stopped, and he didn't think his nose was broken. A fleeting thought of asking Doctor Locke to look at it was hastily dismissed. She was a member of the Bow Street Society, after all.

"We are to dine at the Lillithwaite's tomorrow evening," Oliver Maxwell announced. "After dinner, you will formerly propose to Miss Lillithwaite and present to her this ring." Oliver took a small box from the interior pocket of his frockcoat and held it out to his son but withdrew it a moment later. "On second thoughts, I'll keep it until it's time to gift it to her." He slipped the box back into his pocket and looked to the rain-soaked street ahead. "The necessary financial arrangements for your marriage have already been agreed upon. The Lillithwaite's solicitor will therefore be in attendance, prior to our dining, for Mr Lillithwaite and me to look over the prepared legal documentation."

"P-Pardon me, F-Father, but… what arrangements are those?" Mr Maxwell enquired as he half-lifted his hand to shield his face.

Oliver Maxwell merely glared at him, however. "The *usual* ones." Seeing his son's expression still lacked understanding, he further explained, "A dowry has been offered by Mr Lillithwaite, that I've accepted on your behalf. Furthermore, it's been agreed that Miss Lillithwaite shall relinquish her entitlement to a yearly allowance, from her father's estate, to you, so you may ensure her future wellbeing.

"An insurance policy will also be taken out on your life to guard against Miss Lillithwaite outliving you and losing her financial support as a result. Naturally, any monies paid out by the policy will be put into trust and a yearly allowance given to your wife for the remainder of her days.

"In addition to this, your will—which the solicitor should have drawn up—will stipulate your estate should be placed into the same trust as the policy. To protect your wife from unscrupulous fortune hunters, I will act as executor for both your will and your wife's trust."

Mr Maxwell frowned. "And… and if Miss Lillithwaite should die before me…?"

218

"A will should have been drawn up for her, too," Oliver replied. "You'd inherit all her worldly possessions, and still have full entitlement to her allowance from her father's estate. Should you have had any children by then, it will be your decision as to how much—if anything—they receive by way of an inheritance." Oliver cast a disapproving glance over his son. "Since you can't be trusted with keeping a rat alive, let alone a child, a clause has been added to Miss Lillithwaite's will that stipulates her sister would take in the children." Oliver caught sight of his street's sign and gave instructions to the driver as to where the cab should stop. "The wills, life insurance policy, and legal agreements regarding the Lillithwaite estate shall all be signed by you both immediately after your wedding in two months' time."

"*Two* months?!" Mr Maxwell cried, stunned.

"Yes," Oliver replied as his eyes narrowed. "Miss Lillithwaite named the date this morning." As he felt the cab slow, he opened the doors and climbed out. "My carriage shall fetch you from your apartment at six o'clock tomorrow evening, Joseph." He turned and climbed the steps to his open front door where his butler waited. "*Don't* be late."

"Yes, Father…" Mr Maxwell replied as he sank into his seat.

EIGHTEEN

Mr Maxwell wiped his nose and winced. Bruising had blackened it, and the corners of his eyes, overnight. The cab ride to Gloucester Place, and warmth of the parlour's fire, had made his nose run something terrible. As he sniffed, he checked his handkerchief for bloodspots and returned it to his pocket.

"That's a canny bruise, lad," Mr Verity remarked from other side of the sofa. "How'd you do it?"

"I tripped up the stairs."

"Playing silly-beggars?"

"Pardon…?"

"Not looking where you was going."

"Oh! Yes—no. I meant no. It… it was dark, and I tripped," Mr Maxwell said as he felt his cheeks burn. "I-I'm very clumsy…" When the door opened and Mr Elmore, Jr. walked in, Mr Maxwell leapt to his feet and threw out his hand. "Mr Joseph Maxwell, sir. Y-You've already met Mr Verity, I believe…?"

"Yes," Mr Elmore, Jr. replied as he shook Mr Maxwell's hand. "Please, forgive the delay. My Mother saw you from her window and wanted to know who you were." He attempted to withdraw his hand, but Mr Maxwell's grip tightened. "Would you care to sit?"

"Hm?" Mr Maxwell enquired before he realised he still had his hand. "Oh!" He released it and ran his down his frock coat. "Apologies…"

"Have you come with news of my father's murderer?" Mr Elmore, Jr. enquired while he sat in the armchair, and Mr Maxwell retook his spot on the sofa.

Mr Verity caught the malign undertones of their host's bloodshot eyes. They were in stark contrast to the tired features which, in his opinion, had become more drawn since his last visit. He was further concerned by their host's tight grip of the chair arms. "We're making canny progress toward naming them, but we're not there yet."

"Then why are you here?" Mr Elmore, Jr. enquired in a brusque tone.

"Mr Maxwell?" Mr Verity said as he looked to him.

Mr Maxwell took out Miss Dexter's sketch of the doll's mechanism and passed it to Mr Verity who, in turn, passed it to their host.

"When your Da bought the doll, it had a loaded revolver in its hand," Mr Verity said. "That sketch shows you what was found when we took the doll apart. The wire pulled the trigger, while the cogs opened a hidden door on the case. It's why your Da was shot but the glass wasn't broken. The cogs were started by a key but—as we've been told—the doll wasn't sold to your Da with a key. We wanna know if your Da had one made."

Mr Elmore, Jr. stared at the sketch in silence, the subtle twitch of his eyelid a sign of chaotic emotion beneath. After a time, the malignancy dissolved from his eyes as tears rolled down his cheeks. He pressed a clenched hand against his pursed lips while he continued to stare at the sketch. A loud sob then broke through his composure, and he opened his hand to cover his eyes as his jaw and lips shook. "Forgive me." He dropped his hand to muffle his sobs. The sketch also dropped to his lap and Mr Verity retrieved it a moment later. "It's just…" Mr Elmore, Jr's words were strangled by violent, shuddering breaths.

"Take your time," Mr Verity reassured.

Mr Elmore, Jr. gave a deep nod followed by a curt one. He slouched in his armchair and unfolded his handkerchief to dry his eyes. "It's a relief," he gushed. "To *know* my father didn't commit suicide. *All* these months… he's lain in un-consecrated ground… his reputation *condemned* to that of a despicable sinner." He corrected his posture. "My mother can finally *rest*, assured my father will be waiting for her in the afterlife."

"I know folks in the church," Mr Verity said. "I will do what I can to have your father's remains given the burial they deserve."

"Thank you," Mr Elmore, Jr. replied. He dried his cheeks, wiped his nose, and released a deep breath. "You asked me about a key…" He folded his handkerchief over and put it away. "…Father had a locksmith call to the house on the day he died. They must've made the copy, if that's the only way the doll could've worked…?"

"We believe so," Mr Maxwell replied.

"Do you remember the locksmith's name?" Mr Verity enquired.

Mr Elmore, Jr. steadied himself with another deep breath. "I'm afraid not."

"The doll's new owner didn't buy it with a key either…" Mr Verity said and allowed his insinuation to dangle a moment. "Was that your mam's doing?"

Mr Elmore, Jr. nodded. "She thought my father's death was the result of a demonic possession, so had the doll blessed and its key smelted. In her mind, it was the only way to imprison the demon."

"And now…?" Mr Verity probed.

"She has very little of her mind left."

* * *

Mr Snyder heard the jangle of keys as their bunch was taken from a kitchen drawer. Its guardian—a sixty-year-old, round-faced man with beady, grey eyes behind brown-rimmed spectacles—kept it close as he sat beside him. The guardian picked a key, held it up, and said, "There, that's the professor's old study key." He dropped the key and shook the bunch. "The only key now…" He peered over his spectacles. "And the only spare when he was alive."

"Wot happened to his?" Mr Snyder enquired as he ignored the guardian's cynical tone.

"Buried with him."

Though he was the butler—and therefore the head of the household's servants—his attire wasn't conventional. A stained, cotton apron covered a coarse, dark-brown waistcoat, and creased, black trousers. The loose-fitted sleeves of his white shirt had dust marks on their elbows, while an ink stain soiled a cuff. His red nose, oversized frame, and breathlessness, when he returned the keys to their drawer, all hinted at a comfortable existence. The bottle of port, then brought back to the table, removed all doubt of such. "What is it you do for a living, Mr Snyder?"

"Cabman, Mr Lane," Mr Snyder replied and watched him pour two fingers' worth of port into their glasses. "For the Bow Street Society. Thanks." He accepted the second glass when it was offered and drank half. "How long you been workin' 'ere?"

"Forty years altogether," Mr Lane replied as he reached to top up Mr Snyder's glass.

"Nah, thanks." Mr Snyder covered the glass with his hand.

"Suit yourself," Mr Lane added Mr Snyder's measure to his own and drank half. "Before you ask—*if* you was going to ask—I'm the only one with that drawer's key. It was the same back then."

"You opened the study door when the professor woz done in, then?"

"No… I'm not sure how it was unlocked." He lifted his glass and pointed his little finger at Mr Snyder. "*If* it was locked at all." The remaining port was tossed down his throat, and the glass put down with a thud. "Women get eashily confused—*eshpeshially* when they're frightened. The door was probably unlocked, and they *pulled* rather than *pushed*."

"Is that what you told the coppers?"

"No… I shtayed tight lipped."

"Because you owned the gun what shot him?"

"No… becaushe talking to the police could've got me dishmisshed from thish place."

"You had a Webley Mark I revolver, what you got in the Royal Navy, yeah?"

"*That* wash shtolen." Mr Lane poured—and drank—yet more port. "I found the kitchen door open one morning…" He dangled his fingers and swept them away. "Flour *all* over the pantry floor. The gun wash kept in the flour to hide it from houshebreakers." He hiccupped. "I thought a delivery boy musht've taken it to impressh hish friends." He frowned. "The gun that killed the Professhor wash *never* found. How do *you* know it wash *that* gun— *my* gun?"

"We don't," Mr Snyder admitted. "But we got the gun 'cause it woz where the murderer left it: in the doll's hand."

Mr Lane's glazed eyes widened. While Mr Snyder took a sketch and photograph from his pocket, Mr Lane swayed a little in his chair. Once they were put on the table, he leaned over them and blinked his eyes into focus. Within moments he'd recognised them. "I never knew about that…" He swept them from the table with his arm and poured more port into his glass. "…And I *wouldn't* do that. Not even to a… a *dog*."

"We've never thought you would." Mr Snyder watched Mr Lane draw himself up and set the bottle down. "But puttin' in the wire took some time, ten minutes, or thereabouts. Woz there any time, before the professor died, when someone woz alone with the doll for that long?"

"No… Yesh… Perhapsh." Mr Lane emptied his glass. "I had the only shpare key… but the professhor was never as shtrict in keeping hish key shecure… He'd leave it on… hish deshk when working or out walking. Missh Watkins… his shecretary… she'd be in there alone if the professhor had a lecture…" He rested an arm upon the

224

table to lean upon on as he turned his head to look at Mr Snyder. "Really… anyone could've… walked in…" He swept his other hand up. "And *taken* it from the deshk"—he shook his head—"without Missh Watkins sheeing." He pointed at the wall behind them. "She sat facing the bloody wall, you shee. And the shtudy." He dropped his hand onto his thigh. "*That* wash unlocked in the morning… and left unlocked." His arm swept up and down. "*All* day."

"But, if the key went missin' like that on the day the professor died, he wouldn't of locked it when Miss Watkins woz sent out."

"Like I shaid, women get confushed."

Mr Snyder couldn't accept such an assumption. In his experience—particularly during his time as the Society's cabman—women were as sharp as men, if not sharper. "What do you know abou' an Adam Cosgrove, Mr Lane?"

"He wash Norman's bastard shon."

"He neva married the muvva?"

"No. *Bastard*, Mr Snyder. I shuppose I shouldn't expect shomeone like you to know about the Queen's English." He smirked. "Though your lot's made plenty of bastards to fill the workhoushes."

Mr Snyder's expression hardened, but Mr Lane was drunk, so he resisted the urge to stoop to the provocation.

"Norman shaid she died in childbirth." Mr Lane's drooping, glazed eyes searched for his glass. "The damage wash done when Norman took the child in. The professhor didn't like that, too much shcandal for him to shwallow."

"He disowned him?"

"Absholutely. And… do you know… even *then*… Norman wouldn't give the mother's name. My gueshs's Mrs Cosgrove—but you can't go around shaying such things… can you?"

Mr Snyder gave a weak smile. "Nah."

"Don't matter now." Mr Lane stood, swayed, and sat back down. "Shee yourself out… pleashe…" As he leaned on his arm, again, his eyes rolled, and his headed dropped onto the table with a thud.

After he checked he was still breathing—and just out with the drink—Mr Snyder sighed and patted his back. "It was good talkin' to you." The kitchen was in the basement, so he had to climb the servants' stairs to reach the back hallway. From there, one door led into the main entrance hall while another held Mr Snyder's intended destination. He knocked twice and, through the wood, said, "It's Mr Snyder, can I come in?"

* * *

"The Master won't like me talking to you without him home," Miss Daisy Price mumbled as she smoothed down her apron and skirts. Sat across from Miss Dexter in the servant's parlour, she glanced at the door and mantel clock. "I heard what he said to you before; he wanted you gone."

"We only want the truth," Miss Dexter reassured with a soft smile. "I promise we won't do, or say, anything which would put you in trouble with Mr Cosgrove."

"Are you sure your friends are happy to wait for you?" Miss Price enquired as she, again, glanced at the door and stood. "Maybe I should've put them into the master's parlour…"

Miss Dexter stood and stepped in front of her. "Mr Locke and his wife are very patient." As she felt her cheeks burn, she swallowed back her nervous and said, "Miss Price… two men have died, and we want to know why. I'm sure your master does, too."

Miss Price toyed with her apron but sat with Miss Dexter nonetheless. "He loved his uncle. It's unthinkable that he would've had anything to do with his death." She bowed her head. "Mr Lane took it hard when the professor

226

was murdered. He doesn't say so, but he blames himself. Says how he should've been at the study sooner… and how he could've caught the housebreaker when he climbed out the window."

Miss Dexter took the photograph and sketch from her sketchbook and considered if they might agitate Miss Price further. "Professor Cosgrove wasn't murdered by a thief…" she eventually said. "Someone in this house gave the professor's doll a revolver to shoot him with when he set the doll's mechanism in motion."

Miss Price took the offered photograph and sketch and studied them both for several minutes. "I'd often wondered if that's how it was done," she remarked when she gave them back. "It's clear as the nose on your face, isn't it? Mr Lane's gun going missing, and then the professor getting shot. The doll was holding the only gun they found in the room. Seemed to me like the only thing that made the most sense to me."

"I…" Miss Dexter said, stunned.

"The glass not being broke… I didn't know how that was done. But I know now, don't I?"

"Yes." Miss Dexter gave a weak smile. "Did you tell Inspector Lee of your thoughts?"

"I tried, but he told me not to meddle with things I didn't understand."

Miss Dexter frowned. "And Mr Lane?"

"He gave the same answer," Miss Price admitted. "He doesn't put much stock in women, Mr Lane."

Miss Dexter gave a soft, disapproving hum as she made some notes. "Was anyone alone with the doll in the days prior to the professor's murder?"

"Miss Watkins," Miss Price replied. "The professor, too, of course. Mrs Cosgrove may have asked me to fetch some paper from the professor's desk…"

"And the day of the professor's death?" Miss Dexter ventured. "We believe a Mr Bund paid the professor a visit and there was also an argument shortly before the shot was heard?"

"Between Miss Watkins and him?"

Miss Dexter looked at her. "She told us he'd asked her to leave, but that it was the professor and his wife who argued." She regarded Miss Price with obvious curiosity. "Why did you think it was the professor and his secretary arguing?"

"No reason," Miss Price replied with haste. "I must've been mistaken." She gave a curt nod. "Mr Bund did pay the professor a visit, yes. There was raised voices coming from the professor's study—I don't listen at doors, mind you!"

Miss Dexter offered a warm smile. "Heaven forbid! I'm quite certain you don't, Miss Price." She wrote some more notes. "Did you happen to hear what they were saying though? Perhaps, the argument between the professor and his wife?"

Miss Price glanced at the door for a third time but lowered her voice as she replied, "I *wasn't* listening, *but* I did hear talk of a debt the professor owed Mr Bund. The thing was, it wasn't the professor's debt, but Mr Ned Cosgrove's. According to what I heard, he'd gone to Mr Bund, signed for a loan, but used the professor's name. You could've knocked me over with a feather when I heard that!" She frowned. "When I overheard it in passing, that is."

"Yes, of course."

"Mr Bund still wanted the professor to pay, saying it was him who owed the monies because it was his name on the paper." Miss Price listened a moment when she thought she heard someone outside. Satisfied she hadn't, she lowered her voice again and continued, "The professor refused and that's when Mr Bund said he'd be back the next day to collect what was owed him." She lifted her hand. "*Then*, later, the professor had a *frightful* argument with his wife. I was only walking by, mind you—and Miss

228

Watkins was lurking about besides. She liked to lurk, that one. Her eyes lurked, too. Anyway, I only heard the last few words from Mrs Cosgrove. She told the professor it was impossible, because she'd not known Mr Norman Cosgrove all those years ago."

Miss Dexter's eyes widened. "What do you think she meant by that?"

"The professor must've found out about her and Mr Norman, mustn't he?" Miss Price enquired in return. "We all knew about it, of course. *None* of us dared to say our opinion out loud."

"Did the professor and his wife often argue?"

"Daily," Miss Price replied with a nod.

Before Miss Dexter could enquire further though, someone knocked on the door.

"It's the Master," Miss Price said as she leapt to her feet.

"It's Mr Snyder, can I come in?"

"Yes, Sam," Miss Dexter replied, relieved, as she stood, too.

Mr Snyder stepped into the room and said, "Mr Lane felt tired so 'e's havin' a sleep." When Miss Price's jaw tightened, he knew she'd understood the reality behind his words.

"Excuse me, I should see that he's comfortable," Miss Price mumbled as she hurried out the room.

"You done 'ere, then?" he enquired when Miss Price had gone.

"Yes, I believe so," Miss Dexter replied as she gathered up her notebook, sketch, and photograph and returned them to her satchel. "Miss Price had some very interesting things to tell me. Shall we return to the Lockes?" She followed Mr Snyder into the back hallway. "I'm sure Miss Trent would like to hear what I have to say as soon as possible."

"Yeah, let's go," Mr Snyder replied as he held open the main entrance hall's door for her.

* * *

Doctor Locke opened the library door ajar to watch Miss Price lead Miss Dexter into the back stairwell. "They're gone," she said as she closed the door and returned to her husband.

Mr Locke had taken a seat the moment the maid had shown them into the room. His fair complexion was once more covered by a fine layer of lead-based powder, while the scratches on his hands were concealed under black, leather gloves. Though a slight tremble remained, he was rid of the fever—to Miss Dexter's relief when they'd met earlier. Nonetheless, he endured a minor headache brought on by disturbed sleep. When his wife approached, he had his nose's bridge pinched between his thumb and forefinger.

"Are you quite certain you are strong enough for this, darling?"

"Yes," Mr Locke replied. He dropped his hand and used the chair's arms to push himself to his feet. The velvet roll was then taken from his frock coat and unfurled upon the desk. "Watch the hallway, will you?"

"I heard your yells last night," Doctor Locke remarked as she opened the door ajar and peered out. "You need rest, not Bow Street Society assignments."

"I am enduring, darling," Mr Locke said and slid a pick from the roll. Once he'd compared it to the drawer's lock, he crouched before the desk, and shifted his weight to ensure daylight illuminated the keyhole. "Besides, I have made a commitment, and I must honour it." The pick was slipped into the lock, and he turned his head to listen to the minute clicks. His fingers, meanwhile, detected the small fluctuations in pressure as he manipulated the lock until the pick was driven home. "*Voila.*" He removed the pick, pulled the drawer open, and stood to start his search of its contents. "It is not here…" he said as he removed document after document but found no trace of the professor's will.

"Are you certain?" Doctor Locke enquired as she hurried to join him. Looking over his shoulder, she saw the—now empty—drawer and sighed. "What do we do now?"

"Ned Cosgrove was adamant we should not access this drawer," Mr Locke said and sat. He stared at the drawer for several moments before he lifted it and removed it from its runners. As he turned it over, an unsealed envelope was revealed to be attached to its underside.

"What is it?" Doctor Locke enquired as she watched her husband slide his fingers into the envelope and ease a folded piece of paper out.

The door then opened behind her and she turned to block what Mr Locke was doing from view. While he hurried to insert the drawer and return its contents, she breathed a loud sigh of relief. "You gave us quite a start."

"Sorry," Mr Snyder replied as he closed the door behind Miss Dexter. "Find anythin'?"

"Yes." Mr Locke closed the drawer. As he plucked his pick from the lock and returned it to the velvet roll, he said, "We must return to Bow Street at once."

NINETEEN

"This envelope was attached to the underside of Mr Ned Cosgrove's desk drawer," Mr Locke began as he tossed the item into the middle of the table. When Mr Elliott picked it up and removed its contents, Mr Locke continued, "I think you shall what it contains most intriguing."

Mr Elliott unfolded the piece of paper and read what was written upon it. "I don't understand…" Mr Elliott lowered the document to meet Mr Locke's gaze. "This is Professor Benjamin Cosgrove's Last Will & Testament, but it corroborates everything Ned Cosgrove told us. Why hide it?" Mr Elliott's eyes darted back to the document. "Unless…"

"Unless…?" Mr Locke exhaled his tobacco smoke away from the others.

"It's the genuine will," Mr Elliott replied.

"It is dated a month prior to the professor's death," Mr Locke said and took a second deep pull from his cigarette. His fingers trembled as he flicked its ash into a glass ashtray. "We cannot rely upon its legitimacy, however, due to the simple reason it *was* hidden. If another was written—possibly by Ned Cosgrove himself—it would provide him with a strong motive for murder."

"Mr Bund's loan was also given to Ned Cosgrove," Miss Dexter interjected. "But in the professor's name. Miss Price said it was why the professor refused to pay the debt."

"And if Ned's got more debts…" Mr Snyder said. "He'd wanna get monies fast."

"We can't ignore the possibility the professor may have written another will though," Mr Elliott said. "Norman and Coral Cosgrove were having an illicit affair behind the professor's back. Norman had also recognised his son, despite his illegitimacy. Both reasons could've given the professor ample motivation for disinheriting his wife and nephew."

"But not Miss Watkins," Doctor Locke pointed out. "She loses her legacy in the new will, too."

"That has yet to be substantiated," Mr Elliott replied.

"Miss Price thought I spoke of the professor and Miss Watkins when I asked about an argument," Miss Dexter said. "I didn't think of this at the time, but Miss Price admitted the professor and his wife argued daily. If so, Miss Price had even less reason for assuming I was speaking of Miss Watkins." Miss Dexter's eyes then widened as her hand went to her chest. "*Wait*! Sam, do you recall?" She looked to Mr Snyder who, with a shrug of his shoulder, shook his head. "Miss Watkins. She said the professor had only ever asked her to leave once before. But she didn't say *when* it had been or *why*. She could've argued recently with the professor and that is why Miss Price thought it was them she'd overheard."

"It gives credence to the possibility Professor had disinherited Miss Watkins, too," Mr Locke remarked.

"Disinheriting her on the basis of a disagreement, though?" Doctor Locke enquired. "An overreaction, wouldn't you say, Mr Elliott?"

"Stranger things have happened in court," Mr Elliott replied in his usual monotone. "I would recommend another conversation with Miss Watkins to ask her about the argument Miss Price overheard."

"Me, Miss Dexter, and Mr Verity'll do that in the mornin'," Mr Snyder said. "If the professor woz the one what wrote the will, why'd 'e wanna hide it?"

"To prevent Miss Watkins seeing it, perhaps?" Doctor Locke suggested.

"We'll ask her abou' it," Mr Snyder replied.

"Remind me of the will's contents, please, Mr Elliott?" Mr Locke requested. His memory had failed him, despite having read the will at the time of its discovery and during the carriage ride to Bow Street.

Mr Elliott cleared his throat and read it aloud, "The Last Will & Testament of Professor Benjamin Cosgrove. I, Professor Benjamin Cosgrove, in healthy body and sound of mind, do bequeath a legacy of five hundred pounds to my loyal butler, Mr Ian Lane. To my equally loyal parlour maid, Miss Daisy Price, I bequeath a legacy of two hundred pounds.

"To Miss Henrietta Watkins, my personal secretary of many years, I leave these words: your unerring commitment, impeccable propriety, and unconditional devotion to my work never went unnoticed. With your clerical support, a great number of my academic ambitions were achieved. No monetary amount could ever reflect the place your loyal servitude and friendship hold in my heart.

"In contrast, I leave my false wife, Mrs Coral Cosgrove, an allowance of five hundred pounds to be given annually until the day of her passing. Propriety—and an irrational sense of duty—have compelled me to make this gift. The following conditions are attached to it, however: Mrs Coral Cosgrove must not contest this will, and news of her scandalous behaviour with my nephew, Norman, mustn't be made public. Provided these conditions are agreed upon and met, the first payment will be made a month after my passing.

"To my co-betrayer, Norman Cosgrove, I bequeath a lifetime of misery and destitution befitting one as abhorrent as he.

"I bequeath the remainder of my estate—sans solicitor, burial, and clerical fees—to my only other living relative, Mr Ned Cosgrove." Mr Elliott looked to the bottom of the will. "Mr Carlton Forbes, solicitor, is named as the will's executor and primary witness. A Mr Stephen Spalding is named as the secondary witness. I shall attempt to make enquiries with Mr Forbes." He looked to

234

Miss Trent. "I can't guarantee he'll tell me anything, especially if Mr Ned Cosgrove has forewarned him about the Society's investigation."

Setting the will aside, Mr Elliott took a folded piece of paper from his notebook and placed it in the table's centre. "This is Norman Cosgrove's burial record. As you can see, he was interred on the twenty-ninth of April, 1895. While it's questionable, the possibility of the parish clerk receiving a monetary incentive to falsify the record can't be dismissed beyond reasonable doubt." Mr Elliott, again, turned his attention to Miss Trent. "Where is Mr Maxwell? Was he able to find an obituary in the Gazette's records?"

"He has a prior dinner engagement," Miss Trent replied but paused as she recalled the bruising around his eye. His explanation of falling up the stairs was typical of his clumsiness. Yet, she'd never known a flat step to cause bruising all around the eye. Even its edge would've only affected the skin below. "He and Mr Verity gave their findings earlier. Unfortunately, Mr Maxwell's apprentice was unable to locate Norman Cosgrove's obituary, either in 1895 or during the four years prior. It doesn't mean there isn't one for him elsewhere, of course."

Miss Dexter had bowed her head at the mention of Mr Maxwell. Mr Snyder's large hand upon hers though, coaxed a weak smile. She rested her hand upon his, therefore, as she enquired, "Has the advertisement for Mr Adam Cosgrove been placed, Miss Trent?"

"Yes, it should be printed in tomorrow morning's edition," Miss Trent replied. The tension between Miss Dexter, Mr Maxwell, and Mr Snyder was problematic but, thus far, hadn't been detrimental to the Society's investigations. The sadness felt by Miss Dexter was blatant, however. Deciding she didn't need to hear of Mr Maxwell's black eye—or her misgivings over its alleged origins—Miss Trent turned her attention to Mr Elliott and enquired, "Have you had any success tracing his birth records?"

Mr Elliott shook his head. "Unfortunately not. I found his baptism record but only Norman Cosgrove was recorded as being present. As expected, I was prohibited from seeing the record held at Somerset House. If the advertisement entices Adam Cosgrove to contact us, I'd like him to accompany me back to Somerset House and make the request for his birth records in person—if he doesn't already know who his mother is, that is."

"Did Mr Maxwell and Mr Verity discover if a copy of the doll's key was made by Mr Elmore, senior?" Mr Locke enquired.

Miss Trent consulted her earlier notes. "They did. The key was smelted prior to the doll being sold at auction, however. The doll was also blessed. Mr Elmore's widow believed a demon had possessed it."

Mr Elliott stifled a sigh.

"Torkin' abou' keys," Mr Snyder began. "Mr Lane, the butler, told me the professor's study key woz buried with him but, when he woz alive, the professor would leave it out on his desk, even when he wozn't there. The only spare, Mr Lane told me, woz kept locked in a drawer in the kitchen. That's where the spare is now." Mr Snyder scratched his bearded chin. "Dunno if we should tork to Miss Watkins abou' that again, or not…?"

"You should enquire if a locksmith was hired in the days preceding the professor's death, certainly," Mr Locke replied. "Locksmiths are prohibited from crafting a key from an impression. They must instead rely upon having the lock brought to them or being permitted to enter the premises where the lock is to test one of their keys. If such a visit had been arranged by someone who had no place in doing so, it would have undoubtedly caused suspicion. If, on the other hand, Mrs Cosgrove, a nephew, or even Miss Watkins informed the locksmith they were having the key made under instruction from the

236

lock's owner—in this case, the professor—while in the house, the locksmith would have little cause to doubt their story. Having a copy of the study key would have lengthened the amount of time our murderer could have spent alone with the doll to implement the wire and revolver. It would have been a mere matter of locking the door until their task was complete and, if anyone attempted to gain access, they could have put the locked door down to a slip of the mind." He crushed out his cigarette but kept his gaze upon his trembling hand. "Mrs Cosgrove may therefore recall if a locksmith came to the house, too. I shall visit upon her tomorrow."

"*We* shall visit upon her," Doctor Locke interjected with a hard edge to her tone.

"As you wish," Mr Locke replied with a smile and a playful twinkle in his eyes. Doctor Locke folded her arms across her chest and pursed her lips, however. "If she and Miss Watkins cannot assist us, I may converse with an acquaintance of mine in the Whitechapel Road."

"You should also question Mrs Cosgrove further over Adam Cosgrove's parentage," Mr Elliott said.

"And why is that?" Mr Locke enquired, intrigued. "She told us all she knew during our last visit."

"We gotta be sure she's not Adam's muvva," Mr Snyder interjected.

Mr Locke scoffed. His wife's brow lofted but she otherwise remained silent.

"Begging your pardon, Mr Snyder, but it is a ludicrous idea and one I shan't be putting to her," Mr Locke rebuked as he slid his hand beneath the table.

"You're just sayin' that 'cause you know her from before," Mr Snyder said. "She could've told you a pack of lies."

"My previous acquaintance with Mrs Cosgrove is irrelevant," Mr Locke retorted.

"But why would Norman Cosgrove care for her so and refuse to tell her the truth?" Miss Dexter pressed, her voice and eyes sympathetic.

"Undoubtedly to protect her," Mr Locke replied.

"Arguing about it gets us nowhere," Miss Trent said, firmly. "Mr Locke, if you're unable to set aside your personal feelings then I'll ask another to accompany your wife."

Mr Locke's eyes glanced to Miss Dexter as he parted his lips to toss a cruel rebuttal at Miss Trent. Staying his anger at the last second though, he swallowed it back and said, "As you wish, *Miss Trent.*" He pulled on his gloves' cuffs and rubbed the back of his hand. "I shall enquire after it when I see her."

"Thank you," Miss Trent replied. "Mr Snyder, Miss Dexter, I'll expect your return at eight o'clock tonight, so you may travel to the Hampstead Heath Flagstaff with Mr Skinner."

When the two Bow Streeters gave their agreement, Mr Locke said, "Well, if that is to be all, my wife and I have prior engagements of our own to attend to." He rose to his feet and took Doctor Locke's arm when she joined him. "Good evening to you all."

No sooner had he collected his hat and walking cane from the stand in the hallway though, did Mr Locke hear voices upon the front porch. With a lofted brow, he slipped his arm free, and pushed aside the curtain with his cane's handle to peer out. "Miss Trent!" he called as he turned upon his heel to stride back into the meeting room. "Miss Trent," he repeated with a mild bow of his head and a twinkle in his eyes. "I would suggest you go outside. It would appear the circus has come to town."

Miss Trent's jaw tightened but she, nevertheless, strode past Mr Locke to open the front door.

"And I would recommend everyone else leaves by the back door," Mr Locke suggested as he pointed his cane in that direction.

Miss Trent, meanwhile, took a step back as she not only found Inspector Gideon Lee on the porch, but half of Fleet Street, it seemed. The Kensington Division inspector had his back to her when she'd first opened the door. Upon hearing her movement though, he glanced over his shoulder and smiled. Miss Trent demanded, "*What* is going on—?"

"And here is the clerk of the Bow Street Society, Miss Rebecca Trent," Inspector Lee interrupted as he stepped aside to allow the crowd of journalists to see her. A cacophony of yelled questions erupted from the forty-odd men squeezed onto the porch and steps. Each held a notebook, each cried her name, and each had a wild look in their eyes that came from the relentless pursuit of a sensational story. "As I was saying, gentlemen," Lee continued as he lifted his voice over the din. When the noise subsided, he continued, "I'd like to thank you all for coming at such short notice. Let it not be said the police are unwilling to cooperate with the British press. Some of you already know me. For those of you who don't, my name is Gideon Lee—that's G-I-D-E-O-N L-E-E. I'm the inspector at the Kensington, or T, division of the Metropolitan Police. I'd like to announce that new evidence has come to light regarding the unsolved murder of Professor Benjamin Cosgrove in October of 1890. I'm not at liberty to comment further on what this evidence is. What I *will* tell you is the Bow Street Society is assisting me with my ongoing enquiries into the case."

Miss Trent's eyes narrowed, and she stepped out onto the porch with a hand upon her hip. "*Inspector* Lee, you have no *right* to invite the journalistic press to our door without consulting me—"

"Do you deny the claim, then, Miss Trent?" Mr Baldwin from the *Gaslight Gazette* called.

"Are you calling the inspector a liar, Miss Trent?" a second journalist demanded.

"Doesn't the Society stand for justice, Miss Trent?" a third journalist added.

"*Enough*," Miss Trent commanded. She turned to the crowd and held her head high. "The Bow Street Society does everything within its power to assist the police, and to ensure its clients receive the justice they deserve. Thank you."

"Who's the Society's client, Miss Trent?" Mr Baldwin enquired. "Is it the professor's widow, or his nephew?"

"Our clients' identities are confidential," Miss Trent replied. "Please come in, *Inspector.*" She strode back inside and held the door open for him.

"Do you know, Inspector?" Mr Baldwin called.

Lee grinned. "But of course." As he leaned upon his walking cane, he lifted his other hand to wave over some uniformed constables gathered on the other side of the road. When they followed his line of sight, and saw the constables approach, the journalists dispersed. "You'll receive my full statement in due course, gentlemen." Lee stepped over the threshold and, while Miss Trent closed the door, went into the meeting room. At finding it empty, he commented. "I thought I saw Mr Percy Locke's carriage outside. I was hoping to get his autograph."

"He's left, along with everyone else," Miss Trent said as she put both hands upon her hips. "And I'm entitled to an explanation as to why you invited half of Fleet Street here, simply to take credit for the Bow Street Society's investigation."

"Miss Trent, *please*," Lee replied, disgusted. "It was *never* the Society's investigation." As he walked past the stairs, toward the first door on the left, Miss Trent headed him off. A soft hum sounded in his throat as his mouth's corner momentarily lifted. "In fact, the Society is trespassing on police property." He strolled back to the stairs and scrutinised the hallway. "But, you're lucky I'm a pragmatic man."

The sound of several violent bangs upon the front door tore through Lee's words, however. Inspector Woolfe's unmistakeable voice then followed, "*Open up*! I know you're in there!"

With a frustrated sigh, Miss Trent returned to the front door—only to feel Lee's hand brush against her shoulder. "Allow me," he said and stepped past her to slide back the bolt and open the door. His eyes met Woolfe's jaw yet, despite the height disparity, he extended his hand and said, "Inspector Caleb Woolfe, I presume? Inspector Gideon Lee of T Division."

"I know who you are," Woolfe growled and noticed Miss Trent behind. "What I want to know is why you're here. Holborn's *my* patch."

"And you're welcome to it," Lee replied as he left his empty hand extended. "The Bow Street Society is assisting me with my enquiries into the unsolved murder of Professor Cosgrove."

"What did you need the vultures for, then?" Woolfe enquired.

"Vultures…?" Lee glanced back at Miss Trent. "I assume you refer to the honourable members of the journalistic press?" Lee smiled. "It's important for the police to be seen to be in control of its investigations."

The tension in Woolfe's eyes and shoulders disappeared in an instant. He took Lee's hand and, with a yellow-teeth-stained grin, replied, "I couldn't agree more, Inspector." When he saw Miss Trent scowl, he chuckled. "I'd best be getting back to the station, but it was good meeting you, Lee." He released his hand and opened the door. "Until next time, Miss Trent."

Miss Trent prayed for Woolfe to trip over the step on his way out. Unfortunately, she had no such luck.

"Inspector Conway has been keeping me informed of your latest discoveries," Lee remarked as he, too, stepped out onto the porch once Woolfe was gone. "I will expect an invitation when your group is ready to confront the murderer, however. Goodbye, Miss Trent."

When he pulled the door closed, Miss Trent caught it and followed him outside. She watched him descend the steps and climb into his carriage.

"Home, please," Lee told the driver and looked up at the porch. For a moment, the arrogance slipped from his countenance when he saw a defiant Miss Trent staring back at him. Maintaining eye contact—but expecting her to break it the moment she knew he'd caught her—Lee's lips pursed together when he realised she had no intention of doing so.

"Goodbye. Inspector," she called.

The vexation within Lee's dark-blue hues intensified as he looked away to knock upon the carriage roof.

As the vehicle then started its journey from Bow Street, Miss Trent couldn't help but smirk in triumph. "Never underestimate someone from the Bow Street Society, Inspector," she said and broadened her smile as she went back inside.

TWENTY

*"What do you mean, 'the engagement is over',
Henry? Mrs Fairfax has already bought ten inches of lace
for Georgie's veil. Then there's the time I spent choosing
appropriate hymns for the ceremony. You'd be surprised
how many were too long, or too short, and I don't mind
saying it put my work back a day or two."*

*"I don't want to hear another word about it. The
proposal has been withdrawn. More importantly, our
financial burden is eased until another suitor comes
along."*

*"But, Henry, Mr Maxwell promised to marry
her—"*

Miss Dexter was torn from her thoughts by a
sudden bump in the road that lifted her from her seat. She
threw out her hand and was relieved when Mr Snyder's
took it. She'd no concept of how long they'd been
travelling for. The cloth, that she'd been ordered to wear
by their mysterious courier, prevented her seeing anything
of the carriage's surrounds. Granted, Mr Snyder could've
recognised a mile stone, public house, or crossroads. To
Miss Dexter, all these things would've looked alike in the
darkness. Naturally, she couldn't speak for Mr Skinner.

The Irishman had spoken of his employment as a
protector of… Miss Dexter frowned, *who was it, again?* A
lady, she thought. Yes, that was it. The wife of the captain
Mr Skinner had sailed under during his time in Her
Majesty's Royal Navy. She shivered as she recalled the
preparation of his revolver beneath the Flagstaff. *Would
such a weapon be required tonight?* She wondered. Mr
Snyder hadn't wanted her to come with them. *But why
should I not, simply because I'm a woman?*

"If it was up to me…" Mr Maxwell's voice echoed
within her mind.

"But Henry, Mr Maxwell promised to marry her! He must be took to a judge and made to give an explanation."

"Keep your voice down, or she'll hear you. I told his father we wouldn't involve the courts when I took his money." Miss Dexter's stomach lurched as she replayed the conversation between her parents. She then realised the carriage had stopped. She held her breath and listened for what felt like an eternity. When all she could hear was the wind as it swept through the trees, she enquired, "Sam?"

"I'm 'ere," he replied beside her.

The mere sound of his voice was proof of how foolish her fear was. If *only* she could remove this blindfold—

A gust of cold wind flew into her face, as a thin hand grabbed her arm and tore her from Mr Snyder's side. Startled, she felt air beneath one foot and then gravel beneath the other. "Sam!"

"I'm 'ere!" Mr Snyder yelled in the distance.

"Where are we going?!" Miss Dexter cried as a second, thin hand gripped her other arm and pushed her forward. She stumbled for the first few steps but was then permitted to find her footing by her 'guide'. When she had, she was driven forward by their strength alone. Over the din of the fierce gale, she thought she heard Mr Skinner's Irish drawl. She was unable to distinguish what was said, however.

Miss Dexter felt her toe catch upon a step and, again, she stumbled. This time her 'guide' caught her. They then wrapped their arm around her waist and led her up the remainder of the steep flight.

A burst of warm air struck her next, as many footsteps echoed all around. Her 'guide' released her waist to reinstate their grip upon her arms before she was driven forward again. A plethora of scents and sounds bombarded her senses as her feet shuffled to keep pace.

Then, all at once, the force at her back disappeared, the hands fell away, and a hush descended. She held her breath as she strained to hear anything other than her rapid heartbeat.

"Miss Dexter?" Mr Snyder's voice enquired beside her.

"*Sam*?" she whispered as her heart leapt at the sound.

"Yeah," Mr Snyder said. "I think we can take the blindfolds off now."

"Thank God fer dat," Mr Skinner remarked. "I were startin' to get dizzy."

Miss Dexter untied her blindfold. As she pulled it away, vibrant firelight struck her eyes and caused coloured dots to appear before her vision. She therefore looked at the less offensive wallpaper until her vision adjusted, at which point she realised where they were. She scanned the room and, upon seeing a gentleman stood by the fire, moved closer to Mr Snyder.

"Good evening, Mr Snyder," the gentleman said. "Miss Dexter, Mr Skinner. I was informed of your accompaniment. While I'm disappointed by the Society's indiscretion as far as its members are concerned, I'm grateful for the absence of a certain policeman. Please." He indicated the sofa while he took the armchair. "Sit and tell me of your news."

Miss Dexter looked to Mr Snyder with her hand upon his arm. When he approached the sofa and sat, she followed with Mr Skinner at the rear. While she sat on Mr Snyder's right, he sat on his left, closest to their host.

"Mr Partridge," Mr Snyder began. "What your dinner guest told you woz right. Two blokes have been done in by the doll, but not 'cause of a curse. Miss Dexter…?"

Miss Dexter swallowed hard but—feeling her anxiety ease once she knew their host and client were one and the same—she took the sketch of the doll's mechanism from her satchel.

"Someone in the Cosgrove house put a gun in the doll's hand," Mr Snyder went on while Mr Partridge examined the sketch. "And some wire 'round the cogs inside. When the first owner—Professor Benjamin Cosgrove—turned the key, the cogs started workin' and pullin' at the wire."

"The wire then pulled the trigga," Mr Skinner said. "The gun's a Webley Mark I and, right now, we think it were the Cosgrove's butler's. See, them gun's given to men in the Royal Navy. The butler were in the Navy, like me."

Mr Partridge looked from the sketch to Mr Skinner's iron hand as it lay upon his thigh. Chewing his tongue, Mr Partridge diverted his gaze back to the sketch. "And the second owner…? He died in the same way, I presume."

"Yes," Miss Dexter replied.

"The wire and gun have now been removed…?" Mr Partridge enquired as he set the sketch down upon his lap and glanced along the line of Bow Streeters.

"Yeah," Mr Skinner replied.

"Then I'll arrange to have the doll collected in the morning," Mr Partridge said. He passed the sketch back to Miss Dexter and stood. When he took a deep breath and released it, he smiled. "I'd like to thank you and your Society for getting to the bottom of this. Miss Trent shall receive a generous payment for your efforts. If you would put your blindfolds back on, I'll arrange for you to be taken back to your cab, Mr Snyder—"

"Begging your pardon, sir," Miss Dexter began. When Mr Partridge looked to her, she stood and continued, "We still don't know who put the revolver, or wire, into the doll and there is still the question of why the revolver was fired, here, in an empty room." She looked around. "If

246

I could see where the doll was kept, I could take some photographs and make some sketches—"

"Absolutely not," Mr Partridge interrupted. "The Bow Street Society was asked to ensure the doll was safe enough to send to America for valuation. You have done that. As far as we're concerned, the identity of the murderer is a matter for the police."

"*We*?" Mr Skinner challenged.

"Me," Mr Partridge replied. "As far as *I'm* concerned."

"Maybe you woz thinkin' of the bloke you're workin' for?" Mr Snyder enquired as he, too, stood. Mr Skinner followed and moved behind Mr Partridge.

"I-I don't know what you're talking about," Mr Partridge replied as he glanced over his shoulder at the scarred Irishman.

"What's behind the sheets?" Mr Skinner enquired and nodded toward the covered squares hanging on the walls.

"Whomever asked you to hire us may have a connection to the Cosgrove and Elmore murders, Mr Partridge," Miss Dexter said, her expression and voice sympathetic. "We *must* speak with them."

"Out of the question!" Mr Partridge exclaimed.

"You *are* workin' for someone, then?" Mr Snyder enquired.

Mr Partridge blinked and glanced again at Mr Skinner. "Y-You're putting words into my mouth." He looked between Mr Snyder and Miss Dexter. "Please, you've done what has been asked. Let us leave it at that."

"We can't do that," Mr Snyder replied. "The Society's about justice for *all*, includin' those who've been murdered. All we wanna do is tork to 'em. Then we'll know they had nowt to do with those blokes' deaths."

"We're not goin' 'til we see 'im," Mr Skinner replied as he moved back to the sofa and sat. Miss Dexter and Mr Snyder joined him, each with an expression as determined as his.

Mr Partridge's eyes were wide, while small beads of sweat had appeared on his brow and chin. "More money… is that it? I-I can request an increase in your payment, would that satisfy you?"

Miss Dexter frowned. "We're not blackmailers, sir. It's as Mr Snyder said. The Bow Street Society believes in justice by all and for all." She looked from Mr Snyder, to Mr Skinner, and back to Mr Partridge. "You, and your employer, may be assured we'll act with the utmost discretion."

Mr Partridge dabbed at his temple with his handkerchief while he considered her words. He then nodded as he slipped the damp handkerchief into his pocket. "Very well… I shall put forth your request. If it's refused, do I have your word you'll leave?"

"If we believe you," Mr Skinner replied.

"You've got our words as Bow Street Society members, sir," Miss Dexter said with a firm tone. Seemingly satisfied with this response, Mr Partridge braced his shoulders and left.

As they waited, Miss Dexter twisted the excess material of her skirts between her fingers, Mr Skinner checked the revolver in his hip holster, and Mr Snyder stayed perched on the sofa's edge. The longer they sat, the more curious Miss Dexter became about the paintings. Unable to resist any longer, she stood, and lifted the sheet over the painting above the fireplace. Seeing its plaque first, she read the name. "Oh, my *goodness*!" She dropped the sheet to tell the others. The sight of Mr Partridge in the doorway swept her voice from her throat, however.

"Mr Snyder… Mr Skinner," Mr Partridge said as he waited for one Bow Streeter to stand before saying the name of the next. "Miss Dexter… Allow me to introduce His Lordship, Lord Michael Weeks." Mr Partridge stepped aside as a rugged-looking man, with hair as black as coal and eyes as green as Jade, entered the room.

* * *

"It has already been decided…" Miss Dexter's voice pleaded. A vision of her in Mr Snyder's cab, as she cowered against the onslaught of an unforgiving storm, formed. Then… a masked man materialised in the road. The horse was startled… it attempted to rear up but bolted instead. Rolling… suddenly the world was rolling, and Mr Snyder's cab collided with a tree. "Joseph…" she called, her sweet complexion stained with dirt as her delicate hand reached out from the crushed remains—

"Joseph," Oliver Maxwell growled from across the room. "Don't you agree Miss Lillithwaite is an accomplished pianist?"

Mr Joseph Maxwell realised the melody had ended. Rain beat against the window at his back, while a fire crackled in the hearth. The room was otherwise silent as everyone awaited his response. Aside from Oliver Maxwell, Mr Roger Lillithwaite was also present with his daughter. Miss Poppy Lillithwaite sat at the upright piano in the corner. She was around the same height as him but boasted a stockier frame. The addition of a corset had done little to flatter her broad shoulders, full waist, and wide hips, though. Her face was masculinised by an angular brow, oversized nose, and cleft chin. "Cursed with a pleasant personality," was how her father had described her when she and Joseph had first met. Joseph thought it an apt description, but for different reasons. She was quiet, nervous, and obeyed her patriarch without question. She reminded Joseph of himself, and how 'pleasant' was so easily interchanged with 'compliant'. The fact she was thirty-three—twelve years older than Joseph—hadn't altered her complacency either.

"Very accomplished," Joseph replied as he felt his palms moisten under his father's scowl. As Oliver Maxwell then made a remark to Roger Lillithwaite about how important it was for women to have an emotional outlet, Joseph gave Poppy a polite smile.

"The piano is Poppy's only accomplishment, unfortunately," Roger Lillithwaite replied. "Her fingers are two stubby for needlework, and her water colouring leaves a lot to be desired."

"A wife should only be permitted one outlet, anyway," Oliver Maxwell remarked. "If her emotions are exercised too freely, she may become hysterical." He took a sip of wine. "I trust the solicitor has brought the necessary documentation for us to examine this evening?"

"He has," Roger Lillithwaite replied with a nod. A man of surprising height for his plump build—at least six feet tall—his bent knees almost reached his shoulders while he sat upon the sofa's edge. While the cut of his frockcoat, and quality of his waistcoat's fabric, was inferior compared to Oliver Maxwell's, Roger's clothes were far from a pauper's. Indeed, the silk handkerchief and gold watch chain he wore denoted his wealth better than a cravat or shirt ever could. "They're in my study. Shall we look them over together? I have some vintage port I think you may enjoy, too."

"An excellent idea," Oliver Maxwell replied as he stood and pressed a small box into his son's hand. All the while he kept his gaze upon Roger Lillithwaite who—having hauled himself from the sofa—put his hand on Oliver's back to guide him from the room.

Joseph had recognised the box and fumbled to grasp it in his lap. Poppy Lillithwaite smiled upon seeing his clumsiness but refrained from speaking until their fathers had left them. "Did you really like my piano playing?" she enquired. Her impish voice was in stark contrast to her appearance.

"Yes, it was very…" Joseph frowned. "…Pleasant."

"Good. I've been practising particularly hard." She dropped her gaze to the box. "Is there something… you'd like to ask me, Mr Maxwell?"

"Pardon?" Mr Maxwell enquired, confused. As he followed her gaze to the box, his eyes widened. "Oh! Yes, I do… Erm, let me see…" He fetched a cushion from the sofa and knelt upon it at her feet. When he opened the box and looked up at her though, he saw Miss Dexter looking back. His voice at once deserted him. With a rapid series of blinks, he managed to pull back Miss Lillithwaite's strong features into his vision. Nonetheless his heart sank at the realisation she wasn't who he wanted. His imaginings of a hurt Miss Dexter, beneath the wreckage of Mr Snyder's cab, also returned.

"Joseph…" she called.

"The expectation is you'll formerly propose to her tonight, and present her with this ring," Oliver Maxwell's stern voice explained. Joseph was back in the hansom cab with his father, on their way to the Lillithwaite residence. "Do not shame me by forgetting. Miss Lillithwaite's advancing years oblige her to accept any proposal put to her. Her father's blessing, and generous dowry, obliges you to ask for her hand."

"Mr Maxwell…?" Miss Lillithwaite enquired as the playful nature of her voice was subdued by her concern.

"Yes?"

"You've been kneeling there for a while."

"Have I?" Joseph gave a weak smile. "…I suppose I have…" He bowed his head to look upon the ring. "Miss Lillithwaite, I…" *How can I tell her?* He thought.

Don't shame me, Oliver Maxwell's voice echoed around his head.

"…I don't quite know how to say this…" Joseph continued.

"You don't have to. Father's already explained the arrangement to me." She placed her hand upon his shoulder. "I accept." She plucked the ring from its box and slipped it onto her finger. As she wiggled her finger to entice the firelight to catch the diamond, its sparkle was blocked by Joseph's hand.

"This isn't what I want, Miss Lillithwaite— Poppy."

"The arrangement has been made." She put her hand over his. "We're to be married, Joseph."

"No, Poppy, you don't understand. I love another—I wish to *marry* another. Perhaps, if we speak to your father together, we can explain how this has *all* been a *terrible* misunderstanding—" Joseph was interrupted by Poppy's fingers against his lips.

"I'm afraid it's *you* who's misunderstood, Joseph." She lowered her hand. "Our future together has already been decided. We're to be married. There's no explanation necessary."

"But Miss Dexter—!"

"A memory," Poppy interrupted. As she took his hand in hers, she traced the bruising around his eye with her other. "We both wear the marks of our fathers' will." She withdrew her hand and, as she stood, held both of his while he did the same. "Once we're married, we'll be free from it all. In time, we may even come to love one another. For now, isn't it enough to sleep soundly in a home of our own?"

Don't shame me, Oliver Maxwell's voice repeated in Joseph's mind. Rapid flashes of a belt buckle followed. *It has already been decided…* Miss Dexter's words bounded through his ears, intermingled with the thwack of leather against flesh. A sharp throb erupted in his temple. "I-I'm frightened…" he whispered. "…But I love her… but I'm frightened."

"We'll see this through together, Joseph." Poppy soothed with a soft caress of his cheek. She grasped his

252

hands hard and, with a determined nod, cried out with a broad smile, "Father! Father, I have the most splendid news!" She released his hands to snatch up her skirts and run out the room. She remembered her etiquette at the last moment, however, and let her skirts be. She instead lifted her chin and walked out with all the grace and decorum of a house cat.

Stunned, Joseph stared at the open doorway. The sound of Roger Lillithwaite's booming voice startled him back to his senses, however, and he hurried to join his future father-in-law and fiancé.

"I'll drink to that," Oliver remarked when his son stepped into the study. Despite the joyous news, the stony-faced, elder Maxwell regarded Joseph until his eyes became downcast. Only then did he take his intended sip of port.

* * *

The waves crashed against Brighton's deserted west pier. Out at sea, the thunder rolled over the horizon as lightening shards illuminated the sky. Fishing boats, caught off guard by the encroaching storm, fought their way over innumerable walls of water as they tried to reach the shore. Mrs Coral Cosgrove watched their plight from her vantage point upon King's Road. As she gripped the iron railing to brace herself against the incoming winds, she looked left along the promenade below. The storefronts—so alive in the daylight hours—were shrouded in darkness with their doors locked and shutters secured. Behind her, the glow of electrical lighting, which poured from the windows of the Hôtel Metropole, beckoned to her. She'd abandoned her dry suite, and the warmth of lord Gelding's body, to loiter in the cold and damp for almost twenty minutes, for what? A single, handwritten line of invitation on a note, signed by 'a friend', and given to her by the hotel's assistant manager, no less!

"Pardon the delay," a familiar voice uttered at her back. When she turned toward it, she saw only a pair of dark blue-green eyes peering out from beneath a black, bowler hat. A slender, leather clad hand pulled down the black scarf that covered her companion's remaining features. "You were expecting my husband?"

"I was," Mrs Cosgrove replied. She took in Doctor Locke's frock coat and trousers, which she recognised as Mr Locke's. From a distance, Mrs Cosgrove could've mistaken Doctor Locke for her husband, especially as she'd tucked her dark-blond curls under the bowler hat. "Is he here?"

"No," Doctor Locke recalled the sight of him as he lay upon his study's sofa with the used heroin needle at his side. A wave of sadness swept over her and she turned away to approach the railings. "He has to perform at the Palladium tonight." She looked out to sea and felt the onshore wind weaken a little. "He doesn't know I'm here." When Mrs Cosgrove joined her, she faced her. "I apologise for making you wait for so long, but I had to be certain you were alone. What I want to discuss with you is rather sensitive."

Mrs Cosgrove rolled her eyes. "If you're going to bend my ear over my behaviour toward Percy, I don't want to hear it. We are only good friends."

Doctor Locke regarded her with disdain. "Your awareness of my disapproval is sufficient reason for me not to expend any effort on the matter for now. No, I want to discuss your barrenness."

Mrs Cosgrove's eyes widened for a moment before she turned toward the railings with a clenched jaw and pursed lips. Watching a boat disappear around the pier's edge, she swallowed and said, her voice weakened by adrenaline, "I don't know what you hope to achieve by insulting me like this, Mrs Locke, but it's *most* unbecoming."

Doctor Locke closed the distance between them. "If my intention was to insult you, Mrs Cosgrove, I would have used far more choice words than those." She watched her a moment. "Both first and second marriages bore no children. When this occurs, it's often difficult to determine a cause. He could've had liaisons with exotic beauties while abroad which could've left him unable to conceive. These same liaisons could've led to him infecting his wives with silent diseases which made them unable to conceive, too. Equally, a problematic birth—prior to your marriage to the professor—could've led to you being unable to carry another child. A tragic turn of events which the professor may have had suspicions of, if only due to the failed appearance of a pregnancy in your marriage. Such a reason for his coldness toward you appears logical—on the surface, at least. On the other hand, few men are courageous enough to accept it is *they* who are unable to conceive. It is therefore easier to lay blame at the wife's door. What I want from you, Mrs Cosgrove, is some assistance in clarifying this matter."

"Lies, all of it. You shall have *nothing* from me." Mrs Cosgrove retorted with a desperate edge to her voice.

"Did the professor accuse you of being Adam Cosgrove's mother? Did he tell you the conception and delivery of a bastard child had defiled your womb forever and rendered you nothing more than a common prostitute—"

Doctor Locke caught Mrs Cosgrove's incoming hand. The two women stared into one another's eyes, Coral with a bitter hatred and Lynette with cold stoicism.

Mrs Cosgrove yanked her hand free. "As I mentioned before: you have no idea what it was like being married to a man like Benjamin. Cruel would only begin to describe him." She lifted her chin and folded her arms. "You were right as far as him accusing me of being

Adam's mother, but he finally relented in his torment a month before his death. Though he refused to give me her name, he told me Norman had revealed Adam's mother's identity."

"Did you not press him for the information?"

Mrs Cosgrove shrugged a shoulder. "She meant nothing to me, and Benjamin's accusation of barrenness continued, besides." She tilted her face toward the sea. "Something I found impossible to deny for, you see, Doctor Locke, I did lose a child during a pregnancy that meant I couldn't carry another. It had happened just before I left the stage to marry Benjamin. The doctor at the time said I was no more than a month pregnant. *I*…" She rested her hand upon her bosom. "…had absolutely *no* idea I was until…" She allowed her voice to trail off.

"You have my sympathy," Doctor Locke murmured. "A child's passing… heartrending, tragic, sad—the words sound inadequate against the grief such a tragedy causes."

"Thank you," Mrs Cosgrove replied in a bittersweet tone. "You're *far* too good for Percy."

Doctor Locke chuckled.

"I mean it. He has been the fortunate one."

"Thank you." Doctor Locke smiled.

Both women looked out to sea and, as the wind tossed her hair, Mrs Cosgrove said, "I knew he'd be a heartbreaker. Even all those years ago—even when he was a mere boy of seventeen—he had women fawning over him."

"I can imagine."

"The child wasn't his." Mrs Cosgrove watched Doctor Locke's stoic expression for any hint of relief or surprise. When she saw none, she continued, "He was handsome, and charming, but *too* young for me." Still, Doctor Locke maintained her cool façade. "It was one of the stage hands—the father." She turned her face into the wind. "He never knew, and I intend to keep it that way."

Doctor Locke bowed her head a little but otherwise kept her own counsel, despite being awash with recollections of the previous days' events and paranoia regarding her husband's 'habits'.

* * *

"Mr Partridge has informed me the Bow Street Society is dissatisfied with the proposed arrangement regarding the payment of its fee," a deep voice, as smooth as velvet, said. While Mr Snyder, Mr Skinner, and Miss Dexter were stood by the sofa, Lord Weeks had taken the armchair. Mr Partridge stood to the right of Lord Weeks, but neither had repeated the earlier invitation for the Bow Streeters to sit.

By the light of the fire, Lord Weeks' coal-black hair was revealed to have streaks of grey—as if someone had taken a paintbrush to it—above his ears. Flecks of grey also appeared in his beard and moustache. The beard only covered his chin, while his moustache split beneath his nose and hung in a straight, triangular shape against his skin. Both his facial hair and naturally wavy head hair were trimmed to maintain their neat appearance. While all three Bow Streeters listened to Lord Weeks' statement, only Miss Dexter observed the physical similarities between the peer and a certain surgeon. Namely, the jade-green, semi-circular-shaped eyes, black, wavy hair, prominent nose, and ears.

"Not with the monies, your lordship," Mr Snyder said. "But with what Mr Partridge said. Two blokes are dead 'cause of the doll, and we wanna find out who done 'em in."

Lord Weeks leaned sideways, and Mr Partridge whispered a definition of the slang term into his ear. Shifting his gaze toward the fire as a discreet alternative to rolling his eyes, Lord Weeks then looked back to Mr

Snyder. "An honourable intention, but one irrelevant to the task I commissioned the Society to execute."

"We don't want payin' for findin' the murderer," Mr Skinner interjected. His Irish accent caused Lord Weeks' expression to harden. "The doll just needs to stay at Bow Street 'til we uncover who it were."

"We also wanna make sure you've got nowt to do with it," Mr Snyder said.

"I haven't," Lord Weeks stated.

"So why all dis, then?" Mr Skinner enquired and lifted his hand toward the covered painting above the fireplace. "And the blindfolds, and the man wearin' all black? What are you hiding, if not a part in the murders?"

"Not hiding, protecting," Lord Weeks replied with a tone as hard as his features. "A man in my position must consider public opinion at all times. If it were to be known I commissioned the Bow Street Society to investigate whether an antique doll in my possession was cursed, my peers in the House of Lords would ridicule me out of Westminster."

"Who woz the bloke in black, then?" Mr Snyder enquired.

"You may tell them, Mr Partridge," Lord Weeks said. "Provided their discretion may be relied upon."

"It can," Mr Snyder replied as his fellow Bow Streeters nodded.

"Very well," Mr Partridge said. Lowering his voice, he then hissed, "It was me." With a cough afterward, he continued in his usual voice, "I'm highly recognisable, as Lord Weeks' personal secretary, to those who frequent the Palace of Westminster. Lord Weeks couldn't place his trust in anyone else to act as messenger between him and the Bow Street Society, so it was decided I had better be disguised."

Mr Snyder's hand clenched at his side. "You pushed Miss Trent over," he growled. "And made me and the inspecta come all the way out 'ere, not knowin' who

258

you woz, or what you woz gonna do to us. Tonight, too. You scared the daylights out of Miss Dexter."

"I'm quite recovered now, Sam," Miss Dexter interjected. Moving forward, she rubbed her hands together against her skirts. "And we thank you for allowing us to share your confidence, your lordship, Mr Partridge. Your faith in us—and in the Bow Street Society—shan't be undeserved." She looked to the, still annoyed, Mr Snyder and Mr Skinner. Mr Skinner stood with his iron hand upon his actual arm while he scrutinised the English peer. "But we need to keep the doll, your lordship." She met the peer's gaze and looked to his feet. "We'll take excellent care of it."

Lord Weeks remained silent as his jade-green eyes regarded her with less contempt than her fellows. "Please accept my sincerest apologies, Miss Dexter, if my secretary's methods frightened you," he eventually said. "The ends justified the means, however." He turned his head toward his employee. "Mr Partridge, please show Miss Dexter where the doll was kept and permit her to take as many photographs, and make as many sketches, as she needs to. Then have Mr Snyder. Mr Skinner, and Miss Dexter escorted back to their cab. See to it they are given the receipt and catalogue entry from *Stafford's Auction House* for the doll as well. Please contact Mr Partridge when your work with the doll is completed, Miss Dexter. Mr Partridge." Lord Weeks lifted a clasped hand and Mr Partridge stepped forward to give Miss Dexter a handwritten address for an office in Westminster. "The blindfolds shan't be necessary for the return journey."

TWENTY-ONE

NEW EVIDENCE IN UNSOLVED COSGROVE CASE
read the *Gaslight Gazette's* headline the following
morning. By the time Miss Dexter came down to
breakfast, her father was halfway through his copy. When
he heard her chair draw back from the table, he lowered
the newspaper to peer at her over it and his pince-nez.
"You came home late last night," he said. "Getting
involved in this Cosgrove business, were you?"

"She told us where she was going, Henry," Mrs
Dexter said as she gave Georgina Dexter some toast. After
she'd wiped her hands upon her apron, she refilled their
cups from the teapot, starting with her husband's.

"I know that. I want to know what happened," Mr
Dexter told her.

"We met the Society's client, Pa-Pa," Georgina
Dexter said and gave a soft "thank you" to her mother. She
added some cream and watched its white clouds swallow
the tea's dark liquid.

"Who is…?" Mr Dexter enquired.

"*Really*, Henry. You've never taken this much
interest before," Mrs Dexter scolded as she picked up his
empty plate and carried it to the kitchen.

"I'm concerned," Mr Dexter called after her.

"Concerned, Pa-Pa?" Georgina enquired. Her
fingers toyed with the table cloth, while her hands' heels
rested upon her thighs. "I can't say who he is, Pa-Pa. We
promised we wouldn't."

"It's all over the newspaper," Mr Dexter said as he
closed the *Gaslight Gazette,* folded it lengthways, and
tossed it onto the table so she could read its headline. "I
don't want you hurt because of this Boo Street Society of
yours."

"Bow Street Society," Georgina corrected.

Mrs Dexter returned from the kitchen with two chops which she plonked onto her husband's plate. With one hand on her ample hip, she waved an iron fork at him. "We've gone over this, Henry. Mr Snyder looks after Georgie when she's doing Society work, and there's Miss Trent besides."

"You get *paid* if it's work," Mr Dexter retorted.

"Now you're *splitting* hairs," Mrs Dexter said with a sigh and returned to the kitchen for a second time.

Mr Dexter watched her leave before he took the pince-nez from his nose and pointed them at Georgina. "Your ma-ma and I love you, Georgie, and you'll always have a home here with us. That being said, pennies don't stretch as far as they used to. Your engagement to Mr Maxwell also reminded us how much we want you settled." Mr Dexter rested his pince-nez holding hand upon the newspaper. "Putting yourself in print with the Bow Street Society won't achieve that." He straightened and set down the pince-nez to pick up his knife and fork. "*You* can't be happy either, seeing and speaking to Mr Maxwell after what's happened." He cut into his chop.

Georgina's fingers twisted the cloth beneath the table. "Do you wish me to leave the Society, Pa-Pa? But… I have friends there, Mr Snyder, Miss Trent, Lady Owston…"

"You need a husband to take care of you, Georgie," Mr Dexter said as he chewed. He then swallowed the morsel with a mouthful of tea. "Your ma-ma and me won't be around forever, and we want you to be comfortable. Men of marital age—*competent* and less clumsy men—won't want a wife who behaves like Sherlock Holmes."

Mrs Dexter brought some boiled eggs into the room but put them down the moment she saw her daughter's expression. She put an arm around Georgina's shoulders and brought her head to rest against her bosom while she stroked her hair and cheek. "Oh, *Georgie*, dear," she said with great sadness. "We were all disappointed when Mr Maxwell breached his promise to you—and *surprised*, too! He seemed to *love* you so. Don't worry, I'm sure another one will come along and he'll be *much* more suitable. In the meantime, you can carry on with the Bow Street Society. Can't she, Henry?"

"I was just telling her—" he began.

"Of course, you can, Georgie," Mrs Dexter soothed. "Come on, eat your toast."

Georgina eased her head from the comfort of her mother's warm bosom. Rather than eat though, she said, "It's not the Society's fault my engagement ended, Pa-Pa." She looked to her father. "It was mine."

"It was?" Mr Dexter enquired, confused, as he and his wife exchanged glances.

Georgina nodded. "I kissed him, and now he thinks me immoral." She put her chin upon her chest as she felt her eyes sting and her cheeks moisten. "…You must repay the monies, Pa-Pa." With her gaze downcast, she didn't see her parents' alarmed expressions. "For it's *my* disgrace, not *his*!" She pressed the excess tablecloth against her nose as her shoulders shook, and her violent sobs filled the room.

Mrs Dexter at once pulled Georgina's head against her bosom, while Mr Dexter rushed to take the chair at his daughter's side. "*Georgie*, my daughter," he said as he held her hand tight. "Mr Maxwell's reason for breaching his promise wasn't any transgression on your part."

Georgina lifted her head from her mother's bosom and stared at her father, stunned. "It wasn't…?"

"No," Mr Dexter said as he gave her hand a gentle rub. "He's engaged to another." No sooner had he spoken was he compelled to catch his limp daughter as she fell forward in a faint.

* * *

Mr Elliott alighted from a hansom cab and paid its driver. As he approached the office of Forbes & Son solicitors, the morning sun peeked between the buildings opposite and cast a rectangle of light against the façade. A man in his late-thirties with mouse-brown hair, stern whiskers, and twirled moustache stood within the light while he unlocked the office door. His knee-length, brown overcoat hung from his long, narrow shoulders as if they were a clothes hanger, and his lean body a wardrobe. Even when he turned toward Mr Elliott, his pectorals and deltoids showed no definition whatsoever. "Good morning, sir," the man said as his lower lip jutted out at the last word. "How may I be of assistance?" Mr Elliott presented his business card and the man's expression fell like crockery from a table. "Who's it this time?" The man pushed open the door and went inside.

"Professor Benjamin Cosgrove," Mr Elliott replied and watched the man drop a lump of coal he was about to toss into the cold hearth. "I'm here in my capacity as a member of the Bow Street Society. I'd like to speak with Mr Carlton Forbes, preferably today."

"You're addressing him." Mr Forbes kicked the coal into the hearth and wiped his hands upon his black frockcoat. He then sat behind a desk perpendicular to the door. Intense sunlight poured through a curved, multiple-paned window to illuminate the desktop, while the remainder of the space was gripped by gloom. The dark-oak clerk's desk in the back corner, bookcases of the same make, and beige walls covered in coal dust only served to darken the interior further. "Mr Carlton Forbes the second." He tidied his papers. "But I wager you want my father." He set aside the pile to pick up a chipped, china map and peer into it.

"If he is the man named as executor on Professor Cosgrove's will, yes." Mr Elliott stood by the desk.

"I'd imagine so." Mr Forbes indicated the empty chair opposite. "Please… sit down, Mr Elliott." He straightened the knot of his tie and gave a contrived smile. "But, as much as I'd like to oblige a fellow solicitor, your request isn't one I can grant."

"And why is that?"

"Begging your pardon." The contrived smile grew. "But I'd rather not say." He leaned forward over his hands and inclined his head. "I'm the sole proprietor of Forbes & Son Solicitors, now, and I can tell you—with confidence—that we can't help you."

"Due to your father's absence?"

"Precisely."

Mr Elliott reached into his frockcoat and took out a folded piece of paper. "Were you in your father's service at the time of the professor's murder?"

"Possibly…" Mr Forbes watched the placement of the paper. "What's that?"

"The genuine last will and testament of Professor Benjamin Cosgrove."

"That's impossible, sir, because the professor's will is—" He halted, his finger pointed toward a door at the room's rear. "Er…" He recoiled his finger and gave another—much weaker—smile while he dipped his hand beneath the desk. "…That is, it *was* there…"

Mr Elliott unfolded the paper and pushed it across to him. "The Society has been commissioned to investigate a matter connected to Professor Cosgrove's murder. It's the Society's belief the professor's will may have some bearing upon the matter in question. I'd therefore like to see the copy of the professor's will you hold here."

Mr Forbes' gaze briefly dropped to the document. "Where did you get your copy?"

"Most solicitors' assumption to my statement would be their copy of the will was a forgery—a potentially reputation ruining occurrence. You, on the other hand, are more concerned with the will's origins than its validity, why?" He retracted the document and returned it to his frockcoat.

264

"They're the same thing, aren't they?"

"Mr Forbes, permit me to assist you. Whatever your reasons for concealing the truth of this matter, they shall lead you to the dock if you continue to lie to me. I shall return with Inspector Lee of the Metropolitan Police if you don't start cooperating with me."

Mr Forbes gripped his tie's knot. "You wouldn't."

"I don't condone murder."

"B-But we had no part in that!" Mr Forbes exclaimed as his fair complexion drained of its remaining colour. "Whatever has been told to you is a *lie*!"

"Then tell me your side of the story," Mr Elliott replied but kept his expression stoic.

Mr Forbes adjusted his tie's knot and gripped its strand. "I see you give me little choice, sir... So be it..." He rested the flats of his hands upon the desk. "Ned Cosgrove, the nephew of Professor Benjamin Cosgrove, paid me handsomely to redraft his uncle's will and name him as the sole beneficiary. It was redrafted after the professor's murder, though—God as my witness."

"Wouldn't your father have noticed the will he read after the funeral wasn't written by his client?"

"My father's memory was failing. It failed completely last year. That's why you can't see him; he's in Bedlam." He rubbed his temple. "Ned Cosgrove was in a terrible amount of debt—more than his inheritance would repay. With the police investigation into his uncle's death delaying the reading of the will, Ned saw an opportunity to exchange it with a new one."

Mr Elliott took out his notebook and opened it up at a clean page. "I believe you, Mr Forbes. But I'm still obliged to copy the will you have."

Mr Forbes gave a nod and, with deep forlornness, replied, "One moment, then, and I'll fetch it..." He stood and disappeared through the door at the rear. While he waited, Mr Elliott consulted his earlier notes to ensure there was nothing further to enquire after. "Here..." Mr

Forbes announced upon his return. Untying the ribbon from around the folded document, he opened it out upon the desk.

Mr Elliott leaned over to both read it aloud and copy it down. "The Last Will & Testament of Professor Benjamin Cosgrove. I, Professor Benjamin Cosgrove, in healthy body and sound of mind, do bequeath these words to Miss Henrietta Watkins, my personal secretary of many years: your unerring commitment, impeccable propriety, and unconditional devotion to my work never went unnoticed. With your clerical support, a great number of my academic ambitions were achieved. No monetary amount could ever reflect the place your loyal servitude and friendship hold in my heart.

"In contrast, I leave my false wife, Mrs Coral Cosgrove, a penny. The following conditions are attached to it, however: Mrs Coral Cosgrove must not contest this will, and news of her scandalous behaviour with my nephew, Norman, mustn't be made public. Provided these conditions are agreed upon and met, the payment will be made a month after my passing.

"To my co-betrayer, Norman Cosgrove, I bequeath a lifetime of misery and destitution befitting one as abhorrent as he.

"I bequeath the remainder of my estate—sans solicitor, burial, clerical, and all other fees—to my remaining relative, Mr Ned Cosgrove." Mr Elliott looked up at Mr Forbes. "And *this* was the will read after Professor Cosgrove's funeral?"

"It was, sir."

"Thank you." Mr Elliott finished his copy and folded the document to pass it back to the solicitor. "Your cooperation in this matter shan't go unrewarded."

"And the police…?"

"I cannot speak for them, I'm afraid," Mr Elliott replied. "Good day to you, Mr Forbes."

266

* * *

"It's unacceptable," Miss Watkins said as she led Mr Snyder and Mr Verity into her gloomy parlour. She crossed to the window, drew back its curtains, and lifted the table and talking board both. "Arriving unannounced like this." She carried them from in front of her armchair to place them behind. Going to the hearth, she stirred the hot coals with her poker. "I shan't apologise for the untidiness." She set the poker aside. "What else could be expected at this time of the morning?" As if on cue, the mantel clock struck half past nine while Miss Watkins blew out the candles which lined the shelf. They were all an inch tall, with a mountain of semi-cooled wax that dripped onto their sticks' wide bases. "Make yourselves comfortable." She glanced back at the two by the door. "Where's your associate? The polite, young lady."

"She woz feelin' off so stayed at 'ome," Mr Snyder replied.

"I see," Miss Watkins said with genuine sadness. She lit the gas lamps and, as she sat in her armchair, slipped her brooch from its arm to rest against her thigh. Once she'd arranged her shawl, and the Bow Streeters were settled upon the sofa, she enquired, "What's brought you here this time?"

"We're grateful for your time at such short notice—" Mr Verity began.

"As you should be," Miss Watkins interrupted.

"But we've discovered a new will for the professor," Mr Verity continued.

"Probably," Mr Snyder interjected,

"*Probably*?" Miss Watkins pressed.

"We don't know if 'e wrote it, or someone else," Mr Snyder explained.

"It was found under a drawer in his desk," Mr Verity added.

"He *certainly* didn't hide it when *I* was his secretary," Miss Watkins stated. "The professor wouldn't have engaged in such frivolities. If it was hidden, someone *else* must've put it there."

"Did you?" Mr Snyder enquired.

Miss Watkin scowled but, since Mr Snyder had been so polite with his question, she chose to be courteous with her reply, "No. I did not. As far as I was aware, he'd only made one amendment prior to his death, to add Coral as a beneficiary following their marriage. As was discovered at the reading, however, he'd overturned the amendment. I'd no knowledge of him even thinking about disinheriting her. If you've now found a new will, I couldn't possibly assist you with its origin or authorship."

Mr Verity smiled. "We understand."

Miss Watkins tucked her shawl's corners beneath her arms and retrieved her brooch to clasp it with both hands in her lap. "Will that be all? I have some shopping to do."

Mr Verity, who'd studied the candles during their discussion of the will, caught sight of the brooch and pointed to it. "That's a canny brooch, if you don't mind me saying."

Miss Watkins slipped it from sight. "It's very dear to me."

"That why you been using it in your séances?" Mr Verity enquired with a smile. "That's the professor's silhouette, ain't it?"

"*No*," Miss Watkins snapped. "And what I do with it is my business alone." She looked to Mr Snyder. "Do you have any more questions, or may I be left in peace?"

"I meant no harm—" Mr Verity began.

"*Ask* your questions," Miss Watkins demanded.

"Mrs Cosgrove told us she saw you and Norman Cosgrove comin' out the professor's study the night before his funeral," Mr Snyder said. "What was that about?"

"The professor's manuscript," Miss Watkins replied, bluntly. "What else would you like to know?"

"Why did you speak with Norman Cosgrove about it, and not Mrs Cosgrove?" Mr Verity enquired.

"There were only a few pages to type before the manuscript would be complete," Miss Watkins replied. "Mrs Cosgrove was as ignorant of the professor's academic work as she was of his wellbeing. I therefore asked Mr Norman Cosgrove for permission to finish the task the professor had set me."

"But 'e'd been seein' Mrs Cosgrove behind the professor's back," Mr Snyder pointed out. "You sure you wozn't torkin' to him about the murder? Maybe askin' him if he'd done it?"

"He hadn't," Miss Watkins replied without hesitation.

"How'd you know?" Mr Snyder enquired.

"Because he wasn't *there*," Miss Watkins said.

"Mrs Cosgrove thinks Norman murdered her husband," Mr Verity said.

Miss Watkins glared at him. "Nonsense. Whatever gave her the idea *he*—of *all* people—could've orchestrated a murder? The mere *idea* is offensive."

"He woz havin' an affair with her," Mr Snyder explained. "She thought he'd done in the professor so they could be together."

Miss Watkins snorted. "Norman was never so romantic—*or* intelligent. True, his instincts were his compass, but those instincts weren't the product of his mind."

"Did you know Norman had a son?" Mr Verity enquired.

Miss Watkins swept her gaze over him with a tightened jaw. For several moments, she glowered at him. When Mr Verity didn't avert his eyes though, Miss Watkins said, "I don't wish to speak of it." As Mr Verity parted his lips to reply, Miss Watkins resumed, "The professor was angered by it when he was alive, and I've no desire to anger him with it now he's dead. It was Norman's cross to bear, one he should've carried with all the quiet repentance of a guilty sinner. He should have never tarnished the Cosgrove name with his shame or invited sympathy when the professor duly expelled him."

"Norman told him?" Mr Snyder enquired as he glanced at his fellow Bow Streeter. "When woz that?"

"I don't wish to speak of it," Miss Watkins repeated. She then spoke slowly, but retained her anger, "Ask me other questions if you must, but do it with haste so I may be left in peace." When she felt a weight upon her arm, she looked down to see Mr Snyder's large hand. His gentle smile further eased the pressure of her emotions. "I apologise if I'm being discourteous. I've had trouble sleeping since you told me of Mr Elmore's tragic death. The thought of the professor wandering the Earth in limbo was terrible enough…" She looked to Mr Verity. "I've been trying to reach them both through the talking board. The silhouette on my brooch is of the professor. I had it made after his death… as a reminder of our friendship."

"These are trying times," Mr Verity reassured with a soft smile.

"We won't keep you much longer," Mr Snyder said. "When we woz 'ere last, we asked you abouh the keys to the study. Why'd you not tell us the professor kept his on the desk, even when he woz out?"

"Didn't I?" Miss Watkins enquired in return. When Mr Snyder shook his head, she replied, "It was such a regular occurrence, I thought Mrs Cosgrove might've told you of it."

"Nah, it was Mr Lane, the butler who did," Mr Snyder said. "Do you know if it went missin' for a bit, or if it was sent to a locksmith to be copied?"

"The key was always in my sight whenever I was there," Miss Watkins replied. "The professor could've sent

270

it out to be copied when I wasn't, though." She slipped her hand from beneath Mr Snyder's to retrieve her brooch and wrap it in her shawl. "You'll find no one more willing to put the spirits of Professor Cosgrove and Mr Elmore at peace than I, but I really can't say any more." She stood and held the brooch close to her heart. "If you would excuse me, I'd like to get on with my day." She headed for the door but stopped at the sound of Mr Verity's voice.

"Why did the professor ask you to leave, Miss Watkins?"

Miss Watkins looked back at him with a fierce scowl. "I told you last time."

Mr Verity stood and rested his weight upon his cane. "You did… but you also told us he'd asked you to leave once before. I would like to know why."

Miss Watkins turned on him. "You may like to, Mr Verity, but you shan't." She looked to Mr Snyder who'd also stood. "I've been *more* than generous with my time and patience. There are some secrets which should be kept, and some which should be given away. *This* is one to be kept." She opened the door. "Good day to you."

TWENTY-TWO

The Bow Streeters talked amongst themselves while Miss Dexter finished a line drawing she'd copied, from her sketchbook, onto the blackboard. When she heard several greet Mr Maxwell, she grimaced at the thought of seeing him. She'd spent quite some time considering her situation—following her father's revelation regarding Mr Maxwell's new engagement—and had come to a decision. Any thoughts she had about maintaining a wholly platonic relationship with Mr Maxwell went from her mind though, the moment she saw the dark-purple bruise that corrupted his otherwise pale complexion. Her instinct was to reassure him, to hold his hand as she'd done before. Yet, her pa-pa was right; she didn't feel happy when she saw Mr Maxwell. In fact, she felt like an invisible wall of propriety had been built between them. Her sense of duty to the Society was stronger than her grief at losing Mr Maxwell, however. This, coupled with her decision, meant any abandonment of her membership to avoid him was needless—and unfair to her. Resolute in her determination to remain, therefore, she put down the chalk and sketchbook to greet him. "Good day, Mr Maxwell."

"G-Good day, Miss Dexter," Mr Maxwell replied with a relieved smile.

"Congratulations on your engagement," Miss Dexter said, her demeanour composed despite her tone of voice being restrained. "She is a fortunate woman."

Mr Maxwell stared at her, stunned. "My…?"

"If you could take your seats, everyone, then we'll begin," Miss Trent said.

Miss Dexter did as requested while Mr Maxwell lingered on the spot. When he realised he was the last one standing, he hurried to find an empty chair and sit down.

"These are photographs, taken by Miss Dexter, of the room where the doll was being kept when Mr Snyder and Inspector Conway first saw it," Miss Trent said as she affixed the last to the blackboard. "What you see here…" She placed her fingers beneath Miss Dexter's drawing and stepped back to give the others a clear view. "Is the floorplan of the room." Miss Trent held the back of her chair at the table's head. "What are everyone's thoughts?"

The Kershaw twins left their seats and scrutinised each photograph in turn. Mr Locke joined them and, as they moved onto the next photograph, he took the first to study under his loupe lens. The lens was mounted into a round, brass frame held aloft from the table by three thin legs. "I see no indications of concealed doors or panels," he remarked.

"There aren't any items of furniture, dislodged bricks, or splintered wood on the roof or walls which could've struck the case, either," Bernice said.

"The inclement weather on the night is the likeliest culprit," Brenda added.

"The lock to set the mechanism into motion is not a sensitive one, however," Mr Locke said as he retook his seat beside his wife. Doctor Locke continued to watch the doll's taxidermy rabbit, however. The—now harmless—antique stood in the table's centre.

"The work of a spirit, then," Mr Elliott wryly remarked.

"A coincidence," Mr Verity corrected. "But just as unexplained and possible."

"What we sayin'? A gust of wind fired the gun?" Mr Skinner enquired as he leaned past Mr Snyder. "I don't go along wit that."

"Not the wind, the mechanism," Brenda replied.

"I'm confused…" Mr Maxwell said.

"I doubt we'll ever know for sure, but, with little else to suggest otherwise, we're obliged to assume the wind vibrated the wooden walls which, in turn, caused the case to vibrate. This vibration then agitated the lock's spring enough to set off the mechanism," Brenda explained.

"Sounds good to me," Mr Snyder interjected.

"A possible—if improbable—scenario. What's your opinion, Mr Locke?" Mr Elliott enquired.

"I shall concede the lock could have been affected in such a way. You are quite correct, Mr Elliott. It is amongst the rarer of occurrences," Mr Locke replied.

"If we're unable to uncover evidence to contradict the Kershaws' theory, we're wasting time discussing this any further. For now, then, we'll accept the wind being the likeliest cause of the doll firing its gun in an empty room and move onto the question of our client, Lord Michael Weeks," Miss Trent said.

Mr Elliott's stoicism faltered as he said, "Pardon me, Miss Trent, but did you say *Weeks*?"

"As in a relative of *Doctor Percy* Weeks?" Mr Maxwell enquired.

"Who's Doctor Percy Weeks?" Mr Skinner enquired.

"A drunken, crass surgeon, who assists the Metropolitan Police from time to time," Mr Elliott explained. "It certainly explains the subterfuge during Mr Snyder's first visit."

"We don't know if Lord Weeks' family to Doctor Weeks or not," Mr Snyder said. "We didn't ask 'cause, to my mind, it didn't matter for what we wanted. 'E told us 'e couldn't let folks know 'e was havin' the Society look into the doll and I believed him."

"What did you think of him?" Mr Verity enquired as he addressed Mr Skinner.

The Irishman considered his reply. "Seemed honest enough. Took a shine to Miss Dexter, 'e did."

Mr Maxwell looked sharply at Miss Dexter and enquired, "He did…?"

Miss Dexter hummed and said, "He was the perfect gentleman." When Mr Maxwell parted his lips to question her further, Miss Dexter continued, "In actuality, I'd like to suggest he be removed from our list of suspects, if I may?"

"You may," Miss Trent replied.

"I could make enquires with Inspector Lee about a possible link between Lord Weeks and the original investigation," Mr Elliott suggested. "Simply to be certain of his irrelevance to our case."

"Do you think that wise?" Mr Locke enquired as he scratched his covered forearm. "Lord Weeks has gone to great lengths to guarantee his anonymity. Revealing his identity to a representative of the Metropolitan Police could compromise both his reputation and ours."

"Inspector Lee is the investigating officer; he has a right to know," Mr Elliott retorted.

"And he shall," Miss Trent interjected. "But Mr Locke is correct in his caution. I shall handle the matter of Lord Weeks from this point forward. You may still consider him eliminated as a suspect in Professor Cosgrove's murder, however."

Mr Elliott and Mr Locke exchanged glances across the table but neither refuted the instruction. Instead, Mr Elliott returned to his notetaking while Mr Locke rubbed the crook of his elbow. Satisfied she'd heard the last on the subject—at least for now—Miss Trent informed everyone. "Lord Weeks has agreed for the Society to keep the doll until our investigation is concluded. Mr Partridge also revealed he was the man in black who visited us at the start of this case. He claimed he was too recognisable as Lord Weeks' secretary to risk being seen here as himself."

When Miss Trent noticed Doctor Locke was still staring at the glass case, she realised she'd yet to speak. Miss Trent had a strong suspicion as to why. She glanced at Mr Locke's hands and complexion. His hands trembled while his complexion was pallid. Despite this, Miss Trent saw a marked improvement compared to when she'd seen him the other evening. "Doctor Locke?"

There was a brief delay, wherein Doctor Locke remained absorbed by her thoughts, before she turned her head with slight surprise. "Yes?" She noticed Miss Trent's concern and dragged a smile to her face. "Please forgive me. I'm a little tired. What were we discussing…?"

"Lord Weeks, but we're about to move onto Mr Elliott's report," Miss Trent replied.

Doctor Locke nodded. "I'll endeavour to give it my full attention."

Miss Trent's concern persisted, however. She therefore resolved to keep a close eye on Doctor Locke.

"This morning, I met Mr Carlton Forbes the younger. His father—named as executor on our copy of the professor's last will and testament—was placed into bedlam after losing his memory. After some persuasion—and the suggestion I may return with Inspector Lee—Mr Forbes the younger admitted to drafting an amended version of the will on behalf of Ned Cosgrove. According to Mr Forbes' the younger's story, Ned had gambling debts which exceeded the amount he expected to inherit. The pair therefore took advantage of the delay in burial—and therefore the reading of the will—to draft a new one in which Ned inherited everything," Mr Elliott said and took out a pile of typed documents which he then distributed around the table. "Here is a copy of the professor's will that Mr Forbes the younger showed me. As you will read, Norman Cosgrove and Miss Watkins' inheritances remain unchanged, while Mrs Cosgrove's has changed into a payment of a penny, rather than a yearly allowance of five hundred pounds. Ned Cosgrove paid Mr Forbes the younger a handsome sum for his part in the deception. Mr Forbes insists neither had a hand in the professor's murder, however."

"Which is the genuine will, then?" Mr Maxwell enquired.

"The copy we discovered beneath the drawer in the professor's study," Mr Elliott replied. "I suspect Mr Forbes has already informed Ned Cosgrove of my visit and threat to involve the police. I propose we allow the two to dwell upon my words for a time before confronting Ned about the allegation. If he's panicked when we do, and an olive branch is offered, he is more likely to admit his guilt. As far as the forged will, anyway. Despite it giving Ned ample motive, his presence at the gambling den— corroborated by Inspector Lee—reduces his opportunity to commit the crime to practically non-existent levels. For a gambler—as greedy as he appears to be—to work with an accomplice to commit the murder is also unpalatable to me."

"But he had an accomplice to forge the will," Bernice pointed out.

"Your argument falls rather flat, Mr Elliott," Brenda added.

"I agree with Mr Elliott, and there's a difference between fraud and murder," Miss Dexter said.

"Who does dat leave us wit, then?" Mr Skinner enquired as he rested his faux hand upon his thigh.

"Miss Watkins and…" Mr Locke paused. "…Norman Cosgrove." He read his copy for the third time. "Perhaps you could make enquires about Norman's movements instead, Mr Elliott?"

"Provided Miss Trent is happy for me to do so," Mr Elliott replied.

"I am," Miss Trent said. "Refrain from mentioning Lord Weeks and attempt to prise as much information from Inspector Lee as possible."

"Very well, I'll telephone him this afternoon," Mr Elliott said as he made a note of it.

"I'd still like you and your wife to call upon Mrs Cosgrove, Mr Locke. I presume you've yet to do so?" Miss Trent enquired.

Doctor Locke was startled by the question, but it was her husband who replied, "We shall be travelling to Brighton this afternoon."

"Is that necessary?" Doctor Locke enquired. "Judging by the original will, it seems like she expected to inherit a generous allowance."

"Mrs Cosgrove nonetheless remains a suspect in this case due to the unanswered questions regarding the study key and Adam Cosgrove's mother," Miss Trent replied and rested one hand atop the other. "You've not been yourself since you arrived, Doctor Locke. Has something happened?"

"No," Doctor Locke replied and dragged her contrived smile back into existence. "I'm tired and reluctant to undertake such a long journey because of it, that's all.'

"I shall call upon her, then," Mr Locke said.

Doctor Locke's smile vanished. "You'll do no such thing."

"We three agreed for a second visit to Mrs Cosgrove to be made this afternoon. If you feel unable to honour the commitment due to the demands of your medical work, you must still permit your husband to fulfil his duty as a Bow Street Society member by calling upon Mrs Cosgrove with another," Miss Trent said.

"With all due respect, Miss Trent, I have a right to be unhappy about my husband calling upon other women, even if he does so regardless," Doctor Locke replied and took a deep breath. "Besides, we shan't have to travel to Brighton because I went last night and spoke with Mrs Cosgrove."

Everyone sat in stunned silence.

"You did not tell me your plans," Mr Locke said.

"How could I?" Doctor Locke snapped.

"Why didn't you wait until today?" Miss Trent enquired with a displeased edge to her tone.

"In the course of my medical work, I've encountered both men and women who are unable to bear children," Doctor Locke said and her husband grimaced. "While discussing the possibility of Mrs Cosgrove being Adam Cosgrove's mother, it occurred to me she and the professor had never conceived—despite being married for six years. I wondered if Mrs Cosgrove could—perhaps— be like the women I've cared for in the past. I doubted she'd admit to such a sensitive reality if my husband was present… hence why I went to Brighton last night."

"And what, pray tell, did you discover?" Mr Locke enquired but kept his gaze upon his teacup.

"My suspicions were correct. She is indeed unable to bear children," Doctor Locke replied.

"Did she say why?" Mr Elliott enquired.

"She said she'd lost a child early in pregnancy but hadn't told the professor for fear of his refusing to marry her. I can't be certain if she admitted the truth to me, or if her story is simply a means of hiding the reality that *she* is Adam's mother, because she gave a nameless stagehand as the father of her child," Doctor Locke replied.

"I have no recollection of such an affair— rumoured or otherwise," Mr Locke stated.

"Don't make it a lie," Mr Snyder pointed out. "You woz just a lad at the time."

"And you've no recollection of many things," Miss Trent remarked as she looked to Mr Locke's gloved hands.

"Adam Cosgrove's birth record should confirm who his mother was," Mr Elliott said.

"Am I to be prohibited from disagreeing, now?" Mr Locke challenged as he addressed Miss Trent. "In addition to being deceived."

"I've already explained—" Doctor Locke said.

"You thought she would not divulge her secret if I were present. Yes, I *can* recall that, *Miss Trent*," Mr Locke interrupted and glanced at Miss Trent as he said her name.

He then enquired, before she could reply, "Did she, by chance, divulge a secret regarding a locksmith, Lynette?"

"It wasn't appropriate to ask after we'd discussed her barrenness," Doctor Locke replied. "She was quite upset by it."

"As she would be," Mr Locke remarked.

Doctor Locke's eyes narrowed, and, for a moment, it seemed as if she would rise to her husband's bait. She instead turned toward Mr Snyder. "Did Miss Watkins mention keys at all?"

"She said the study key woz in her sight all the time when she woz there, but that the professor could've sent it to be copied," Mr Snyder replied.

"A visit to my acquaintance in the Whitechapel Road is in order then," Mr Locke said and gathered up his cigarette case and matches. "If he did not tend to the lock personally, he shall know who did."

"I'll go wit ye," Mr Skinner said.

Mr Locke ran his green eyes over the man's horrific appendage with more than a hint of distaste. "My acquaintanceship with the gentleman has been forged through absolute trust and discretion. With all due respect, Mr Skinner…" He stood. "Your presence may frighten him into silence."

Mr Skinner followed Mr Locke's line of sight to his iron hand and dragged it from the table. "Suit yeself."

"I shall," Mr Locke replied. "Good day to you all." He turned on his heel and left the room.

"Please, forgive my husband," Doctor Locke said when she heard the outer door close. "He hasn't had his medicine yet."

"He needs to," Mr Elliott remarked.

"No. He doesn't," Miss Trent replied.

Mr Verity allowed a moment for the tension to ease a little and said, "Y'nah what else Miss Watkins told us? She's started trying to talk to Mr Elmore's spirit, on top of the professor's. There was bags the size of trunks

280

under her eyes and, when we got there, she blew out candles which looked to've been burning all night. Her talking board was out, too—*with* the brooch she wears, the one that's got the professor's silhouette. She said it was made *after* he died."

"How morbid," Bernice remarked.

"Terribly so," Brenda added.

"I think it rather romantic," Mr Maxwell remarked.

"How would you know?" Mr Snyder replied with a glare.

"Miss Watkins lamented not being the professor's wife in place of Mrs Cosgrove. Did she explain why the professor had asked her to leave?" Miss Dexter enquired.

"Nah," Mr Verity replied. "She said it was a secret to keep."

"An intriguing choice of words," Mr Elliott mused.

"Yeah, there's something in that," Mr Verity agreed.

A knock then came from the outer door.

"This may be an answer to our advertisement," Miss Trent said and left the room to answer the door. Voices were soon heard in the hallway and everyone stayed quiet to listen to the brief conversation. "Allow me to introduce Mr Adam Cosgrove," Miss Trent announced upon her return. A young man of seventeen years then entered the room behind her.

TWENTY-THREE

"I read the advertisement this morning, but was only freed from my work at midday," Mr Adam Cosgrove said. His left hand held his double-breasted overcoat's lapel as his right rested on the mantel shelf. Despite his oversized overcoat, his trim physique was plain to see, while his fair complexion was without malnutrition's pallor. Though his voice was refined, its trepidation surpassed the keenness of his large, chestnut brown eyes. "If I'd known you were searching for me, I would've come sooner."

"You're here now," Mr Elliott said. "Do you know why we've sought you out?"

"The matter of my great-uncle's murder, I presumed, since there was also an article about the Bow Street Society assisting the police with their investigation," Adam replied.

"Reverse the order, Mr Cosgrove, and you shall have something akin to the truth," Mr Elliott remarked.

"Is it the Society's investigation, then?" Adam enquired, somewhat taken aback.

"We are acting on behalf of our client, yes," Mr Elliott said. "Your great-uncle possessed the antique doll you see on the table. It's our belief his murderer altered the doll's mechanism to fire a gun."

"But what of the housebreaker?" Adam enquired.

"You know of that?" Mr Maxwell enquired.

"My father—"

"Norman Cosgrove?" Mr Verity interrupted with a raised hand.

"Yes, he told me of the night his uncle—my great-uncle—died, and how my great-aunt Coral was convinced he'd been responsible," Adam replied.

"And was he?" Mr Elliott enquired.

"My father was innocent," Adam insisted.

"How can you be so certain? You were—how old?" Mr Elliott enquired.

"Eleven," Adam replied.

"You would've been at boarding school, then. Additionally, you've only heard your father's version of events," Mr Elliott said.

"I have more than that, sir. My great-uncle died on a day when my father was visiting me at boarding school. Several schoolmasters confirmed he was there when the police made their enquiries," Adam said.

Mr Elliott frowned. "Be that as it may, I don't know how scrupulous your father was in the months prior to his death last year, but those scruples didn't extend to his uncle's wife—your great-aunt, Coral. I shan't patronise you by concealing our discoveries, Mr Cosgrove, for you are clearly a man with wife and home now. In plain terms, your father was in an illicit relationship with Coral Cosgrove. There is also the possibility this same relationship may have given your father motive for murdering your great-uncle."

"If you're referring to my great-uncle's will, you're mistaken. My father inherited nothing but, more importantly, he expected to inherit nothing," Adam told him.

"Because he'd told Professor Cosgrove about your illegitimacy?" Mr Elliott enquired.

"Yes." Adam frowned. "My father provided for me—*raised* me—when others would've condemned me to the workhouse." Adam's shoulders stiffened. "My so-called great-uncle was more concerned about his reputation amongst the academics than the welfare of his own flesh and blood. I, for one, am proud of my father for having the strength to defy him, despite knowing hardship would follow."

"I can imagine. Yet, I was referring to the identity of your mother, Mr Cosgrove. Do you know it?" Mr Elliott enquired.

"No, I'm afraid not. My father told me she'd died giving birth to me," Adam replied.

"We believe your father may have murdered the professor to prevent him from discovering that *Coral* was in fact your mother," Mr Elliott said.

"That's impossible," Adam replied, confused. "I was already born by the time my great-uncle and aunt married."

"Last night, Mrs Cosgrove told me she'd lost a child in early pregnancy prior to marrying your great-uncle. The loss meant she couldn't bear any more children. She claimed the father of her deceased child was a stage hand at the Paddington Palladium. I don't know if you're aware, Mr Cosgrove, but she was an act there prior to her engagement," Doctor Locke said.

"Why isn't her word sufficient?" Adam enquired.

"Because, she could've done in your great-uncle, too," Mr Snyder replied.

"She was there when he died," Brenda said.

"And could've accessed the doll at any time," Bernice added.

"We may settle the question once and for all if we're able to see your birth certificate," Mr Elliott said.

Adam frowned and sat at the table. "I don't have it."

"Well, if you know your date of birth, you and I may visit the Registrar General's offices at Somerset House to request a copy," Mr Elliott said.

"I don't understand… if my great-aunt Coral was my mother, why would she marry my great-uncle when she knew he was related to my father?" Adam enquired.

"Perhaps, she didn't know," Miss Dexter pointed out.

"Until she'd accepted the professor's proposal," Brenda interjected.

"Which she couldn't break for fear of causing a scandal," Bernice added.

"Made all the worse for the cause of the engagement's failure," Brenda said.

Miss Dexter looked across the table to Mr Maxwell, but his attention was on Adam.

"And my father, still in love with Coral, resumed their past affair…" Adam sighed. "Forgive me… this is rather overwhelming."

"An understandable reaction," Doctor Locke reassured.

"What is your date of birth, Mr Cosgrove?" Mr Elliott enquired with pencil poised.

"The sixth of May, 1880."

"Have you talked with your uncle Ned, or your great-aunt, since the professor died?" Mr Verity enquired.

Adam scowled at the mention of Ned's name. "My uncle Ned treats me no better than a piece of manure stuck to his shoe. When I was due to be married, I wrote him with an invitation to the ceremony. The response I received shouldn't be repeated in the presence of ladies. As for my great-aunt, we've only communicated on the occasion of our meeting."

"What about the servants, or Miss Henrietta Watkins?" Mr Snyder enquired.

"The servants always kept a respectable distance, and I don't know who Miss Watkins is," Adam replied.

"She was the professor's secretary. I presume you never met her, then?" Mr Elliott enquired.

"Not that I recall. My great-uncle's disapproval meant my father was reluctance to expose me to the hostility of the Cosgrove residence," Adam replied.

Mr Elliott nodded and made some notes. "If there's nothing further to discuss, I'd like us to visit the Registrar General's office as soon as possible. I also intend to telephone Inspector Lee to confirm your father's whereabouts at the time of your great-uncle's murder, Mr Cosgrove. If what I've discovered at the office of Mr Forbes is to be believed, and your father wasn't even in London, our circle of suspects is reduced dramatically."

* * *

Mr Locke wiped his brow and put away the damp handkerchief. As he put his head out the carriage window, he saw his destination and tapped on the carriage roof. The driver pulled on the horses' reins and brought the carriage to a standstill while Mr Locke alighted and put on his top hat.

"Wait here," he told the driver and crossed the street to a stall strewn with keys of all shapes, sizes, and materials. Many were dirty or covered in rust. A battered key was preferred by the working classes over a pristine one. Older keys tended to be cheaper than the newer ones.

"Good aft'noon, Mr Locke!" Mr Daniel Holland greeted as he doffed his flat-cap. His tanned, leather-like skin added ten years to his fifty, while the dark-brown suit he wore appeared older still. Though as tall as Mr Locke's shoulder, his jovial countenance and sharp wit often increased his perceived stature. As he shook Mr Locke's hand, he remarked, "Beggin' your pardon, sir, but you've got the look of someone who's spent too long in China town."

"Something along those lines," Mr Locke replied with a wry smile. "Perhaps, you could turn your powers of observation to business?"

"Always 'appy to do business with you, Mr Locke. You needin' anuva lock fitted?"

"No, nothing so elaborate." He picked up a key and turned it over. "Six years ago, Professor Benjamin Cosgrove was murdered at his home in Chelsea." He returned the key to the pile. "Cast your mind back to the

October of 1890, Mr Holland. Can you recall if anyone approached you with the request to supply a replacement key for the professor's study door?"

Mr Holland slid the flat cap off to scratch his pale scalp. The little hair he possessed was thin and straw-like. "If you'd asked me that yesterday, I couldn't of told you out. But I read about the murder in the 'paper this mornin' and remembered goin' to the house to check the lock. A woman—can't remember her name or what she looked like—come by 'ere and said a Professor wanted a key for his study 'cause 'e'd lost the old one. I told her I couldn't give her one, 'cause it wasn't her lock, and I'd need to match the key to the lock b'sides."

"What did she say to that?"

"She didn't like it. The day after though, she got me to the place in Chelsea and had me sort the key out."

"Did no one question your presence there?"

"Nah, she let me in at the front door—*right* high class, it was—and took me to the study. I looked at the lock and, as luck had it, had a key that almost fit. I filed it down, put it in, and gave it her when I was done."

"What happened next?"

"She paid me and saw me out—oh, we come by another woman in the hall." Mr Holland thought a moment. "Dunno who she was, just that she was young and looked like she had money."

"Thank you, Mr Holland. I believe I may know who she was and, by consequence, your customer." He took the man's hand. "Once again, you have proven you are worth your weight in gold."

* * *

Somerset House, that overlooked the Victoria Embankment, was named after the Protector Somerset. In 1549, he began construction of a palace that was never completed and demolished in 1766 after his death. The

House's façade was almost eight hundred feet long and rose from a terrace fifty feet high. It was all but hidden by the trees which lined the Embankment. Overall, Somerset House stretched from the Embankment to the Strand. This marked it as a prominent building in not just its function but also its size.

Mr Elliott and Mr Adam Cosgrove sat in a government office housed within the immense establishment. They'd been directed there when they'd arrived over an hour earlier. The clerk—to whom the office belonged—had been absent for the bulk of that time under the guise of searching for Adam's birth record. Mr Elliott consulted his pocket watch and found four o'clock was almost upon them.

"I hope he returns soon. I don't want my lost pay to be for nought," Adam said.

"The Bow Street Society will compensate you," Mr Elliott replied as he stood and opened the door ajar to peer out into the corridor. He heard echoed voices and hurried footsteps in the distance but perceived no sign of their elusive clerk. "I will permit another ten minutes before I commence a search." He closed the door and returned to sit beside Adam.

"He could be anywhere."

"Most likely amongst the records," Mr Elliott said and looked to the door as he heard the faint sound of someone approaching. Their footfalls became lounder until, finally, the red-faced clerk bust into the office with some paper clutched in his hand.

"I *have* it!" he cried. "I. Have. *It*." He dropped into the chair behind the desk and mopped his brow with a handkerchief. "Dear *Lord*, the incompetence of *some* people here is enough to send a saint to drink." He slammed the paper onto the desk. "*Please*, take it. *Do* with it what you will, for I *never* wish to lay my *poor*, tired eyes upon it *again*."

Mr Elliott stood and shook the clerk's hand while Adam took the paper. The two then left the room. While Mr Elliott closed the door, Adam turned over the paper and located his mother's name. As soon as he'd read it, he passed it to Mr Elliott and said, "You were correct." He turned and walked away. "…*All* those years he *lied* to me…"

Mr Elliott read the name and felt immediate confusion. "But how…?" He mused as each piece of the puzzle ran through his mind. None of it made sense at first but, when he read the name again, a picture began to form. "Norman and…" His eyes widened at a recollection. "Of *course*." He looked up but found Adam was gone. "Lee," he mumbled and returned to the clerk's office to demand the use of his telephone.

"But who are you calling?" the clerk enquired.

"Inspector Gideon Lee of T division. It's imperative I speak with him at once."

TWENTY-FOUR

Thunder rumbled overhead as torrential rain beat against the window. Dense cloud blocked the moonlight and kept Oakley Street in pitch blackness. Inside the Cosgrove's library, a fire was the sole light source. Shadows therefore stretched across the walls and floor to transform the faces of those gathered.

Sat in a circle at the library's centre were Ned Cosgrove, Adam Cosgrove, Coral Cosgrove, Henrietta Watkins, the butler—Ian Lane, the parlour maid—Daisy Price, Edgar Elmore, Jr., Carlton Forbes, Jr., and the moneylender—Paul Bund. All had an unobstructed view of the infamous doll as the fire's reflection danced upon its glass case and caught the maniacal smile and polished revolver.

A second circle of Bow Street Society members framed the first. Each stood behind a specific individual. Mr Skinner was behind Ned with Miss Dexter behind Adam, the Lockes behind Coral, Mr Verity behind Henrietta, Mr Maxwell behind the butler, Brenda Kershaw behind the maid, Bernice Kershaw behind Edgar Elmore, Jr., Mr Elliott behind Carlton Forbes, Jr., and Mr Snyder behind the moneylender. Inspector Gideon Lee sat behind the late professor's desk and surveyed the scene with a pleasant smile that failed to reach his eyes.

"I don't take to being pulled from my game, Inspector," Ned said and lifted his open hand. "A *royal flush* I had!"

"You will sit, and you will do, as you are told, Mr Cosgrove," Lee replied.

Ned slid his cigar from one side of his mouth to the other and puffed upon it several times. The abundance of thick smoke caused Coral, Daisy, Henrietta, and Edgar Elmore, Jr. to cough and wave their hands about.

"Do you *mind*? We *all* have to breathe this air," Coral said.

"It's my house," Ned replied and continued to smoke. "Which is *another* thing, Inspector." Ned plucked the cigar from his mouth. "What *right* have you to treat my servants like cows?"

"The right bestowed upon me by the Metropolitan Police," Lee replied. "Don't concern yourself over your servants' wellbeing, Mr Cosgrove. They were rather cooperative once I explained the purpose of our visit."

The butler and maid exchanged worried glances.

"Which is *what*?" Ned enquired as he placed his cigar between his teeth. "All I see is people I've no care for seeing, and a doll I sold months ago."

"To my father," Mr Elmore, Jr. replied. "Who *died* because of it, so, you'll sit there, be quiet, and listen to what has to be said." He plucked the cigar from Ned's mouth and tossed it into the fire.

"You *demmed* rogue!" Ned yelled as he leapt to his feet and brandished his fist at Mr Elmore, Jr. "I've a good mind to—"

"Sit down at once," Mr Elliott commanded.

"You've got a *demmed* nerve, too, sir!" Ned yelled.

"Sit down, Mr Cosgrove, or you shall be handcuffed to your chair," Lee stated.

Ned puffed out his cheeks and chest while his face turned a bright red. "This is an *outrage*—!" When he saw Lee stand though, he dropped onto his chair like a sack of potatoes and muttered a string of obscenities.

"I mean what I say," Lee said and allowed his words to settle in Ned's mind. When no further ruckus came from the man, Lee turned his attention to Mr Elliott. "Please proceed."

"Thank you," Mr Elliott replied and took a thick file from the bookshelf behind him. "Six years ago—at eight-thirty on the twenty-second of October, 1890 to be precise—Professor Benjamin Cosgrove was murdered in this room. It was his study at the time." He went through a gap in the chairs and placed the file atop the doll's case. "The Bow Street Society was commissioned, by the doll's current owner, to investigate the circumstances which surrounded not only Professor Cosgrove's death, but the death of the doll's more recent owner, Mr Edgar Elmore, Snr. Mr Elmore died six months ago—at four o'clock on the sixth April, 1896—in the library of his home at Gloucester Place. Our client wished to ensure the doll was safe before he shipped it to America for valuation."

"Both gentlemen were in locked rooms, alone, when they were fatally wounded by a single gunshot," Mr Locke said. "In each instance, the doll was found as you see it now, smiling down at the dying men from behind its—undamaged—glass case."

"The glass in one piece is what made our client, and the Bow Street Society, think the doll may be haunted," Mr Verity said as he turned the silver, skull-shaped handle of his cane toward Miss Watkins and rested his weight upon it. "Since the year of our Lord, 1882, a children's toy maker in the Midlands, called *Joseph Maskelyne & Sons*, has made dolls for use in séances. Bereaved parents use them to encourage their deceased children to come forward. They are made with a clay and salt mixture—the salt to stop evil spirits using them—and blessed by the spiritualist church." He pointed at the doll. "As you can see, this one isn't made of clay, but…" He lifted a finger. "That didn't mean it hadn't been used in a séance. The Bow Street Society wanted to make sure a demon, or a malevolent spirit, hadn't possessed it. We therefore held a séance."

Mr Elliott cleared his throat and shifted his weight from one foot to the other when he caught Inspector Lee's smirk out the corner of his eye.

"Even if *some* of us didn't agree," Mr Verity remarked with a glance at Mr Elliott. "When our séance

292

didn't reach anyone—*or* anything—we all decided the doll's problem didn't come from beyond the veil but had more Earthly causes."

"Professor Cosgrove was found slumped over his desk with his right arm dangling and his left raised above his head," Doctor Locke said. "The attending doctor— Doctor Walters—concluded a single gunshot wound to the back of the head was responsible for his death. The bullet, according to Doctor Walters' preliminary examination of the body, had entered the skull at an, approximate, ninety-degree angle.

"Mr Elmore, Snr, was still alive when his son, wife, and groomsman found him. With his dying breath, he pointed to the doll." Doctor Locke entered the inner circle and took the file to read aloud, "Superficial examination of the corpse, by Doctor Wren while still at the location of passing, revealed a single bullet wound. The use of a bullet probe upon the corpse further revealed the bullet had entered the torso at an angle of approximately two hundred and forty degrees. The trajectory then grazed the left ventricle, thereby piercing the heart, and ended when the bullet became lodged in the deceased's rib."

"Good *God*," Elmore, Jr., interjected with disgust.

"If the wound was inflicted by another person, they would have had to have been at least seven feet tall to achieve the bullet's angle of entry. This is a supposition based upon the angle itself and the fact the measured height of the deceased is five feet," Doctor Locke said in a subdued tone. "A full post mortem examination failed to uncover any symptoms of disease which may have led to death. As the stomach was empty, it was Doctor Wren's opinion poison wasn't a factor either. He therefore had no alternative but to categorise Mr Edgar Elmore Snr's cause of death as a self-inflicted gunshot wound to the chest."

"Despite no gun being found within the vicinity of Mr Elmore, Snr's body," Mr Locke said.

"If someone shoots 'emselves," Mr Skinner said. "The gun's gonna drop next to the body."

"A gun was not found near to Professor Cosgrove's body, either," Mr Locke said. "Why?" He held his bent arm against the small of his back and walked out the circle, to the window. As he saw his own reflection in it—and that of the room behind—he turned to face the others. "This window was found to be open when the professor's body was discovered by his wife, Mrs Coral Cosgrove, and his secretary, Miss Henrietta Watkins." He rubbed his clasped hands behind his back and looked to Inspector Lee. "A housebreaker was the natural choice for Professor Cosgrove's murderer, therefore, in the eyes of his wife *and* the police." He half-turned to glance out the window. "When I made my own inspection of the window, the surrounding walls, and railings, I was baffled as to why *anyone* would surmise a housebreaker could either enter, or leave, without sustaining a serious injury to their person. There was also the additional detail of no footprints on the walkway below to consider. In short…" He walked from the window to the circle. "There was *never* a housebreaker at all. The open window was a mere ploy—created by the professor's murderer—to put the idea of a fictional housebreaker into the minds of those who surveyed the scene." Mr Locke smiled. "It succeeded. When Mrs Coral Cosgrove saw the open window, and the professor's dead body, she naturally assumed a housebreaker had murdered her husband during a robbery that had gone awry."

"A housebreaker she thought you'd sent, Mr Bund," Mr Snyder said.

The moneylender chuckled. "Not my way of doing business."

"It was a mere supposition on the part of Mrs Cosgrove," Mr Locke replied. "You and the professor had argued earlier in the day, after all." Mr Locke rested his hand upon the doll's case. "But now, I put the request to all of you, to dismiss the idea of a housebreaker from your mind and, instead, look to your neighbour."

"One of *us*?" Miss Watkins replied as her hand reached for her brooch.

"This is *demmed* nonsense!" Ned growled.

"I shan't sit idly by and allow you to accuse me, Percy," Coral said.

"The truth must be known, Coral," Mr Locke replied as his smile faded. "Whatever the cost." A hard shiver coursed through him and he left the circle to approach the fire. "Earlier, Mr Verity spoke of Joseph Maskelyne," Mr Locke said as he held his gloved hands against the heat. "When he mentioned it during our other meeting, it reminded me of an illusion performed by magicians John Nevil Maskelyne and George A. Cooke. It comprised of a doll, named *Psycho*, who they claimed could not only play cards but *think* about its next move. For a time, audiences were coerced into believing the charade, simply because they could not fathom how the doll worked. In the end, an indiscreet patent, filed by the magicians, revealed *Psycho*'s secret. The air within the tube, upon which the doll sat, was manipulated, off-stage, by a set of bellows. By manipulating the air, the bellows' operator could manipulate the doll's movements to give the illusion of thought. It was rather ingenious, since the tube was always in plain sight of the audience, yet, no one had ever made the connection. My recollection of *Psycho* gave me cause to ponder about our doll. Could it, like *Psycho*, have a hidden mechanism which our murderer could manipulate from another room?"

"And could the gun in its hand be real," Mr Skinner said. "When Miss Trent asked me to take a look, and I saw it, I knew the gun at once. It's a Webley Mark I, and they're mostly found in the Royal Navy. Ye see, the gun wasn't found by the professor's body, because it was where it's now—where the murderer left it—in the doll's hand. There stayed the question about the glass not being broke, though. There's been no bullet made, yet, that can pass through solid glass and not break it."

"Hence my suggestion, to Miss Trent, to invite a clockmaker to examine the doll," Mr Locke said as another hard shiver coursed through him.

"Which me and my sister did," Brenda Kershaw said as she retrieved the file from Doctor Locke and found Miss Dexter's sketch of the internal mechanism to show the others. "What we discovered was the doll's mechanism allows it to open its case."

"Thus, allowing it to fire the revolver without damaging the glass," Bernice Kershaw interjected.

"The doll was never built with murder in mind, however," Brenda Kershaw resumed, "As you can see, a piece of fine wire was added to the mechanism. Thus, when the key was turned—"

"And the mechanism was set into motion," Bernice Kershaw interrupted.

"The cogs pulled the wire taut as they rotated. The wire then, in turn, squeezed the revolver's trigger," Brenda Kershaw said.

Miss Dexter next took the file and showed her sketched floorplan to the room as she said. "The doll was kept on a tall table to the right of the window, within touching distance of the professor."

"And at a perfect angle for the bullet's entry wound," Doctor Locke said. "According to Ned Cosgrove, the professor was hard of hearing. He therefore wouldn't have heard the tick of the mechanism behind him."

"Whereas Mr Edgar Elmore, Snr., would've heard the mechanism, but would've had no notion of what was about to befall him," Bernice Kershaw said.

"Mr Elmore, Snr., was able to set the doll's mechanism into motion as he had arranged for a locksmith to visit his home on the day of his death to replace the doll's missing key. It is important to note, ladies and gentlemen, that the doll's original key disappeared following Professor Cosgrove's death," Mr Locke said but paused as he failed to recollect the Elmore key's fate. He therefore took the file from Miss Dexter and consulted the relevant passage. "Ah yes." He set the file down on the doll's case. "Following Mr Elmore Snr's death, his son and wife arranged for the replacement key to be smelted. The doll was also blessed as, according to Mr Elmore, Kr., his mother believed the antique to be cursed."

"The doll's current owner don't have a key, either," Mr Snyder said.

Mr Locke nodded and returned to the fire as he felt the onset of another shiver. "As I explained earlier, the universal—albeit misplaced—assumption was a housebreaker had murdered the professor. I also said the doll's original key disappeared following the professor's death. Due to the assumption, it was therefore unlikely the key had been removed by the police as evidence."

"That's correct," Inspector Lee interjected.

"If any—innocent—person had suspected the doll was the murderer." Mr Locke looked to the maid, Miss Price. "It is logical they would have left the key in place, even if they then neglected to air their suspicions to the police or others within the household."

Miss Price gave a curt nod.

"Our murderer, on the other hand, would have had the perfect reason to remove the key," Mr Locke said. "For they—and they alone—*knew* the doll's secret would be exposed should the key be used. Our murderer could *not* risk the doll's mechanism being set into motion before they removed the wire and retrieved the—still loaded— revolver."

"Dear *God*," Mr Elmore, Jr. said, disgusted.

"The murderer was determined to see Professor Cosgrove dead," Doctor Locke said.

"Unfortunately for our murderer, the police weren't easily satisfied," Mr Elliott said. "They frequently returned to the Cosgrove residence to speak with its inhabitants and conduct searches for the murder weapon—as attested to by Inspector Lee."

"That's correct," Lee replied with a smile.

"Threading the wire through the intricate maze of rods and cogs wouldn't have been a simple task," Brenda Kershaw said.

"It would've required ten minutes or more," Bernice Kershaw added.

"When Bernice and I removed the wire, it took us at least twenty minutes, for the wire had become tangled," Brenda Kershaw said.

"The murderer would've needed just as long to do the same, therefore," Bernice Kershaw said.

"Yet, with the police's frequent visits, the murderer couldn't arrange to be alone with the doll without arousing suspicion. Soon, their small window of opportunity closed completely when they were obliged to leave the residence—and the doll—behind," Mr Elliott said.

"Our murderer had no knowledge—or expectation—of the doll being sold at auction to Mr Elmore, Snr.," Mr Locke said and dabbed at his forehead as his core became hot.

"This fact doesn't make them any less responsible for his death," Mr Elliott said and looked to Mr Elmore, Jr. "Mr Elmore, Snr. would be still alive today if our murderer had not supplied the doll with a loaded revolver."

Miss Watkins took in a sharp breath as she clutched her brooch.

"It is our suspicion that the murderer still has the doll's original key in their possession," Mr Locke said as he walked to the window and opened it an inch. The sudden introduction of the cold wind caused the fire to flicker. Nonetheless, Mr Locke sat on the window's internal ledge and allowed the wind to cool his sweat-soaked back. "We also suspect our murderer arranged for a copy of this room's key to be made so they could ensure they would not be disturbed while they thread the wire through the doll's mechanism and put the revolver into the doll's hand.

"An acquaintance of mine, who is also the proprietor of a street locksmith's stall on the Whitechapel Road, described how a woman approached him and put forth the request for a new key to this room's lock. Given the strict rules all locksmiths must abide by, my acquaintance could not grant her request because—by her own admission—she was there under instruction from Professor Cosgrove, the lock's owner. The woman was displeased by my acquaintance's answer. Yet, the next day, she arranged for him to visit this house and form a new key to that door."

"Would the murderer still have that key, too?" Inspector Lee enquired.

"I doubt it," Mr Locke replied. "The doll's key holds greater significance for our murderer. As a result, they would have felt unable to part with it. The copied study key, on the other hand, was a mere means to an end."

"You certainly speak as if you know the murderer's identity," Lee remarked, dryly.

"We do, Inspector," Mr Elliott replied. "But, first, we shall tell you who we suspected and explain our reasons why."

"Startin' with this bloke," Mr Snyder said as he slapped Mr Bund's shoulder. "You woz heard havin' words with the professor on the afternoon before 'e was done in."

The moneylender shrugged off the broad hand and scowled. "A matter of business"—he pointed a crooked finger at Ned—"started by *that* one there. He took out a loan he couldn't repay, using a name that weren't his."

"A loan of one hundred pounds with one hundred per cent interest added, to be exact," Mr Elliott said.

"You planned to return the next day and take items to sell," Mr Maxwell pointed out.

"Yet, despite your threat, the professor was resolute in his refusal to pay," Mr Elliott said.

"And you think I done him in 'cause of that?" Mr Bund chuckled.

"No," Mr Elliott replied. "As unsympathetic and devious as you are, Mr Bund, it's evident you wanted the money rather than a pound of flesh."

Mr Bund smiled. "Debtors aren't any good to me *dead*, sir." He stood but his shoulders remained hunched. "And, unless you're going to arrest me, Inspector, I've business elsewhere."

Inspector Lee and Mr Elliott's eyes met across the room.

"We have no further need of you," Mr Elliott said.

"You may leave," Lee added.

"*Thank* you," Bund replied and shuffled from the room. The butler followed to show him out while Mr Elliott's hand rested on Carlton Forbes, Jr.'s shoulder. He didn't speak but instead allowed the sounds of the fire, the door, and Mr Bund's footsteps to fill the room.

Ned stroked his moustache. When Carlton Forbes, Jr's eyes met his, he rubbed his lips and gave a subtle shake of his head.

"What an *awful* man," Coral muttered.

"Moneylenders often are," Miss Watkins replied as she still held onto her brooch.

"Mr Cosgrove, would you ask your maid to put some more coals onto the fire, please? I do believe Mr Forbes is cold," Mr Elliott said as he felt the man shiver beneath his hand.

Ned chewed his tongue but looked to his maid and jerked his head toward the fireplace. While she stood and tossed additional coals into the flames, the butler returned and went to assist her once he saw what she was doing.

Mr Elliott followed Carlton Forbes, Jr's panic-stricken gaze to Ned and said, "I wouldn't seek counsel from him if I was you. His advice would reserve a seat for you in the dock. Inspector Lee already has plans to interview you both."

Ned's eyes widened. "I *beg* your pardon?! *I'm* not responsible for Uncle Benjamin's murder! As you well know, Inspector!"

"Perhaps," Mr Elliott replied and held Carlton Forbes, Jr's other shoulder. "But, with this gentleman's assistance, you are responsible for fraud, namely, the forging of your uncle's last will and testament to ensure you—and only you—inherited his entire estate."

"That's *demmed* slander!" Ned growled.

"It would be, if it were false, yes," Mr Elliott replied. "Mr Forbes has already confessed to assisting you, however, and that makes it true. According to his account—that I believe, by the way—you required the entire estate to cover your outstanding gambling debts. We've already had evidence of such from Mr Bund in the form of his loan. You shall gain nothing by denying the allegation."

"But I *shall*, sir!" Ned yelled as his face turned bright red, again. "And I *do*! If Mr Forbes drafted a false will, then it had nothing whatever to do with me!"

"You paid me to do it, you bugger!" Carlton Forbes, Jr. yelled.

"Are you willing to swear to that under oath?" Mr Elliott enquired.

"Yeah, on the Pope's life, even," Carlton Forbes, Jr. replied.

"*Leech*, that is what you are, Ned Cosgrove," Miss Watkins hissed. "A *leech*."

Mr Elliott removed his hands from Carlton Forbes, Jr. and the two advanced upon Ned as Mr Elliott explained, "Mr Carlton Forbes, Snr was the executor of your uncle's will. Yet, his memory had been failing prior to your uncle's murder. He was therefore unable to recognise the forgery—that his own *son* had written—when he read it after the professor's funeral. Unfortunately, Mr Forbes, Snr, isn't well enough to confirm this, but his son is. I'm obliged to ask you. Therefore, do you still deny your guilt, Mr Cosgrove?"

"I had no choice," Ned yelled as his voice shook as much as his body. "You've seen the kind of men I'm forced to do business with—and Mr Bund isn't the worst! My gambling debts could've never been repaid with my original inheritance. I *had* to have it all. I... I knew Uncle Benjamin had disinherited Norman, and-and was unhappy with Coral. Mr Lane and Miss Price would keep working for me, so I knew they'd be taken care of. Mr Forbes, Jr. agreed to write the new will because he could *see* how much trouble I was in. I *swear* to you, Mr Elliott, Inspector, the new will was written *after* my uncle was murdered. Tell them, Mr Forbes, tell them!"

"It's true," Carlton Forbes, Jr. said.

"How do you know Ned didn't murder my husband, and persuade you to forge a new will after the fact?" Coral enquired with suspicious eyes.

"But I didn't!" Ned yelled. "I shall swear it to God, Almighty! I was at the gambling den at the time! Inspector, *please*, tell her! I was at the table, remember?"

"Yes, I remember," Lee replied. "It was as he says, Mrs Cosgrove."

"And we believe the inspector's testimony," Mr Elliott said. "It—and Mr Forbes' genuine fear at being found out—has exonerated Mr Ned Cosgrove of any wrong doing as far as the professor's murder is concerned."

"But not over the will," Adam Cosgrove interjected with a glare cast in his uncle's direction.

"Hold your tongue, you," Ned said as he whirled around. "You've no right to even be here."

"Norman Cosgrove was my father," Adam replied. "I intend to redeem his reputation and claim what's rightfully mine."

Ned grunted and, with a sneer, said, "Norman was already written out of Uncle Benjamin's will, boy. You'll get *nothing*, and my brother can rot in the ground as the murderer he is."

"Your brother was innocent," Mr Maxwell interjected.

"He couldn't of done it 'cause 'e were wit his boy at his boardin' school," Mr Skinner said.

"When I telephoned Inspector Lee earlier today, he confirmed the account given by both Adam and Norman during the original investigation," Mr Elliott said.

"I had no idea…" Mrs Cosgrove said with great sadness. "…If I had…" She pressed her hand to her mouth to stifle a sob. "Oh, *Norman,* please forgive me." She turned her gaze to Adam. "And you"—she reached across to put her hand on his—"I'm sorry for ever thinking your father could've…" She dabbed at her eyes with her handkerchief. "He was a good man—a far better man than Benjamin ever was."

"How *dare* you," Miss Watkins said with a scowl. "Benjamin loved you—for all the good it did him. If anyone was contemptible, it was you."

"So speaketh the woman who longed to take my place," Coral retorted.

"And what of it?" Miss Watkins replied. "He would've been happier with me—he would still be alive today, if he'd married *me* instead of *you*."

"But he didn't," Miss Dexter said. "Coral was his wife, and you made no secret of your disapproval of her relationship with Norman."

"It was *disgusting*," Miss Watkins remarked.

Coral's eyes narrowed as she stood. "Benjamin was *beyond* cruel to me; he treated me no better than a prostitute when we couldn't bear a child."

Mr Locke stood in between the two ladies.

"An appropriate reaction," Miss Watkins replied with a sneer.

Coral lunged forward with a raised hand, but Mr Locke caught her wrist and held it tight. "Unhand me, Percy!" she yelled and swung her other hand toward him. Again, he caught her wrist and held both against her sides.

"You had no business being Mrs Benjamin Cosgrove," Miss Watkins said as she stood. "You brought him nothing but heartache."

"Pardon me, Inspector," Carlton Forbes, Jr. whispered as he leaned over the desk. "But may I go…? If you don't require me any longer, that is."

Inspector Lee regarded the scene. "Very well," he said and gave Carlton Forbes, Jr. his calling card. "Be certain to present this to the sergeant when you arrive at Kensington Police Station tomorrow morning."

"I shall, inspector," Carlton Forbes, Jr. replied as he pocketed the card.

"Sit *down*, Coral," Mr Locke said and guided her back to her chair while Carlton Forbes, Jr. slipped from the room.

"You, too, Miss Watkins," Mr Verity said as he tapped the back of her chair. "It's time for our séance."

TWENTY-FIVE

Miss Watkins spun around as her hard gaze vanished. The rigid lines of her jaw and mouth had also eased into a look of utter astonishment. "Séance…?" she enquired while Mr Verity took her by the elbow and eased her into the chair, she said. "You don't think the doll is haunted, though."

"It isn't. This room may be, however," Mr Verity replied with a smile. "I know how much you want to talk to the professor—and Mr Elmore, too. I dunno about Mr Elmore, but I think we'll have better luck reaching the professor here. It was the place he died—where he was murdered. That connection should make it easier for him to cross the veil."

Ned Cosgrove muttered an obscenity as he stood. "Are you going to allow this *nonsense*, Inspector?"

"I wish to satisfy my curiosity," Lee replied. "Sit down, Mr Cosgrove. The sooner Mr Verity completes his séance, the sooner we may leave."

Ned grunted but plonked back down onto his chair with a zealous chewing of his tongue and another string of mumbled obscenities.

"I don't approve of this debacle, either, Percy. If you intend to accuse one of us, then do so. Don't hide behind smoke and parlour tricks," Coral said.

"Perish the thought. My illusions are *far* more elaborate than that," Mr Locke replied with a smirk. As he felt another wave of heat rise from his core, he wiped his brow and returned to the open window.

"I doubt we'll be successful, Mr Verity," Miss Watkins said as she grasped her brooch and watched him wander over to Carlton Forbes, Jr.'s vacant chair opposite. "Even if we *could* reach Benjamin and Mr Elmore, what would you expect them to say? As you've already explained, the doll was used to murder these gentlemen. Neither would know the identity of their murderer."

"True," Mr Verity replied and accepted his bag from Mr Snyder. From it, he took his bible, salt vessel, and bottle of Holy Water. "The professor, or Mr Elmore, Snr, may recall something—a detail, a memory, a *word*—which could shed light on this whole thing." He thumbed through his bible while Mr Snyder moved his bag. "Provided I have permission to contact your father, Mr Elmore?"

"Anything to cleanse the sin of suicide from my father's memory," Mr Elmore, Jr. replied.

The butler wiped his hands upon his waistcoat and enquired, "Will you be needing Miss Price and me?"

"I'll need everyone," Mr Verity replied as he looked across his shoulder at the servants. "First, to bless the gathering." He cleared his throat and read the relevant, biblical passages aloud while he sprinkled the air with Holy Water. "Please, can everyone join hands? You too, Inspector. We'll also need *absolute* silence."

The members of the Bow Street Society occupied the gaps between the chairs and took the hands of those sitting on either side. Mr Locke was between Coral and Miss Watkins, Doctor Locke was between Miss Watkins and the butler, Brenda Kershaw was between the butler and the maid, Bernice Kershaw was between the maid and Mr Elmore, Jr., Mr Maxwell was between Mr Elmore, Jr. and Miss Dexter—who'd taken Carlton Forbes Jr's seat, Mr Snyder was between Miss Dexter and Mr Verity—who's taken the moneylender's seat, and Mr Elliott was between Mr Verity and Inspector Lee who was also stood. Mrs Cosgrove's other hand took the inspector's to complete the circle.

Everyone looked to the doll in the circle's centre as the thunder increased and the wind gust through the open window to pull at the fire and howl within the chimney breast.

306

"Professor Benjamin Cosgrove," Mr Verity boomed. "If you're here with us now, please, come forward. We mean you no disrespect." Brilliant white light filled the room as thunder crashed. As the library was plunged back into darkness, the pitter-patter of rain sounded outside. Within moments though, the rain became heavier and struck the pavements, window, and walkway without mercy. "Professor Benjamin Cosgrove! Please, come forward!"

"This is a *demmed* waste of my time—" Ned said but a thud against the ceiling cut him off. "What was that…?" The colour drained from his face as he—and everyone else—looked up.

"Professor Cosgrove, did you make that noise?" Mr Verity enquired. "One knock for yes, two knocks for no."

A single thud followed.

"But it *can't* be Benjamin," Coral said in a voice choked by fear.

"It's got to be someone upstairs," the butler remarked as the maid gripped his arm.

"Shall we see…?" Mr Verity enquired with a smile as he stood with the aid of his cane. He then walked to the door when no one moved. "If it's someone living, you've got nothing to fear, have you?"

Coral grimaced as she glanced up.

Ned shifted his weight from one side to the other, while Miss Watkins' fingers trembled as they grasped her brooch. She, too, was looking up, wide eyed.

"I, for one, want to speak to whomever thinks this is amusing," Mr Elmore, Jr. said as he followed Mr Verity from the room. He was joined by Mr Locke, Mr Elliott, and Mr Skinner, while Miss Dexter and Mr Maxwell left at a more cautious pace. The room's remaining occupants stayed sitting until Inspector Lee ventured after the others. At which point they raced one another to avoid being the last in the library.

"'Ere's where the noise came from," Mr Snyder remarked when they stepped onto the landing to join him. He stood by a closed door on the left side of the house.

"Benjamin's bedroom," Miss Watkins whispered.

Mr Snyder tried the handle but found it to be locked. Another loud—and clear—thud came from within the room and both Miss Watkins and Mrs Cosgrove shrieked.

"I'll put a stop to this!" Ned yelled as he shoved the others aside to unlock the door. No sooner had he threw it open and peered inside though, did he stumble backward and shield his face with his arm. "It's *empty*!" He then lunged to grip the balustrade as everyone piled into the bedroom.

"It *is* Benjamin," Miss Watkins declared when she saw the vacant bedroom. As she ran her wide eyes over it, she brought up her shaking hands to cover her mouth.

While Mr Elmore, Jr. opened the wardrobe to reveal the clothes within, Mrs Cosgrove dropped onto the edge of the bed and gripped her chest to ease her racing heart. Most of the Bow Street Society members loitered around the door and fireplace, but Mr Locke went to the window to look east down Oakley Street. He gave a smirk and subtle nod before he drew the curtains and watched Inspector Lee check the unoccupied space under the bed.

"Professor Cosgrove," Mr Locke said. "We thank you for stepping across the veil to reach out to us tonight." He wiped his brow and walked toward the bed. "If you are still with us, please make yourself known."

There were three taps against the window.

Everyone listened to the rain in the moments which ensued.

Three more taps sounded, and Mr Locke threw open the curtains in one, swift, movement.

"*Benjamin!*" Miss Watkins yelled as she saw a figure, entombed in black robes, crouched upon the ledge. Its pale fingers tapped at the glass as ran poured from its hand. "It *can't* be…" Miss Watkins wailed and the figure's hand slammed, repeatedly, against the glass. "*No!*" Miss Watkins threw herself against the wall and dislodged a painting. As it landed with a loud thud, she gave a more indiscriminate wail and attempted to flee the room. Inspector Lee, Mr Snyder, and Mr Skinner blocked the door, however. "Let me out!" She clawed at their arms, shoulders, and clothes. "*Let me out, I beg of you!*"

The hand continued to slam against the window.

"No, *please!*" Miss Watkins yelled as she pressed her body against Inspector Lee's and he gripped her arms to hold her still. "I *swear* I never knew the truth until it was too late, Benjamin!"

"What truth is that, Miss Watkins?" Mr Verity enquired as he stood beside the window where the hand continued to slam against the glass. "*What* did you *do?*"

Bang. Bang. Bang.

"I thought he despised me," Miss Watkins said as she kept her gaze on the malevolent apparition.

Bang. Bang. Bang.

"*Confess*, Miss Watkins," Mr Verity ordered. "Confess so he may know some peace!"

BANG. BANG. BANG.

"I *can't!*" Miss Watkins wailed.

BANG. BANG. BANG.

"Confess!" Mr Verity yelled and pointed at Adam Cosgrove. "*Confess* that *you* are this lad's mam!"

BANG. BANG. BANG.

"*Confess* that *you* wanted *nothing* to do with him, and *that* was why Norman Cosgrove lied about his mam dying!" Mr Verity urged.

BANG. BANG. BANG.

"*No!*" Miss Watkins yelled.

"Your name is on his birth certificate!" Mr Verity boomed as he took the document from Mr Elliott and held it in front of her face. "*YOURS*, Miss Watkins! *Not* Mrs Cosgrove's. She couldn't have any bairns; a lost pregnancy in her youth put an end to those hopes! *YOU* are Adam Cosgrove's mam."

BANG. BANG. BANG.

"*Stop* it, Benjamin, *please*!" Miss Watkins wailed.

"*Confess* that *you* had the study key copied!" Mr Verity boomed. "That *you* took Mr Lane's revolver from the flour pot! That *you* put the wire into the doll and gave it the loaded revolver! *Confess* to you *murdering* the man you loved because he *turned* you away when he was told the truth of your *shame* by Norman!"

BANG. BANG. BANG.

"*CONFESS*!" Mr Verity shouted as he unhooked the latch on the window's doors.

Violent winds threw them open, and a deluge of rain exploded into the bedroom. Black robes billowed around the figure as its fingers gripped the window frame and it lowered its foot to the floor.

"*I CONFESS!*" Miss Watkins screamed, and her legs gave way beneath her. Lee released her arms and she collapsed onto her knees while the figure straightened to its full height to tower over her. "No, *please*, no! I beg of you, Benjamin!" Miss Watkins fell forward onto the rug and buried her face into its pile. Her fingers also dug into it as her entire body shook. "I confess! I *confess*… I murdered you!"

Mr Locke closed the window and reapplied the latch.

The robed figure meanwhile pushed back its hood to reveal dark-brown hair and the youthful, stubble-covered face of a man in his late-twenties. Looking to Lee, he enquired, "Is it done, sir?"

"Yes, Sergeant Gutman," Lee replied with a grave tone. "It's done." While the sergeant nodded and removed his damp robes to hang by the fire, Lee ushered Coral, Adam, Mr Elmore, Jr., the butler, and maid past Miss Watkins. "Come on, everyone, back downstairs." As Ned joined them on the landing, Lee closed the bedroom door.

Doctor Locke, concerned by her husband's appearance, put her hand on his arm and looked at him with questioning eyes. With a weak smile, he said, "I am well."

Mr Verity, meanwhile, placed a gentle hand upon Miss Watkins' back and rubbed between her shoulders. "Shhhh," he said. "The professor's spirit is now at peace." He stood a chair beside her prone form and reached down to take her hands. "Come on, now, sit down."

Miss Watkins lifted her head and sobbed when she saw Gutman. Nonetheless, she allowed Mr Verity to help her onto the chair while the tears poured from her eyes.

"Perhaps, if you talked us through what happened, lass," Mr Verity said and put his hand on her shoulder. "It'll make you feel better."

"I-I shall never feel p-peace again," Miss Watkins said through shuddering breaths.

"But you may commence your road to redemption by completing your confession," Mr Verity said.

Miss Watkins bowed her head and wrapped her body in her arms. Her breathing continued to warble as more sobs escaped her lips. "I-I should *never* have done what I did…"

The other Bow Street Society members sat upon the bed to listen.

"…I thought he d-despised me for having Adam, for lying with Norman," Miss Watkins said. "Before he knew the truth, he was kind and generous with me. Afterward, he was *cruel* and *despicable*. He'd often yell and chastise me for the most minor mistakes in my work."

"The arguments Miss Price overheard," Miss Dexter remarked in a soft voice.

Miss Watkins nodded. "Eventually, I reached the end of my tether and decided to silence his hatred." She swallowed as she unpinned the brooch and held it in her lap. "I knew how the doll moved, and how deaf Benjamin was. I had the key copied by Mr Holland on Whitechapel

Road. He came to the house and I told him Benjamin wanted it made. I took the revolver from the pot of flour in the pantry and made a mess by tossing the flour onto the floor, so it would look like a delivery boy had stolen the gun. I-I knew Mr Lane wouldn't miss it until after…" She pressed her trembling hand to her lips as she gave another sob. "Oh *God…*" She wrapped her hands around the brooch as she closed her eyes. "Who art in Heaven… hallowed be thy name…" Her voice trailed off and she broke down into violent sobbing.

"The professor asked you to leave when Norman told him you were Adam's mother," Miss Dexter said.

Miss Watkins nodded but couldn't speak.

"You loved him," Mr Maxwell said with sadness. "You wanted to be his wife but he… spurned your affections in light of your betrayal. The same betrayal committed by Coral." Mr Maxwell's gaze drifted to Miss Dexter and he felt a tremendous wrench deep inside his heart. "And when he was cold toward you after his argument with her, you decided to see your plan through."

"Yes." Miss Watkins pressed the brooch to her heart. "I'd locked myself in the study that morning to thread the wire through the mechanism and put the revolver into the doll's hand."

"And you used your spare key to the study to unlock the door following the gunshot," Mr Locke said as he held his trembling hands behind his back. "Entering the room ahead of Mrs Cosgrove… you opened the window while her attention was on her husband's dead body. Then, you pocketed the doll's key." Mr Locke held out his gloved hand.

Miss Watkins looked to it and then her brooch. For several moments she stared at it as her shoulders bounced from her silent sobs. "It's true," she whispered before she kissed the silhouette and pressed the brooch into his hand.

"You also kept the study key, using it again following your conversation with Norman on the night before the funeral," Mr Locke said while his fingers closed around the brooch. "Mrs Cosgrove had seen you two leave the study but could not recall who had locked the door. She only knew it was locked due to a requirement she had to enter the study later. The door was locked then. She even assumed—wrongly—she had unlocked the study door following the gunshot since, according to her recollection, you never had a spare key."

"Ye could've taken the professor's key," Mr Skinner said. "But ev'ryone were so used to seein' it on his desk, ye couldn't risk 'em noticin' it were gone."

"You felt your act of murder was justified in the circumstances," Mr Elliott said in his usual monotone. "You had given the professor many years of selfless, loyal, loving service but he had turned against you over one foolish mistake that resulted in you bearing a bastard child."

"After his first wife died, I continued to serve him in the hope of winning his love," Miss Watkins said as her gaze remained fixed upon Mr Locke's closed hand. "But he was either ignorant or dismissive of my affections, for he never once returned them. I was hurt, and Norman took advantage of my weakened state."

"You thought you'd gotten away with your secret when Norman took in the lad and told everyone his muvva had died," Mr Snyder said. "But then he told his uncle—why?"

"He had the *ridiculous* expectation I should be part of Adam's life, if only in secret," Miss Watkins said with a sneer. "I told him, in no uncertain terms, that Adam was *no* child of mine."

"When the professor's last will and testament was read out after the funeral though, you discovered the truth of his affection toward you, and the guilt burrowed its way into your heart," Mr Maxwell said.

"That's why you've been trying to talk to him, and Mr Elmore, to ask their forgiveness," Mr Verity said.

Fresh tears rolled down Miss Watkins' face. "I never meant for anyone else to die… I thought, by taking the key, I could stop it. I'd planned to retrieve the wire and revolver but there was no time. The police kept searching the house. I was never alone with the doll for longer than a minute. If I'd known Ned had sold the doll…" She sobbed some more. "Please forgive me, Benjamin… Mr Elmore…"

"Where's the doll's key, then?" Brenda Kershaw enquired.

"Yes, where's that key? You said the murderer should still have it, Mr Locke," Bernice added.

"She does," Mr Locke replied as he held up the brooch for the twins to see and pressed its side. Its front popped open with a click to reveal a small, brass key with a chipped tooth and rose engraved upon its handle. "Only Miss Watkins knew of the key's chipped tooth." Mr Locke took the key out and snapped the brooch shut. "The rose marking is a generic one; most would attach it to the key as a means of identifying it, rather than the tooth. Yet, after six years of—allegedly—not laying eyes upon it, Miss Watkins named the key's unique feature. It is unlikely she could have remembered it if she had not seen the key recently. It was therefore only logical she was lying when she claimed to not know the key's whereabouts."

"And the brooch?" Brenda enquired.

"Yes, how did you know it was in there?" Bernice added.

"I did not," Mr Locke replied. "In Miss Dexter's report from her first—and only—meeting with Miss Watkins she remarked upon Miss Watkins' tendency to hold this brooch."

Miss Dexter nodded. "Yes, that's correct. She was most fond of it."

"When I saw the brooch this evening, therefore, I suspected it was large enough to conceal a key," Mr Locke said.

"And the silhouette bein' the professor also gave the game away," Mr Snyder remarked.

Mr Locke smiled. "Indeed." His smile faded when he looked down at Miss Watkins though. "Darling…" He looked to his wife. "Would you escort Miss Watkins downstairs with the inspector, please?"

"I shall," Doctor Locke replied and put her arm around Miss Watkins' shoulders.

"I'll take good care of you," Inspector Lee reassured as Miss Watkins stood and turned her bloodshot eyes toward him.

"My conscience is clear now that Benjamin and Mr Elmore may rest in peace," Miss Watkins replied. "I… I am ready to face the judgement of my Creator." She slowly looked to Mr Locke's hand. "May I have my brooch, please?"

"Of course," Mr Locke replied and placed it in her hand. "Keep it close."

"I will," Miss Watkins said as she closed her fingers around it. "Thank you…" She allowed Inspector Lee to take her by the arm and lead her from the room. Behind them went Doctor Locke and Mr Verity, while the other Bow Street Society members and Sergeant Gutman sat in silence to digest what they'd just heard.

EPILOGUE

COSGROVE MURDER CASE SOLVED

The long-standing, unsolved case of the murder of Professor Benjamin Cosgrove has been solved by an inspector of the Metropolitan Police's T Division, Gideon Lee. The individual responsible—Miss Henrietta Watkins—made a full confession at the Kensington police station where Inspector Lee brought the case to a close after six years of dogged police work.

In an exclusive interview with your correspondent this morning, Inspector Lee revealed, "Miss Watkins became distraught with guilt once the facts were laid out before her. Her confession was not coerced in any way and was given with repeated expressions of remorse." The inspector went on to describe how Miss Watkins had also accepted responsibility for the death of Mr Edgar Elmore. Due to the circumstances which surrounded his death, a verdict of suicide was returned at the inquest several months ago. According to the inspector, Mr Elmore had "purchased the antique automaton Miss Watkins had used to murder Professor Cosgrove with. She'd armed the automaton with a loaded revolver to shoot the professor while she was elsewhere. She hadn't intended to murder Mr Elmore and deeply regrets her actions."

Miss Watkins is due to appear before a judge in the Central Criminal Court at the Old Bailey later today. In light of her unadulterated confession, it's expected the judge will show clemency and pass down a sentence of life imprisonment.

Mr Elliott lowered the *Gaslight Gazette* with a deep sense of disappointment. He'd come across the newspaper by chance in the Law Society's library. When he'd read the headline, he'd expected the article to describe the Bow Street Society's triumphant exposure of a cold-blooded murderess.

Mr Oswald Baldwin. Mr Elliott didn't recognise the journalist's name and wondered if Mr Maxwell knew he'd published the story first. Ever since the Oxford Street murders, it had become routine for Mr Maxwell to write about the Bow Street Society's cases in the *Gaslight Gazette*. Mr Elliott also doubted Miss Trent had allowed Inspector Lee to claim the recognition for the Society's hard work. He read the article, again, and his disappointment turned into anger as he realised there was little they could do to overturn Inspector Lee's deception. If the Bow Street Society cried falsehood, the journalistic press would no doubt accuse it of attempting to ride on the coattails of Inspector Lee's success. Even if, by some miracle, the Bow Street Society's claim was believed, its relationship with the police would become even more problematic.

"Fulfilling your duty, I see," Inspector Lee said from above.

Mr Elliott put the newspaper down and reached for his book. "I doubt if you know the meaning of duty."

Inspector Lee pulled out the chair opposite and sat. While Mr Elliott pretended to read, Lee reached for the newspaper and read the headline. "I know chapter and verse," Lee replied with a smirk. "As demonstrated by Mr Baldwin's superb article."

"Perhaps, I should've used the word 'honour', then. For you clearly don't possess such a quality," Mr Elliott said and glared at him with a clenched jaw.

"My conscience is clear. The investigation into the murder of Professor Benjamin Cosgrove was mine at the start and mine at the end. I'll concede the Bow Street Society leant its assistance—"

"We *solved* it for you. Without us, you would've still been searching for your fictional housebreaker."

"But the Bow Street Society doesn't have the authority to arrest the murderers it exposes, or to make them answer for their crimes in court," Inspector Lee said. "All it can do is give a name and pray the investigating police officer believes their theories." He smiled. "Like I did."

"I shan't allow you to perpetuate a lie."

"Shan't you?" Inspector Lee stood and walked around the table. "I rather think you shall." He sat beside Mr Elliott and placed a hand upon his leg. Though they were alone in the library, he was careful to ensure the gesture was hidden by the table. "I enjoyed your company," he said as he leaned close to Mr Elliott's ear. "I'd like to enjoy it again."

"I'm reluctant to spend my time with deceivers," Mr Elliott replied and pushed the hand away.

"As I told you before, Mr Elliott, I'm the protector of Chelsea's wealthy elite. They expect me to maintain order within their little idyll, and I have…" He remained close to Mr Elliott's ear but kept his hands to himself. "It's imperative to the success of my police work that I share a

318

mutual respect with them. They reveal interesting—often scandalous—pieces of information with me when they believe in my discretion." He smiled. "Such as the identity of your actual client, Lord Michael Weeks."

Mr Elliott turned his head.

"I rather thought that would catch your attention." Lee smirked. "It certainly caught mine." His hand rested upon Mr Elliott's leg once more. "I suspect Lord Weeks is reluctant to be associated with murder and deadly dolls." He glanced at the newspaper. "It's why I neglected to tell Mr Baldwin of his connection to the case." He moved his lips closer to Mr Elliott's face and continued in a hushed tone, "That could all change, however, if you, Miss Trent, or anyone else associated with the Bow Street Society attempt to sully my good reputation by printing an alternative version of events."

"You'd sully your reputation by exposing Lord Weeks," Mr Elliott pointed out.

"Measures have been put in place to ensure the British press describes the Bow Street Society as a negligent bunch of buffoons, should it try to refute my account of this case." Inspector Lee pulled the newspaper across to sit in front of Mr Elliott. "It could never hope to recover from such a scandal."

"I see you've given me no choice but to comply," Mr Elliott said through a grimace.

"There's always a choice. You've just made the right one." Inspector Lee smiled and patted his leg.

"But why come to me and not Miss Trent?"

"I trust your conviction more than hers. She has a wholly disagreeable attitude of defiance toward authority." Inspector Lee withdrew his hand to rest on his own knee. "I'd also like to think you and I have a connection—a mutual respect." He picked up the newspaper. "This article wasn't written to undermine your good work, Mr Elliott, but to shore up the fragile face of police respectability in the public consciousness." He tossed the newspaper aside.

"You're an intelligent and honourable man, and I admire you for it."

Mr Elliott's jaw clenched as he swallowed hard. Nonetheless, he kept his gaze upon Inspector Lee's intense, dark-blue hues while his intellect conceded the policeman's deception had been a masterful stroke. "The business of Mr Ned Cosgrove and Mr Carlton Forbes Jr. forging the professor's Last Will & Testament, what will come of it?" he enquired once he'd decided to return the discussion to less emotive matters.

"Both gentlemen wrote, and signed, full confessions. Based upon this—and the fact that six years have passed and the professor's estate is all but gone—it was decided no further action would be taken against the pair," Inspector Lee said.

"Doesn't Mrs Cosgrove, and Mr Adam Cosgrove, want to pursue their rightful inheritances?"

"Mr Ned Cosgrove has agreed to grant Mrs Cosgrove a yearly allowance, as per the terms of the original will—at a greatly reduced amount, of course. Mr Adam Cosgrove isn't entitled to anything since his father inherited nothing from the professor in either version of the will."

Mr Elliott frowned. "It doesn't seem fair."

"Life isn't, I'm afraid," Inspector Lee replied and stood. "Mr Lane and Miss Price's legacies shall be granted as outlined in the original will." He leaned down to place his lips beside Mr Elliott's ear once more. "I meant what I said about enjoying your company again, Mr Elliott. Think it over." He then left.

* * *

The birdsong outside Mr Locke's study window invaded his consciousness like nails down a chalk board. As his eyelids flickered and opened, the dull daylight hurt his bloodshot eyes and caused his temples to throb. With a

320

groan, he lifted his hand to shield his eyes and heard the clatter of the empty needle as it fell from the sofa and onto the floor.

Another, prolonged, groan sounded as he rolled onto his side and peeled his dry tongue from his mouth's roof. "Jam—" His hoarse voice broke as he coughed and gripped the sofa's edge. "James!"

The door was unlocked at once and his valet entered to assist his master in sitting up.

"What time is it?" Mr Locke enquired once his back was against the sofa's.

"Noon, sir."

"Close those curtains, will you?" Mr Locke requested as he turned his face away from the window.

While he carried out his master's request, James announced, "Your bath is prepared, and your clothes are laid out for your approval. Will you be taking breakfast this morning, sir?"

Mr Locke grimaced. "No… I could not stomach it. Is my wife tending to her clinic?"

"Your wife is behind you," Doctor Locke said.

Mr Locke looked to the open doorway but could only distinguish her silhouette in the gloom. "Good afternoon, darling."

"Is it?" Doctor Locke enquired as she came into the room and pulled back the curtains. Mr Locke winced and shielded his eyes the moment the daylight poured in. "You and I have a great deal to discuss, Percy. Starting with your unacceptable behaviour at Bow Street yesterday." She stood before the window with her hands upon her hips. "I've never felt so *embarrassed*."

"Could we have this discussion in private, darling?" Mr Locke enquired with a glance at James.

Doctor Locke gave a frustrated sigh. "You're a fool if you think the servants aren't aware of your habits." Nonetheless, she turned to James and said, "Please fetch my husband a glass of milk and a bowl of gruel."

"Do as my wife said, James," Mr Locke said to his valet and watched him leave. When they were alone, he looked to Doctor Locke with hardened eyes. "If you wish to discuss unacceptable behaviour, Lynette, let us not neglect your impromptu visit to Brighton." He gripped the sofa's arm as he stood. "You speak of your embarrassment, but what of mine? I was obliged to sit, in silence, while my wife lied to my associates."

"I didn't lie. Everything that happened during my conversation with Mrs Cosgrove was as I described it," Doctor Locke replied.

"I am not referring to your conversation with her, but the reason you gave for having it at all." Mr Locke crossed to his desk to light a cigarette. "You have *never* treated a barren woman in all your years of medical practise."

"And how would you know? You're too busy injecting heroin to have the first clue about my work."

"Do not attempt to divert the blame onto me, Lynette." Mr Locke exhaled the smoke away from her. "I have enough of the burden to last a lifetime." He moved closer to her. "Did you tell Coral of the true reasoning behind your suspicions?"

Doctor Locke looked away with a grimace as she folded her arms. "Don't be absurd."

"Why is it absurd? By your own admission, you were looking to gain her trust. What better way is there than to admit you suffer from the same affliction as she?"

"I wasn't going to uncover the truth at the cost of my own dignity, *Percy*," Doctor Locke said as she looked back at him. "Nor was I going to *humiliate* me—and, yes, *you*—by admitting to the *entire* Bow Street Society that I'm unable to bear you a child!" She walked past him to sit on the sofa's edge and turn her bowed head away.

When Mr Locke heard the delicate sobs, he discarded his cigarette, and sat beside her. As he tried to embrace her though, she slipped free and retreated to the window. "I've rescheduled the appointments I was due to have today," she mumbled through bitter tears. "Once you've taken your bath and had your breakfast, I expect you to rest in the parlour for the remainder of the day."

"I have rehearsals at the Palladium to attend—"

"It was *not* a request." Doctor Locke glared at him. "Your body needs time to adjust to the reduced dose, and I will *not* have you feverish in front of the performers."

Mr Locke's brow had lofted at her admission. When she was finished, he considered her terms and stood to crush out his discarded cigarette in the ashtray. Without meeting her gaze, he said, "If you were to give me an additional dose, I would not have the fever."

Doctor Locke's eyes narrowed. "I hope you're not being serious."

"It is only logical, darling," Mr Locke replied. "You are concerned about my performers seeing me in a fever and I am reluctant to miss rehearsals. An additional dose would solve both our problems—"

The impact of his wife's hand upon his cheek cut him off.

"You are *unbelievable*, Percy Locke," she said with fierce eyes and a fiercer scowl. "After *everything* we have endured this week—everything we *discussed*— because of your dependency, you have the bare-faced audacity to request *more*?!"

"I was simply suggesting—"

"There is *nothing* simple about it! Just look at yourself. You're weak, pale, and in the same clothes you wore last night—it's despicable."

"I have only just awoken—"

"At *noon*," Doctor Locke retorted. "Following a slumber induced by heroin that you all but *begged* me for last night. We made an agreement when you almost humiliated yourself in front of the Bow Street Society. You came *very* close to doing so, again, last night. Shivering, trembling, sweating—*absentmindedness*, where shall it end? How much of a degradation will you tolerate before you realise the heroin is *destroying* you?"

"I am in perfect control, Lynette." He picked up the empty needle, but his wife held out her hand.

"*I'm* the one in control," she replied. "You simply surrender to temptation and expect me to pick up the pieces."

He placed the needle onto her hand. "I can stop whenever I want."

Doctor Locke pocketed the needle and, with a sad frown, replied, "No, Percy, you can't. That's why we are where we are." She went to the door and looked back at him. "Your bath water will be getting cold. I'll be waiting downstairs for you." She turned to leave but, again, stepped back. "The front door is also locked, and I have the key and your picks." She strode onto the landing and, as she passed James, said, "My husband is ready for his bath. Please serve his breakfast downstairs once he's dressed."

"Yes, ma'am," James replied with a bow.

Mr Locke sighed. "Come, then, James." He left his study. "A gentleman does not keep his fair lady waiting, after all."

"Yes, sir," James replied with another bow and followed his master.

As Mr Locke went along the landing he removed each item of clothing and tossed it onto the floor. He was therefore nude by the time he entered the room where a high-backed, ceramic bath stood. His valet—who'd collected the items as soon as they were dropped—followed him inside and closed the door.

* * *

"Yes, I understand that, Mr Maxwell—" Miss Trent paused as she listened to his panicked voice on the other end of the telephone. "You couldn't have known Inspector Lee's intentions—Mr Maxwell, it's done. Please,

324

calm yourself." She rolled her eyes at his continued histrionics. "*Mr Maxwell…*" She took a moment to calm her irritation. "Mr Maxwell, I don't place any blame for the article upon your shoulders. Cease your worrying and have a cup of sweet tea." She listened. "Yes, that's correct." She nodded. "Yes, very well. Thank you, Mr Maxwell. Goodbye." She leaned toward the telephone's box. "*Goodbye*." The receiver was hooked back onto its cradle and she sat back with a sigh. "I swear that man pushes me to the limits of my patience at times."

"Jones' not gonna like this," Conway remarked as he read the *Gaslight Gazette* article for the second time. "I always knew Lee was a devious bugger."

"Richard can't openly contradict one of his inspectors without questions being asked," Miss Trent replied. She took a file from the top drawer of her desk and passed it across. "Here, my final progress report on the case. It includes another that you may give to Inspector Lee."

Conway opened its cover and flicked through its pages. When he reached a particular passage, he paused, read it again, and looked up at her with clear confusion upon his worn features. "Am I reading this right?"

Miss Trent tore open an envelope and pulled out its letter as she enquired, "What are you reading?"

"It says 'ere some bloke called Lord Michael Weeks was the Society's client."

Miss Trent hummed and read Mr Partridge's name at the bottom of the letter.

"That's not in the 'paper."

"Because we haven't revealed the fact to Inspector Lee," Miss Trent replied as she returned to the letter's start. Its contents were as expected. Their mutual friend was very grateful. The doll had been dispatched to America for valuation, and a generous payment would be made to the Bow Street Society in recognition of its work.

"Why not? I thought you was being open with coppers now."

"We are." Miss Trent put the letter away. "But, aside from being the doll's current owner, Lord Weeks was unconnected to the case. Revealing his name to Inspector Lee would've served no purpose, other than exposing him to ridicule."

"And what about Doctor Weeks?"

"What about him?"

"Lord Weeks is his dad, yeah?"

"There's no evidence to suggest that," Miss Trent said as she opened another letter and discovered it to be from her aunt in Tonbridge, Kent. She therefore set it aside to read later. "I don't want you putting a cat amongst the pigeons, John. Lord Weeks expects discretion and, thus far, the Society has given it to him. I only revealed his identity in the report to Jones because of his connection to the Society. It's not an official piece of information so, please, forget you ever read it."

Conway frowned but, with a deep exhale, closed the file and picked up his trilby from the desk. "Woolfe been 'round to gloat yet?"

"First thing this morning," Miss Trent replied with a frown. "He was smiling from ear to ear as he basked in the Society's 'failure' to 'humiliate the police at their own game'. He suggested we rethink our existence because, as he put it, 'the police aren't as incompetent as the public assumes' and we should 'quit while we've still some reputation to salvage'."

A knock then came from the front door and they both stood.

"I don't doubt he'll say the same to you the next time you meet," Miss Trent said as they crossed the hallway.

"Yeah," Conway replied and waited as she unbolted and opened the door.

"Mr Elmore," Miss Trent said, surprised, when their visitor was revealed. "I wasn't expecting your visit."

"I've come to thank the Bow Street Society," Mr Elmore, Jr. replied.

Conway put on his trilby and stepped out onto the porch while Miss Trent invited Mr Elmore, Jr. inside. "I'd best be gettin' back to the Yard. Good day to you, Mr Elmore." He touched the brim of his hat and looked to the clerk. "Miss Trent."

"Goodbye, Inspector," Miss Trent replied and closed the door. "I'm afraid there's no one else here at the moment."

"I expected as much," Mr Elmore, Jr. replied with a frown. "I had to arrange for Doctor Wren to sit with Mother while I came, you see, and his schedule is rather chaotic. Otherwise, I would've written ahead of time."

"How is Mrs Elmore?"

"Still unwell—I doubt she'll ever fully recover—but she's greatly comforted by the knowledge her love will be waiting for her on the other side." His smile faded. "I was wondering—if you'd like to, of course, and if it isn't too inconvenient—if you and the other Bow Street Society members would care to attend Father's funeral? He's to be reburied in the churchyard with full Catholic rights in a few days' time."

Miss Trent smiled. "I would be honoured to, Mr Elmore, and I'm sure the others will be, too. Thank you." She lifted her hand toward the open, parlour door. "Would you care to join me for some tea?"

Mr Elmore smiled and, in an instant, ten years were taken from his tired face. Yes, I would." His smile grew. "Very much so."

"Perfect," Miss Trent said as she led him into the parlour. "I hear the teapot's whistle now."

* * *

Lyons, the butler, was waiting in the hallway when Doctor Locke came downstairs. He gave a shallow bow and said, "A Mrs Coral Cosgrove is in the patient waiting room, ma'am."

"Please, give her my apologies, but I can't see her at the moment," Doctor Locke replied as she rubbed her temple and walked toward the parlour.

"She was rather insistent in her request to see you, ma'am," Lyons said.

Doctor Locke sighed.

"As she intends to return to Brighton within the hour," Lyons added.

"Isn't it Mr Locke she wishes to see?" Doctor Locke enquired with exasperation.

"No, ma'am," Lyons replied.

Doctor Locke stilled when she heard his reply and looked to the waiting room door. With her curiosity piqued, she went through it and approached Mrs Cosgrove, who stood when she entered. Doctor Locke enquired, "You wished to see me?"

"Yes. I suspect my visit has taken you by surprise—"

"I wasn't expecting you, but I'm not surprised," Doctor Locke interrupted. "My husband is unavailable at the moment. If you wish, I'll tell him you were here."

"He isn't my reason for coming," Mrs Cosgrove said in a hard tone. "As improbable as it may sound, I want to thank you."

"The solving of your husband's murder was a collective effort by the Bow Street Society," Doctor Locke replied as she tidied the magazines and newspapers which littered the low table in the centre of the room. The large, potted plant in the corner also garnered her attention. "I shall pass on your gratitude, nonetheless." She stopped in her tracks when Mrs Cosgrove stepped into her path.

"I'm very grateful for Benjamin's murderer being brought to justice—*finally*—of *course*, I am." Mrs

328

Cosgrove adjusted the fox fur stole draped around her shoulders and placed her hand upon her chest. "*I* know the truth of it, even if that *dreadful* police inspector has printed lies about *him* being the master detective." She allowed her hand to drop to her side as a wave of sadness overwhelmed her features. "But I'm *most* grateful for you, Doctor Locke. You *listened*—without judgement—as I poured my heart out to you about my poor baby. You *believed* me and *comforted* me, when others' words have caused me to feel nought but *shame* and *disgust*." She placed her hand upon Doctor Locke's arm. "You reminded me I am *still* a mother, even though my child has passed." A smile warmed her face. "Norman may be gone, but his son is still with us. I intend to do right by them both, Mrs Locke. Ned has agreed to give me a yearly allowance from Benjamin's estate. It's not as high as I should have received, but I will give half of every penny to Adam all the same. I will be his mother in spirit, if not in fact."

Doctor Locke felt her eyes begin to well as she listened to the heartfelt words of a woman she'd hated. Her irritation at Mrs Cosgrove's behaviour toward Percy, her frustration at Percy's uncontrollable dependency—*all* of it melted away as she beheld the warmth, love, and new-found life in Mrs Cosgrove. Without consideration for propriety, Doctor Locke embraced her visitor and said— with full sincerity—"I'm so *very* happy for you."

* * *

The modest laughs of ladies and eloquent drawls of gentlemen drifted through Inspector Woolfe's open window. He watched the admirers of music alight from their pristine carriages and file into the opera house. It was an ambition of his to take a box at that palace of the arts and converse over a glass of champagne at the interval. On the meagre pay of a police inspector though, the dream had to remain that—a dream. He lifted his glass of whiskey in a silent toast and tossed it back before he sensed someone at his office door.

"What are you doing here?" he enquired as he turned toward his desk and set the glass aside. Night had drawn in, but Woolfe was conscious of how much gas he'd used that day. The lamps were therefore low. Nonetheless, he recognised his visitor's fine-cut suit, manicured eyebrows, and flawless fingernails. "I read the Cosgrove case was solved."

"It is," Inspector Lee replied. He closed the door and took the chair opposite Woolfe's. "But a mutual rival of ours still exists."

"The Bow Street Society," Woolfe said through gritted teeth as he picked up the glass and slammed it down.

"The one and the same. Upon my return to Kensington, I found a directive from Chief Inspector Richard Jones of Scotland Yard on my desk. In it, he revealed the Head of the Mob Squad, Inspector John Conway, has been assigned to lead the ongoing surveillance of the Society. Inspector Conway is to also inform any investigating officer of the Society's involvement in their case, and which members have been assigned."

Inspector Woolfe grunted.

"Is it true you and Inspector Conway are friends?"

"Yeah." Woolfe's eyes narrowed. "What's your point?"

Inspector Lee smiled. "A desire to rid the Metropolitan Police of the nuisance that is the Bow Street Society."

Woolfe sat back and his chair groaned under the strain. "I think every honest copper has the same desire," he said as he poured another finger of whiskey. "Me more than others; they've not only set up shop on my patch but on my bloody street." He tossed the dark liquid down his throat while Lee leaned forward with his smile still in place.

"I had suspected as much during our first meeting," Lee said. "Your friendship with Inspector Conway does provide you with a unique advantage over the rest of us. As his confidant, you will, undoubtedly, be told everything Miss Trent of the Bow Street Society has told him."

Woolfe grunted again and peered into his empty glass. "I wouldn't put my last farthing on it." He put the glass down. "Conway's my friend, yeah. He's also told me *not* to investigate the Bow Street Society as per the orders of Chief Inspector Jones."

Lee's brow quirked. "Is that so? How curious… Did Inspector Conway tell you *why* Chief Inspector Jones didn't want you to investigate?"

"The same reason he's given you. The Bow Street Society is a gang and Conway's the Head of the Mob Squad." Woolfe put his glass and a bottle of whiskey into his desk. "I'd threatened to search the Society's house for evidence of their members because I suspected—actually, I *still* suspect—one of the surgeons the Yard uses has been giving the Society privileged information. I gave Miss Trent twenty-four hours to produce the list of members before I went back to search. During those twenty-four hours she went to Conway—he was the first copper she dealt with—and told him what I'd said."

"Did you ever receive the list?"

Woolfe shook his head.

"Aren't you still curious about the surgeon—about the Bow Street Society as a whole?"

"Yeah, of course I am," Woolfe growled. "But my hands have been tied." He stood and took his fur coat from the stand.

Lee also stood. "*Your* hands, yes, but not *mine*." He watched as Woolfe stilled with one arm in his coat. "Chief Inspector Jones has ordered you not to investigate the Bow Street Society. The directive he sent to me—and, I presume, to the inspectors of the other divisions—included no such clause. Furthermore, I have recently made the acquaintance of one of the Society's own. I therefore propose an alliance between you and me, Inspector, to expose the truth behind the Society through whatever means we have at our disposal."

Woolfe's mouth grew into a yellow-teeth-stained grin. Coupled with his bushy eyebrows and unkempt hair, it gave his feature an altogether animal-like appearance. He discarded his coat upon his chair to circle his desk and take Lee's hand in a firm shake. "Consider me your ally, Inspector Lee."

**If you enjoyed the book, please leave a review to help more readers discover the Bow Street Society.
www.bowstreetsociety.com**

Notes from the author

Spoiler alert

The original title of this book was *The Case of The Deadly Doll*. When I wrote the scenes in which the Society are commissioned, and Inspector Conway and Mr Snyder are taken to speak with Mr Partridge, I realised the tension I had built was nullified by the title. In other words, there could be no curiosity about what Mr Partridge would tell Inspector Conway and Mr Snyder because the title had given away the punchline.

The Case of The Spectral Shot became the next logical choice due to the book's theme of spiritualism (spectral) and the murder weapon: a Webley Mark I revolver (shot). The title had to comprise of alliteration to match the previous two books in the series—*The Case of The Curious Client* and *The Case of The Lonesome Lushington*. I wanted this book to have the spiritualism theme for several reasons.

First, spiritualism began in the Victorian era and grew in popularity throughout the period. Arguably one of the most famous spiritualists of the era was author and creator of Sherlock Holmes, Sir Arthur Conan Doyle. In his book, *The Secrets of Houdini*, J.C. Cannell relates Houdini's account of a private séance he attended with Sir Arthur and Lady Doyle, in the Doyles' suite. Paper and pencils had been laid out on the table. Soon after Sir Arthur had said a prayer, Lady Doyle was—apparently—taken over by a spirit. She beat the table, shook, and began writing. When she'd completed a page, Sir Arthur gave it to Houdini who read a message—supposedly—from his late, beloved mother. The Doyles had held the séance in the hopes of convincing Houdini there was an afterlife and it was possible the living could communicate with the

334

dead. This was a belief the two firmly held and their intentions behind the séance were wholly honourable. Once the séance had ended, Houdini was disappointed because the message had been written in English and his mother's main dialect was Yiddish. The 'spirit' hadn't mentioned Houdini's mother's birthday, either, despite it being on the same day when the séance was held. Due to the Doyles' blatant sincerity in trying to convince Houdini, he didn't tell them of his disappointment.

According to Dr Keith Souter's book, *Medical Meddlers, Mediums and Magicians: The Victorian Age of Credulity*, the history of spiritualism began in New York, USA, when the Fox family experienced unexplained knocks and tapping in their home in 1848. The youngest of the three Fox sisters, Kate, soon realised she could communicate with the cause of the noises by assigning one knock for "yes" and two for "no." The alleged spirit wasn't particular about who it communicated with, either. Kate's mother—and soon, their neighbours—used the system of knocking to garner the same responses as Kate had. After a time, during which the Fox family continued their communication with the spirit, they ascertained from it that it was a murdered peddler. This suggestion led the Fox family to dig up their cellar and make the discovery of hair and bones which were later identified as human remains. Naturally, the newspapers picked up the story and it wasn't long before the Fox sisters were widely known as mediums. Spiritualism as a movement also gained momentum and, by the late 1880s, Kate had given séances, under experiment-like conditions, which had convinced many non-believers. In 1888, however, another of the sisters, Margaret, demonstrated to the press how she could create the tapping noises by simply cracking the joint in her big toe. She and Kate had seemingly denounced spiritualism by this point though, and had become estranged from their sister, Leah, as a result.

Prior to the Bow Street Society holding a séance to determine if the doll is haunted, Mr Elliott suggests they should bind Mr Verity's feet to the chair if they hear knocking. Mr Elliott enquires if alleged mediums use their big toes to tap upon the floorboards. This is a subtle reference to Margaret's demonstration.

Magicians were often the ones who actively sought to debunk spiritualism by exposing the frauds of so-called mediums. Mr Verity makes a passing reference to this, and Mr Locke later remarks upon John Nevil Maskelyne & George A. Cooke's exposure of the Davenport Brothers. The Brothers were exposed by the two magicians as fraudulent mediums in 1865. This incident is what made Maskelyne & Cooke famous.

My second reason for having spiritualism as the book's theme is, it allowed me to pay homage to the "uncanny" which was prevalent in gothic literature of the period, e.g. the monster in Mary Shelley's *Frankenstein*, Mr Hyde in R.L. Stevenson's *The Strange Case of Dr Jekyll & Mr Hyde*, etc. Victorian gothic literature also had brooding landscapes, tumultuous weather, and intense sensationalism.

All these elements are brought together in Mr Snyder and Inspector Conway's midnight visit to a blustery Hampstead Heath to meet the enigmatic man in black. This same mad had earlier shoved Miss Trent aside to escape the Bow Street Society's house. There's also a subtle nod to Bram Stoker's *Dracula* in this scene on Hampstead Heath. When Mr Snyder first sees the man in black's carriage, he's only able to distinguish two bright, white, glowing balls from the carriage's lamps. I intentionally wrote this to mirror Jonathan Harker's description of Dracula's carriage as it neared him on the Pass.

I've always had a fascination (read 'fear') of the paranormal. When I was younger I'd scare myself silly by watching television programmes like *Strange but True?*

with Michael Aspel and *Unsolved Mysteries* with Robert
Stack (the opening sequence of *Unsolved Mysteries*, with
its menacing music, was enough to frighten me as a child.
While writing *The Case of The Curious Client*, I
discovered Rob Dyke's YouTube series *Seriously Strange*.
From there I discovered other YouTube channels, such as
Wacky Wednesday, Unexplained Mysteries, and Top 5
Unknowns, which tended to show a lot of paranormal
based lists. I must confess I binge watched so many
'ghosts caught on camera' videos I started to believe my
home was haunted. This belief was further strengthened by
the fact I kept waking up to my bedside lamp being on—
on an almost nightly basis—despite my having turned it
off when I went to bed. It wasn't until I woke up and
caught myself turning the lamp on that I realised I'd been
doing it in my sleep. After this, I curbed my paranormal
video watching (but the odd one still gets my attention
every now and then).

My third reason for using the theme of
spiritualism stemmed from my obsession with YouTube
videos about the paranormal. An episode of *Seriously
Strange* centred on haunted/cursed dolls. It was the first
time I'd seen or heard about this subject in detail and it
fascinated me. When it came to planning the mystery for
the third Bow Street Society book, therefore, I knew I
wanted to have a haunted doll somewhere in the story. The
addition of a spiritualist Society member, in the form of
Mr Verity, meant the Society could take advantage of
spiritualism as a means of determining the validity of the
doll's alleged curse. Practically all the dolls in the videos
I've seen moved. I therefore wanted to not only have my
fictitious doll do the same, but for the doll's movement to
be the means by which the murderer kills their victim.

Despite the inclusion of spiritualism and curses
etc., I wanted the mystery's solution to be based on
tangible fact rather than abstract concepts. The Bow Street
Society books have always been clue-puzzle mysteries

which are investigated using reason, logic, and indisputable facts. I didn't want to undermine this unwritten rule by including actual spirits and/or curses, even if they were just an add-on to the main mystery. The doll's movement was thus put down to an internal mechanism akin to those found in clocks. These clockwork dolls, or automaton as they were also known, had proven popular during the decades prior to the mystery's in-book year of 1896. They'd also been used in illusions, as described by Mr Locke's account of Maskelyne & Cooke's *Psycho*.

Mr Verity explains the manufacture of séance dolls by toymaker, Joseph Maskelyne, while the Society is discussing the possibility of their doll being haunted. He also makes a reference to *Frozen Charlotte* dolls. Originally made of unglazed porcelain in Germany in 1850, and used by children as a bath toy, these dolls were usually left nude with the only colour being on the hair, cheeks, lips and eyes.

The dolls became known as *Frozen Charlotte* in America due to people associating it with a popular poem by Seba Smith in 1840. The poem describes a young woman who had been frozen to death while riding in an open sleigh with her love on New Year's Eve. According to the poem, the woman hadn't wrapped up warm enough despite her mother warning her to do so.

To buy a *Frozen Charlotte* doll set people back a penny and the dolls were sometimes sold in coffin-shaped boxes with blankets. At Christmas in Britain, the dolls would be baked in puddings, or cakes, to amuse any child who found them. The whole concept of a *Frozen Charlotte* doll may seem shocking to our modern sensibilities. In the Victorian era though, it was treated as a cautionary tale with morbid amusement.

A gun was chosen as the murder weapon because it could be manipulated by a mechanism and I'd yet to use it in any Bow Street Society mystery. Those with a keen interest in modern day forensic science may feel bemused by the Society, and the police, not using the grooves on a bullet—made by the barrel from which it was fired—to marry the bullets which killed the victims to the Webley Mark I revolver. There's a simple explanation for this: this kind of identification wasn't done until 1899, three years after the in-book mystery is set.

Thank you for taking the time to read these notes. I hope they've helped to clarify the historical context of the mystery and my thought process as its author. Please leave a review, or just a rating out of five stars, on Amazon if you enjoyed the mystery, disliked it, or were indifferent about it. Reader feedback helps me to improve my craft and enhance future instalments in the Bow Street Society mystery series. Reviews and ratings also help the Bow Street Society books to reach a wider audience.

Subscribe to the Bow Street Society's official newsletter, the *Gaslight Gazette* to read brand-new Bow Street Society Casebook short stories before they're published on Amazon, and to receive Bow Street Society news straight to your inbox for free.

Thank you for your support.

~T.G. Campbell
June 2018.

MORE BOW STREET SOCIETY

The Case of The Curious Client
(Bow Street Society Mystery, #1)
NOVEL

**WINNER OF FRESH LIFESTYLE MAGAZINE BOOK
AWARD APRIL 2017**

In *The Case of The Curious Client,* the Bow Street Society is hired by Mr Thaddeus Dorsey to locate a missing friend he knows only as 'Palmer' after he fails to keep a late night appointment with him. With their client's own credibility cast into doubt mere minutes after they meet him though, the Society is forced to consider whether they've been sent on a wild goose chase. That is until events take a dark turn and the Society has to race against time not only to solve the case, but to also save the very life of their client…

The Case of The Lonesome Lushington
(Bow Street Society Mystery, #2)
NOVEL

In this sequel to *The Case of The Curious Client,* the Bow Street Society is privately commissioned to investigate the murder of a woman whose mutilated body was discovered in the doorway of the London Crystal Palace Bazaar on Oxford Street. Scandal, lies, intrigue, and murder all await the Society as they explore the consumerist hub of the Victorian Era & its surrounding areas, glimpse the upper classes' sordid underbelly, and make a shocking discovery no one could've predicted…

The Case of The Toxic Tonic
(Bow Street Society Mystery, #4)
NOVEL

When the Bow Street Society is called upon to assist the *Women's International Maybrick Association,* it's assumed the commission will be a short-lived one. Yet, a visit to the *Walmsley Hotel* in London's prestigious west end only serves to deepen the Society's involvement. In an establishment that offers exquisite surroundings, comfortable suites, and death, the Bow Street Society must work alongside Scotland Yard to expose a cold-blooded murderer. Meanwhile, two inspectors secretly work to solve the mystery of not only Miss Rebecca Trent's past but the creation of the Society itself…

All titles are on sale now from Amazon and available for free download via Kindle Unlimited.

SOURCES OF REFERENCE

A great deal of time was spent researching the historical setting of *The Case of The Spectral Shot* prior to my even starting to write it. Thus, a great deal of information about the period has been gathered, to inform me of the historical boundaries of my characters' professions and lives, which hasn't been directly referenced in this book. Where a fact, or source, has been used to inform the basis of descriptions/statements made by characters in the book, I've strived to cite said source here. Each citation includes the source's origin, the source's author, and which part of *The Case of The Spectral Shot* the source is connected to. All rights connected to the following sources remain with their respective authors and publishers.

BOOKS

St Martin-in-the-Fields Trafalgar Square chapter, Humphrey, Stephen London's Churches and Cathedrals: A guide to London's most historic churches and cathedrals (Mew Holland Publishers, London) pp.90-93
St Martin-in-the-Fields church's exterior's appearance and parish including royal palaces.

AA Exploring Britain's Churches & Chapels: Inspirational Journeys of Discovery (AA Publishing, Basingstoke, 2011) p.85
St Martin-in-the-Fields church's interior's appearance

Eveleigh, David J., Firegrates and Kitchen Ranges (Shire Publications Ltd) p.20
The open range in Conway's kitchen.

Fowler, Will, North, Anthony, and Stronge, Charles <u>The Illustrated History of Pistols, Revolvers and Submachine Guns</u> (Lorenz Books, 2014) p.52 & 53.
Info about Webley Mark I revolver.

Ware, J. Redding, <u>Victorian Dictionary of Slang & Phrase</u> (Bodleian Library, 2015)
"Put the lights out" and its definition: kill.

Gray, Henry, 1825-1861; Spitzka, Edward Anthony, 1876-1922 Anatomy, descriptive and applied (Published 1913)
https://archive.org/details/anatomydescript00gray
Heart in place structure diagram on p.553
Doctor Locke's description of the structure of the heart

Bradshaw's Rail Times for Great Britain and Ireland: December 1895 (Middleton Press)
The time of the train to Brighton and name of the Metropole Hotel

Steinmeyer, Jim <u>Hiding the Elephant: How Magicians Invented the Impossible</u> (Arrow Books, 2003) pp104-105
Maskelyne & Cooke's Psycho doll, how it worked, and how its secret was discovered.

Bondeson, Jan <u>Strange Victoriana: Tales of the curious, the weird, and the uncanny from our Victorian ancestors</u> (Amberley Publishing, 2016) pp.76 & 77
Chard house ghost, Berkeley Square haunted room's victim and victim's disbelief in supernatural

Cannell, J.C. <u>The Secrets of Houdini</u> (Dover Publications Inc, New York) pp.16-17
Houdini's séance with Sir Arthur Conan Doyle and his wife, Lady Doyle

Souter, Dr. Keith <u>Medical Meddlers, Mediums and Magicians: The Victorian Age of Credulity</u> (The History Press, 2013)
Tying Mr Verity's feet to the chair and explanation in Notes from the author.

Jaffé, Deborah <u>The History of Toys: From Spinning Tops to Robots, 11: Automata and Mechanical Toys</u> (Sutton Publishing, United Kingdom) p.182
Fernand Martin and his work

McCrery, Nigel <u>SILENT WITNESSES: A History of Forensic Science</u> (Random House Books, 2013) pp.56-57
Gun identification by its bullet markings first being used in 1899.

WEBSITES

Lee Jackson's *The Victorian Dictionary*
http://www.victorianlondon.org/index-2012.htm
The following sources are all taken from The Victorian Dictionary website

Cassell and Company Limited, <u>The Queen's London. A Pictorial and Descriptive Record of the Streets, Buildings, Parks and Scenery of the Great Metropolis in the Fifty-Ninth year of the reign of Her Majesty Queen Victoria,</u> 1896

- *Photograph of Hampstead Heath: The Flagstaff, with approach to "Jack Straw's Castle" and accompanying description used as historical reference sources for basis of the in-book description and history of Jack Straw's Castle.*

- *Photograph of Hampstead Heath, from the flagstaff, looking West and accompanying description used as historical reference sources for basis of the in-book description of Hampstead Heath's appearance and the history and appearance of the Flagstaff*
- *Photograph of Piccadilly Circus and accompanying description used as historical reference sources for basis of the in-book description of Piccadilly Circus and adjoining streets.*
- *Photograph of South Kensington Museum: The Sculpture Hall and accompanying description used as historical reference sources for basis of the in-book description of sculptures and room etc*

J. Thomson and Adolphe Smith, Street Life in London (THE STREET LOCKSMITH chapter) 1877
Rules for locksmiths and lock ownership and Whitechapel Road being location to find Locke's locksmith acquaintance

The Pocket Atlas and Guide to London, 1899
The Grove, Heath Street, and Heath End Hill locations.

Edmund Yates, His Recollections and Experiences, 1885 [chapter on 1847-1852]
Gambling houses in Piccadilly, Gambling House entry process, gambling room appearance, and supper room

The Criminal Prisons of London and Scenes of London Life (The Great World of London), by Henry Mayhew and John Binny, 1862 – Introduction THE CONTRASTS OF LONDON. (chapter)
Genteel used to describe Gloucester Place.

About London, by J. Ewing Ritchie, 1860 - Chapter 13 - Breach of Promise Cases
Mr Maxwell's breach of promise to Miss Dexter and the threat of court.

***

The history behind your birth certificate article, Anglia Research website
https://www.angliaresearch.co.uk/articles/the-history-behind-your-birth-certificate/
Name of the Act for the Registering of Births, Deaths, and Marriages in England passed in 1836, the requirement for life events to be recorded by a local registrar, and the collated indexes sent to the Registrar General at Somerset House.

Birth, marriage and death records in England & Wales article on Find My Past website:
https://www.findmypast.co.uk/content/expert-bmd
Local registrars in registration districts, Months when indexes collated, year of the enforcement of compulsory registration

London Metropolitan Archives Information Leaflet Number 41 coroners' records for London and Middlesex: https://www.cityoflondon.gov.uk/things-to-do/london-metropolitan-archives/visitor-information/Documents/41-coroners-records-for-london-and-middlesex.pdf
Coroners keeping their own records, coroner districts, name/definitions of inquisitions and depositions

Sinks of London Laid Open, [--pub. J. Duncombe--], 1848 - Flash Dictionary.
http://www.victorianlondon.org/index-2012.htm
"Thrown a hatchet" and its definition: "to tell a marvellus story, or a lie, and swear its true"

"A Few Words on the Art of Canoodling" article, dated SEPTEMBER 8, 2014
https://victoriandictionary.wordpress.com/tag/flirting/
The Dictionary of Victorian Insults & Niceties by Tine Hreno.
"Pisser" and its definition: Penis.

Dolly Darko – The Séance Doll
http://www.danbaines.com/dolly-darko/
Masklyne & Sons, the makers of Séance Dolls and Séance Dolls' construction.

John Nevil Maskelyne article on Britannica
https://www.britannica.com/biography/John-Nevil-Maskelyne
John Nevil Maskelyne's name, his performing partner, George A. Cooke, and their exposure of fraudulent spiritualists, the Davenport Brothers.

FROZEN CHARLOTTE: THE CREEPY VICTORIAN-ERA DOLLS THAT SLEPT IN COFFINS AND WERE BAKED INTO CAKES http://dangerousminds.net/comments/frozen_charlotte_the_creepy_victorian-era_dolls_that_slept_in_coffins_and_w Via Nourishing Death, Pretty Awful Things, Alex Bell, Katherine Barrus and eBay and h/t Coilhouse on Facebook / Posted by Paul Gallagher

Frozen Charlotte dolls.

North Laine Community Association website http://www.nlcaonline.org.uk/page_id__305.aspx
When Gloucester Place was built, and gardens having been removed by 1896 to widen the road.

Gloucester Arms, Gloucester Place, Westminster LB: by Park Place photograph from London Met. Archives (https://collage.cityoflondon.gov.uk/tempFileHandler.php?f=print8825203801512739373.html&dn=Image&WINID=1515426617422)
Balconies and cobbled street on Gloucester Place gardens having been removed by 1896 to widen the road.

London Metropolitan Archives' Collage, Various interior photographs of Gloucester Place homes https://collage.cityoflondon.gov.uk/
Staircases, size of hallway, high window, and arch

Sussex, Brighton Beachfront circa 1890's http://www.oldukphotos.com/sussex-brighton4.htm
Description of promenade, including Jungle Shooting Gallery

Sussex, Brighton, Entertainers on the Beach circa 1890's
http://www.oldukphotos.com/sussex-brighton4.htm
Description of the bathing huts

VIDEOS

BRIGHTON 1896 - NO SOUND video by British Movietone
Published on 21 Jul 2015
https://www.youtube.com/watch?v=8yvGqCrK9V0
Description of bathing suits = YouTube video bookmarked in Brighton bookmark folder.

MAPS

Booth, Charles Booth's Maps of London Poverty East and West 1889 (reproduced by Old House Books) *purchased from* **Shire Books**
http://www.shirebooks.co.uk/old_house_books/
Classification of Ballance Road in Hackney, and location of nearby roads and Hackney Union Workhouse.

Printed in Great Britain
by Amazon